PRAISE FOR

The Witches of Echo Park

"A dark compelling page-turner."
—Kelley Armstrong, #1 *New York Times* bestselling author of
Otherworld Secrets

"Great characters, great story, great setting—Amber Benson's
got it. Get it for yourself."
—John Scalzi, *New York Times* bestselling author of
The End of All Things

"Dark, delicious, and devilishly intricate. A spellbinding winner."
—Seanan McGuire, *New York Times* bestselling author of
A Red-Rose Chain

"*The Witches of Echo Park* is dark, thoughtful urban fantasy about
destiny, the ties that bind us, and the power of women who rely on
themselves—and each other—for strength. A fantastic read."
—Christopher Golden, #1 *New York Times* bestselling author of
Dead Ringers

PRAISE FOR THE CALLIOPE REAPER-JONES NOVELS

"Benson knows how to tell a good story, and she ratchets up the
tension with every page." —Seanan McGuire

"Amber Benson does an excellent job of creating strong characters, as
well as educating the reader on some great mythology history . . . A
fast-paced and very entertaining story." —*Sacramento Book Review*

"An urban fantasy series featuring a heroine whose macabre humor
fits perfectly with her circumstances. Sure to appeal to fans of Tanya
Huff's Vicky Nelson series and Charles de Lint's urban fantasies."
—*Library Journal*

"A beguiling blend of fantasy and horror . . . Calliope emerges as an
authentically original creation . . . The humorous tone never gets in
the way of the imaginative weirdness of the supernatural events."
—*Locus*

continued . . .

Ace Books by Amber Benson

The Calliope Reaper-Jones Novels

DEATH'S DAUGHTER
CAT'S CLAW
SERPENT'S STORM
HOW TO BE DEATH
THE GOLDEN AGE OF DEATH

The Echo Park Coven Novels

THE WITCHES OF ECHO PARK
THE LAST DREAM KEEPER

The Last
Dream Keeper

AMBER BENSON

ACE BOOKS, NEW YORK

ACE

An imprint of Penguin Random House LLC
375 Hudson Street, New York, New York 10014

This book is an original publication of Penguin Random House LLC.

Library of Congress Cataloging-in-Publication Data

Benson, Amber, 1977–
The last dream keeper / by Amber Benson.
pages ; cm. — (An Echo Park Coven Novel)
ISBN 978-0-425-26868-1 (trade)
1. Witches—Fiction.   2. Magic—Fiction.   I. Title.
PS3602.E685L37 2016
813'.6—dc23
2015027251

PUBLISHING HISTORY
Ace trade paperback edition / January 2016

PRINTED IN THE UNITED STATES OF AMERICA

10   9   8   7   6   5   4   3   2   1

Cover illustration by Larry Rostant.
Cover design by Diana Kolsky.
Interior text design by Kelly Lipovich.

Penguin
Random
House

The Last
Dream Keeper

Eleanora

I am dead.

It's strange to think those words and feel nothing. One spends an entire lifetime pushing the thought from one's mind, pretending it doesn't exist, and then suddenly it's over: Your partner whirls you off the dance floor and you are no longer among the quick . . . Now the dead beckon you to their side of the ballroom.

Only I have chosen not to join them just yet. I stand in the middle, caught between this world and the next. We blood sisters, or witches, as society has deemed us, are allowed to make this choice upon our death. We can stay behind and become Dream Walkers, traversing the dreamlands without corporeal form, using our powers to help those we've loved during our lifetimes—though many of them will never see our invisible hand helping to guide their destinies.

One might think this means we are only "ghosts" who cannot affect the human world, but Dream Walkers are more than mere shades. Unlike the rest of humanity, we have magical powers that we carry with us to the other side—because magic transcends death, it seems.

What lies beyond the veil of human consciousness, you ask? What does one see when one is no longer blinded by mortal wants and needs?

That I cannot say.

For I still linger here, drifting between the Earth and the dreamlands—and I will stay this way, unaware of what lies beyond, until I cut the final tie, severing the connection that holds me here in self-imposed purgatory: my love for my granddaughter, Lyse, and my worry for her safety in these desperate times.

I stay because something terrible is coming; something that seeks to wash away our human world and install a new regime. They call themselves The Flood, but they are so much more than that . . . and their will shall be enacted across the land unless someone stands against them.

So I have chosen to throw in my lot with the living. Like Hessika, the coven master before me, I will remain a Dream Walker, and together we will help Lyse and her coven mates mount a defense against what is to come. Whether they know it or not, they will need all the help they can get.

For if they fail (*no, they cannot fail*), a darkness unlike any other will blanket the Earth, and all will be lost. The world as I have known it will cease to exist, and another kingdom will rise in its place.

A kingdom of horror that begins with the arrival of a bloodred moon.

Lyse

I dreamed that I murdered someone last night.
   But was it a dream?

Lyse woke up on the floor in her underwear, blood from the reopened wound on her calf smeared across the rag rug she'd used as a bed. There were bruises all over her body (dreams did *not* leave bruises) and she was bone tired. The kind of tired that made your whole body ache.

She lay there on the floor, staring at the ceiling, too worn out to get up. The jangle of the landline screamed through Eleanora's bungalow like a war cry. It was the impetus Lyse needed. With a sigh, she climbed to her feet and threw on a pair of flannel pajama pants, padding out of the bedroom.

She didn't bother to clean the blood off the rag rug.

She took the call in the kitchen. It was a wrong number. Some kid from the *L.A. Times* wanting to renew Eleanora's subscription. Lyse hung up on him. After that she was wide awake, her body thrumming like she'd swallowed a carafe of coffee. More than anything, she decided, she needed to clear her head. There were just too many questions she didn't know the answers to, and she wanted them all to go away. Wanted the silence of sleep to fill her head again.

I want to disappear, Lyse thought, the weight of her guilt making her heart hurt. *But I think I might've killed someone last night, and, if I have, I need to do the right thing and turn myself in. And if I'm wrong? If I've imagined it all? Then I need to confirm my insanity with my own eyes.*

This was not something she relished doing, but it was necessary. She would go down to Echo Park Lake and look at the scene of her "dream" crime. Then, if fantasy proved to be reality, she would call the police.

She slapped a couple of Band-Aids on her calf and got dressed. Wearing sweats and her red hoodie, she stuffed the house keys in her pocket and closed the front door softly behind her. She crossed the deck and took the footbridge that led over the koi pond—which had always been the focal point of Eleanora's front yard—taking the steps two at a time. She made her way onto Curran Street, her Converse sneakers squeaking against the cool asphalt.

She loved the way Echo Park smelled: a clean scent without any trace of the pollution you got when you ventured into other neighborhoods in the city. There were strains of eucalyptus, flowering jasmine, freshly mown grass, and sizzling meat from the neighborhood taco trucks all woven together—but there was another smell there, too. Just out of reach. A strange, indefinable note she could never place. It sat apart from the other scents, almost as if it weren't really a smell, but the musk of magical energy transfusing the air.

Eleanora had once told her that Echo Park sat on a flow line, a place where there was a confluence of supernatural energy, making it the perfect setting for a coven of blood sisters to do their work. If that was true, then why *couldn't* there be a taste of magic in the air?

It only took Lyse fifteen minutes to reach the lake, her nervousness making her move quickly. As she walked, she let her brain default to autopilot, hoping this would keep her from turning back for home. Fear held on tight to her gut, squeezing her insides until she thought she might throw up. The abject horror at what she'd done the night before—*you murdered some- one,* her brain screamed—lingered like a virus, feeding on her unconscious worry even as she tried to push it away.

The only thing you can do now (if you didn't dream the whole thing) is to take responsibility for your actions. It was an act of self- defense. He would've killed you if he could have—

Stop it, she shouted at her brain, *you don't dream things like this!*

She cleared her thoughts, focusing instead on the staccato hum of traffic and the chatter of other pedestrians as she took the crosswalk at a jog. It got quieter as Sunset Boulevard dis- appeared behind her, and soon she found herself accompa- nied only by the sound of her own footsteps . . . the silence serving to highlight the fear buzzing inside her head.

Just keep moving. Don't think. Don't second-guess—

Her heart skipped a beat as she stepped off the sidewalk and saw that there were no policemen or women anywhere on the grounds of Echo Park Lake, no cordon blocking the jog- ging path, no ambulances encircling the park.

"What the hell," she said out loud, the sound of her own voice startling her.

She scanned the horizon, eyes squinting against the sun's reflection as it skipped off the surface of the lake and blinded her. She jogged over to the newly constructed playground, but its swings and bright-colored plastic slides were empty. She could see swirling mandalas in the sand made in kid-sized foot- prints, but the squealing laughter of giddy children was miss- ing in the crisp morning air.

It was early enough that there were only a few plodding joggers and a flock of spandex-clad mothers pushing expensive baby carriages around the circumference of the lake. The little café was open and a burly man in a green army jacket stood outside, holding a cup of steaming coffee in his hands sans lid.

She wished she could swap lives with him, wished she were the one standing there holding a cup of coffee while *he* had carnivorous butterflies in his belly, eating him from the inside out.

Sadly, there would be no life-swapping today.

She relinquished her wish for what could've been and returned to what was. Thus began the slow trudge around the lake that would lead her to the (imagined?) horrors of the previous night and to the destruction she'd rained down (or had she?) on the Lady of the Lake, the art deco stone statue that had stood sentry over the park for decades.

Last night (in her dream?) the statue had been struck down by a ghostly flash of lightning, crushing Lyse's homicidal uncle into a pulpy mass of exposed human entrails underneath its massive weight. Now as she rounded the corner and the far end of the lake came into view, Lyse was prepared to see the statue's shattered remains. To her shock, she found the Lady of the Lake wholly intact. There was no sign the statue had saved her life the night before.

Even though she'd guessed this would be the case when she hadn't seen any signs of police activity at the lake, it was still a bit of a shocker. The night before had felt so real. She couldn't believe it was a figment of her imagination. That she'd *dreamed* it.

Part of her brain—the part that held on to things that were considered "rational"—insisted someone must've come along and cleaned the whole mess up, fixed the statue, paid off the police, and uncrushed her uncle's body.

But that's impossible, she thought. *No one could or would do any of that* . . . unless they were using magic.

This was the only way for someone to fix a statue and dispose of a corpse with no one ever the wiser.

Until a few weeks ago, Lyse would've laughed at the idea, found it repugnant even. The people who believed in magic were right up there with the idiots who swore the Loch Ness monster existed and that Stanley Kubrick faked the moon landing. But since then her world had been upended and everything had changed.

Life turned on a dime and either you could roll *with* it, or it would roll over you. It was your choice.

She'd arrived on the West Coast expecting to be there for a brief visit. Just enough time to take Eleanora to another doctor, get a miraculous second opinion that said the cancer was surmountable and Eleanora would make a full recovery. Then Lyse would've hopped back on a plane to Athens, returning to the simple life she'd built for herself in Georgia.

Nothing had gone as she'd planned.

Instead, Eleanora had sprung a trap. She'd pinned Lyse to Echo Park with a deathbed promise: Stay in Los Angeles and take Eleanora's place as the master of the Echo Park coven of witches.

Lyse was shocked to learn that the woman who'd taken her in and raised her as her own after she'd been orphaned was, in fact, a witch—or blood sister, the name they preferred because of the connotations associated with witchcraft. Lyse hadn't known such things existed in the world—and now because of the promise she'd made, she found herself in the thick of powerful magic she didn't understand.

Circling the statue, she looked for telltale signs of cracking and repair—but there was nothing. The Lady of the Lake was as pristine as the day she was created. As was every inch of ground around the statue's square perch.

She stared at the statue.

If only you could talk, Lyse thought.

But the Lady remained stubbornly silent.

Lyse fished her cell phone and headset from the pocket of her red hoodie and jammed in the earbuds. She didn't care what she listened to, just fired up the music and let shuffle choose the song.

Flustered, she turned away from the shining water. She

spent the long walk back across Sunset and up into the hills questioning her sanity.

Lyse stayed to the left side of the road. This way she could keep an eye on the oncoming traffic and get out of the way quickly if need be. Shafts of sunlight shot through the tree line, bathing the sidewalk in an undulating kaleidoscope of shadows. She'd made the executive decision that it was okay to enjoy her late-morning constitutional now that she didn't feel like a fugitive.

Though she hadn't been prepared to permanently stay in Los Angeles, after Eleanora died Lyse was forced to accept the changes her death had wrought. The night before—dream or no dream—she'd finally understood this. As Eleanora had foreseen, her life no longer belonged to her.

It had been appropriated by the coven.

At first Lyse had been angry with Eleanora. For shielding her from the truth. For lying to her. But her anger had quickly evaporated. How could she blame Eleanora for wanting her to have a normal life before being dragged—kicking and screaming—into a world she had no control over?

Yes, she probably should have told me a bit sooner, Lyse thought, as she hit the top of Echo Park Avenue and started down the backside of the hill. *But so be it. What's done is done.*

She passed through a tree-lined bohemia, tiny wood-slatted bungalows and Spanish-style stucco houses dotting the side of the hill like wildflowers. Her eyes followed the sloping curve of the stairways that were built into the hills, the concrete steps spiraling off through the trees before disappearing into the woodland. A few cars passed Lyse as she walked, but none going so fast they couldn't see her coming and make allowances—and she did the same, stepping off into the grass, or hopping onto a curb to give the vehicles more room.

An old Jeff Buckley tune came on—"Last Goodbye," a song she loved—and she pressed the repeat button.

Yes, she was *that* girl. When she was obsessed with a particular tune, she'd listen to it over and over and over until she'd worn out her love for it. Then she'd move on to her next musical obsession. This quality drove her best friend and business partner, Carole, insane. Lyse would be working in The Center of the Whorl, the nursery they co-owned back in Georgia, blasting a ridiculous rock song on repeat because she'd broken up with some jerk, and it would send Carole on the warpath.

I told you not to date that asshole, her friend would say—and Lyse, who hated anyone saying *I told you so,* would just turn the stereo up louder.

She'd spoken to Carole twice since Eleanora's funeral. Once to tell her Eleanora had died and she needed to stay longer to sort out the estate. The last time they'd talked, she'd told Carole most of the truth: Lyse wasn't coming back to Georgia anytime in the near future.

Carole had taken the first call like a champ, worry for her friend apparent in her voice—the second call, well, she'd yelled at Lyse and then immediately apologized. Needless to say, she was not pleased with Lyse's news.

Carole had a little boy, and Bemo occupied all the time her friend didn't spend at the nursery. Lyse understood that Carole wasn't really mad at her, that she was just worried about losing her livelihood. What she didn't know was that the coven had recently placed a large sum of money in Lyse's account, and that a cashier's check for her half of the business was already on its way to Carole's bank in Athens—and it was double what Lyse's share was actually worth.

She hated that the Athens part of her life was over. It left a hole in her gut, an empty place that would never be filled, no matter how long she lived. With her normal existence gone, and Eleanora dead and buried, Lyse felt rootless. Add to this the fact that she'd ruined the only possible love connection she'd had in ages, and she felt more than lost. She felt alone.

Weir, her friend Lizbeth's ridiculously hot older brother, had been smitten with her until she'd behaved like a terrified child and demanded he give her "space." She'd acted like an emotionally unavailable asshole who wasn't ready to get involved in anything serious—which wasn't really true. It was just with so many changes in her life, she felt overwhelmed. And as much as she wanted a relationship with him, she was just too scared of getting hurt, especially when she was already feeling emotionally bruised.

It was ridiculous how intense their connection was. They hadn't even had sex yet and she was kind of in love with the guy. There was just something special about Weir. Something that made him unlike any other man she'd ever dated. She desperately wanted to be with him: He was sexy and sweet and compassionate and smart . . . and it was only her fear of being hurt that had pushed him away. Like an idiot, she'd run her mouth off and screwed the whole thing up.

She realized she'd been walking without paying attention to where she was going and was now almost to her favorite spot in all of Echo Park. It was the place she used to run away to when she was a teenager living with her great-aunt Eleanora and they'd have a fight. (It was only recently she'd learned the truth. That, in actuality, Eleanora was her *grandmother*, not her great-aunt.)

She didn't know why she found the hidden glen so glorious. Maybe it was because of the light, or maybe it was just the giant weeping willow tree that grew there. The one with the thick trunk and heavy boughs peppered with soft green leaves. Or possibly it was the rope swing lovingly looped around one of its branches, on the seat of which someone had written the loveliest of quotes: *This Is Where Memories Are Made.*

Lyse had chosen to come to this particular spot because it was a happy place from her childhood and she wanted to sit on the swing, listen to music, and think about Eleanora.

She wanted to remember her life before.

Before. Whatever, exactly, that meant.

She just wanted to get lost in the memories she'd created

when Eleanora was alive . . . because maybe then she could forget that the woman she loved so dearly was dead.

But dead *doesn't mean what it used to,* Lyse thought as "Last Goodbye" cycled through her earbuds for the umpteenth time. *Eleanora is here. Just not physically here.*

She reached the edge of the Elysian Park expansion and hopped over the metal guardrail separating the road from her hidden glen. Her mood was improving. She was looking forward to staring out at the city as she pumped her legs and made the swing go higher and higher.

The view from up there was amazing, the little valley packed full of crumbling houses and twisting stairways and overgrown greenery. These were the hills Lyse liked to trek through best, the ones upon which Eleanora's bungalow still stood. Though yuppies and aging hipsters peopled the area now, once upon a time Echo Park had belonged to the new bohemians. Sadly, what was once a home for all the liberal-thinking, left-wing-leaning communists, artists, and politicos of Los Angeles had changed its makeup completely. A restaurant at the bottom of Echo Park Avenue called Red Hill was the only reminder of what Echo Park had once been.

Time marched forever onward—and it waited for no one. It hadn't taken her long to realize the old neighborhood was changing again. Slowly but surely it was being absorbed by the rest of Los Angeles, and soon it would lose the last remnants of its bohemian charm.

Oh, well, it was inevitable, Lyse thought as she made her way past the dirt and scrub grass that made up the floor of the glen, her eyes on the willow tree. Her heart lifted even though she couldn't see the swing, which was obscured by low overhanging branches.

Take us humans. We live and die and live and die on an endless loop. Nothing, not even love, lasts forever.

As she reached the tree, Lyse stopped in her tracks. Someone had viciously cut one length of the thick rope anchoring the swing to its branch, so it half hung in the dirt. The same someone had taken a can of spray paint and covered the wooden plank in a dripping layer of black, obscuring the words that had made Lyse smile as a teenager—no matter how miserable she'd been on the inside.

Lyse felt eyes scuttling along her back. She looked up and saw a lone house on the far side of the field. Lyse could just make out the shadow of a person standing on the porch. They seemed to be watching her. She wondered if they even knew the swing existed, or that some jerk had destroyed one of the most magical places in all of Echo Park.

Lyse was heartsick. Seeing that kind of destruction in a place she loved so well made her livid with anger. She whipped around, hair flying, and began to walk away from the tree, Jeff Buckley wailing in her ears. Her anger drove her to walk faster and soon she was running, feet pounding the dirt as she tried to escape the rage rippling through her. She hit the edge of the field at top speed and, in her blind fury, almost slammed into the guardrail. But some sixth sense kicked in and she was able to stop herself before she cracked her shins on the metal.

Breathing hard, she sat down on the guardrail's precarious edge, her back to the road. Somewhere along the way, one of her earbuds had popped out and was hanging at her side, only a few inches from the dirt. She made a grab for it, but, like a pendulum, it swung away from her grasp.

"Stop it!" she snapped at the earbud, feeling an irrational spike of rage toward the inanimate object.

It swung back in her direction and this time she was able to scoop it up, jamming it back into her ear. Distracted, she was unaware of the figure standing behind her. It wasn't until the person dropped a tentative hand on her shoulder that Lyse realized she was not alone. This, coupled with a well-developed fight-or-flight instinct, made her jump up off the guardrail, a scream lodged in her throat.

"Who the what—" she cried, the words all jumbled in her

mouth as she backed away, almost tripping over her own feet. The earbuds flew out of her ears in the confusion of the moment.

It only took her a few seconds to realize this was a friend, not a foe.

Her coven mate, Lizbeth, stood on the street side of the guardrail, staring back at her. She obviously hadn't expected this kind of reaction from Lyse because she looked terrified.

"You scared me," Lyse said, feeling guilty for scaring the girl. Lizbeth frowned.

"What're you doing here?" Lyse continued, not expecting a verbal answer because Lizbeth was mute and could not reply in words.

Lizbeth shrugged, pulling a small Moleskine notepad from the bib pocket of her faded cream overalls. With her scarf, purple thermal shirt, and a grungy orange-checked flannel looped around her waist, she looked like an escapee from a Pearl Jam music video. Lyse watched as the girl produced a violet-colored pen from another pocket and began to write.

She ripped the page out of the notepad and handed it to Lyse:

Following a dream. Are you okay?

"I couldn't stay in the bungalow. Alone . . ." Lyse said, trailing off as she folded the piece of paper and put it into her pants pocket. "I needed to escape."

Lizbeth nodded her understanding, and Lyse wondered if the girl had ever felt a similar urge to run away from her life and disappear into the shadows.

"But then I came up here and someone had vandalized my fucking swing—"

Lyse's throat tightened. She gritted her teeth until her jaw ached and the urge to sob disappeared. Lizbeth, in her infinite patience, waited for Lyse to continue.

"Sorry about that," Lyse went on, stuffing her hands into the pockets of her hoodie. "You know the swing, right?"

Lizbeth nodded, her long braid slapping against her back. Something about the girl's eyes, the way they shone in the sunlight, pierced Lyse's cracked heart and all her hard fought composure melted away. First the swing and now the innocent look of pity on Lizbeth's face . . . it broke Lyse open. She felt hot tears burning the corners of her eyes, but she refused to wipe them away.

"I killed someone last night," she whispered, the need to confide her sin greater than she'd realized. "I mean, at least, I *think* I did . . . and now I'm not so sure."

She found no recrimination in Lizbeth's eyes. Instead, the teenager reached out and wrapped her arms around Lyse's shoulders, hugging her tight. They stood like that for a long time, the sun cresting over their heads as it lit up the whole of the L.A. River basin. From their vantage point high in the Echo Park hills, they did not see the water meander slowly down its man-made channel, or the 5 freeway come to life with the flow of morning rush-hour traffic.

Lyse was on edge as she made coffee in the stovetop espresso maker. She sat down at the round oak kitchen table to drink it and felt like thousands of pairs of eyes were watching her, spying on her comings and goings, so they could file away information about her every move. Maybe some giant computer somewhere was collecting all the info for further tabulation, turning her life into a series of ones and zeroes—which sounded rather comforting if it got rid of all those pesky emotions like guilt.

Guilt. She was tortured by it. The image of her uncle David crushed and bleeding underneath the Lady of the Lake statue filled her mind. The way his fingers twitched, bloody and pale white in the moonlight; the sound of stone driving flesh and bone into asphalt, compressing a living being into mush. His scream had been the worst. Like an earwig tickling her eardrum, it wiggled around inside the labyrinth of her ear canal, repeating itself over and over again.

She fought to push the image out of her brain, to banish it to some nether region of her cerebral cortex where she could pretend it didn't exist—even though the whole strange night was, of course, burned into her gray matter for eternity. She had hoped that telling Lizbeth would make her feel better, but it had only done the opposite: She felt crushed underneath the weight of her own anxiety.

Because even though there wasn't a body and the statue was still intact, Lyse *knew* she didn't dream her uncle's death.

The ringing phone cut into these morbid thoughts, throwing her a lifeline. Someone out in the real world was thinking of her—or, at the very least, was thinking of Eleanora—and wanted to connect.

Lyse got up from the table, the scrape of her chair competing with the jangle of the telephone. She grasped the receiver of the avocado-green corded telephone that hung on the wall by the refrigerator and slid it from its hanging cradle.

The jarring noise stopped midring.

"Hello?"

It was strange to stand there, an adult in the house where she'd spent her formative years. The last time she'd really used this phone, she'd hidden in the cupboard with the door closed, the cord wrapped around her finger as she'd tried to get some privacy. That was what it was like being a teenager: You felt constantly harassed, were always looking for an escape (especially from your own head), and you didn't want *anyone* knowing your business. The adult version of Lyse was an entirely different person from the angsty teenager, and she found it hard to reconcile the two aspects of herself.

"I just wanted to check in on you, make sure you were holding up okay?"

Dev's voice was warm and reassuring, and she could imagine her friend in the kitchen of the cozy Victorian she shared with her partner, Freddy, and their two daughters, holding a mug of something hot and autumn-spicy in her hand.

"You must be psychic," Lyse said, then realized the old adage actually kind of applied in this situation. Dev was a diviner, the tarot her divination tool of choice. Though Lyse hadn't seen Dev at work, from what Eleanora and the other blood sisters said, she was very talented at her craft.

"What's wrong?" Dev asked, instantly picking up on the fact that something was amiss.

Lyse twisted the rubbery telephone cord around her finger. She was desperate to pour out the horror of the previous night's encounter with the man who claimed to be her long-lost uncle David. She'd tell her story—the kidnapping, the attack, the ghost causing the Lady of the Lake statue to topple and crush her uncle to death—and Dev's maternal instincts would kick in and she'd tell Lyse it wasn't her fault, that her uncle's death was his own doing. And this would happen before she'd even told Dev the worst of it: that this horrible human being, this uncle she'd never known, was the murderer responsible for Eleanora's death.

Something he'd told her, wearing a look of glee on his hateful face, before he'd tried to murder her, too.

"It's not something . . ." She paused, unsure of how to put it. "I mean, uh, maybe I can come to you. We can talk? I don't want to do it over the phone."

"Of course, come now," Dev said. "Come whenever . . . I just want you to know you can tell me anything and I won't judge. It's always a safe space at the Montrose house."

Lyse wasn't worried about being judged. She was worried about going to jail if a body ever turned up.

"Give me an hour—I wanna shower and get dressed."

"Of course," Dev replied, a breathless quality to her voice.

"And get hold of the others," Lyse added. "I'm really sorry, but I think we're in way over our heads."

Even then she knew the sentence was an understatement.

Lyse

❧

The knock at the door scared her.

Showered now and dressed in a flannel shirt and a pair of old acid-washed jeans, she made her way through the living room, finding that the sunlight streaming through the skylights gave the space a hazy, ephemeral quality. Like looking at the world though a layer of gauzy cotton fabric, or a camera lens greased with Vaseline in an attempt to blur the edges of an already dreamlike reality.

A second knock on the door made Lyse jump. She stopped at the stone fireplace to scoop up the black wrought-iron poker and held the makeshift weapon aloft, feeling its heft in her hand. No matter who was at the door, she wanted to be prepared, and just holding the heavy poker made her feel more secure.

Moving with as little sound as possible, she crossed the hardwood floor, reaching the front door just as another volley of knocks echoed through the bungalow. She stopped at the threshold, letting the abrasive knocking wash over her. Holding her breath, she hoisted the poker in front of her like a lance.

"I have a weapon, but I don't want to hurt you!" she yelled, her words ringing with what she hoped was authority.

The banging stopped.

Her heart, which was already beating faster than normal, started to hammer in staccato sixteenth notes—so fast Lyse began to feel light-headed. She waited for the person on the other side of the door to say something.

There was only silence.

She reached out with her free hand and unlocked the deadbolt. Her other arm was shaking from the effort of holding up the poker, so she let the weapon drop to her side—but that didn't mean she couldn't brandish it again at a moment's notice.

I'm an idiot, Lyse thought. *I should go call the police. Only a vapid scream queen opens the door when there's clearly something monstrous waiting on the other side.*

She grasped the handle and turned, but didn't open the door. Instead, she stood there, hand on the cold metal, willing herself not to be a coward. She slowly began to count to ten under her breath, steeling herself to rise to the occasion—and as the number eight passed her lips, she threw open the door.

There was no one there.

Of course there wasn't.

She sagged in the doorway, and the adrenaline, which up until a few seconds earlier had been coursing through her veins like fire, evaporated. She felt nauseated and weak with exhaustion, her legs boiled noodles that could barely hold her up. Black dots flickered at the edge of her vision, and if she hadn't just downed two espressos' worth of coffee, she might've given in to her body's demands and passed out.

Then she noticed the tarot card poking out from underneath the woven sisal doormat. She knelt down, her fingers sliding the card from its resting place. She held it up so she could get a better look at The Fool from the Rider-Waite tarot deck.

She turned the card over and saw someone had scrawled a message in black pen on the back.

Beware the Fool.

She stood in the doorway for a few long minutes, back pressed against the doorframe as she peered out into the late-morning light, the tarot card held tightly between her fingers. A prickle on the back of her neck told her whoever had left the tarot card was still in close proximity, watching her carefully. She squinted, eyes roaming the confines of the wooden deck and koi pond, looking for some sign of her visitor.

Nothing. Only the lingering scent of a spicy men's cologne.

Her eyes cut through the wall of bamboo separating Eleanora's bungalow from the neighboring house, but she couldn't discover her watcher's hiding place. Human eyes can only see so far, and, in the end, Lyse was not a formidable adversary. Cold and sick-feeling, she finally gave up the search and went back inside, closing the door behind her.

The *click* of the deadbolt being thrown into place was quick and sharp, the sound dying almost as soon as it was born. Anyone who was close enough to hear it would know its meaning:

Lyse was scared.

Lyse placed the tarot card on the kitchen counter faceup. She didn't want to see the spidery writing on its back, and holding it made her feel strange.

She began to pace, not sure what her next move should be. She didn't want to leave the house, but there was nothing for it. She'd told Dev she was going over there, to the old Victorian that had been in the Montrose family for over a century, and Dev would've made sure the rest of the coven—Arrabelle, Daniela, and Lizbeth—would be coming, too.

Wait.

Daniela lived across the street. If Lyse asked, she would totally come over and walk with her to Dev's house.

She felt foolish as soon as the thought entered her head. She

was a grown woman, not a child. She should be able to leave her
house without an escort. But once she'd had the idea, it wouldn't
leave her mind and so she crossed the kitchen, picking up the
phone receiver one more time.

She realized she didn't know Daniela's phone number—but
Eleanora's old handwritten address book was still sitting on the
shelf below the telephone. She thumbed through it, recognizing few of the names inside. Finally, she found the page where
Eleanora had written Daniela's name and phone number. It
looked more recent than many of the other entries, written in
pencil instead of the blue ink Eleanora had used for the rest of
the address book.

She dialed Daniela's number and waited, holding the
receiver tightly to her ear. The line rang three times before
Daniela picked up.

"Lyse?"

She must have Caller ID, Lyse thought.

Daniela was an empath, and that meant her magical abilities were completely unconnected to fortune-telling or pre-
cognition. Caller ID was the only way she could've known
Lyse was on the other end of the line.

Thank God for technology.

"Hey, yeah, it's me," Lyse said, twirling the cord tightly
around her finger, so the tip went a bloodless white. "Not
sure if Dev called you or not, but I'm heading down to her
place and thought we could walk together?"

"What's up? You don't sound so good."

Daniela was astute when it came to reading human emotion.
She didn't have to touch Lyse to know something was wrong.

"Long story," Lyse replied. "Long one that's best told to
everyone at once. And I'm gonna need you guys to tell me
what to do. Some bad shit . . ."

She stopped there, her throat constricting as she felt hot tears
burning her eyes.

"Lyse?"

Real concern in Daniela's voice.

Lyse fought back the tears, pushing all the swirling emotions away.

"I'm okay," she said, fighting to sound a little brighter. "Nothing we can't figure out."

"When do you wanna go?"

Lyse thought for a moment before answering, then decided she didn't care how immature her vulnerability made her seem. She really didn't want to be alone.

"Can you come get me now?"

She hung up the phone and felt better almost immediately. The coven mates Lyse inherited from Eleanora were more than just friends now, more than family even . . . it was as if they'd become a part of her soul. Her connection to these women went beyond the physical world.

Another knock at the door drew her from her thoughts— but something was wrong. It was too soon. There was no way Daniela could've gotten ready and made her way over to the bungalow in such a short amount of time. True, Daniela only lived across the street, but in her gut, Lyse knew the petite, rainbow-haired woman was *not* the person standing outside.

The knock came again and Lyse grabbed the poker, moving to the door. She pressed her palm against the wood.

"Go away! I'll call the police if you don't get out of here!"

There was a slight hesitation and then:

"Lyse? It's Weir. Will you open the door, please?"

She dropped the poker and unlocked the door, disengaging the deadbolt with a loud *thunk*. In a moment he was standing in the doorway, filling it with his strong, solid presence. His blond hair was mussed, sticking up at odd angles, windblown because he'd walked over from the house he shared with his sister, Lizbeth.

Weir was gorgeous, firm, and *real* when nothing else in her life felt that way. She liked him, liked the way he looked and smelled. Liked that he was covered in beautiful nautical tattoos—something she'd meant to ask him more about but hadn't gotten around to doing yet.

"Is Lizbeth here?" he asked, his voice taut.

She shook her head.

"Is something wrong?" Lyse asked. Weir wasn't here for her, and she felt disappointment bloom in her heart. "I saw her this morning. Up by the swing. But that was a while ago."

"Dammit, I told her to stay in the house today."

He turned to go, distraction like a film over his eyes.

"If she's not here, then maybe she's in Elysian Park," he muttered, almost to himself. Then addressing Lyse: "Two detectives came by the house—a man and a woman. There was something really creepy about them. They wanted to talk to her, but when I went looking . . . she was gone. They were not happy."

The mention of the word *detective* shot a bolt of fear through Lyse's heart. *Had they come to question Lizbeth about Lyse's uncle? That didn't make any sense—how could they have known Lyse mentioned anything about the previous night to Lizbeth?*

Weir turned to leave, but Lyse grasped his arm, her fingers wrapping around the thick bicep underneath the light corduroy jacket. Touching him—even through fabric—made her shiver.

"Wait, I'll go with you."

He nodded.

"Okay, yeah, more eyes the better."

She released her grip on his arm and he went for the door. It appeared her touch didn't ignite the same electric feeling in him that it did in her. She knew he was worried, that fear might be jamming the circuits—or maybe it was just the terrible way they'd left things the last time they were together.

"Wait. Daniela. She was coming over," Lyse called out to Weir as she grabbed one of Eleanora's shawls from the coat rack by the door and slipped it around her shoulders. "We can stop and pick her up. More eyes, right?"

She realized she'd almost forgotten her keys on the kitchen

counter. She quickly scooped them up, then locked the door behind her.

"Wait up!" Lyse called, jogging to catch up with Weir, who was already halfway across the street to Daniela's house.

Running made the wound on her calf split open again—the damn thing just wasn't healing properly—and she had to slow down. She crossed Curran Street at a limp and headed for the front door where Weir was already waiting. The girls, Verity and Veracity—Daniela's two gorgeous black cats—were lazing on the rickety front porch, but they both snapped to attention as soon as Lyse and Weir arrived. Apparently they liked the cut of Weir's jib because before Lyse could call out to them, they were twining around his legs like two sensuous snakes.

"Daniela?" Weir called, and knocked on the front door.

Lyse knelt down and stroked the two cats, who were meowing for attention.

"They sure seem to like you," Lyse said, using the stair's handrail to keep herself balanced.

"We're friends."

And what does that mean? Lyse wondered. Why was Weir friends with Daniela's cats? She thought Daniela didn't go for men.

Just for you, Lyse's mind teased.

She knew her coven mate thought she was cute. It was obvious from the way Daniela looked at her. As flattering as it was that Daniela found her attractive, Lyse only had eyes for Weir.

Lyse felt the blood rush to her cheeks as the door opened and Daniela stared down at her. From the quirk in her friend's lopsided grin, Lyse began to worry that Daniela had a hidden talent for mind reading.

"I thought I was coming to you, hotcake," Daniela said in a teasing voice. Then her face became serious as her eyes shifted from Lyse to Weir. She frowned. "Okay, the vibe you're giving off? Not good. What's going on?"

She stepped onto the porch, joining them, and Lyse thought her paint-spattered Dickies and wifebeater made her look about twelve years old—but then she slipped on a Members Only jacket, and that, coupled with her black leather gloves, took her from "teenybopper" to "Hillside Strangler" in the blink of an eye.

"The police came to their house. They wanted to talk to Lizbeth, but Weir can't find her. We think she might be in Elysian Park," Lyse said.

"I don't think they were real police," Weir said quietly. "Something was off about them. I don't know what the deal is, but since Eleanora died, things have been strange up in these hills."

"Shit," Daniela said, eyes wide. She shot Lyse a look that said: *This is not good.*

"I know LB likes to go for walks up in the park," Weir continued. "And yesterday, she was chomping at the bit to get out to the Dragon. I think she might've gone out there on her own."

Daniela narrowed her eyes and nodded.

"I'll text the others."

She pulled her phone out of her pocket and Lyse watched as Daniela's fingers flew across the screen.

"Something happened last night," Lyse blurted out. Weir and Daniela both turned to look at her. "I may or may not have killed my uncle. But only after he tried to kill me."

Lyse crossed her arms protectively over her chest, waiting for Daniela and Weir to respond—but they both just stared back at her, shocked by this surreal revelation.

"And I think he killed Eleanora, too."

"Is that why there were police at my door this morning?" Weir asked, anger rippling through his words. "Jesus, what did you drag Lizbeth *into?*"

And from the fury on his face, Lyse worried their relationship might never be the same again.

Daniela

෨෨

"You said you 'may or may not' have killed someone?" Daniela said, and watched Lyse's face contort into an expression of uncertainty.

"I went down to the lake, but the Lady of the Lake was totally fine and there was no body, no police—"

"Hold up," Daniela said. "Did this happen or not?"

Lyse frowned.

"I don't know. It might've been a dream . . ."

Lyse was one of those women who had no idea what kind of impression she made on the people around her. Classically beautiful with an angular face and deep blue irises the color of a sailor's dream, even when frown lines etched the skin around her mouth and eyes, she was still gorgeous.

"And you'll tell us about it after we find Lizbeth," Daniela said as Lyse faltered for words.

Lyse nodded.

"Okay, I just wanted you guys to know. In case this is all my fault."

Daniela watched Weir's frown deepen. She felt sorry for Lyse.

Weir was like a mama bear: Anyone who hurt his little sister was gonna get their ass kicked.

"I just want to find LB," Weir said, shaking his head. "I don't care about anything else."

"I told Arrabelle to meet us there," Daniela said, "and I let Dev know where we were going, too."

Weir seemed happy to have Daniela take charge.

"Thanks. I appreciate you doing this."

He directed his words to Daniela, not Lyse.

"Girls, be good and watch the house. We'll be back soon," Daniela said, kneeling down so the two black cats could nuzzle against her legs. Like the Sphinx, their faces remained forever inscrutable.

"Well, I know they love me," Daniela mused. *At least, the way a cat loves any human: with a touch of pity because we're not lucky enough to be cats ourselves.*

Daniela stood up and indicated that they should head back up Curran. Lyse and Weir followed her without comment, letting her lead the way. She took them around Eleanora's old bungalow, away from Echo Park Avenue, and toward the park.

Weir was much taller than either of the girls and he quickly stole the lead, so Daniela had to jog to keep up with his longer gait.

"Can you slow down a bit?" she asked, dripping with sweat after only a few minutes.

"Sorry," he said, looking back at her sheepishly. "Was in my head."

No shit, Daniela thought. Instead, she said out loud, "I'm sure she's up at the Dragon."

They were halfway down Cerro Gordo, a street whose houses crowded together like an overgrown brick, wood, and concrete forest, shading them from the worst of the sun. Weir looked so sad Daniela almost reached out and touched his arm.

Thankfully, she stopped herself before their bodies actually connected.

"It'll be okay," Daniela added a bit lamely.

She wanted to reassure him, but she didn't trust her empathic talents not to behave oddly. Things had been strange and unpredictable since Lyse's arrival in Echo Park, and it had reached the point where even with her gloves on, Daniela was afraid to touch anyone.

They were the conduits to her powers as an empath—and they would also be the instruments of her demise. It wasn't a matter of *if* her empathic powers would kill her, but *when* . . . because every time she used her talents, she blew out a little bit more of the neural circuitry in her brain. It was an absolute certainty that one day she would cross the fail-safe point and this would be the end: Vegetable-Hooked-Up-to-Heart-Lung-Machine City.

"I just worry about her," Weir said. "She's physically an adult, but more like a child on the inside."

At that moment, Daniela thought he looked just like a little boy himself: eyes wide with concern, brows lifted in exasperation.

"She's smart," Daniela said. "I know you worry—and you have good reason to—but she's not a little kid anymore."

Lyse had moved ahead of them and was nearing the end of the street where a set of stairs led down to one of the entrances to Elysian Park.

"Let's go," Daniela said, eyes on Lyse, getting farther away from them.

"Thanks," he said, smiling. "I needed to hear that. She's *not* a little girl anymore. You're right."

"Glad I could ease your mind," Daniela replied—and they took off in pursuit of Lyse's retreating back.

Behind her, Daniela could hear Weir's heavy work boots hitting the asphalt.

"I know you and Lyse have a *thing*—" Daniela began.

"Had," Weir said, looking glum.

"Okay," Daniela said, "didn't know that. Well, anyway, there's something you should know about us . . . about Lyse and me and Lizbeth."

She stopped, realizing she actually couldn't walk and talk at the same time. She turned and faced him, marveling at how rough he looked in the sunlight, fear and worry cutting deep grooves into his handsome face.

"There's no way to say this that doesn't sound utterly ridiculous," Daniela continued, not sure what to do with her hands as she spoke. Whenever she felt passionate about a subject, she tended to pinwheel her arms around her head as she talked.

He gave her a funny look, but she ignored it.

"I . . . we . . ."

"Go on," Weir said, eyes flicking past her shoulder to where Lyse was still trudging toward the stairs without them.

"Argh, I don't know!" She threw up her hands, letting out a protracted breath.

Screw it, she thought. *This "need-to-know information" is now needed.*

"We're witches. We prefer the term 'blood sisters,' but we answer to either/or." She planted her fists on her hips and held them there. "I know it sounds crazy, like something out of a bad movie, but it's the truth. I'm not fucking with you."

Daniela felt Lyse's return before she saw her.

"She's not," Lyse said, coming to stand beside Daniela. "Fucking with you."

The crudeness was obviously for Daniela's benefit.

We haven't spent a whole lot of time together, Daniela thought, *but she's already got my number.*

"I didn't know any of this before I came back to be with Eleanora when she got sick," Lyse continued. "They just sprang it on me, too."

"What are you talking about?" Weir asked, eyes narrowing.

"That there's more going on here than you know," Daniela added. "And I wanted you to be aware of this before we run into anything out of the ordinary—"

"I'm confused here," Weir said, turning to Lyse. "You say you may or may not have killed someone, but you don't know?"

From the look on Lyse's face, it was obvious she was embarrassed.

Killing someone or not killing someone—would seem pretty black-and-white to Weir, Daniela thought. *But when you stepped into the world of the covens . . . well, all bets were off.*

"And you—" His eyes fixed on Daniela. "You just drop 'I'm a witch' on me, totally out of the blue like it's nothing?"

"I just wanted you to be prepared—"

Weir shook his head.

"Are you guys on drugs?"

"Weir," Lyse said, reaching out to touch his arm—but he pulled out of her grasp. "I know it sounds crazy to you, but it's real. I swear it. I didn't believe it at first, either. Eleanora raised me like you've raised Lizbeth, and I had no idea she was the head of a coven of witches—"

Weir's eyes narrowed further, and, seeing the change in his expression, Lyse stopped speaking.

"I'm not talking about this right now," Weir said, tone prickly. "I can't even . . ."

He turned away from them, his words trailing off. His body language let them know he was done with the conversation.

"I just want to find my sister," he added, not looking at either of them. "I don't care what you guys do on your own time. I just want LB safe."

Denial is strong in this one, Daniela thought, channeling her inner Yoda. It was easier to ignore the obvious than to change your perception of how the world worked.

She didn't blame Weir for not wanting to dig deeper into the conversation. She knew being forced to deal with the supernatural could make normal human beings switch off. They weren't interested in facing things that went beyond their realm of comprehension. Were eager, in fact, to put magic, and all the weird stuff that went along with it, into a nice little box and chuck it out the window, enjoying the supernatural only when they experienced it in the guise of "entertainment"—like in a movie or book.

"Me, too," Lyse said. "I want to find Lizbeth. Anything else we can talk about later."

Daniela nodded her agreement, relieved Weir hadn't had a complete and total freak-out—and she was more than ready to let him live in denial, if it kept him from losing his shit.

Why does everyone hate change so goddamned much? Daniela wondered as she followed Lyse and Weir down the stairs leading into the park.

There was no answer from the powers that be—and she wasn't about to stir things up.

Not until they found Lizbeth.

The park was quiet. There were only a few intrepid hikers and dog walkers on the path, so they were able to keep a steady pace as they made their way down the dirt trail that took them deeper into the heart of the park. Daniela was in the lead, Lyse and Weir neck and neck behind her. Above them, the clouds amassed like a murder of angry crows, dark feathered and full of menace. It was going to rain again—which was good for the drought-starved state of California, but it worried the hell out of Daniela.

It feels like someone's tampering with the atmosphere, she thought— her empathic abilities had always made her very sensitive to magic use. *Drawing out the darkness and making the air heavy with rain.*

Normally Daniela didn't give in to negative thinking, but every day there seemed to be more to worry about . . . and then there was the blood moon on the horizon. Daniela had never been a fan of these total lunar eclipses—and this year there'd already been two of them—but with the third only days away, and all the bad things happening here and abroad, it made Daniela nervous. The blood moon was bad business, and its influence made people behave strangely, the world getting even crazier—if that was possible—than usual.

She wished her mother were still alive. Marie-Faith Altonelli would know how to handle everything. She was by far the most formidable human being Daniela had ever known. Her mother didn't let a little thing like fear stop her from doing what needed to be done—and Daniela wished she were more like the slender woman with the olive skin and hooded eyes . . . eyes that saw everything, belying their sleepy appearance.

Daniela felt a ping of magical energy and knew they were near the grove of ancient eucalyptus trees where the coven met and performed their rituals. Through the influence of spellcasting, the grove was impossible to find unless you knew what you were looking for. Long ago the Echo Park coven had chosen it for its remote locale, but as the city of Los Angeles had grown up around it, the grove had lost its isolated quality, forcing the blood sisters to use spells and charms to keep the trees hidden from prying eyes.

Daniela had felt an affinity for the sacred grove from the first moment she'd laid eyes on it. There was something wild about the place, a feeling of raw power in the air. So many blood sisters had used their talents here that the trees no longer just existed in the physical world. The grove had become a clearinghouse of psychic and magical energy extending far beyond the earthly plane.

"We're close," Daniela said, turning to look at Lyse and Weir as they moved away from the magic encircling the grove.

Weir nodded and tried to smile back, but Daniela could see the strain on his face. She knew he saw himself as more of a parent than a big brother. Deciding to save Lizbeth from a life of institutionalization made him feel responsible for her continued well-being.

"It'll be okay," Daniela heard Lyse say to Weir. "I'm sure she's up there."

Daniela knew Lizbeth had not enjoyed a great childhood. Weir's father didn't like having a daughter "on the spectrum," thought it reflected badly on his genetic line. After Lizbeth's mother divorced him, he distanced himself from their child. He'd had nothing further to do with Lizbeth until her mother died, and then, as her legal guardian, he'd had her institutionalized.

She was barely functioning already—the trauma of losing her mother had been a terrible blow to the little girl—and the shock of being sent away to such a cold and inhumane place had pushed her inward. And it was there, alone in that facility, where she'd become locked inside herself, mute and unable to connect to the outside world.

Then Weir had come to rescue her.

He'd petitioned the courts to make him her guardian and her entire world had changed. Under his constant care, she'd come out of her shell and started interacting with other people via notepad and pen. She'd come a long way in the intervening years, but she still couldn't speak—an affliction her doctors believed was purely psychological.

"I haven't thought about the Dragon in years," Lyse said. "God, I used to go up there and spend hours reading books and writing bad poetry in my journal."

The Dragon was actually an outcropping of rocks local vandals had spray-painted with graffiti, making it resemble the head of a massive reptile. Daniela thought it looked more like the basilisk from the Harry Potter movies than a dragon, but she seemed to be alone in her opinion.

"Why would she be going there?" Lyse asked Weir, as a drop of rain hit her on the nose.

"I don't know," Weir said, crossing his arms over his chest. "She was hell-bent on getting up there last night, and then she had one of her episodes. I had to take her home after that."

"Well, whatever the reason," Daniela said, looking at the sky and not liking what she saw, "I just hope she's up there."

They remained silent as they made their way through the trees, hiking deeper into the woods. A drop of rain hit Daniela's arm, and when she looked up again, the clouds had grown even darker.

"It's really gonna pour," Lyse said, following Daniela's gaze heavenward.

Daniela nodded, picking up her pace. She jogged through the trees until she found the trail she was looking for and veered onto it.

They passed an elderly couple walking a German shepherd, and she gave them a wave. She'd seen them out in the park before, assumed they lived somewhere in the neighborhood, but they'd never exchanged names. It was one of the things she loved best about the Echo Park hills. You spent time outside, and even if you didn't know someone's name, they still smiled and said hello. It didn't matter if they were old hippies, funky artist/musicians, or one of the slew of younger hipster families that had recently infiltrated the hood; everyone was reasonably nice to everyone else.

They left the trail, striking off into the trees, and it was all uphill from there. Lyse had a little trouble with the incline, but Daniela was used to walking and spent more than a few mornings a week down at the Echo Park Pool.

"Should we slow down?" Daniela asked, but Lyse shook her head.

"Not on account of me. I'm fine. It's just my stupid leg. I sliced it open and I thought it was better, but it's just not."

Daniela hadn't wanted to slow down and was glad Lyse didn't want to, either.

"It's close. Not too far now," Daniela said.

Lyse nodded, her pale cheeks pink with exertion.

"I know," she said. "You never forget how to find a place like the Dragon."

"Do you see her?" Daniela asked as they rounded the bend and the Dragon came into view.

The outcropping of gray rock extended out of the hillside like a Paleolithic monster. If anything, it was covered in *more* graffiti than the last time Daniela had seen it. There were the requisite gang tags—swooping lines of color representing the initials of the various East L.A. gangs—and then the more artistic endeavors, which included ghost-white eyeballs encapsulated inside teal-blue circles of electric color that made the Dragon appear as if it were staring right at you.

"Lizbeth!" Weir yelled.

Daniela followed his gaze up to the top of the Dragon, where Lizbeth lay stretched out across the rocks, her body inert, long russet hair covering her face.

Weir took off, Lyse right there with him, her stride almost matching his own. Daniela watched as they scrambled across the rocks, clawing their way up the steep embankment that led to the top. Daniela let them go and doubled back, choosing to take the trail rather than climb up the stonier outcropping.

She reached Lizbeth just before the others and was able to step in front of Weir, blocking his path.

"Out of my way," he said, moving past her.

"Look at her—*she's not touching the ground!*"

Daniela's words penetrated and Weir stopped in his tracks to stare down at his kid sister.

"Don't touch her," Daniela continued. "I think she's *dreaming.*"

He looked back and forth between Daniela and Lizbeth's prone body, uncertainty in his eyes.

"Weir," Lyse said, touching his arm. "Lizbeth is breathing—I can see her chest rising and falling—and she's not in any obvious danger. Let Daniela go to her. She can help your sister in a way neither of us can."

Weir turned to Daniela for confirmation.

"Let me try first," Daniela said. "She's having a different kind of 'episode,' but I can get to her. I can reach her."

Weir nodded, totally out of his element.

"Okay."

"Okay, you'll let me do my thing? You won't try to interfere?" Daniela prodded.

Weir nodded his agreement.

Daniela could see how hard this was for him. His instinct was to rush in and save Lizbeth, and giving over control of the situation to someone else was not in his nature. But given the surreal situation, he appeared to trust them enough to let them intercede.

Daniela shot Lyse a look that said: *Keep him occupied.*

Lyse nodded her understanding and wrapped her hand around Weir's arm, pulling him closer to her.

"Lizbeth?" Daniela said.

And turning away from the others, she began to remove her black leather gloves one finger at a time.

Lizbeth

I t had begun with a dream.

All her life Lizbeth's dreams had been more vivid, more *alive* than any of her waking hours, and this was still the case even when, for all intents and purposes, she was no longer a child.

In this particular dreamtime adventure, the tall lady—Hessika, she was called in real life—came to visit her and they'd gone to Elysian Park, moving along the wooded trails like ghosts. The tall lady wanted to show her something special, something Eleanora had left behind for Lizbeth at the Dragon. Eleanora had done this because she knew it was the place Lizbeth loved best. So it was here Lizbeth must go and go quickly, the tall lady had impressed upon her, because the item had to be retrieved before anyone else could steal it away.

Once upon a time, the tall lady had not visited Lizbeth often. But with Lyse's arrival in Echo Park, the tall lady's visits had become more regular, almost as if Lyse were their catalyst. So with the dreaming, the need to get to the Dragon began to grow—and then, regardless of the dream, the urge to find whatever was waiting for her there took on a life of its own. As if it were a living, breathing creature calling out to Lizbeth through the ether, demanding she come find it.

Which was how she'd ended up in Elysian Park, moving through the woods as fast as her feet could carry her. The scarf she'd wrapped around her throat, a pale peach knitted thing Dev had given her as an eighteenth-birthday gift, was not enough to keep her warm. She wished she'd had the forethought to bring a jacket; the overalls and flannel she had on did little to warm her body now that the clouds had covered the sun and were threatening a downpour.

Lizbeth had easily found her way to the Dragon, her long-legged stride helping her cover ground quickly. But when she'd gotten there, she'd realized she had no idea what she was looking for. She'd stood beneath the Dragon's sleepy-eyed gaze, scanning the ground around her. Nothing had caught her attention. Whatever Eleanora had left behind for her, she could be assured it was well hidden. The former master of the Echo Park coven was nothing if not thorough.

If I were a secret thing, where would I be? Lizbeth had wondered as she'd climbed up the incline, her sneakers gripping the rock, helping her not to slip on the loose stones as she'd worked her way up to the Dragon's head. Finally her fingers had found purchase on the edge of the cliff and she was able to pull herself up and over the precipice. Crawling to her feet, she'd brushed away the dirt that coated her hands like chalk.

She'd looked around, hoping she'd see things differently from another, loftier vantage point. But the woods were just woods. Full of trees with heavy branches held up toward the sun, and doe-brown dirt trails leading into the brush before disappearing entirely.

There had been nothing new in the park, nothing special clamoring for Lizbeth's attention.

She'd been mad at herself for being so stupid and not asking the tall lady to give her a clue. At the very least, a hint that would've guided her in the right direction.

If only she were asleep, she could've dreamed of the tall lady and asked—

Like the strong dark scent of the coffee Weir liked to brew in the mornings, an idea had caromed through Lizbeth's brain and jolted her awake. *Why couldn't she be asleep right now?*

The answer was simple: *She could be.*

Lizbeth lay down on the rock, letting the heat rise up through the stone to warm her body. Soon she felt the Sandman's pull, his lulling presence pushing her into sleep as the daylight disappeared.

I'm falling. I can feel it, she thought, having a strange out-of-body moment before everything began to slip away from her. Her thoughts, cognizance of her own body, the chill of the air as it whipped across her . . . all of it ceased to exist for Lizbeth as she began to drift far, far away . . .

Only she wasn't far away. She was there. At the Dragon—and she was still inside her body.

Time to get up, *she thought, and then, almost without meaning to, she was sitting. Only her body didn't come with her. She swiveled onto her hip and looked behind her. Her body, hair spread around her head like a slash of reddish-brown blood, lay sprawled on the ground, lips and skin blue as a corpse.*

Lizbeth was used to this kind of thing, so instead of being frightened, she calmly climbed to her knees and looked around. Everything was the same. The trees, the dirt, the trails, the gray sky—nothing had changed. She began to wonder if she'd fallen asleep for nothing. The only difference she noticed was that she no longer felt chilly. In other dreams, she'd been cold as ice, but here, in this particular one, that was not the case.

I'll be right back, *she thought to her unconscious body, and stood up. Her legs felt a little wobbly underneath her, but she ignored the sensation. It was a dream and her legs did what she wanted them to do. She began to move around the top of the rock outcropping, searching for the secret thing Eleanora had hidden under the Dragon's watchful gaze.*

Her lifeless body stayed exactly where it was.

"Hello?" Lizbeth called out, but her voice died on her lips.

Of course, *she thought.* Even in this dream—like all the other times I've explored the dreamlands—I'm mute.

She walked over to the edge of the Dragon's nose—or where its nose would be if it were a real dragon—and that was when everything shifted. It was like a tiny earthquake concentrated on the spot where she was standing, rolled through the ground, and took her legs out from underneath her. She fell forward, her face slamming into the ground. The impact of delicate skin on sharpened rock should've hurt like hell. There should've been bones cracking, blood flowing everywhere . . . but there wasn't.

The ground was still buckling underneath her as she reached up and touched her face.

Everything was intact.

No wound.

No blood.

There were strange rules in this dream.

Lizbeth felt her body rolling to the side, heading straight for the side of the Dragon's head. She tried to grab hold of something to stop herself from going over the edge, but her fingers slid across the dirt. They dug into the rock, grasping in desperation, but caught nothing. Another shake, another forceful wave of motion, and she was sailing into empty air, arms and legs flailing as she fell.

She hit the ground hard, her left side taking most of the brunt of the fall. She expected her body to start screaming, but after a few seconds, when there was no pain, she flipped onto her belly and raised her torso.

There was nothing to speak of in the way of hurting. Only a sense of lightness that served to remind her she was still in a dream and that the rules of Earth physics didn't seem to apply to this part of the dreamlands.

Thank God, Lizbeth thought—because she'd been in other dreams where things like gravity did apply and it hadn't been pretty. Once she'd even broken her wrist in a dream (and it had stayed broken in real life), but that had been in the days "before." When she was in the institution and no one believed anything she said . . . and then she'd stopped talking.

And that had been the end of that.

The horrors of the institution had robbed her of her voice, rendering her mute and almost catatonic. Then Weir had rescued her from a fate worse than death and her whole life had changed. Only she'd realized—with dawning horror—that no matter how safe she felt in Echo Park, her voice would not come back. It had been swallowed up in the darkness of her lost life—

"Do you DARE to wake me!?"

The voice wasn't a pleasant one, and Lizbeth craned her neck to see whom, exactly, the voice belonged to. At first, she couldn't get a bead on the owner, but then the voice came again, and she quickly realized what she was dealing with: the Dragon.

"You crawl upon my back and stomp across my nose! You have no decency or respect whatsoever—"

Only in her dream, he wasn't made of stone anymore. He was flesh and blood. Other than that little detail, he looked exactly as he did in waking life. His gray scales were covered in gang tags and graffiti and lovers' initials wreathed in rough-hewn hearts. Even his eyes were the same: dark teal pupils and white eyeballs encircled in electric-blue paint.

She opened her mouth to speak, to apologize to the Dragon for treading on its head, but the words wouldn't—couldn't—come. They sat like hard glass marbles taking up real estate in her mouth. She wanted to spit them out, but it wasn't an option. Instead, she stood up and took a deep bow. Her hope was the beast would accept this as a polite response to his tirade.

"Do not bow at me," the Dragon roared, slithering down from the cliff like a snake, its body long and lean and sinewy.

In her fear, Lizbeth took a step backward and tripped over an exposed tree root that ran across the ground behind her. She lost her balance and fell hard against an old pine tree. Luckily, she was able to grab hold of the tree's massive trunk and stay on her feet—but in the process she'd made a pretty good fool of herself in front of the Dragon.

She heard laughter coming from behind her, and she spun around to face the creature. Coiled like a garden hose in the yard, his serpentine body glittered with silvery light despite the fact the sky was dark with thunderheads. The creature was shining from the inside out, as if he were powered by a tiny sun instead of a heart.

Maybe he was.

"Cat got your tongue?" the Dragon asked after he finished laughing at her—not that she minded. Better to be laughed at than roasted alive, even in a dream.

While she tried to find a way to communicate with him, the beast continued to stare at her. Up close, he was very beautiful, his huge eyes fringed in thick black lashes.

"Aha!" the Dragon said, head rising up from the coil and looming over her. "Maybe this will be better for you, mute. I'll just put my voice inside your head."

—Can you hear me?

Lizbeth started, unsettled. The feeling of having someone speaking directly to her brain was surreal.

—Well?

She nodded.

—You can speak back, silly mute.

Oh, *Lizbeth thought.* This is strange.

The Dragon let out a long guffaw, revealing nubby herbivore's teeth. Which made Lizbeth relax a little. Obviously the Dragon wasn't a meat eater—unless he torched his prey into soft, overcooked meat kabobs first. And if that was the case, then all bets were off.

"I can hear everything you're thinking," the Dragon said as he slithered over to her, unwinding himself to his full length.

For the first time, Lizbeth could really appreciate the monstrous size of the beast. His head was as big as a golf cart, but much more shapely, and his scaled body was probably fifty feet long. Lizbeth tried to remember if the Dragon was this big in waking life, but it was hard to remember back to the real world when you were inside a dream. It was also hard to think clearly when something so large and imposing was freaking you out by reading your mind.

"I can still hear you," the Dragon said out loud, looking displeased that Lizbeth couldn't rein in her thoughts. "Although, it is a lot more fun to watch you squirm, so thank you for that."

Sorry, *Lizbeth thought.* I'm not used to anyone being able to hear me. Even though I'm talking to you with my head and not my mouth, it's . . . just . . . an odd sensation. Being understood.

The Dragon nodded. He really did seem to understand.

I'm here, in this place, because a friend left something for me, *Lizbeth thought.* Maybe you can help me find it—

The Dragon physically recoiled from Lizbeth, swaying his head far away from her.

"But you're still just a child!" *he cried, almost spitting the words at her.* "Not even full grown. I can smell childish things on you."

He blinked so rapidly Lizbeth could tell he was actually upset and not just teasing her.

I'm not a child, *Lizbeth thought, trying to protest, but the Dragon rose high above her head, shadowing her with his body.*

"You are, too!" *the Dragon said, his voice rising an octave in annoyance.* "Hold up a moment. I need to change form. This is all too much for this body to handle."

Lizbeth blinked and the Dragon was gone. In his place stood a beanpole of a man with pale gray eyes and a shock of pitch-black hair shaped into an impressive mohawk.

Whoa, *Lizbeth thought, unprepared for the transformation— and, if she was being honest, for the fact that this man was the handsomest thing she'd ever laid eyes on.*

"Mwahahaha!" *the Dragon-man crowed, dancing in a circle in front of her, his long arms and legs swinging like a whirling dervish as the long, green leather coat he wore flapped around him.* "Tell me what you really think? Handsomest thing ever, eh?"

Lizbeth felt her cheeks flush pink. She had to remember this thing/creature/man *could read her thoughts. Otherwise she was just going to keep embarrassing herself.*

"You're not so bad for a half-caste mute yourself," the man said, arching one black brow in a charming—and very flirtatious—manner.

Half-caste? *Lizbeth thought, not understanding.* What does that mean?

The man stopped shifting back and forth on the balls of his feet and clasped both hands behind his back.

"Ah," he said, nodding thoughtfully. "I forget so many of you don't know a thing about your heritage."

Our heritage? *Lizbeth echoed in her thoughts.*

"You call yourselves Dream Walkers/Dream Keepers . . . or something just as silly. That's humans for ya."

Lizbeth was feeling even more confused now.

I don't understand, *Lizbeth thought.*

The man unclasped his hands so he could scratch the tip of his Roman nose, and Lizbeth saw very long and delicate fingers, the kind one often found on a musician—

"Magician, actually," the man said and grinned down at her. Always the tallest person in a room—except for Weir, whose height made her look demure—Lizbeth was unused to someone towering over her. "And the name is Temistocles—sounds like Tim."

Temistocles offered her his hand, which was so huge it eclipsed her own.

I'm Lizbeth, *Lizbeth thought.* And explain what you meant before. What's a half-caste?

Temistocles looked up at the sky and frowned. Above them the dark clouds bunched together into a thick mass, their fluffy bodies braided so tightly the sky was almost impossible to see. Lizbeth felt a cold chill start at the nape of her neck and travel down the length of her spine. She decided it had more to do with the malevolent look of the clouds and sky than the actual temperature.

"You can't stay much longer," Temistocles said, a thread of worry woven through his words. Then he changed his tone and grinned at

her: "*Half-caste means one of your parents was a normal Earth human and the other . . . well, the other is like me. A creature from another dimension—*"

Are we in another dimension now? *Lizbeth thought, the idea popping into her head without warning.* Is that what dreams are? Other dimensions?

Temistocles smiled at her, seemingly pleased by the way her brain worked.

"*You are a clever one, indeed. Dreams are their own dimension,*" *Temistocles said, eyes still clocking the trajectory of the clouds above them.* "*Anyone can enter the dreamlands, but the majority of visitors don't remember their time here. Just a little quirk in their wiring, I guess.*"

Where do you come from? *Lizbeth thought, curious to discover more about the strange man.*

"*That's for another conversation. But, suffice it to say, I didn't possess a mastery over the dreamlands—*"

A mastery? *she thought.* Over what?

"*What I mean is that I didn't have the ability to manipulate things here in the dreamlands until I was dead.*"

Lizbeth's heart caught in her throat.

You're dead? But . . . you seem so alive! *she thought.*

With an abrupt snort, Temistocles turned away from her, green coat swinging. He was already on the move before Lizbeth realized he was going. When she didn't immediately follow him, he turned around and rolled his eyes at her.

"*Come on,*" *he said, gesturing with a long finger.* "*I have to give you your present before they get here.*"

They? *Lizbeth asked, but Temistocles was even farther away from her now. Afraid to lose him inside the thicket of trees bordering the space where the Dragon rock had once stood, she began to jog after him.*

"*Pick up the pace!*" *Temistocles called over his shoulder, his eyes searching out her own. There was a darkness there, in the hollows of his face and behind his pale gray eyes—and all Lizbeth wanted to do was reach out and soothe his worries away.*

"*Stop trying to mentally mother me, mute child,*" Temistocles yelled back at her, but there was an amused tone in his voice.

Lizbeth caught up to him but was now too mortified to look him in the eye. Instead, they traipsed through the darkening woods together, Lizbeth hyperaware of her new friend's nearness but trying desperately to pretend he wasn't there—she didn't need to embarrass herself further.

They were no longer in the dreamlands version of Elysian Park. Somewhere they'd taken an unexpected turn and ended up in a much more wicked place. The trees, tall white birches with peeling gray bark, shot straight up to the heavens. There, they came together in a massive canopy that blocked out any sunlight stupid enough to try and reach the forest floor. The smell of the place was rich and loamy, but with an undertone of decay that tickled the back of Lizbeth's throat.

She'd experienced lots of strange things and places when she was dreaming, but Temistocles and this odd forest were the creepiest of them, by far. Plus, realizing that dreams existed in an alternate universe . . . well, that was a bit creepy, too.

I'm not scared, Lizbeth thought, her long legs carrying her deeper into the spooky environs of the birch forest.

"*You should be,*" Temistocles whispered, and then he reached out and took her hand.

She had all of two seconds to register she was being touched—and by whom—before Temistocles threw her to the ground with enough force that she had no option but to comply. She cried out in pain as her ankle twisted beneath her, but Temistocles was already on top of her, covering her mouth with his hand, shushing her. Fear wrapped around Lizbeth like a blanket, smothering her. Her breath, what little of it she could catch with Temistocles's hand over her mouth and his body pressing against her, came in shallow staccato bursts that made her light-headed.

—*They're coming. Be bloody quiet.*

Temistocles was in her head again, but instead of it feeling like a violation, it was strangely intimate. Like he was bypassing her skull and whispering into the folds of her brain. She shivered, but the heat *and nearness of Temistocles's body was a good antidote to the terror she was feeling.*

Who are "they"? *she thought.*

—The Flood. The bad guys, as you humans like to say. Always looking to put things in perfect little black-and-white boxes.

There was a tremendous crash above them, and then the rush of running water filled Lizbeth's ears.

What the—*Lizbeth started to think, but then Temistocles removed his hand from her mouth and leaned down, pressing his lips to her ear.*

"You'll wake up with the book in your hands. Hold on to it tightly, my little half-caste love," he whispered before covering her mouth with his lips.

The rush of water, metric tons of the freezing stuff, hit them both at once—that and the kiss taking Lizbeth's breath away.

Temistocles?! *she thought frantically.*

—We will meet again. I promise you that.

Lizbeth opened her eyes to find she was underwater. She could see nothing for the moment . . . but then something bone white caught her attention and she screamed, water filling her mouth and lungs.

She was holding on to a skeleton. One clothed in a long, green leather coat.

Lizbeth woke from the nightmare feeling trapped, her mind spinning faster and faster as it tried to come up with a way to escape the lockdown her body had begun in its sleep.

I will not have an episode, she thought, anger shooting through her.

It was as if there were two parts of her, both acting of their own accord. Her brain was cognizant of everything and wanted to stay engaged in the real world—*save me from the dreamlands, where poor Temistocles is only a skeleton*—while at the first sign of trouble, her body battened down the hatches and went into survival mode.

This problem had started when she was a small child. Not long after her mother died. Now just thinking about the time "before," when her beautiful young mother had loved and protected her, made her shut down. It was hard to believe, but somehow the good memories were more difficult to handle than the bad ones.

No, you can't hide the past away anymore, Lizbeth thought. *If you want to stop all of this and break the cycle, then you have to remember. You have to embrace the good times. Own them and break the spell they hold over you.*

Remembering was so painful she could hardly stand it. But to remember her mother, and the good life she'd had before the institution, was the most important thing—

This was when reality intruded, and she felt Daniela's bare hand hovering inches above her face.

Arrabelle

❧

Arrabelle woke late, dark dreams dogging her sleep. She felt unrested, her brain lost in a fog, eyes bleary. The last few weeks had been painful for her. So hard to process that she found her dreams doing the bulk of the lifting. Because when it came to rebalancing her emotional state, she just couldn't bear to deal with it in her waking hours.

All her life she'd prided herself on being immune to emotions. Not that she didn't feel them—she did—she just didn't let them control her life or influence how she saw the world. But ever since Eleanora's death, her ability to remain calm in any situation had begun to unravel.

It started with small things. Like burning her hand on her espresso maker and knocking its aluminum pot over in anger, or dropping a carton of milk onto the tiled floor, or stubbing her toe on the leg of the kitchen table and crumpling to the ground in tears.

It was adolescent angst behavior. Not at all appropriate for an adult woman. But she found she couldn't help herself. She was a pot boiling over on the stove, a totally out-of-control emotional wreck—and the poor sleep she was getting didn't help things.

Still groggy, she pushed the thick brown duvet away from her body and climbed out of the king-sized teak bed. She slid her feet into a pair of soft slippers then pulled on her powder-blue chenille bathrobe, letting the plush fabric enfold her in its warmth. She walked over to the vanity and sat down to stare at her face.

She looked awful. Hungover even. Her usually handsome features were drawn, the ebony skin too taut over the razor-sharp cheekbones she'd inherited from her mother—who was now only a faded memory, having died when Arrabelle was four. Leaving the curious little girl behind so she had been raised by a loving, yet eccentric, physician father and a revolving door of nannies.

"Who are you?" Arrabelle asked the image in the mirror, but if she expected a reply, she was disappointed. The tired-looking woman in the glass did not answer.

She left the vanity and dragged herself to the bathroom, where she brushed her teeth and washed her face, slathering on moisturizer. This was the same ritual she'd performed for years, eschewing makeup and the other accoutrements of femininity because she was just too damn busy doing other things. Worrying about what she looked like did not rate high on her priority list.

The late-morning light filtered through the living room windows as Arrabelle made her way to the kitchen for her morning coffee. Unlike makeup, espresso rated high on that priority list, and she was no good to anyone before she'd had her first shot of the day.

After decades of living among the detritus of her father's folk art collection, Arrabelle had become almost immune to the West African and South Asian ceremonial masks and ornamental sculptures that decorated her living room—but not quite. Somehow these same collectibles seemed apropos to their environment when they resided in her father's dilapidated old row house in San Francisco, but here in the Southern California sunshine there was something macabre about them.

Their brightly colored faces followed her, eyes ogling her back. Her slippers made no sound on the hard surface of the living room floor, no echoing footfalls to carom off the cathedral post-and-beam ceiling. She'd bought the house for its good bone structure, but she'd ended up redoing the whole space, shaping it into a modernist version of a wooden cabin—large plate-glass windows juxtaposed against the original, more traditional, wooden structure. It was an impressive bit of architecture, something she was proud of creating.

Still, her father's collection felt strange in the space, like a flea-ridden squatter hiding out in the palatial expanses of Versailles. All those faces watching and whispering from their spots on the wall, their gazes malevolent and hostile. Even the benign ones—the smiling masks with wide eyes and grinning mouths, or the animal avatars with their paintwork stripes and spots and fur.

And then there were the vertical-eyed monsters with serrated teeth and pointed tongues, the plain wooden masks that seemed like blank slates ready to take on the emotional state of whatever shaman wore them. For some reason, their expressionless faces terrified Arrabelle the most.

She didn't think of herself as easily upset, but more and more she found she averted her eyes when she had to go through the room.

. . . Bella boo . . .

The words flowed around her as though someone were whispering them inside her head, the imagined fluttering of lips and teeth making Arrabelle shiver.

. . . Bella baby child . . .

Her body went rigid, feet stopping her in place. She felt like a bug trapped in amber in the middle of the living room. All the hair on her body stood on end; the voice—and the words it spoke—was not something she'd heard for a very, very long time.

. . . Bella baby . . .

It was her dead mother's voice, calling out the pet name she'd used when Arrabelle was a small child. After that, no one had ever called her Bella. The truncated version of her given name had been buried along with her mother's bones, never to be resurrected.

Until now.

"Maman?" Arrabelle called out—the urge to connect to the voice so strong she couldn't control her response.

Tiny pinpricks began to cover her body, starting at her feet and then, in a wave of nerve-tingling sensation, traveling up the length of her firmly muscled body until she was consumed. Her eyeballs burned like coals and she scratched at the searing hot flesh with her nails, trying to rip away the skin as if this action would stop the pain. She flailed around the room, slamming against the edge of the couch and falling forward, her head cracking into the wooden coffee table.

"Maman!" Arrabelle cried, acid tears scalding her cheeks as they streamed down her face.

. . . Bella baby, beware . . .

"Maman?!" she screamed, every inch of her body in pain.

The foul stench of charred human flesh filled her nostrils and Arrabelle choked back a scream, terror overloading her brain. She prayed she wasn't smelling her own body cooking, but, of course, she knew that was exactly what was happening. She cracked open a gelatinous eyelid and saw her terror realized: She was roasting like a pig on a spit. Flames leapt from her body and traveled along the couch, engulfing the room and threatening to destroy all the masks and artifacts her father had bequeathed to her upon his death . . .

The burbling of the espresso maker and the smell of percolating coffee replaced the stink of her own fiery death. She shuddered, tension pouring off her in undulating waves, until she felt limp and wrung out.

She was standing in front of the stove, one gas eye lit up in iridescent blues and oranges, the flames licking along the angular aluminum bulb at the bottom of the espresso pot. She reached out to pluck the pot from the gas burner but thought better of it and pulled her fingers back before she burned them.

No more burning today, Arrabelle thought, shivering as she remembered how real the lucid dream had been. *What else could it be* but *a lucid dream? Her mother wasn't a ghostly voice in her head, and she wasn't burning to death. Shit like that only happened in dreams.*

Arrabelle's Cornish Rex kitten, Curiosity, brushed past her ankles, and Arrabelle could feel the thrum of the kitten's purr against her skin.

"Hey, little one," she said as she picked up the skinny beast and pulled her close.

Ordinarily, Curiosity didn't care to be held. But she must've sensed Arrabelle needed the closeness and so the kitten allowed it.

"Nothing bad will ever happen to you, baby girl," Arrabelle said as she gave the kitten one more cuddle, then let her go. "I won't let it."

But who will protect me? Arrabelle thought. *Who will protect us all when the end comes?*

She shook her head, not liking the words that had just come unbidden into her head. She was not a woman who kowtowed to hysteria, but the strange intensity of the lucid dream had freaked her out. As much as she enjoyed the privacy that came with living alone, at that moment she would've given anything to have someone there to hold her like she'd held the kitten.

Dev is the luckiest. She has those little girls at her feet and that flirtatious scamp of a man in her bed. She's never alone.

She turned the eye of the stove off and poured the sludgy brown liquid into a small ceramic espresso cup. She took an orange from the refrigerator and sliced it into four sections, then cut off a wedge of rind from one of the quarters and placed it on the saucer next to her cup. She took her coffee and orange sections to the scarred wooden table and sat down at one of the long benches, wishing it were cold enough to set a fire in the stone hearth that took up the entire back wall of the kitchen.

The heady scent of sage and lavender lingered in the air, a remnant from the poultice she and Lizbeth had been working on the day before—but underlying those enticing aromas were other smells: the pungent manure stench of asafoetida or Devil's Dung, the cinnamony heat of betel nut husk, the crisp mint of pennyroyal, the foul-sweetness of valerian root, the spicy warmth of clove, the decaying odor of cuttlefish bone. Usually, the scents infiltrating her kitchen, via the two Chinese apothecary cabinets that housed her herbal collection, put Arrabelle into a Zen state. But as she drank her espresso, she discovered she just couldn't relax; the strange lucid dream permeated her thoughts, making it impossible to calm down.

To try to change the flow of her thinking, she got up and grabbed a stack of mail she'd left lying on the kitchen counter and brought it to the table. There, she found the requisite bills and junk mail clamoring for her attention, but buried underneath the unwieldy pile was a padded manila envelope simply addressed to *Bell*.

The delicate, looping script was immediately familiar to Arrabelle—and its presence was completely unexpected, filling her belly with both excitement and dread.

Evan, she thought, the name both a blessing and a curse—because the sender of the letter was none other than Evan Underwood, the only man she'd ever loved.

She tore open the envelope, slicing her palm on the metal clasp so that bright red blood smeared across it. A Rorschach of color against the plain beige of the wrapping.

"Stupid," Arrabelle hissed, annoyed with herself for being so clumsy—and for the way her hands were shaking.

Just the thought of Evan was enough to make her heart start to race. It had always been this way. The calm, cool, collected woman she'd worked so hard to create was instantly washed away by a flood of emotion, and she was left as naïve and vulnerable as she'd been when she was eighteen.

I'm like a golden retriever puppy, so excited, tail wagging, tongue lolling out of my mouth like an ecstatic idiot, Arrabelle thought as she pressed her palm to her lips, stanching the trickle of blood with her mouth.

She willed her body to chill out, to just take a moment to process the excitement it was feeling and then to calmly put that excitement away. *Compartmentalize* was her mantra where Evan was concerned—otherwise she could get very, *very* hurt by expectations.

It wasn't as if there were anything she could do to change things. As much as she loved him—and always would—they didn't work. Not as a couple, at least. They were like night and day, oil and water . . . all those ridiculous idioms that basically implied she and Evan were polar opposites who did not combine well. But their attraction to one another defied their differences. Arrabelle didn't know another human being who could light up her life the way Evan did. Just his voice set her ablaze, made her feel alive. Her world was cast in grayscale, and his presence turned everything Technicolor.

Just stop it, she chided herself, inhaling deeply. She held the breath—the lack of oxygen calming her down—then slowly released it through her nostrils in one long exhale.

She slipped her hand into the manila envelope, removing the small leather-bound book that was tucked inside. As she lifted it up from its nest of padding, a folded square of paper fell out and landed on the tabletop. She set the book down and picked up the paper, opening it with shaky hands. A sense of foreboding, so deep she could literally taste its metallic tang, overwhelmed her. She had the bizarre urge to stuff the paper and book back into their envelope and burn them.

Even with the horrible feeling swirling around inside her gut, she knew she would read whatever Evan had sent. Her curiosity was too great.

Dear Bell—

This sounds so trite, but if you are reading this it's because I'm gone, or near to it. Niamh will take this to the general store and post it to you. She's trustworthy—and my last remaining blood sister. She won't let either of us down.

You will know what to do with its contents.

I should have said this to you twenty years ago, but it just never seemed like we were in a place for it to not be misconstrued: I love you. I always will. You are my soul mate. Now and forever.

Be careful. The Flood is coming . . . no, The Flood is already here. We were all just too stupid to realize.

All my love,
E.

Arrabelle stared at the letter, her brain disbelieving its contents. She reread Evan's words again, trying to process what he was telling her.

Evan was gone? How could that be? Wouldn't she have felt it?

Nothing in the letter made any sense.

Except the part where he told you he loved you, Arrabelle thought, her throat tight as she fought back tears. *All these years and only when the world is ending, only when he's gone does he say it . . .*

She hated him in that moment—but hate was just the flip side of love.

Arrabelle pushed back the wooden bench and got to her feet, her body off balance, legs unsteady. Her heart was slamming in her chest, banging against her rib cage, begging to be let out. She laid her palms flat on the scarred tabletop, feeling the deep grooves her knives had made in the wood. Her life's work as an herbalist had created those scars, and once upon a time, they would've reassured her. But in light of what she'd just read, she felt untethered . . . *lost*.

Her work meant nothing when her heart was broken and the man she loved wasn't there, standing beside her. All these years she'd lied to her heart, telling the poor hardworking muscle that it was superfluous. She didn't need it. She could choose to be cold and unemotional, tough as nails. That way she'd be safe.

Ha! What a joke. Only in this moment could she see just how big an idiot she'd been.

She needed love just like everyone else.

She wasn't immune.

She wanted Evan.

She pressed *redial*, but the outcome was the same. The number was no longer in service.

"Damn," Arrabelle muttered, ending the call and setting her cell phone down on the table. It had been so long since she'd spoken to Evan, she didn't know for sure if this number was even his most recent one. She should never have let it go so long between phone calls.

She and Evan would always be connected, no matter the time and space that physically separated them. And even though she'd always felt inextricably drawn to him, she'd been able to stuff those "love" feelings away. Because there were just so few people you met in life who really *got* you, and so when you found one, you held on to them for dear life. Even if that meant you weren't honest with yourself about how they really made you feel.

But now she wasn't sure what to think. Evan was unreachable, *gone*—as he'd said in his letter—and all that was left of him was a leather-bound book. Whatever information it contained, she knew it would only upset her.

She picked it up, weighing it in her hands. It felt very light. The plain leather cover was dark with dirt and ash, and when she lifted it to her nose, the scent of burnt paper leapt out at her. There was a thin brass hasp where a lock had once been, but it was long gone.

It took Arrabelle a moment to realize this was someone's journal.

All those private thoughts on display and now it's available to anyone who cares to read it, Arrabelle thought, feeling guilty for even holding the book in her hands. *But Evan wanted me to have it and I trust his judgment.*

With a silent apology, Arrabelle flipped open the cover. Inside, someone had written: *Property of Niamh Gunderson.*

Arrabelle smiled when she saw the small red heart Niamh had used over the *i* in her given name—but the smile faded when she saw that a number of pages had been ripped out of the beginning of the book, jagged chunks of lined notebook paper left behind in the gluey binding.

"Damn," Arrabelle murmured, a sinking feeling in the pit of her stomach. She knew something terrible lurked within these remaining pages.

Arrabelle stared down at Niamh's journal. With trepidation, she began to read from the first intact entry, the girl's halting voice slipping into her head like the beginnings of a dream.

And then Niamh's past became Arrabelle's reality.

Niamb

They came tonight. This time there were so many I couldn't count them all. The first time they knocked on Yesinia's door, there had only been two—and I had already predicted their arrival with my tarot cards. They identified themselves as belonging to the enforcement arm of the Greater Council, but they didn't give their names.

In retrospect, they never gave their names to us.

At her urging, I opened the door of Yesinia's small cottage, a found-wood structure by the beach she'd built herself over one spring and summer, and there on her driftwood porch stood two people I didn't know. They reminded me of census takers. The man wore his hair so short that I could see the pink of his scalp under his brown hair. He was in his middle age, the paunch of his belly hanging low over the waist of his pants, so that even his black suit could not disguise it. He was so big the suit seemed too small, the buttons straining to stay closed.

"We're looking for Yesinia Arroyo. We're here on official Greater Council business," the man said. He indicated the woman beside him, who nodded coldly. "May we come in?"

I turned to Yesinia, and she shrugged.

What could we do but let them in?

They sat at the square kitchen table with the yellowed linoleum top, their presence filling the room. I stood in the corner, watching, having quickly scooped up my tarot cards from the tabletop. My instincts had told me to remove the spread—one I'd pulled three times that morning, and the impetus for coming to Yesinia's house—before the man and woman could see it. The World, The Magician, The Hierophant, The Devil, and The Fool . . . the message was clear: The advent of these two was only the harbinger of worse things to come.

Yesinia looked small in comparison to these two strangers. And Yesinia had always been the biggest personality I knew.

"We have a writ from the Council," the woman said as she spread her stubby, ringless fingers across the tabletop. She lifted her chin and the man took this as his cue, retrieving a folded piece of parchment from the inside of his coat pocket and tossing it at Yesinia.

I watched the woman pick up the paper, a sneer curling her lips. She was a large creature with hungry gray eyes and thick, fleshy lips that bore no sign of ever having seen a tube of lipstick. The off-putting sneer stayed curled in place for the rest of the conversation.

"Read it," the woman said, greedy to watch—but Yesinia didn't oblige her.

The woman reeked of camphor, as if she'd spread muscle liniment all over her body and then hid her glistening skin underneath her clothing, so no one could see it. Even if they could smell it.

"What kind of business is this you bring to me?" Yesinia asked, looking down at the parchment in her hands.

I knew the clipped cadence of her voice as well as I knew my own. She was born in Guadalajara, and her first language was Spanish. English came to her slowly, her brain forever searching for the correct word or phrase, and often failing.

But she'd found that the slower she spoke, the fewer grammatical errors she made.

"We've been asked to bring you this writ of dissolution," the woman replied, eyes locked on Yesinia as she answered the question. "We believe your coven has been contaminated. Compromised."

Neither Yesinia nor I had any idea what they were talking about. No one understood what was happening in our world; that evil had infected the Greater Council. The gossip channels had not begun to speak of the atrocities being enacted upon our sister covens in distant locales. The West was in the dark as to what was happening in poorer countries, places where human beings still feared magic . . . and where it was easy to destroy women like us.

We didn't realize we could be next on the chopping block.

"I don't understand," Yesinia said as she ran her callused fingers through her thick dark hair.

Even though she was in her late forties, she didn't have a hint of gray in her hair. Her face was unlined, her skin as soft and supple as a child's, her dark eyes always alert and wary. This wariness came from being illegally transported into this country when she was a small child. She knew persecution and fear well, was always aware of what was happening in a room, where any strangers stood, and what they might be thinking.

She was protective of her privacy, and the privacy of our coven. From the rigid set of her shoulders, I could see that her instincts told her there was something very wrong with this man and woman.

"We will give you . . ." The man paused, seeming to enjoy the words as they rolled off his tongue. "Twenty-four hours. Twenty-four hours to dissolve your coven—anything you do that contradicts this edict will be considered a hostile act, and actions will be taken."

"But that is not at all possible. We cannot—" Yesinia tried to protest, but the woman cut her off.

"It's not a question of whether you can or cannot. It *will* happen. This coven—these blood sisters—will not meet again. It's over."

The woman's words were well rehearsed. She'd given this speech before—I was certain of it.

"Who are you?" Yesinia asked.

If they were truly from the Greater Council then, I decided, the world had gone insane.

"We're just the messengers," the woman said, grasping a silver pendant she wore around her neck. It was the image of an ouroboros—a snake eating itself. "Understand. If you do not dissolve this coven of your own doing, it will be dissolved for you. One way or another."

It was a threat—and not a veiled one.

"We will do no such thing," Yesinia replied, her face alive with anger.

"Suit yourself," the man said. "There will be repercussions. You have doomed yourself and your sisters."

They left Yesinia's house, but a residue of evil remained.

Yesinia called the coven together that night. Laragh, Honey, Evan, and I met there beneath the night sky in our secret spot, a grove of ancient madrone trees only a few feet from the edge of the Salish Sea. For centuries, blood sisters had done their work for the Goddess underneath the watchful eyes of this same moon and these sacred madrones.

We didn't know that this night would be our last.

"We have been threatened," Yesinia began after we called the protective circle and gave thanks to the Goddess. "Someone or something evil is on our island and they would want to stop us from doing our business here."

The others—Evan, with his shy smile and curly hair; Honey, the oldest of us, but the most childlike; and Laragh, my identical twin—were unprepared for Yesinia's words. I alone had divined the coming of the Devil with my spread.

"What can we do to stop it?" Evan asked "Can't we go to the Greater Council ourselves?"

I loved Evan and his logical herbalist's mind—and under different circumstances, he would not be wrong. But the world had spun off its axis and things were not normal anymore. I tried to explain this to the others, but they were bullheaded. Even my own twin, Laragh, our coven's empath—and the one who was usually the most sensitive to change—did not believe something terrible would happen to us if we didn't comply with the man and woman's demands.

"It's the twenty-first century, Niamh. Something as awful as the Salem witch trials could never happen again. Not here. Not in the United States . . ."

Everyone was in agreement. How could something so horrible happen now, in our modern-day world? Well, we didn't have to wait long to learn the answer. It was as if Laragh's words were the catalyst for the beginning of the end. For the evil my spread predicted to become reality.

Like silent beasts birthed from the night, they descended on the madrone grove with only one agenda: to destroy us.

The words had no sooner left Laragh's mouth before I saw the first of them. I couldn't tell if it was man or a woman, its gender swallowed whole by the pitch-black robe it wore. The gray mask tied to its face was like a second, more malevolent skin. Each of them carried an object of dark device: a palely glowing knife with serrated blade, a scythe borne on a stem of green metal, a machete with a blade as long as my arm, a rope coiled like a sleeping snake in its master's hand . . . every item my eyes alighted on cut another wound into my heart.

Without thinking, I bent down and scooped up some smooth pebbles from the ground, slipping them into the pocket of my jeans.

"What the hell—" I heard Evan say as they fell on us, each

member of their ranks armed with weapons of violence while we possessed none.

They streamed out of the woods like ants, their targets pre-arranged. Yesinia was the master of our coven, and they had decided to subdue her first. Circling her like dancing demons, seven of them stretched out their hands as if she were a bovine animal that needed corralling. She screamed as they attacked, a guttural cry of impotent rage, her face wild. She tried to fight them off with her bare hands, but she was outnumbered. There was little she could do but persist in fighting a losing battle.

At the same time, three of them surrounded Honey, who was so shocked by their arrival that she stood stock-still, eyes wide like a woodland creature caught in a car's glaring head-lights. They grabbed her roughly by the arms and forced her to her knees, pinioning her arms behind her back.

I watched as tears trickled down her cheeks, glistening like diamonds in the moonlight—but I could do nothing to help her. I was already dealing with monsters of my own.

Laragh and I stood back to back, our identical faces wear-ing (I assumed) the same fierce expressions. Dark brown hair worn long and loose, pale green eyes, lashes dark even without makeup, and pale skin. She was me and I was her . . . and nei-ther of us would be taken down without a fight.

"Don't touch us," I growled through clenched teeth.

Feeling Laragh at my back gave me the confidence to lash out, and lash out I did. I pulled the first pebble from my pocket and found my target, never before so glad to have learned to skip stones as a child. My aim was true, the pebble catching one of the masked creatures square in the face, shattering its nose. It howled in agony and dropped to its knees.

Of course, another one immediately took its place.

"No!" I heard Laragh shriek, the sound coming from a few feet away. I turned and saw my sister being dragged away from the open grove of trees, toward the darker, more thicket-like section of the wood.

It wasn't a decision. I ran toward my twin, pain screaming through my body as one of the robed figures pulled out a serrated knife and slashed Laragh across the back. I saw the blood, a wave of dark liquid soaking the fabric of my sister's cream brocade blouse. I could feel her pain like it was my own and it was as exquisite as the sound of a bow being drawn slowly across the taut surface of a violin string.

I fell to my knees, skinning my hands on the rocky ground.

—Niamh

Laragh was in my head—something that hadn't happened since we were small children.

—Run, Niamh . . . please . . . don't let them . . . get . . .

The words died away. I lifted my head, looking up through wet lashes, but all I could see were the robed figures disappearing into the woods with my sister, her limp body held aloft in their arms.

"Laragh!" I screamed. "Laragh!!"

My throat burned as I called out to her one more time. My only answer was the whoosh of the wind as it whistled through the madrone trees.

My sister was gone. Dead or unconscious . . . I did not know which.

A hand gripped my shoulder and I automatically slammed my elbow into its owner's thigh. I heard a grunt and then:

"Niamh, it's me. It's okay. They're gone."

Evan stood in the moonlight, holding his leg where I'd elbowed him. He had a bloody nose and a split lip, and he held most of his weight on his left side. A horrific gash—from what horrible instrument of violence I couldn't guess—had split apart the flesh at his waist, soaking the hem of his T-shirt in blood.

"Evan," I gasped, but he shook his head.

"I'll live."

I stood up and threw my arms around Evan's shoulders. I was afraid if I didn't hold on to someone, I would lose my mind.

Laragh.

An anguish unlike anything I'd ever known ricocheted through me. I could hardly breathe. My sister was gone and my soul felt as if it had been ripped in two. Evan understood and held me tight. Even though I'm sure with his wound that it was beyond painful for him to do so.

When I was finally calm enough to look around, I saw we were the only ones who had not been taken. Laragh, Honey, and Yesinia were gone . . . and the grove felt empty without their presence. I'd spent so many lovely hours here in this magical place, and now it was destroyed forever.

"Where did they take them?" I asked—even though I knew neither of us possessed the answer. "We have to find them."

That was when I heard the sound. A clanging of bells that rippled through the air and shook me to my very core. Someone was at the Red Chapel in the Woods.

Evan took my hand and we ran.

I grew up on this island. I know those woods like the back of my hand, but somehow, that night, they were alien to me. Every branch, every root and stump blocked my way or caught my flesh, pulling and tearing at me as if to stop me from my fool's errand.

As we crashed our way through the woods, it became apparent that the gash in Evan's side was not okay—that it was bad and only getting worse with the wear and tear we were putting it through. I realized he was not going to be able to keep up with me. But when I stopped, both of us out of breath and almost wheezing, he glared daggers at me.

"I'm going with you."

He leaned against a gnarled old shore pine, hand pressed to his side. Even there in the semidarkness of the moonlit night, I could see the blood seeping out between his fingers. He could argue all he wanted, but his own body was going to betray him.

"Stay. Please. I'll be back," I said—and I meant it. Even then I think I knew I would not be able to save anyone else that night. And maybe not even myself.

He took out his cell phone and tried to dial the police, but he gave up quickly.

"My cell won't work, they're probably using a signal jammer . . ."

He slipped the phone back into his pocket and winced, then tried to rouse himself enough to follow me.

"We were always on our own," I said, and gave him a sad smile. I took off and never looked back—especially when I heard his sobs.

The moon was not my friend. It illuminated things I didn't want to see. Or maybe it was my only true friend, letting me see the event that would purify my heart and start me on the quest. The one from which I will probably not come back.

No one knows who built the Red Chapel.

(But I know who burned it down.)

The building was here on this island seemingly from the start—almost as if it had been created by inhuman hands and left as a gift. Island legend offered many possible architects, but I'd always liked the idea of a ghostly builder the best. Thick planks of redwood—trees that are not indigenous to these parts, so where did they come from?—red cedar, and red alder all planed with precision and care. It was a building built by someone who knew of the golden ratio and had incorporated it into their design.

Normally I found the chapel pleasing to the eye, with its parallel lines and crisp angles, but now in the dead of night it looked menacing. Set back away from the woods, the square building had been built on a piece of flat grassland overlooking the water. The bell tower—with its leaded, stained-glass windows—stood out from the peaked roof as though it were in bas-relief, the shadows giving the steeple that topped it a sinister air.

I stayed away from the clearing and its grassy carpet, keeping myself well hidden among the trees. To step beyond their protective canopy would've been madness. The robed men and women were at the Red Chapel in force, gathered on its front lawn.

Wrapped in the faraway darkness, I couldn't tell if there was anyone within their numbers that I knew. This was my island and I was friends with most of its year-round residents—and quite a few of the summer people, too. I was sure that none of them would've participated in anything like this—something so violent and cruel and unnecessary . . . at least I hoped not.

They'd crafted a pyre of driftwood on the rocky shoreline behind the chapel, a column of wood piercing the middle of the thing like a divining rod buried in the dirt. I watched as they wound Honey and Yesinia through the crowd, robed figures on either side of them keeping them in line. Yesinia could barely walk, her face puffy and bruised. Her captors were holding her up by the arms, dragging her along. They'd beaten her until she'd given up and now she looked just like a dead woman walking.

The powerful coven master I'd once known was broken.

Honey had fared better because she probably hadn't put up much of a fight. She was always the first among my coven mates to run from confrontation, and I was sure this time was no different. Her face was clean, but her eyes flicked back and forth in their sockets like those of a hunted animal. She had to know what was going to happen to her, but she managed to stand tall even in fear—and I was proud of her for this small show of confidence. She was not the kind built for hardship. When Death rode the land on its pale horse, she would be among the first of its followers.

I searched the crowd for Laragh, but she was nowhere to be found. I hoped this meant they had other plans for her . . . but in my heart I was terrified she was already dead. The only thing I could hold on to was that the part of me connected to my twin still felt intact. I decided that if she were gone, I would've felt her go.

"—been charged with witchcraft—"

I'd been so wrapped up in my own worries for Laragh that I'd missed my blood sisters arriving at the pyre. Now they both stood at the foot of the wooden mound, Honey clinging to Yesinia—or holding her up, I couldn't tell which.

Perched on the bed of a red pickup truck, one of the masked men towered above all the others. From the timbre of his voice as he led the others with his skillful oration, I was certain that he was in charge.

"—how do you plead? What is your answer to this charge?"

Yesinia refused to speak, but I saw that some of the fire had come back into her eyes.

"Please, why are you doing this?" Honey cried, desperation riding on the back of her words. "We don't hurt anyone—"

I saw Yesinia lift her hand, trying to silence Honey, but it wasn't any use.

"Then you plead guilty as charged!" the masked man shouted back at her.

Honey turned white as a ghost.

"No! That's not what I said—"

The masked man was on a roll. Like a frothing evangelist at a tent revival, he lifted his arms in the air and began to scream at her:

"You are an abomination, witches! You retard the evolution of mankind and keep us in the Dark Ages. You separate us from our fated destinies—"

"No, no, no!" Honey wailed, but the wind had picked up, stealing away her piteous sobs.

"The Flood is coming, and you and your kind will no longer hold it back—"

Honey wailed and kicked out at her masked captors as they dragged her against her will up onto the pyre. They yanked her arms behind the wooden column, securing her wrists together with thick coils of rope. They wrapped more of the same fibrous rope around her ankles, binding her to the wood and preventing any chance of escape. She sobbed as they worked, tears flowing harder with each subsequent binding.

Yesinia bore the same treatment without comment. There were no tears from her, only the stillness of stone. Part of me wanted her to rail against the injustice of what was happening, but I knew in my heart it was fruitless to fight. No one was coming to rescue either of them.

The end would arrive one way or another.

Of course, we witches know that "the end" is not really what it seems. That our physical forms may die, yet our spirit/energy goes on. But it's one thing to intellectually understand that death was a doorway to a different plane of existence, and another to be a human being who desperately didn't want to die.

Yesinia was a master. She had merged these two parts of herself and was ready for the leap forward.

Unlike Honey, she didn't fear death.

"Light the pyre," the leader of the robed figures called out to the crowd, two of them coming forward with gas cans in their hands.

They soaked the wood with gasoline. It was so strong, I could smell its pungent, oily stink even from my faraway hiding place. Set against the stark white moonlight, the whole abomination seemed surreal. It was as if I were watching a horror movie and I couldn't turn off the television screen.

The robed figures encircled the pyre like faceless judges. They'd called out their verdict and now they were waiting for punishment to be meted out. The smell of the gasoline melded with the rotting-salt stench of the nearby sea—and I knew I would never be able to separate them again.

The ground underneath me was cold, my legs cramping as I crouched there, waiting for it to all be over. I don't know why I felt so helpless, why I didn't think I could do anything for my blood sisters. A fatal apathy had settled over me and I couldn't shake it. I stood up, pain shooting from the small of my back down into my legs. As much as my brain told me that staying hidden was my only option, my body was moving me forward, letting me know there was something else I could do.

I didn't have a plan, at least not a conscious one, but I sensed a hand guiding me, steering my course through the trees toward the back of the Red Chapel. I stayed clear of any sight lines, following the path that led me along the rocky ground beneath the old-growth shore pines, the ones whose feathery boughs cast long shadows over the grassy clearing. I hadn't spent much time at the chapel in recent years, but I knew the door was never locked. There was a specific reason for this—a hammered bronze sign nailed above the front entrance that read:

Deo Oscailte Chun Gach Cé An riachtanas is gá succor Ó An Dark.

This roughly translated to: *Forever Open to All Who Need Succor from the Dark.*

The Dark had built a bonfire near the shoreline in order to murder two people I loved. If anyone needed succor, it was me.

When I reached the back of the chapel, I paused, realizing I was going to have to cross a stretch of ground lit up by the moonlight. I would be vulnerable for a few moments, completely on view to anyone who happened to look in my direction. There was nothing I could do but take a deep breath, run, and hope for the best.

Luck was not on my side. As soon as I leapt forward, a robed figure exited the back of the chapel, holding a can of gasoline. Our eyes locked and I did the only thing I could think to do in the situation. I threw myself at the figure. My elbow slammed into its throat, while the weight of my body knocked its feet out from under it. We fell to the ground and I rolled on top, pressing my advantage. I wrapped both hands around the figure's throat, my fingers digging through layers of black cloth to get to skin. The figure gagged as I straddled it, pinning its arms to its sides. And though it flailed like a dying fish, I did not let go.

After a few seconds, the brown eyes behind the mask rolled out of sight and I released my grip. I dropped my head, listening for breath, and relaxed when I felt the gentle rise and fall of its chest. With shaking fingers, I removed the mask and was pleased when I didn't recognize the man's face. Clean-shaven, tan skin, dark lashes and brows—he was completely unknown to me.

I left him lying there, unconscious, but I took the gasoline can he'd been holding and tucked it under my arm. With this weapon, I could create a distraction and maybe stop the robed figures from setting my blood sisters on fire. Laragh had been right. It was the twenty-first century. No one needed to be burning any witches.

Not on my watch.

I stole the man's robe and mask, slipping them on so I could move more easily through the crowd. They were large on me, but in the darkness it wouldn't be noticeable. Besides, I was carrying a full can of gasoline. No one was going to mess with me.

I reached the pickup truck without much trouble and stood there staring up at the robed leader as he brought the crowd to a frenzy with his aggressive rhetoric. I felt hate burbling inside me, pushing me to do my worst. I closed my eyes and whispered a silent prayer to the mother of the world that I might live through this night. Then I uncapped the can of gasoline and climbed into the bed of the pickup.

The robed man turned around to stare at me.

"What the hell do you think you're doing?" he growled, but I didn't answer him. Instead, I poured the contents of the gas can over his head and went for my Hail Mary pass. I pulled out the Zippo I'd used earlier in the evening to light the coven's ritual candles and flipped it open. The lighter roared to life.

"Untie the witches, or I set him on fire!" I screamed at the crowd.

At first, there was only stunned silence, and I thought I was going to get what I wanted without a fight.

"You can kill me, but The Flood will still come," the robed figure said as he stepped toward me, stinking of gasoline.

He grabbed my wrist and the lighter fell from my fingers. It only took a second for him to go up like a Roman candle. He jumped out of the back of the truck, screaming. There was nothing I could do; he ran right for the pyre. The fumes alone were enough to set it ablaze.

But he wasn't finished. He turned and, with what I imagined was the last of his sanity, ran toward the Red Chapel. With all that wood, it never stood a chance, going up like tinder. I stared at the Red Chapel as it was engulfed in flame.

I was dumbfounded by what I'd become part of.

And since there was nothing left for me there except death— I ran.

Devandra

"I can't find my butterfly shoes, Mom!"

Ginny's voice cut through Devandra's thoughts, and she set her deck of cards down on the lemon damask tablecloth, letting her mind clear. Instinct kicked in and she was able to quickly search her memory, scanning her mind for the last place she'd seen her seven-year-old's pink light-up sneakers.

"They're in your closet!" Dev yelled back.

"No, they're not," Ginny said as she cleared the doorway leading into the kitchen and frowned down at her mother. With her hair and eyes as shiny and brown as new buttons, it always amazed Dev that this child belonged to her—that *any* child belonged to her. Let alone two beautiful girls with intelligent, fierce little faces who favored their Filipino father's exotic coloring.

"Mom?" Ginny asked, a questioning lilt at the end of the word. She stood on her tippy-toes in the center of the kitchen, hand on hip, bare feet pressing against the thick planks of the hardwood floor. "You went away again."

Ginny held a pair of pink pompom socks clutched in her

right hand and rolled her eyes at her mother. Long and lean for her age, she was still tan even though it was October and the weather had finally turned wet and chilly.

Good-bye, Indian summer, Dev thought.

"And you look funny, too."

"Sorry, kiddo, didn't mean to disappear," Dev said, smiling affectionately at her younger daughter. "Just thinking."

"'Bout the lady?"

Dev frowned as fine lines crosshatched her pale forehead. Ginny was very observant and extremely blunt. She called it like she saw it, regardless of anyone's feelings.

The night before, Dev and the girls had experienced a visitation from beyond: a ghostly apparition that led them to find a letter written by Dev's great-great-grandmother Lucretia over a hundred years before Dev was born. The letter was hidden inside the frame of the Victorian mourning wreath Lucretia's daughters had crafted shortly after her death. Dev had always loved the memento mori the women had made to memorialize their mother—five flowers woven from the thick strands of Lucretia's raven hair and set against a mother-of-pearl disc—but now she felt connected to it on a whole new level. It was a bridge linking Dev and her daughters to the Montrose women of the past.

She just wished the experience hadn't scared her older daughter so badly.

Dev sighed and pushed her spindle-backed chair away from the table. She was glad the previous night's ghostly encounter hadn't affected Ginny, but it was worrisome that Dev's older daughter, Marji, was so frightened she couldn't go to sleep until the sun came up.

Marji was her sensitive child. Fragile as an antique china doll, she didn't like to leave her glass display case unless there was a protector at hand—which usually turned out to be Ginny. It niggled at Dev, the pattern of younger sibling acting as a spokesman for the older one. She worried their relationship might become too symbiotic, too insular—but her partner, Freddy, told her to stop helicopter parenting and just let the girls be.

"Did you check your closet?"

Ginny nodded, long hair flying.

"I already did. Marji looked, too," she said with a slight lisp. Missing baby teeth were in the process of being replaced by larger, permanent ones. "Can you braid my hair?"

"I can. And are you telling me that you need a special set of mom eyes to find your shoes?" Dev asked.

Ginny's head tipped back and forth on the long stalk of her neck.

"Yup."

She followed Dev out of the warm kitchen, past the antique O'Keefe and Merritt stove, the hanging rack of copper pots and pans, and out into the living room where the staircase led up to the second floor.

It was an old Victorian house that had belonged to Dev's family for more than a hundred years—long enough for everyone in the neighborhood to refer to it as the Montrose House—though it hadn't actually been built in Echo Park. A Montrose woman had won the house in a high-stakes game of poker (a royal flush in a suit of clover) and had relocated the home from Bunker Hill to a plot of land in the wilds of the Elysian Valley.

This was the very same parcel where the house still stood. And since that time, the house had been passed down to each eldest Montrose daughter upon the arrival of her twenty-first birthday. Dev and Freddy lived there now, but as soon as Marji came of age, she would take possession. She would either invite them to stay on, or they would move out, as Dev's parents had done.

With four daughters in as many states—three of whom had children—her mom and dad were more than happy to be homeless, tooling around the country in their truck and Airstream trailer, visiting their various progeny for weeks at a time. Her parents both worked as literary translators (her father was fluent in German, her mother French), so they'd always been free to live and work wherever they chose. They'd both officially retired a few years earlier, but when they were still working, Dev would get postcards from her mom telling her about the translations they were doing while visiting the Grand Canyon, or Café du Monde in the French Quarter, or a sweat lodge in New Mexico.

She and Freddy had offered to turn the Mucho Man Cave— the garage where Freddy hosted a neighborhood weekend bar—into a guesthouse, but her parents had happily declined. They enjoyed their freedom and the Gypsy lifestyle it afforded them. Dev had a hard time imagining her own life being so rootless. As much as she enjoyed traveling, she liked having a fixed address and a place to display all her things.

The old wooden staircase creaked as it took Dev's weight, but Ginny's footsteps hardly rated a whisper as she trailed along behind her mother. As she trod upon the squeaking thirteenth step, Dev promised herself (for the umpteenth time) that she'd get out the toolbox and fix it. Just a few taps of her hammer and it would stay silent for a couple of weeks, at the least.

That was the only problem with having stewardship of an older home: You were responsible for all the bits and pieces that needed looking after. Because just when you got the thirteenth step to stop squeaking like a scared mouse, the roof would spring a leak or the water heater would go on the blitz. It was frustrating to be fixed, taped, drilled, and caulked into oblivion. The constant upkeep drove both her and Freddy crazy.

At the top of the stairs, Dev took a right and headed for the girls' rooms. Behind her, she could hear the soft shuffle of Ginny's feet on the wooden plank floor. The long hallway was quite narrow, thick wooden doors branching off into the home's three upstairs bedrooms, a half bath, and the full bathroom the girls shared.

The rule of the house was you left it (mostly) as you'd found it, the décor unchanged unless something broke or was destroyed by calamity—then could you make updates or add modern conveniences.

Like the new low-flow toilet Dev added when one of the water pipes burst, flooding one of the upstairs bathrooms and giving them the opportunity to install a shower, said low-flow toilet, and a double-sink vanity. With no fights over who got to brush their teeth first in the mornings, it made getting the girls ready for school a much easier task. Especially because Marji was notorious for climbing up on the vanity, sticking her feet into a stoppered-up basinful of hot water, and falling asleep—*Please, just ten more minutes, Mom!*—her face pressed against the mirror.

Until the arrival of the double vanity, this quirk of Marji's nature made Ginny, who wanted to brush her teeth in a foot-free sink, absolutely lose her mind with annoyance each and every morning.

"It's cold up here," Ginny said, trailing alongside her mother.

It *was* noticeably colder up here than in the rest of the house. Dev shivered and wrapped her soft cotton shawl around her shoulders. The light was dim upstairs, one small porthole window feeding natural light into the space.

Dev felt Ginny's small hand grasping at the folds of her purple peasant skirt.

"I can see my breath, Mommy."

This had happened the night before, this sharp and unexpected drop in temperature. It was something Dev associated with the arrival of a ghostly presence.

"Marji!" Dev called out, her voice high-pitched with worry.

When there was no reply from her elder daughter, a thin film of sweat broke out on Dev's upper lip. She quickly wiped it away.

"Marji!!" she called again. She turned to Ginny, whose face was pinched with uncertainty, and asked, "Where was your sister when you saw her last?"

"Her room before," Ginny replied in a tiny voice.

Dev grabbed Ginny's hand, and together they made their

way toward Marji's closed bedroom door. Decorated with some of Marji's favorite poems—handwritten on lined notebook paper in sparkly silver and pink gel pens—the door was a glittery homage to E. E. Cummings, Emily Dickinson, and Shel Silverstein.

Dev wrapped her fingers around the brass doorknob as a gust of arctic wind blew across the hall. Ginny's head swiveled like a bird's, dark eyes wide with worry. She gripped Dev's hand harder, and Dev could feel the slick sweat of fear in between their entwined fingers.

"Do you hear the voices, Mama?" Ginny whispered.

Dev narrowed her eyes and listened hard, trying to catch whatever it was her daughter was hearing. But there was only the soft hiss of the heater turning on downstairs.

Inching the doorknob to the left, she pushed open the heavy door. Its metal hinges creaked with her effort. A ray of sunshine shot out from inside the room, piercing the gloomy hallway. Dev blinked as the light temporarily blinded her. She didn't see the man step out of the room, fist raised. She didn't see his knuckles as they shot toward her face, their aim true and swift. Only the tug on her skirt from Ginny's tiny hand saved her from taking the hit directly to the bridge of her nose.

Instinct (and the need to see what Ginny wanted) made her turn her head slightly so the punch landed on her left cheekbone. The pain was jarring, ricocheting through her face and snapping her jaw shut tight, nearly severing her tongue between her teeth. She'd never been hit in the face before and didn't recognize what was happening to her until the second time the man's hand connected with her face. This time the pain flared through her and she felt something *crack* underneath her skin. Tears sprang to her eyes. Everything was happening so quickly she didn't get a chance to look at her assailant.

Somewhere outside herself, she heard a child's scream of utter rage—and it terrified her. As darkness descended like a sheet, she heard a voice whisper inside her head: *Don't worry. I'm here.*

Dev's heart squeezed at the sound of Eleanora's voice, and then she fell back into an abyss of black fire.

Dev opened her eyes to find herself standing in exactly the same place, only now everything around her was shimmering like stardust. She felt a tug at her belly and her eyes dropped to her navel, out of which emerged a long filament of glowing light that coiled down to the ground and disappeared. Dev gasped as her eyes followed its path and she discovered her own body sprawled at her feet, the other end of the glowing cord connected to its navel.

"Don't be afraid."

She looked up. Where only a few moments earlier there'd been no one, now Eleanora stood at her side, floating a few inches above the floor.

This was not the Eleanora that Dev had known as an adult. This was a much younger version, hale and hearty and full of life. Dev remembered this incarnation from her childhood, when, as a little kid, she'd seen the former master of the Echo Park coven around the neighborhood. She'd had no idea that when she turned twenty-one, Eleanora would seek her out. That this beautiful, mysterious woman would become her blood sister and induct Dev into the world of the covens.

"Look," Eleanora said, pointing to the far end of the hallway. There, by the top of the stairs, Dev saw something terrifying and exhilarating.

Marji and Ginny stood against the wall, hands linked in an unbreakable bond, their bodies wreathed in a shimmering firestorm of light. Behind them, her body so translucent Dev could see the small brown-and-beige chevrons on the antique wallpaper behind her, stood Hessika, the giantess who'd been the head of the Echo Park coven before Eleanora.

She did not look nearly as young as her ghostly counterpart. In this incarnation, Hessika was late-middle-aged, her hair soft and feathery around her thick-lashed eyes. Her Cupid's-bow mouth, painted in over her thin lips, was compressed so tightly it resembled a rosebud.

She kept one hand on each girl's head, and Dev realized she was the source of the light. Her love and power were blanketing the girls, protecting them so they wouldn't be scared of the strange man crouching at the top of the stairs, his hair falling in a long sheet across his face.

Dev watched, transfixed, as the girls lifted their intertwined hands into the air, calling into being a powerful whirlwind that spiraled through the hallway. It sucked up bits of dirt and detritus from the floor, so that it began to take on a visible shape as it barreled toward the man on the stairs. Marji's ponytail whipped across her face, obscuring her dark eyes just for a moment, but not before Dev saw the look of unbridled joy on her elder daughter's face.

She was loving this.

Ginny, too, seemed to thrill at the power they held between them. Her long hair eddied around her face in curlicues, her eyes shining in their sockets like living flame. Together, they lifted their hands higher, and the whirlwind grew stronger, now threaded with the same glowing luminescence Hessika was using to protect the girls.

The man grabbed the stair railing, using it to hold himself in place as the wind screamed in a furious maelstrom of magic. The sheet of hair was blown away from his face, and Dev found an emptiness there that was horrible to behold. Even in the middle of the frenzy, he appeared calm and collected, the human version of the eye of a hurricane. With his high cheekbones and long dark hair, he should've been very handsome—but his pale blue eyes bore the ugliness of evil, ruining the picture. Flat and empty, they held a promise of terrible things to come.

And then, as if someone had turned off a light switch, the man was no longer floundering, no longer fighting to remain upright as he gripped the railing. Instead, the winds appeared to break around him. Like an invisible barrier was now protecting him from the girls' power. The man opened his mouth, lips stretching wide to emit a cloud of pitch-black sulfur. Dev gagged, covering her mouth and nose with the heel of her palm.

The cloud swirled around the man's head like a whirling dervish, and those dead blue eyes locked on her daughters, eyeballs skittering back and forth in their orbital sockets, trying to memorize every curve of their faces.

"No!" Dev screamed just as the foul cloud gathered itself into a ball and shot toward the girls.

The glittering light surrounding her daughters took the hit, swallowing the dark energy.

The man growled, eyeballs popping out of his head. His face began to change, the pale skin rippling as if something alive moved underneath the flesh. Dark purple marks gouged themselves into his skin, creating elongated bruises that ran across the length of his cheekbones.

Or maybe, Dev thought, *the scratches are being made from the inside out, fingers trying to tear their way into our world.*

This idea terrified her, but she couldn't tear her eyes from the sight. The marks began to fade, disappearing as quickly as they'd been made and leaving no trace of themselves behind.

The man drew in a deep breath and exhaled another dark cloud of foul-smelling sulfur even bigger than the last. Dev knew exactly what he meant to do with it.

"Leave them alone!" she screamed.

She ran forward, wanting to protect her daughters from the man, but the glowing filament connecting her to her unconscious body (the real, living one) snapped her backward. Without thinking, she grabbed the cord with both hands, meaning to yank it from her belly.

"Stop, or you'll be lost here forever, Devandra."

Dev froze, having forgotten Eleanora was still beside her. She shook her head, her stern expression chiseled from granite. A

New Englander by birth, Eleanora was as tough and implacable as the land she hailed from and never shy with her opinion.

"Don't be an idiot," Eleanora said.

"But my babies need me," Dev cried.

As though Eleanora had timed it this way, a high-pitched scream tore through the air, drawing Dev's attention. Heart in her throat, she was certain it had come from one of her girls—but her ears had deceived her: The girlish scream belonged to the strange man at the top of the stairs. Apparently, while Eleanora had kept Dev otherwise engaged, the man had sent over his dark cloud and it had proved no match for Hessika and the girls.

The man's face twisted, and he broke out in the same dark bruises as before, the thing inside him lashing out in fury. Dev could sense its rage, its utter disbelief that the man it possessed was unable to touch Marji and Ginny.

The man let loose another earsplitting scream and ran at the girls, hands outstretched. It looked like he was going to scoop them up and steal away with them into the shadows.

"No!" Dev screamed. There was no way she was going to let this abomination touch her children.

But before she could take a step forward, destroying the delicate link between her spirit and her body, a tall figure in a long green coat swept up the stairs. Moving with the grace of a dancer, the figure leapt up the last step and threw himself at the evil man, grabbing him around the middle and pulling him away from Hessika and the girls. The evil man was caught unawares, and the figure in the green coat used this to his advantage, wrapping an arm around the evil man's throat and yanking him back toward the stairs.

The evil man's body began to writhe, fighting for oxygen as the figure in the green coat looped his arm into a choke hold. The purple bruises across the evil man's face became raised and swollen. Whatever was inside him was still struggling to get out, but after a few minutes, the evil man's energy was tapped and he lost steam. The will to fight ebbed out of him until he went limp and stopped moving.

The figure in the green coat seemed to relax, eyes full of sadness at what he was being forced to do. Then the evil man opened his eyes, a sly gleam flickering behind lowered lashes. Dev realized it was all a ruse.

"He's faking it!" Dev cried, trying to warn the figure in the green coat.

Too late.

With a guttural grunt, the evil man twisted away, throwing his weight into the figure in the green coat. The two of them fell backward off the top of the landing, and Dev watched in horror as they disappeared into the darkness.

She just wished she could blot out the sound of flesh and bone cracking against the wooden stairs.

"It's okay, Mama."

Marji's voice drew Dev's attention away from the empty stairs.

"Mama?"

Marji spoke the term of endearment again, her dark eyes uncertain—and Dev realized her daughter wasn't looking at the inert body on the floor but at Dev's spirit self.

"You can see me?" Dev asked, astonished.

Marji nodded, her usually tan face pale.

"Mama can't hear you," Ginny said, looking up at her older sister. "She's sleeping."

But Marji shook her head.

"Mama's right there by Auntie E."

Auntie E was what the girls had always called Eleanora, and Dev saw her ghostly friend smile at the use of the nickname.

"Where?" Ginny asked, looking around the hallway, obviously seeing nothing.

"There," Marji said, pointing at spirit Dev—but Dev knew Ginny couldn't see her by the confused expression on her younger daughter's face.

"Don't you see?" Marji continued as she looked back at Hessika, who stood behind them. "Why can't anyone else see you guys?"

"No one else can see the Dream Walkers, *ma belle*," Hessika said, her lisping Southern-inflected voice soothing to Dev's ear. "Not unless we choose to exert our energy and show ourselves to them, that is. But you're special. You have the gift of second sight. To see what others cannot."

Marji looked sad.

"Not even Ginny?"

"Not even me, what?" Ginny asked, as Hessika smiled and rested an unseen hand on Ginny's head.

"Don't worry about your sister, sweetness. She has plenty of other gifts," Hessika said, her voice laced with a glorious sugary slowness that drew out each individual word like taffy.

Dev found herself transfixed by the woman, wanting to stay in this half-alive/half-dream state purely so she could observe Hessika's movements, languish in the sibilant sound of the giantess's voice.

"And you, *ma belle*," Hessika continued, her focus shifting to Dev. "It's time for you to wake up."

Dev felt Eleanora's hands on her shoulders, pressing down into and through her noncorporeal flesh—

—and then she opened her eyes.

Above her the hammered tin ceiling slowly came into focus, illuminated by the weak sunlight filtering in through the porthole window above the stairs. She felt like a cockroach flipped onto its back, and quickly remedied this by rolling onto her side. A dull pain radiated from her cheek and mouth. When she pressed a hand to her lips, her fingers came away bloody.

"Mama!"

Marji's skinny arms wrapped themselves around her neck, squeezing hard. She felt Ginny squirm up on her other side, pressing the top of her dark head into the crook of Dev's neck.

"It's okay, babies," she whispered, her busted lower lip making her words sound funny.

She sat up and pulled her daughters in tight.

"Mama," Ginny said, brows furrowed. "The man's still downstairs and he's not moving."

Marji nodded, her skinny shoulders almost up to her ears. Dev could feel the tension rolling off her older daughter in waves.

"Stay here," Dev said, and crawled over to the stairs, using the curved wooden banister to pull herself to her feet.

She looked back at the girls, but neither seemed to have any intention of disobeying her. Instead they huddled together like two frightened animals, shivering despite the warm air circulating around them from the downstairs heater.

"I'll be right back."

She checked the hallway, looking for any signs that Hessika and Eleanora were still there. She decided that if they were, she was blind to their presence. Slowly, she followed the stairway down, taking each step with the utmost caution. Her head pounded in time with her heartbeat, and she knew she was going to have to take some ibuprofen *sooner* rather than *later.*

When she reached the bottom step, she stood there, unwilling to leave the safety of the stairs. The evil man was on his back, unconscious or dead—she didn't know which—his long hair splayed around his head like a charcoal crown. His eyes were closed, and his chest remained stubbornly flat. No telltale rise and fall to let her know he was still breathing.

She looked for the figure in the green coat, but he was gone. *Or maybe he was never here at all,* she thought.

"Marji!" Dev called, not bothering to turn her head. "Did you see the man in the green coat?"

She heard the sound of scurrying feet on slippery wood and realized the girls had taken that as a cue to come downstairs. She didn't want them to see this man laid out on their living room floor, so she called back up at them: "Stay at the top of the stairs!"

The pounding of feet stopped just short of the top step,

and Dev turned to see both girls on the landing, watching her with wide eyes.

"I didn't see a green—" Ginny started to say, but Dev shushed her.

"Let Marji answer first, please." Her tone brooked no argument from her younger daughter.

At first, Marji only nodded.

"Tell me," Dev said.

"He came up the stairs and got the evil man," Marji said, finally finding her tongue.

Dev nodded, encouraging her daughter to continue.

"And then, after they fell, he came back up to tell you something, Mama, but you were asleep again. You weren't there for him to talk to."

"What did he say?" Dev asked, trying to keep her voice light. She knew putting pressure on Marji would only cause her to clam up.

"I didn't see any man in a green coat," Ginny chimed in, not liking that she was being left out of the conversation.

"Ginny, please," Dev said, her exasperation making Ginny pout.

"It's not fair. I never get to see *anything* and Marji sees *everything*—"

"He said to tell you," Marji began, and Ginny instantly quieted down, letting her sister speak, "that Temistocles sends LB his love. I think he meant Lizbeth."

"That's all he said?" Dev asked, confused by the man's words. Marji shook her head.

"He said that you need to call Grandma and our aunts," her daughter intoned, the words spilling from her lips in a rush. "That they need to come and stay. That the others are going to have to go away and it won't be—it's already not safe anymore."

With the entirety of the message fully revealed, Marji began to cry.

Lizbeth

"Don't!" Lizbeth cried, her voice hoarse from years of disuse. She rolled away from Daniela's outstretched hand, narrowly avoiding being touched. She wasn't sure how she knew this, but if Daniela's hands ever came into contact with Lizbeth's skin, it would most likely be the end of her.

"Holy shit, you just said something!" Daniela said from her seat in the dirt. She'd landed there when Lizbeth rolled away, and her surprise had kept her there.

Lizbeth climbed onto her knees, clutching a tattered notebook in her hands. She stared down at it, unable to believe something real and solid had come through with her from a dream . . . the other side . . . *wherever* she'd been with Temistocles.

Temistocles.

Her heart beat faster at the mere thought of his name. It startled her because she'd never experienced a feeling like it before. No one had ever brought out that part of her. She'd thought she was immune, maybe even asexual. That she was incapable of feeling attracted to another person.

"Why are you crying?"

She looked up and saw Lyse standing nearby, a worried expression in her blue eyes. Weir was with her, but he didn't look scared like Lyse, or surprised like Daniela. He looked angry.

"You can't just go off like that—" he began, in a booming voice.

Lyse put a hand on his shoulder in an attempt to calm him down.

"She's clearly upset," Lyse said. "You don't need to yell at her—"

Daniela scooched toward Lizbeth, trying to slip her gloves back on her hands at the same time.

"Wait—she was talking. Did neither of you hear that?" Daniela demanded.

Weir's face was getting red.

"—anything could've happened to her—"

Lyse spoke with the voice of reason:

"—please, just let her have a minute—"

Daniela was climbing to her feet, brushing the dirt off of her pants:

"—uhm, *hello*, guys, she's *talking*—"

It was all too much for Lizbeth. She was used to silence, to whispers, to the quiet of her own internal world. She felt herself shutting down; the gates in her brain—the ones that protected her when she became overwhelmed—began to slam tight.

No, she thought. *I won't let it happen. I won't. The past is past.*

Of course, this was all so much easier said than done. Lizbeth had no experience telling her body no. Just as she had zero experience with being kissed by someone.

When she was a little girl, Lizbeth's mother would sing her Korean lullabies as she rocked her to sleep. Her mother had died when she was still pretty young, so her memories were kind of blurry and dreamlike. She had a vague recollection of a slight, dark-haired woman with soulful brown eyes holding her, and pushing her on a swing, making her eggs

for breakfast . . . and then her mother got sick and Lizbeth
hardly saw her after that.

But she remembered her mother's singing voice: the husky
half-whispered lyrics and the loving way she sang them, her lips
right next to Lizbeth's ear. Lizbeth had been so young, her world
so insular and small, that those murmured words made more of
an impression on her than anything else about her mother.

They were, those songs, the thing that came to her mind
when she was gasping for breath. When she couldn't keep her
head above water and was terrified she'd sink into the abyss
of her own mind. She needed to learn how to stay present—
and her mother's warm contralto and the sugary smell of her
mother's skin . . . these memories were what Lizbeth held on
to, what gave her the strength to remain above the murky surface of the water.

"LB?"

She opened her eyes. Hadn't even been aware that she'd
closed them. Saw Weir's handsome face, worried now, and
only inches from her own.

"You didn't . . ." He stopped, suddenly choked up. "You
didn't shut down."

She frowned, reaching out to place a slender hand on his
cheek. Strange how she described her hand as *slender*. Until
that very moment, she'd always thought of her hands as com-
ically huge, too big and bony for a girl. Now she stared at
them, surprised by how graceful they looked.

It appeared as though something inside her had broken
irretrievably and there would be no going back. She didn't
know what Temistocles—*what that kiss*—had done to her,
but she was not the same person she'd been when she'd lain
down on top of the head of the Dragon.

"No, I didn't," she said, pleased by the sound of her voice.
It was husky and melodic just as Bit-na's voice had been.

Bit-na.

Her mother.

She wished Bit-na were with her now, still alive and smiling. She'd have been so proud of Lizbeth.

"What happened?" Weir asked. He crawled closer, his knees buried in the dirt.

"I don't know."

She was distracted by her mother's voice. It still lingered in her head but was slowly fading away even as she tried to hold on to it. She wished Weir could hear it, too. He'd loved Lizbeth's mother, had confessed to Lizbeth once that he wished his stepmother had been his *real* mother. Especially because his own mother—the Nordic Ice Queen, as he liked to call her—had very little to do with him when he was growing up, preferring to spend her time abroad, acting like she didn't even *have* a kid.

Lizbeth suspected his love for Bit-na colored how he felt about Lizbeth. That he loved her more, felt more protective of her because of a debt he thought he owed her mom for being there for him when his own mother was not. Why else would he have saved her from the horrific institution their shared father had dumped her into after her mother died? He was not the responsible party. He received no financial compensation for taking care of her—the opposite, actually—but still he'd come for her. Plucked her out of hell and brought her back to Echo Park, and for that she would be eternally grateful.

Daniela sat down beside Weir. She held out her gloved hands, her eyes on the spiral-bound notebook resting in Lizbeth's lap.

"May I?"

Lizbeth looked down at the dog-eared book. Once upon a time the front cover had probably been brown, but now it was a sad beige, the metal spirals rusted through. But despite its age and discoloration, the inside was still in decent shape as Lizbeth flipped open the cover. The paper was oatmeal brown and curling around the edges, the blue lines faded to a soft violet. Lizbeth traced a finger along the top, and saw that someone had written the word *Evolvo* in neat and precise script in one of the margins.

She turned the notebook around so Daniela and Weir could see. Weir frowned.

"It's blank."

Lizbeth stared at him: *What was her brother talking about?* She looked at Daniela, who nodded in agreement.

"Is there something on the page that you can see?" she asked Lizbeth. "Something that maybe we can't?"

Daniela held Lizbeth's gaze, waiting for an answer.

Lizbeth blinked.

"Yes."

She returned to the page, eyes running along the rigid lines of script that cut across the paper, the handwriting tight and restrained. How could they not see it? She looked up again, catching Lyse's eye.

"It's not a Dream Journal, but it's something like it, right?" Lyse asked.

She was still standing, hands on hips, a worn expression on her face. She'd pulled her shawl over her head and her eyes stayed on the gray sky above them as it threatened to douse them in rain. "And we should get out of here."

"Why? The rain?" Weir asked, confused.

"Just a feeling," she said. Then to Lizbeth: "I can't read it either, but I know you can. Eleanora has more of these things back at the house. Dream Journals. She showed them to me—and I'm betting she's shown them to you, too."

Lizbeth shook her head.

"The tall lady did. Not Eleanora."

"Same difference," Lyse said, and gave Lizbeth a wan smile. "What one does, the other already knows about."

Lizbeth agreed with that sentiment.

"The notebook. It wasn't here in our world?" Daniela asked, sitting back on her haunches and looking up at the sky.

Lizbeth shook her head.

"No."

Daniela pursed her lips together thoughtfully.

"You brought it back with you from the other side."

Yes, that's exactly what I did, Lizbeth thought. *I have the ability to do strange and terrible things. I don't even know the half of it yet.*

Like a carcass pecked clean by carrion birds, she felt as smooth as bone. The years of fear and uncertainty had been washed away. What remained was clean and glistening, waiting for her destiny to begin. Not that she said any of this to her brother or to Daniela. She would talk to Lyse later—Lyse, to whom she felt a kinship that went deeper than just being blood sisters.

"What the hell does that even mean? Dream Journals, notebooks with stuff in them no one can see?" Weir asked, frowning.

The sky chose that moment to split apart. A sliver of electric light arced across the sheet of gray clouds. A cold rain began to fall, large droplets that burst like ripe berries as they hit the ground. It wasn't a normal California rain—it came in a torrent, cutting tributaries into the dirt and sluicing down the sides of the Dragon, sheets of water cascading across the outcropping of rock before splitting off into mini-waterfalls.

"We need to go!" Lyse cried, reaching for Lizbeth's arm. "Too much rain and it's moving quickly."

Lizbeth tucked the spiral-bound notebook under her shirt where it would stay drier and took Lyse's hand. She might have towered over her friend in height, but there was a quiet strength about Lyse that made Lizbeth feel safe.

"C'mon," Weir said, appearing at Lizbeth's side, his blond hair plastered down to his head by the rain. Daniela was right behind him, looking as pissed off as a waterlogged cat.

"I fucking hate rain," she murmured, peeved. "Look, we can go to my house and get my car. Head to Devandra's, check out the notebook there—"

A crack of thunder rolled across the sky, and it was so loud all four of them instinctively looked up. Daniela opened her mouth to say more, but another loud boom drowned her out as a pillar of darkness amassed in the sky above them.

"Holy hell!" Weir said, grabbing Lizbeth and wheeling her away from the edge of the rocks. "Let's go!"

He pushed her toward the slope leading back to the trailhead, but Lizbeth couldn't move. She stood transfixed by the towering funnel of dark cloud as it shot swiftly toward her, scooping up trees and rock wherever it touched the Earth. Lizbeth knew she needed to move, but she felt drawn to the darkness, curious to see what was at its core.

"Go!" Lyse said, and pulled on Lizbeth's arm, yanking her out of her stupor.

Whatever hold the dark had over her was broken. She let Weir take her arm, guiding her down the slope. Lyse was ahead of them, trying to keep her balance as she slid down the rocky incline.

"Daniela!" Lyse screamed when she realized Daniela wasn't with them. She turned back, staring up at the top of the ridge. "Where the hell are you?"

Daniela popped her head over the side of the Dragon and grinned down at them.

"I'm gonna go back," she called out, pointing in the opposite direction. "I wanna see what's on the other side of it."

"Are you insane?!" Weir yelled back at her. "You're gonna get yourself killed."

"I'm not! I promise!" she shouted over the sound of the storm—and then she was gone.

"She's nuts," Weir said. Not wasting any time, he pulled Lizbeth with him as he searched for the trail leading them back to the heart of Elysian Park.

Lizbeth wasn't worried. She knew Daniela would be okay because, like a cat, Daniela always managed to land on her feet.

"Hold up!" a voice called out ahead of them.

Arrabelle stood in the middle of the trail, waving at them. Weir tried to dodge her but tripped on an exposed root. He fell hard, and Lizbeth went down with him, his hand still clutching hers. He was running on big brother mode, and to that end he was already climbing to his feet, his sole focus getting Lizbeth to safety.

Lizbeth noticed the change in barometric pressure and the sudden silence.

"Weir!" she cried, but he ignored her.

She could see that the sky had changed, was nothing like the steely black mass of clouds that preceded the funnel. She dug in her heels, weighing him down like an anchor. He kept pulling her, but she was not a waifish thing, and after a few seconds he stopped trying to do the impossible.

"Look, it's gone," she said, squeezing his hand as she pointed up at the sky.

Shell-shocked, Weir followed her gaze. There was absolutely nothing funnel-like on the horizon, no uprooted trees, and no destroyed property. It was as if the rain and the funnel had never happened—which she was beginning to suspect was the truth of the matter.

That's where Daniela went, Lizbeth thought. *She knew it wasn't real. She was looking for the source of the magic.*

"It was an illusion," Lyse said, pulling the shawl from her head and wrapping it around her shoulders. She turned to Arrabelle, who was still standing in the middle of the hiking trail, eyes fixed on Lizbeth: "How did you find us?"

Arrabelle blinked when she realized Lyse was speaking to her.

"Text from Daniela. Just got it," Arrabelle said. "I have my car up the way."

"We need Daniela—" Lyse started to say.

"Daniela's here." Daniela crunched her way through the underbrush, her hair disheveled, but a wide grin on her face. She turned to Arrabelle: "You got my message."

Arrabelle nodded, eyes still lingering on Lizbeth—which made Lizbeth feel weird. She didn't like being stared at like a specimen under a microscope.

"Things are getting weird and I think it's best if we recon-vene at Dev's. We need to talk as a coven," Daniela contin-ued. "Besides, I'm beat from running. I scared the crap out of a bunch of hikers, but when I got down to the other side, I was too late. Whoever cast that spell was gone."

She held up a pair of binoculars.

"But I found these at the grove—which we're gonna have to reconsecrate, by the way, since someone's breached our wards. They were watching their handiwork."

"Agreed," Arrabelle said, taking off her green sweater and slipping it over her arm.

Arrabelle was usually so put together, but today her face looked puffy, her eyes red and swollen like she'd been crying. Lizbeth had worked as the herbalist's assistant for months and she'd gotten used to Arrabelle's cool reserve. In all that time, she'd never once seen Arrabelle get emotional.

"You heard her talk?" Daniela said to Arrabelle, tilting her head in Lizbeth's direction. "Stupid crazy, right?"

Lizbeth blushed, wishing she were back in the dream-lands with Temistocles. He didn't embarrass her the way her blood sisters did, didn't look at her like she was some kind of freak. He treated her like an adult. Which she technically was—and he'd *kissed* her like she was one, too.

"Lizbeth and I are going home," Weir said, reaching for Lizbeth's arm. "Then we're packing a bag and getting the hell out of Dodge."

Everyone turned to face Weir. He'd been silent up until this moment, but now he looked ready to fight. From experi-ence, Lizbeth knew once Weir had made up his mind about something, it was almost impossible to change it—and his mind looked pretty made up.

"We can't let you do that," Daniela said. "It's not safe for either of you out there on your own."

Weir began to shake his head, his mouth fixed in a tight grimace. Any emotion stopped at his eyes, which were cold and unreachable. He looked from Daniela to Arrabelle, and finally to Lyse, who took the bullet and stepped forward.

"Weir, I know all of this sounds crazy—"

"There was a massive storm and then it was just *gone*—"

"I saw it, too. It was scary—" Lyse said, and tried to touch his arm.

He stepped out of her reach.

"Fuck scary," Weir said, glaring at Lyse. "It's not safe for LB. You think you guys are going to be able to protect her? There were police at my house—"

"We don't know what they were," Daniela said. "But that's beside the point right now. We need to get somewhere safe. All of us and the sooner the better."

"If there even *is* a safe place," Arrabelle murmured softly.

Weir wasn't having any of it.

"No way. It's not gonna happen, Daniela." He turned to Lyse and Arrabelle. "You're all welcome to come with us."

"I'm sorry, Weir," Lyse said. "There is so much you don't know or understand . . . We're needed here. We can't just run away because we're afraid."

She sighed, letting her hands fall to her sides, where they clenched into tight fists.

"And Lizbeth can't, either. We need her. And we need you, too."

Weir bit his lip, a lost child in a grown man's body.

"I . . . my job is to take care of Lizbeth."

Lyse nodded.

"Let us help you with that."

Weir turned to Lizbeth, waiting for her to weigh in. She didn't want to disagree with him, but she knew Lyse and Daniela were right.

"Well?" Weir asked, his fear manifesting as impatience. "You can talk now, so what the hell do you want to do?"

What do I want? Lizbeth thought. *I want to go back to the*

dreamlands, but if I can't have that then I want . . . to do what
would make Eleanora proud.

"Dev. Let Dev show you the cards and then you'll see."

Weir nodded, capitulating to Lizbeth's request.

"Okay, we'll do what you want. For now . . . but if anything, and I mean *anything else*"—he let the words hang in
the air so Lyse, Arrabelle, and Daniela would know he meant
business—"happens, we're done. I don't care what you want, LB."

"We read you loud and clear," Daniela said, crossing her
arms over her chest.

"Good," Weir replied. "That was the point. Now let's get
the hell out of here."

"The car's just over here," Arrabelle said, pointing up the
trailhead.

They trudged up the path in silence, cutting through the
trees. It seemed like everyone had forgotten about the notebook, so Lizbeth kept quiet, waiting until she was in Arrabelle's backseat, between an angry Weir and a distracted Lyse,
before pulling it out and opening its cover.

She traced the word *Evolvo* with the tip of her index finger . . . and then she began to read.

Hello, last of the Dream Keepers. Last one born under the old
moon, last one born before the blood moon heralds the coming of
the others . . . my name is Marie-Faith and I sit here hold-
ing this notebook with no idea whether my sly trick will work.
The dreamlands mirror our own reality, and some things, like
a Dream Keeper's consciousness, can pass between the two.
Francesca believes we can use this to our advantage, to keep
this sensitive information safe. In case something happens to
me, or to her . . . Francesca is a Dream Keeper, like yourself,
and she lies on the bed nearby me, asleep. She is traveling in
another realm as I dictate this story to her. She will write it
down there, in a mirror image of this notebook, my words in

her head, so that only those who can walk in dreams might read it . . . strange the way these two worlds work, each bleeding over into the other. But that is neither here nor there . . . what I need to say to you, last of the Dream Keepers, is brief, and I only hope it will be enough to prepare our world for the oncoming Flood—out of the darkness, on quiet feet, it will arrive at our door before we know it—and then we must band together to prevent it from destroying everything we hold dear. Already it has slipped into our ranks . . . the Council has not been impervious—this is a truth . . . trust no one, *last of the Dream Keepers.* No one . . . *not even the members of your own coven, barring Eleanora. She is the only one who can be counted on. Listen to her for she is wiser than me . . . I'm sorry to be so harsh, but you must be made to understand, and all I have at my disposal is this notebook. A paltry sheaf of pages that might never see the light of day . . . but I have hope . . . although time is running out. Even now, Francesca starts to stir . . . You must come to Rome. In the old Jewish catacombs beneath Villa Nomentana, you will find a secret way that will lead you into the vast, underground heart of the catacombs. Here they have been doing unspeakable things . . . locking away souls that have no business being trapped . . . release them . . . we will need their power, the power of* all *the Dream Keepers, once The Flood is at its fiercest . . . Francesca will be there waiting for you with my last gift . . . You will know her when you see her. Godspeed, last of the Dream Keepers . . . you must get there before the blood moon or it will be too late . . . may you save us from ourselves.*

Lyse

Lyse was confused by her feelings for Weir.

She appreciated that he was worried about his sister, that he had no idea what kind of crazy shit Lizbeth was involved in, and that he'd been overwhelmed and thrown into the deep end of their world without any preparation. She knew it wasn't fair to ask him to accept everything he'd seen without question— and yet that was exactly what she wanted him to do. Because she was the master of a coven and anyone she dated needed to be okay with that part of her life.

Until this morning, she'd been ridiculously smitten with Weir, his presence making her feel as giddy as a schoolgirl with her first crush. Even though she'd screwed stuff up, leaving things with him on shaky ground, she'd been hopeful she could fix it.

Now she wasn't sure if Weir liked her anymore, wasn't sure if he even *wanted* to mend things between them. Not that she was writing him off, but his silence made her wonder about any kind of future for them.

If both of them wanted it to work, anything was possible. If they didn't, it was over.

God, she hoped she wasn't turning into Eleanora. She didn't want to be a spinster. Didn't want to be alone forever. She was interested in having a partner, a man who was her equal and could match her in everything. Someone she could trust to be there when she needed him and who wasn't scared of her independence. A tall order. She knew it. But he was out there—and maybe it *was* Weir. Maybe he'd surprise her.

"You have a funny look on your face," Daniela said, twirling a strand of pink hair around her index finger.

They were in the Mucho Man Cave waiting for Dev to get back from taking the girls their bag lunches, which had been forgotten in the craziness of the morning. Lyse had never been in the actual bar before, only the backyard, where every few weekends Dev and Freddy threw an outdoor brunch for the neighborhood, but it was exactly as she'd imagined it: beat-up rattan tables with matching chairs, dodgy green carpeting on the former garage floor, a real working tiki bar with twinkle lights and a puffer fish hanging from the top of its crossbeam.

The place even smelled like she'd imagined. Stale beer and Nag Champa incense—not as odd a combination as you would think. It was safe and homey inside the Mucho Man Cave, which made Lyse kind of love it.

The only thing out of sync with the rest of the bar was the man sitting in the corner, bound to a rattan chair with a thick coil of rope. It was a pretty thorough job, and Lyse would never have guessed Dev possessed a talent for binding. But she supposed when someone broke into your house and used magic against you and your children, it would bring out the mercenary in anyone.

He was handsome with sharp features, pale skin, and long dark lashes. He had a thin build, but Lyse could see that he was lithe and muscular, too. If he hadn't been a horrible waste of a human being, she would've found him rather attractive. He was still unconscious, had been since Eleanora, Hessika, and a stranger wearing a green leather coat had had their way with him. After that, it hadn't been too hard for Dev to drag him out to the Mucho Man Cave and tie him up.

Arrabelle sat across from the man in one of the matching rattan chairs, her dark eyes fixed on him. She looked as if she expected him to jump up from unconsciousness at any moment and attack her. Lyse didn't want to wager on the man's chances if that happened. She didn't recommend crossing Arrabelle. Her friend was ruthless and could do serious damage if she wanted.

On the other side of the room, Weir and Lizbeth were cozied up at the bar, the two of them huddled together like co-conspirators. An articulated skeleton wearing a blue Hawaiian print shirt, aviator shades, and a straw hat sat on the stool beside Lizbeth. Its bony hand was wrapped around a beer can ensconced in a foam rubber coozie. Someone had placed an unlit cigar in its mouth, and when seen from the right angle, the skeleton kind of looked like it was smiling at you.

Slightly creepy.

Lyse and Daniela were sitting by the door, the tiny table between them stopping Daniela from accidentally touching Lyse. She felt bad that they had to be so aware of their proximity to each other, but Daniela's empathic powers were too erratic.

"I keep thinking about the future, about what's coming . . . what Marji said to Dev about needing to circle the wagons and call in reinforcements," Lyse said, playing with the fringe of her shawl. "That we'd be going away. It's chilling."

Daniela narrowed her eyes.

"It's been a long time coming. When my mom—"

Daniela stopped speaking, the words refusing to come. Lyse wanted to reach out and touch her friend, offer her some solace, but once again it wasn't an option.

"I'm sorry."

Daniela nodded, jaw set and eyes as steely as flint.

"It is what it is now. But I know her death wasn't what it seemed."

"Just like Eleanora," Lyse whispered, her voice so low that Daniela had to lean in close to hear. "I know how you feel."

Daniela nodded, sitting up straighter in her chair.

"You never really told me what happened."

Lyse swallowed hard, emotion flooding through her body.

"He tried to kill me, but Eleanora stopped him. She just appeared. Like this morning. With Dev and the girls? She's a Dream Walker now."

"So what happened to him? Where's the body?" Daniela asked, eyes on alert. Lyse thought she looked ready to go down to the lake and do battle right then and there.

"I went back early this morning, and there was nothing there," Lyse said. "Seriously, it was like it didn't even happen."

Daniela sighed and leaned onto her elbows, dropping her chin into her gloved hands.

"I don't know. It's all so messed up." She shook her head but kept her eyes fixed on Lyse. After a moment of silence, she changed the subject: "Those two over there are thick as thieves. I just want to see what's in that damn notebook she found. But she's not gonna let it out of her sight."

"She will," Lyse said, following Daniela's gaze to where Lizbeth was sitting, hunched over the bar with Weir. "She knows we need to see it."

"And I love Weir, but he was such a mess up there in the park," Daniela added as if Lyse hadn't just spoken. "I think it's too much for him. Some people can't handle the massive shift in perception that comes from exposing them to our world."

Lyse nodded. She'd been thinking the exact same thing.

But before she could reply, the door to the Mucho Man Cave opened and a shaft of sunlight cut across the darkened bar. Lyse and Daniela looked up at the same time, with an unspoken promise that they would pick up the thread of this conversation later.

Lyse was surprised by how easy it was to be with her blood sisters. She was growing to rely on them more and more, to the point that they were becoming like the family she'd never really had. After all those years of feeling alone, it was hard for Lyse to give over and be open with other people. Her best friend, Carole, had been the only person she'd ever felt comfortable enough to share her deepest, darkest secrets with.

But after Eleanora's death, Lyse had changed.

She'd allowed Arrabelle and Dev to pick up her slack. They'd arranged for the memorial service at the house and not asked Lyse to do anything other than be present. At the time, that was all Lyse *could* do. Eleanora's death, and then the subsequent discovery that Eleanora was *actually* her grandmother and not her great-aunt, had been difficult for Lyse to process. But her coven mates hadn't pushed her, hadn't forced her to deal with things until she was ready.

It was strange to feel like she'd been given four new sisters out of the blue. With all the good and bad that went along with the gift.

"Well, the girls are taken care of and my mom and my sister, Delilah, are on their way now," Dev said, closing the door behind her and shutting out the sunlight. "They'll be here in the morning."

It took Lyse's eyes a few moments to adjust to the darkness again, but when they did, Lyse saw that the man in the corner had woken up—and he was looking right at her. Their gazes locked and a visceral thrill ran through Lyse's body. Her fingers gripped the edge of the table and she swallowed hard before dragging her eyes away from his.

The bizarre connection threw her and she scanned the room, hoping no one else had caught the interaction. To her dismay, the only person who'd noticed was Weir. He refused to meet her gaze, eyes shifting away before she could catch them, a frown on his face.

Dammit, she thought, mentally chastising herself for even looking in the stranger's direction.

"—they're here in my house. They saved Ginny and Marji from that son of a bitch."

Lyse tried to focus on what Dev was saying, but her brain only wanted to think about whether Weir was ever going to talk to her again.

"Well, we'd planned on doing Eleanora's releasing spell tonight," Arrabelle said, eyes still on the man, watching his every move—which consisted of him testing his bonds while making bemused faces at the thoroughness of his bindings. "But maybe that's not a good idea."

"I'm afraid it might be the last ritual we'll do together as a coven," Lizbeth said from her perch at the bar, the timbre of her voice smoother than before. Her vocal cords were finally warming up.

She stood, holding the notebook in her hands.

"It's like a Dream Journal, but not," she said, then turned her attention to Daniela. "It's from your mother. She didn't write it, but she dictated it to a Dream Walker on the other side. In the dreamlands."

Lyse watched Daniela's face tighten. She wondered if her friend was jealous that she'd received the notebook, and not her.

"Dreamland?" Arrabelle asked, raising an eyebrow. "That's H. P. Lovecraft stuff, isn't it?"

"Maybe. I don't know. But it's where we go when we dream," Lizbeth said.

Her eyes slid away from Arrabelle, done with the question.

Lyse understood that the Lizbeth they were dealing with now was not the Lizbeth from before. The girl she'd first met was shy and withdrawn, frightened of her own shadow. The new Lizbeth was no longer a wilting teenager. She was a strong and assertive *woman.*

"Marie-Faith left something for me in Rome. I need to leave tonight, and I want Weir to go with me. The blood moon is coming and I need to be there before—"

Daniela's chair slid away from the table and she was up on her feet before Lyse realized what was happening.

"I don't think so," Daniela said, striding across the room until she was face to face with Lizbeth. It would have been comical— the tall, willowy girl towering over the petite rainbow-haired pixie—if the air hadn't been so fraught with tension. "Where you go, I go. No *ifs*, *and*s, or *but*s about it."

The old Lizbeth would've been intimidated. This one was not.

"No."

Daniela didn't back down.

"It's not up for negotiation. I will be going with you. Get over it."

There was a protracted silence and then Arrabelle spoke: "I agree with Daniela. You can't go alone, and Weir isn't a member of this coven, or a blood sister; he would be useless in some situations"—she shot Weir an apologetic smile—"sorry, Weir, but one of us should be with you, LB. Probably Lyse or Daniela."

"And what about you?" Lyse asked Arrabelle. "Don't you want to go?"

Lyse didn't think Arrabelle was capable of showing intense emotion. She'd spent so long beating her feelings into submission that they'd ceased to exist. Well, Lyse was dead wrong.

"I . . ." Arrabelle began, and then her eyes filled with tears. "They're burning witches. I had word from my friend Evan, whose coven is just outside Seattle. They've burned them out, destroyed them utterly. I need to go and see if I can help. And then I need to travel, begin spreading the word, letting our world know that we're at war with something evil. Do this now. Before it's too late to make a difference."

Dev crossed the room and wrapped her arms around Arrabelle—and Lyse was shocked to see Arrabelle not only allow it, but reciprocate. Who was this Evan person and how important was he to Arrabelle? For her to lose her composure like this, Lyse decided he had to be important.

"I'm so sorry," Dev said, holding Arrabelle close.

"It's . . . it's not good, Dev," Arrabelle sighed. "I didn't want to believe any of this was possible. The world should be long past destroying what it doesn't understand. It's the twenty-first century, dammit."

Lyse wished this were the case, but time and again, humanity proved to have one foot stuck in the Dark Ages. Being different was no easier in the twenty-first century than in the Stone Age.

"Why are we doing this in front of him?" Daniela said, her voice a sharpened knife cutting through the emotion in the room. "We're going to Rome"—she looked at Arrabelle—"and you're going to Seattle. This guy could escape with that info and then we're all screwed."

At this, the man in the chair perked up. His dark hair was wild and he looked lean from hunger, but when his piercing blue eyes settled on Lyse, her cheeks burned.

"Why would I go anywhere? I'm bound to this chair, for one—well done on that, by the way," he said, and grinned at Dev, who glared back at him. "And Temistocles freed me from the spell I was under, so—"

Lizbeth took off like a shot, her hands on the man's shoulders, squeezing them tightly.

"Temistocles. You said Temistocles. Do you know him?"

She was a teenager again, frantic to get information from the strange man who'd come to do them harm.

"Of course I know him," the man said. "He's my brother."

The color drained from Lizbeth's cheeks.

"But . . . you're alive."

The man's face fell and he looked away, miserable under Lizbeth's intense stare.

"How do you think I ended up this way?" He kept his eyes

on the ground, on the walls, on anything but Lizbeth's face. "They came. We fought them, and Temistocles was killed. But he chose to stay. Like your friends—"

He finally looked up, finding Dev's face.

"The women. They're Dream Walkers. Powerful ones. They protected your daughters . . . not that the older girl needed it."

Dev frowned.

"What do you mean?"

He flicked his gaze to Lyse for a moment before returning to Dev. Lyse took this as an indication that he was going to talk about her like she wasn't in the room.

"Your daughter? She's like that one there"—yep, as Lyse had expected, he was talking about her—"a hybrid. The next evolution, they say. A jack-of-all-trades and a master of none. But that's not really true. With the power of all five talents— Clairvoyance, Divination, Dream Keeping, Empathy, and Herbalism—the magic evolves, becomes exponentially stronger than when you have one talent alone."

Lyse had no idea what the man was talking about, and she didn't like the looks the rest of the coven were giving her.

"I'm not a hybrid," Lyse said, anger spilling out with her words. "That's ridiculous."

"Of course it's not ridiculous," the stranger said to Lyse. "You'll see exactly what I'm saying, if you really think about it. You have a talent for each of their disciplines . . ."

His eyes slid from Arrabelle to Lizbeth to Dev before finally settling on Daniela.

"Don't look at me," Daniela said, glaring at him.

"Why do you think your powers have been so out of control, empath? I can see you steering clear of everyone, even with your gloves on."

Daniela's glare softened.

"Oh, yeah?"

He nodded, then turned his attention back to Lyse.

"You're the cause. Deny it or not, it's merely a truth. And The Flood has been keeping tabs on you. On all of the hybrids, actually . . . even the children . . . in all the worlds. And now they've started taking them for their own purposes, using them for the high concentration of magic they possess. This is why Temistocles and I were fighting them . . . once they take the children, it's all over."

This last bit was directed at Dev.

"What's your name?" Daniela asked, stepping closer to him. She was the first to accept that the stranger's words might hold some truth.

"Of the two of us, I received the more pedestrian name," he grinned. "Thomas. And I am the doubtingest Thomas of all."

His good humor was infectious, and Lyse felt herself smiling back at him against her better judgment. Out of the corner of her eye, she saw Weir frown, and she quickly wiped the grin from her face and looked down at her hands. The skin was rough and dry, the nails bitten down to the quick. She was a nervous wreck—all the things she'd been dealing with over the last week had really taken a toll.

"I'm Daniela, and the hybrid is Lyse—"

"I don't think you should—" Arrabelle began, but Daniela held up a hand.

"Seriously, Arrabelle, the guy isn't going anywhere, and maybe his information can help us," Daniela said, frowning. "Because we know that what happened to your friend is happening in other places, in other worlds even, and that means we're gonna need all the help we can get."

Arrabelle looked away, eyes unfocused for a moment as she processed Daniela's words. Then she nodded slowly.

"Yes, okay, I see," she said, her face relaxing. "We need help. Maybe he can help us."

"I want your permission to go to someone on the Greater

Council. I think they can help us," Daniela added. "My mother trusted them implicitly and I do, too. We can meet with them now . . . today even."

Lyse didn't know if this was a good idea or not—but because she was the leader of the Echo Park coven, everyone was looking at her.

"No," Lizbeth said, shaking her head. "The notebook says the Council can't be trusted."

"Well?" Daniela asked, looking from Lizbeth to Lyse.

"I think we should hold off for now, okay?" Lyse said.

"We don't know how far up this goes," Dev chimed in, and then she looked at Thomas. "And we don't know who or what *he* is, or why he's here. I don't believe a word that's come out of his mouth—and you wouldn't either if you'd seen what he did to my girls. He stays right where he is, tied up good and tight."

It was an impassioned speech from someone who rarely raised her voice.

"I think we should let him go," Lizbeth said, coming to stand behind Dev. "I think he's telling the truth about the hybrids. It makes so much sense when you think about what's happened since Lyse got back to Echo Park."

"I'm sorry about your friend, Arrabelle," Lyse said. "Go if you need to. We'll do what we can on this end."

She touched Arrabelle's hand.

"I have to go and see for myself," Arrabelle said, nodding, and she didn't pull her hand away. "I don't even know if Evan is alive or dead . . . and if he is . . . I want to help what's left of his coven. Then I want to spread the word. I want our blood sisters to know what's going on."

"You're like an apostle," Lyse heard herself say. She had no idea where the words had come from. They'd just slipped out.

"Doubting Thomas and Bella. The first two," Thomas chimed in from his spectator's seat.

"You're not in this conversation—" Dev said to him.

"How do you know that name?" Arrabelle asked, getting upset. "No one else but my mother ever called me that."

Thomas shrugged and sat back as far as his bindings would allow. Then he began to wiggle his nose.

"Itchy nose. Will anyone oblige me?"

No one moved.

"Well, I'll stay out of this then," he continued in a teasing voice. "Don't want to upset you, ladies. Any more than you already are."

Arrabelle and Dev glared at him, but Daniela laughed.

"What? He's funny," she said and shrugged.

"He's not from our world," Lizbeth said, smiling at Thomas. "His brother said they come from another dimension—"

"*Shh,*" Thomas whispered, and Lyse wasn't sure if he was serious or not. "The Flood isn't just in your world, it's in every world. And what it doesn't kill outright, it absorbs into itself. A prisoner becomes part of the whole and must do its bidding . . . like the hybrids . . . *especially* the hybrids."

Finally, Weir couldn't stay silent any longer. Lyse had expected this—maybe some part of her even craved it—and he did not disappoint her. He got up from his seat at the tiki bar with enough momentum to knock the beer coozie out of the skeleton's hand. It rolled across the floor, and Weir nearly missed stepping on it as he began to pace back and forth in front of the bar.

"Am I losing my mind?" he asked, running his hands through his hair, almost as if he were trying to wring answers out of the wily blond strands. "Witches, magic, monsters from another dimension—"

"Monsters are in every dimension," Thomas interjected.

Weir ignored him.

"I think you're all crazy. And I actually have a pretty open mind, considering," he said, and shook his head. "But I saw some impossible things today that I don't have answers for. So, if you're crazy, I guess I am, too."

This was the Weir Lyse knew and loved. He wasn't inflexible or rigid in how he saw the world, but willing to give over to things he didn't understand. Things he'd deemed impossible only seconds before. This was why she'd fallen for him—it was true, she cared more for him than she'd even realized—and it made her very happy to have been wrong about him.

"What I'm saying is . . . use me how you will," Weir continued, staring pointedly at Lyse. "What's your plan? Let's go. I'm game to help."

Lyse hadn't exerted command over the coven before, had been scared of the responsibility, but now she channeled her inner Eleanora.

"Tonight, we perform the ritual releasing spell for my grandmother."

She locked eyes with Thomas.

"You stay here, bound, under lock and key. Weir, you said you're game?"

"I am," he answered.

"Then you're on security duty"—Lyse smiled at Dev—"and when Freddy gets home, you have to tell him everything. Weir is gonna need help. This doubting Thomas is a sly one."

At the mention of his name, Thomas sat up and winked at her.

"You've got my number," he said. "Though I still wish someone would itch my nose."

Lizbeth knelt down in front of him. Reaching out a long index finger, she gave his nose a scratch.

"Much obliged. I can see why my brother's so smitten with you."

Lizbeth stood back up, pushing her long hair out of her face.

"Stop it," Lyse cut in, not liking the way Thomas was playing with Lizbeth's feelings. "Keep your mouth shut, 'cause you're not winning any friends when you open it."

She turned her attention away from Thomas and back to the rest of the room.

"We're not getting anyone from the Greater Council involved," Lyse continued. "Not after what happened to your mother, Daniela, and to Eleanora. At this point, we just make a decision not to trust *anyone*. Not even someone from the Greater Council. Arrabelle, go to your friend, but come back to Echo Park afterward. Dev will need you here."

"You think keeping this to ourselves is best?" Arrabelle asked, not convinced.

"For now, yeah. Yeah, I do," Lyse replied, trying to sound firm. "If we talk to the wrong person . . . it could be catastrophic."

"Then what happens?" Daniela asked, eyes narrowed. Lyse could tell she didn't like being told no. "You're just gonna let Lizbeth and Weir leave the country alone?"

Lyse shook her head.

"Of course not—"

"You can't do that," Lizbeth cried, glowering at Lyse. "I have to go to Rome. It's imperative—"

"—and you *will* be going to Rome," Lyse interrupted. "But Daniela and I are coming with you. As Daniela said: It's non-negotiable."

For the first time in her life, Lyse understood what it felt like to be a general leading an army into battle—and it was exhilarating.

She wondered why she'd ever been scared of it.

It was the greatest job in the world.

Lyse

Lyse placed the tip of the match against the side of the match-box, pausing for a moment as her hand trembled slightly—not from anxiety, but exhaustion—and then she dragged the cherry-red head against the striker. The acrid scent of burning sulfur filled her nose and she sneezed, almost blowing out the match she'd just lit.

"Dammit," she said, sneezing again, and then once more for good measure.

Lyse always sneezed in threes. Unless she was sick, and then all bets were off.

She grasped the delicate wrist of the hand holding the match, steadying her arm. She knelt down beside the stone altar and lit the wick of the long white taper resting atop it. The candle flared to life, a pulsing pillar of flame that gradually settled into a squat orange-and-gold triangle of fire. The match was beginning to gutter, so she quickly moved to a second white taper, and it, too, blazed to life beneath her fingers.

She stared at the flames, at the living fire she'd trapped on pale white columns made of string and wax. The fire wanted to be free. To leap from her hands and take root in the brittle brown leaves carpeting the floor of the eucalyptus grove and the clearing.

"*Ow*," she yelped.

She almost dropped the match as it burned down to its end and singed the skin of her fingertips. That was what it wanted: to catch her off guard and force her to help it escape. Instead, she shook the flame out, a trail of smoke issuing from its burnt black end. She dropped what was left of the match onto the top of the stone altar, then stuck her burned fingers into her mouth. The pain was sharp and fierce, and it woke Lyse from her exhausted stupor.

She swiveled on her heel, turning back to look at the others. "It's done."

There was so much Lyse needed to learn now that she was the master of the Echo Park coven of witches—and since there were no books for her to read, no lesson plans to follow as a guide, the four women standing behind her would be her de facto teachers.

"Good," Arrabelle said as her lips twisted into the facsimile of a smile. There was no warmth in her serious dark brown gaze; she was too emotionally raw for that.

With her muscular athlete's body and perfect posture, Arrabelle cut an imposing figure. She'd taken a pair of shears to her hair that afternoon in preparation for the Releasing Ritual they were about to perform. Now her once thick hair was a blanket of soft fuzz against the skin of her scalp.

She was wearing a flowing scarlet sheath dress belted in at the waist with a cord of cream sateen. Offset by the rich brown of Arrabelle's arms and throat, the red fabric shimmered like silken rubies. Pinned just above her left breast was a small brooch made of hammered bronze, its intricate woven pattern reminiscent of a Celtic knot. Yet when Lyse observed it more closely, she saw that it was, in fact, an abstract representation of the eternal aspect of the universe: an infinity symbol that resembled a swooping figure eight.

"Your grandmother would be pleased with all of this," Arrabelle added, and this time she gave Lyse a real smile.

The word *grandmother* sounded surreal to her, felt rough on her tongue whenever she said it out loud. She'd spent over a decade in the dark, thinking Eleanora was some distant relative with very little blood connection—and it was only upon her death that the truth had finally been revealed to Lyse. It was still bizarre to think she was so closely tied to Eleanora. She was just sorry it had taken death to right this wrong.

Not that death was the end. She knew this now . . . and even in death she would always be aware of how much Eleanora loved her—and she, Eleanora. That was a given.

"Come join us," Dev said, and Lyse's gaze shifted from Arrabelle.

Short, round and maternal, she was Arrabelle's polar opposite. In the moonlight, her strawberry-blond hair hung loose down her back, the ends curling slightly as they reached her shoulder blades. Her freckled skin was milky white with undertones of pale peach, and she wore the same scarlet sheath dress as Arrabelle.

Actually, they were all wearing the same outfit, but each had chosen a unique object to add to her ensemble—like Arrabelle's brooch—almost like a reverse version of the bridal saying: "Something borrowed, something blue . . ." To this end, Dev was wearing a burnished gold cuff on the meaty part of her left forearm, with a beautifully etched pentacle cut into the wide gold band.

"We should begin," Dev continued, "before the candles start to burn too far down—"

"Give her a minute," Daniela said, interrupting Dev. Her pink Louise Brooks bob had been pinned back, giving her a less quirky, more regal look for the evening. "She needs a second to collect herself. She's fucking exhausted. We all are. And we need to be focused to reconsecrate the circle."

Someone had breached their wards, using the power of the flow lines running through the grove to create some kind of storm spell . . . Lyse really didn't understand all the magic stuff yet—but she promised herself that she soon would. Daniela, who was the coven's resident badass, had explained it as "someone calling up a mass illusion"—which still didn't one hundred percent explain things to Lyse.

Petite and delicate-boned with intense eyes that never stopped moving, Daniela had learned some serious fighting skills in her life, and she would most likely kick the living crap out of anyone who tried to cross her. She was the kind of woman you only wanted to meet in a dark alley when she was on *your* side of the fight.

The red sheath dress she wore was too big for her tiny frame, making it seem like the dress was wearing her instead of the other way around. Her piece of ornamentation was the most gaudy: a small tiara of copper and the clotted merlot of Brazilian garnet. It perched high above the curve of her bangs but kept sliding forward because it was too big for her.

"I'm okay," Lyse said, standing up, her own red sheath dress pooling around her feet, its hem dirty from the walk through Elysian Park. "Sleep hasn't been my friend lately. That's true. But I'm fine. Really."

She caught the eye of each of her blood sisters, in turn, reassuring them with a wan smile. Only Lizbeth remained silent on the topic of how tired Lyse looked. She didn't comment on the dark circles ringing Lyse's startlingly blue eyes, or the deepening hollows underneath her already sharp cheekbones— not eating or sleeping would do these small damages to an otherwise healthy body.

Lizbeth fixed her gaze in Lyse's direction and flared her eyes, letting Lyse know how sorry she was that the others were harassing her. Lyse gave a slight shake of her head in reply: *It's okay.*

Lizbeth lowered her eyes, and Lyse felt an outpouring of maternal love for the girl.

Not a girl anymore, Lyse thought. *She's changed. Something happened up at the Dragon. Something to do with a man named Temistocles.*

Yes, Lizbeth was a teenager no longer. She'd always been the tallest of them, but now she carried that height with confidence. Gone was the super-shy child who could only communicate through pad and pencil, her newfound preternatural self-assurance setting her apart even more.

A stunner even without makeup, she'd inherited her beauty from both sides of her parentage: thick russet-colored hair streaming down past her shoulders, golden-brown sphinx eyes, glowing olive skin dotted with freckles. No more was she the coltish and awkward beauty not quite comfortable in her adult body . . . now she was a willowy goddess.

Earlier in the afternoon, Lyse and Lizbeth had combed through Eleanora's jewel box, each choosing a piece of jewelry to wear for the Releasing Ritual. Lizbeth's choice was a pair of earrings that were a favorite of Eleanora's: flat metal discs split down the middle with carnelian on one side and smooth copper on the other. Lizbeth said they represented the last quarter moon, or the Crone aspect of the Goddess; they also signified release, which both of them thought was apropos for the night.

Lyse had chosen something simpler, more intimate even, for her ornament. Buried deep within the smooth balsa wood jewel box underneath tangled skeins of gold and silver chain, cut-glass jeweled rings, sparkling bracelets, and other sentimental trinkets, she'd unearthed a small silver charm suspended from a short sterling silver chain.

"What's this?" Lyse had murmured, plucking the necklace out of the box and holding it up to the light.

It was fashioned in a curling Gothic script that made it hard to decipher at first, but then, with a start, she'd realized what it was.

"*E* for *Eleanora*," she'd whispered. The tiny charm caught the afternoon light streaming through the quartered panes of the casement window, throwing reflections all around the room.

Now she let her fingers drift to her throat, where the charm lay nestled in the hollow of her throat just above the neckline of her own scarlet dress.

"I feel strange leading this ceremony," Lyse said as she joined her blood sisters inside the circle of burnt ash they'd sprinkled in the clearing.

Their first order of business would be to consecrate this circle, making it safe to perform the Releasing Ritual that would be the coven's final memorial to Eleanora.

It's strange to be here, in this place again, Lyse thought. *I spent so many years being frightened of it, and now it's where I'll help my blood sisters give Eleanora a proper send-off.*

Before Lyse became a member of the coven, her only experience with the grove had been in her dreams. It was the scene of a recurrent nightmare she'd had all through her teenage years, in which she was stalked by something outside the circle of ancient trees, an evil presence that wanted her dead and would wait as long as necessary to taste her flesh and blood. Even thinking about it now gave her the chills, and she felt goose bumps peppering her arms.

"It's your job," Dev said, giving Lyse's shoulder a reassuring pat. As if she'd guessed what Lyse had been thinking. "Give it a try and soon it'll be old hat—"

"Tell her it's just like riding a bicycle, Dev," Daniela said, and giggled.

Dev rolled her eyes, but then something in the sky caught her attention and she fell silent.

"No making fun of me," Dev said finally, eyes still heavenward like she expected something to drop out of the sky. She looked back at Lyse and smiled. "I'm used to talking to little girls, not grown-ups."

Lyse imagined that living in a house with two kids changed

your brain. For one thing, you always had to be careful about saying inappropriate things. Just in case one of them decided to repeat it at school. It was something she'd been highly aware of when she'd spent time with Carole and Bemo. Especially now that Bemo was starting to parrot back everything the adults said.

Damn, she missed Athens.

"But seriously," Dev added, shivering as the temperature dropped and the wind began to shake the boughs of the trees. "Daniela's right. It kind of *is* like riding a bike. Once you do a spell, it tends to stick with you and never get lost."

"You have what I wrote out for you?" Arrabelle asked, and Lyse nodded. Arrabelle had been kind enough to write out the spell so Lyse could say it without fumbling the words.

"Thanks for that."

Arrabelle smiled, and once again it reached her eyes. If only for a moment.

"Of course."

Lyse knew Arrabelle had wanted to be the master of the Echo Park coven. That she'd thought the job was hers until Lyse had shown up and taken it away. Now Arrabelle was forced to help Lyse learn the ropes.

Funny how things work out sometimes, Lyse thought, grateful to Arrabelle for being so kind to her. Had the roles been reversed, she wasn't so sure she'd have been as gracious a loser.

Lyse cleared her throat, stalling a bit out of nervousness. She looked at the faces of her blood sisters, taking comfort from their presence and from the beauty of the clearing, which had been decked out for the evening like an autumnal fairyland. Because it was so close to Halloween, Dev had asked her daughters to carve miniature pumpkin lanterns for the event. They'd risen to their task, gouging out the pumpkins' flesh in strange swirling shapes and then stuffing the innards of the small gourds with tea lights.

Dev and Lizbeth had festooned the trees with the lanterns,

then added garlands made from brown leaves and dried garlic. Small burlap bags filled with dirt, seeds, and spices sat like stones around the edges of their about-to-be-consecrated circle. This would give them even more protection for the evening's ritual.

Lyse had only learned that evening, as she'd helped Daniela fill the burlap bags, that powerful charms were buried underneath the roots of the trees, protecting the grove from evil interlopers and keeping the location of the witches' ritual grounds secret from prying eyes.

Which was why Daniela finding those binoculars in the grove had been such a frightening blow. It meant the wards had become weakened . . . or worse, one of their coven mates had broken the others' trust and allowed something evil into their midst.

I don't believe that's the case, Lyse thought. *Maybe no one has considered this, but what if The Flood is just stronger than us?*

Even *she* didn't like to think about that, but it was an idea she hadn't been able to shake. The Flood wanted to own their world. To do so, it would have to wipe the covens off the face of the map. She didn't one hundred percent understand their motivation . . . but she knew that discovering this key piece of information would be integral to defeating them.

"Shall we?" Daniela said, her words a gentle nudge to get Lyse moving.

"Yes," Lyse said, and took a deep breath.

The moon had risen high above them, the moonlight making it easier for Lyse to see what she was doing.

"So let's make this happen," Lyse said, shaking out her shoulders and rolling her neck back and forth like a prizefighter.

Daniela snorted.

"You planning on taking a run before we work?"

"I don't know why I feel like I'm about to start a triathlon," Lyse said, and smiled.

"You'll be great," Dev chimed in.

"Don't worry," Daniela said, clapping her gloved hands together in excitement. "No swimming will be necessary."

Lizbeth shot Lyse a secret smile. Even though she'd gotten her voice back, Lizbeth was still judicious about what she said, weighing the necessity of each word before she spoke.

"I call the protective circle now, right? To reconsecrate the ground?" Lyse asked, ninety-nine percent sure this was correct but wanting a little reassurance.

"Yes, now would be a perfect time to call the cardinal elements," Arrabelle replied evenly, as if she were speaking to a small child. "Now that we've added more protection to the grove, we'll reconsecrate the circle, and then we can start the Releasing Ritual."

Lyse opened the box of matches she held in her hand and plucked one from the inside, lighting it. It flared to life with a sulfurous spark, and she cupped its flame with her hand to keep it from going out. She walked over to the first candle, a fat pillar with alternating white and canary-yellow swirls, and lit its wick.

"We call to the powers of the Air," she said as she held the guttering candle. "To Wisdom and Intuition. Be with us this night."

The others intoned their part of the call and response: *"Be with us tonight."*

A gust of wind blew through the clearing, tendrils of cold air encircling Lyse as gooseflesh pimpled her arms. She stood back up and grinned.

"Well, that wasn't too bad."

"Three more to go before we start patting ourselves on the back," Arrabelle said.

"Okie-doke," Lyse said, moving to the second candle and kneeling beside it.

Another fat pillar, but this one was made of striped blue-and-white beeswax.

"We call to the powers of the Water," she said, striking another match. "To Love and Fertility. Be with us tonight."

"Be with us tonight," the others intoned in unison.

They repeated the call and response twice more, using a red-and-white candle to signify Fire, and a green-and-white pillar for Earth. These two joined Water and Air to complete the invocation of the cardinal elements. With that done, Lyse began to say the spell that would reconsecrate the circle of protection:

"The cardinal candles have been lit—"

Another powerful gust of wind shot through the branches of the eucalyptus trees, the leaves rustling like whispering children. A number of the tea lights inside the pumpkin lanterns went out, but the moonlight more than made up for the lack of candlelight.

"Just the Santa Anas," Dev said.

Daniela wrapped her arms around herself and shivered.

"Let's hope that's all it is."

Arrabelle nodded to Lyse.

"Go on."

The wind picked up again, cold air rushing through the circle and nipping at the cardinal candles, almost as if it were trying to extinguish their light. A chill set in, one that had nothing to do with the weather.

Lyse realized her teeth were chattering.

"Keep going," Arrabelle said, eyes imploring Lyse to continue. "We're not good until you finish the spell."

"But you said we were safe here—"

"It is . . . *mostly* safe," Daniela added. "Just finish it, Lyse."

Lyse nodded and bowed her head, her body shivering uncontrollably.

"We cast out . . . anything unwanted . . . from the circle—"

The wind lashed at Lyse as she went on with the invocation. It was like a living creature, tearing through the trees and swirling around the women as they fought to remain upright. The wind whipped hair across faces, yanked on hems of dresses, its insidious fingers pinching and prodding, battering at them without end.

Anything to stop them from finishing their spell.

A lone howl ripped through the air, and Lyse's blood froze, time seeming to stop as the eerie sound ricocheted through the park. Every hair on Lyse's body stood on end as the sound, a constant in every one of the nightmares she'd had as a teenager, gripped her brain, making her want to sprint into the trees, leaving her blood sisters alone and the circle unconsecrated.

"Say the rest of the damn spell!" Arrabelle yelled over the screaming of the wind.

"But you guys have to repeat after me—"

"Just finish it, dammit! It doesn't matter if we don't call it back to you," Daniela cried. "C'mon, here. This wind isn't a coincidence. Close the goddamned circle, Lyse!"

Another stygian howl echoed through the clearing, but this one was different. It belonged to a creature that was smaller and weaker than the first one, its song one of desperation and terror, not aggression.

This second cry wrenched at Lyse's heart.

It came again, that same piteous howl. Closer now, and followed seconds later by a cry from the first creature—the one that had instilled terror in Lyse's heart during all those nightmares.

"There're two," Lyse cried over the sound of the wind, turning toward the edge of the circle and pointing out into the woods. "Can't you hear it?! The weaker one's in trouble. It needs our help!"

"No!" Arrabelle called back to her. "Don't leave the circle . . . you're not safe out there!"

She took one step toward Lyse, her foot stepping just outside the bounds of the circle, and she froze in place.

"Arrabelle?"

Eyes wide and imploring, she stared back at Lyse.

"Don't touch her," Daniela called out to Dev as she started to move toward Arrabelle's frozen form. "She's on the edge. You touch her and you'll be sucked in, too."

Daniela turned to Lyse.

"Don't go outside the circle. Whatever you do."

Lyse nodded.

"Okay."

The wind licked at Lyse's back, pushing her forward as if it were encouraging her to venture outside the protected circle and disappear into the deep, dark woods . . . though Lyse doubted she'd make it two steps before something nasty came calling for her. An evil creature lurked in the shadowy depths of the woods, and she was glad her baser instincts for self-preservation were keeping her rooted to the ground where she stood.

"No!" she yelled up at the sky, hoping whatever was out there would hear her. "I'm not falling for your trap. But I *am* closing the goddamned circle—"

The words were no sooner out of her mouth then her dress came flying up around her waist, the wind circling her like a cyclone, pushing her dark hair into her eyes and mouth. With flailing hands, she fought back, but she wasn't strong enough.

"Lyse!" she heard Dev scream.

The wind shoved her with inhuman hands and she fell backward, her head hitting the ground as a starburst of pain shot through her brain. She gasped, the throbbing intense, but then she felt a pair of hands grasping her shoulders, pulling her back into the circle.

No, they were pulling her out *of the circle!*

She wanted to cry out for help, but her voice was gone, locked away so she couldn't access it. Cold fingers wrapped around her living warmth, sucking away her energy, leaving her paralyzed and unable to escape. She fought to open her eyes, but her eyelids felt sewn shut. With superhuman effort she was finally able to tear them apart, and the night sky slipped into view above her. The swaying branches of the trees, their boughs laden down with the remnants of the twinkling pumpkin lights, acted like a proscenium arch, emphasizing the grinning face of the harvest moon.

No, it wasn't the moon at all, she thought; it was a monster.

She screamed as a misshapen jaw and two bulging yellow eyes drifted above her, a string of drool dangling inches from her face. She closed her eyes, trying to banish the image, pretending the creature was not touching her. But she could feel its fingers digging into her skin, its will bullying her into submission.

"*No!*" she cried, opening her eyes to stare into the creature's ravenous yellow gaze.

She'd never seen anything so hideous. It was humanoid in shape, but with ropy red scar tissue belting its corroded gray skin like a corset. Bits of its rotten flesh flaked off onto Lyse's face as it grinned down at her, and she shook her head to keep them out of her mouth and nose.

"You're not in your circle anymore, witch," it said as flecks of foul-smelling saliva rained down on her, making her gag.

She shuddered, disgusted by the stench of its breath— which strongly reminded her of raw meat left out to sour in the sun—and sensing her revulsion, it threw back its head and howled in pleasure. The creature's howl was followed by a string of maniacal laughter, which chilled Lyse to the core of her being.

After all the years of nightmares, Lyse realized she'd never actually seen the face of the monster that had stalked her in her dreams . . . until now.

The spell, she thought. *I have to finish the spell.*

She opened her mouth and nothing came out.

Only a moment before, she'd been able to scream, but now her lips were frozen solid. She racked her brain, trying to think of a way to counteract the creature's power over her.

"Don't let it drag you out of the circle!" she heard Dev scream, but the words sounded like they came from a thousand miles away.

Lyse turned her head, fear dawning on her as she realized most of her torso was already outside the circle, bits of ash clinging to her hair. The creature was trying to drag her out of the circle and into the trees—and God knew what it would do to her if it got her out there. For now, it could only dominate her with its will, using magic to lock her words inside her.

Outside the circle, she thought, *all bets are off.*

In her peripheral vision, she saw a flash of movement. Dev and Daniela were holding on to Lizbeth, trying to prevent her from coming to Lyse's aid.

"Lyse!" Lizbeth cried as their eyes locked.

Let me go, Lyse thought, wishing she were a telepath. *You're the last Dream Keeper. You're the important one. We're supposed to be looking after you, not the other way around.*

The monster seemed to read Lyse's thoughts and replied by digging harder into her shoulders, its fingers pressing through flesh and muscle to get at the bone. Its face hovered over hers, scarred skin and pale yellow irises now only inches away. She turned her head, wishing this were a nightmare and not her reality.

This was it, her life ending before it could really begin. She imagined the creature biting down on her cheek, tearing into her skin, its foul breath enveloping her.

She began to cry, silent tears running down the sides of her face.

I'm sorry, Eleanora, she thought, a strange sense of calm settling over her. *I've failed you. You were so wrong to have left all this at my door. I wasn't strong enough. I couldn't save any-one . . . not even myself.*

It would be easier to remain calm if she didn't have to see the monster coming. She closed her eyes and waited to meet her death.

Hands encircled the soles of Lyse's feet, and their warm, human touch woke up something deep inside her, a small kernel of power that moved through the rest of her body, setting her on fire. The creature howled in pain and released her, its fingers blistered from touching Lyse's heated skin.

Lyse closed her eyes and whispered the last two lines of the spell, her body free now that the creature's hold had been broken: "And we draw together our power here in this protected circle with the promise it shall only be used in good works. Your blood is our blood."

Though she could not see them, Lyse heard the others murmur their reply: *"Your blood is our blood."*

There was a bright flash of white light as the magical wards flared into life and the circle was reconsecrated, the evil banished—for now—from their sacred grove.

Lyse had beaten death, her life saved by the soles of her feet. But she was unconscious at this point and had no idea that the monster hadn't eaten her, after all.

Lizbeth

ஐ

L izbeth could feel the creature's fury like a live current, its
anger electric. It reached out to Lizbeth through Lyse, her
friend's inert body a conduit right into the creature's mind,
but then the connection was severed, and Lizbeth pulled
Lyse's unconscious body back into the circle.

The creature was repelled by the current of magic, an
electric-blue light that emanated from the circle, creating a
wall of power both she and the creature could see—and that
the creature could not cross.

Lizbeth wasn't scared of the beast. She'd been inside its
mind long enough to know it was here against its will.
Forced to do The Flood's business when all it wanted was to
be put out of its horrible misery. It had been a man once, a
member of The Flood's army, but its sacrifice to the cause
had been too great. Its scarred and broken form was the pay-
ment it received for its service. A test subject that had volunteered for the honor, but had not understood the depth of
what it was signing up for.

Lizbeth blinked back a wave of images. Dark places that

gave way to fiery infernos and then stark, sterile rooms with cages full of . . .

She couldn't see farther. The connection had been broken too soon. She sighed and looked back at the beast where it paced outside the circle, hungry and alone.

As the blue light began to fade from the circle, the creature let out a desperate, inhuman howl and bounded off into the woods. Lizbeth watched it go. Her pity for the beast was endless.

"Lizbeth, you could've been killed," Dev murmured as she knelt down beside her.

Lizbeth didn't want to upset the others, but she'd known as soon as she'd seen the creature that once she touched Lyse, she would be able to overpower its magic. What her blood sisters didn't seem to understand was that Lyse's proximity increased their powers exponentially. This was what Thomas had been trying to tell them back at the Mucho Man Cave. Lyse was a hybrid, but more than that, she was like a signal booster for their individual talents.

"Dammit, LB," Daniela said, anger tingeing her words.

Lizbeth looked up, surprised to see Daniela wiping away a trickle of blood from one of her nostrils.

"What happened?" she asked, and Daniela raised an eyebrow.

"To my nose?" Daniela asked.

Lizbeth nodded.

"*You.*"

"What?" Lizbeth asked, confused.

"You pushed me out of the way to get to Lyse, and that's when my stupid nose started bleeding."

Daniela's empathic powers are getting more and more out of control, Lizbeth thought. *Just another example of the result of Lyse's presence.*

"I don't understand," Dev said. "One minute we were reconsecrating the circle and the next . . ."

Arrabelle had collected herself enough to join them. She looked the worse for wear, but the encounter had kicked some fire back into her.

"What the hell was that thing? I've never seen anything like it before."

"A monster The Flood created," Lizbeth said. "It should be pitied, though. It didn't want to be here, but it's under their control."

"What *thing?*" Daniela asked. "What're you talking about?"

"There was nothing there—" Dev started to say, but Arrabelle interrupted her.

"I'm not fighting anyone on this. I saw it and so did Lizbeth—"

Lizbeth tuned the argument out, wanting a minute to think. She needed to process what she'd seen, understand how it was visible to her and Arrabelle, but not to the others. And Lyse couldn't comment because she was still unconscious.

Lizbeth pulled the hem of her dress up, knotting it between her knees like a makeshift sarong, so she could move more freely. She didn't like the red dresses, found it too tempting to the fates to wear a color so reminiscent of blood.

"It's because we were out of the circle. Arrabelle and Lyse and then me when I touched Lyse."

Actually, Lizbeth had seen the monster even before she'd touched Lyse. She didn't have an answer for how that was possible, so she kept the information to herself.

The others stopped arguing and looked at Lizbeth.

"I'll buy it," Arrabelle said, giving Lizbeth's answer some credence. "It makes sense. The circle wasn't fully reconsecrated, but we'd called up enough magic that we were partially protected."

Lizbeth picked up Lyse's hand, curling her fingers around her friend's wrist and giving it a squeeze. The skin was so cold to the touch that Lizbeth wished she had a blanket to drape over Lyse. Dev took Lyse's other hand, rubbing it in between her palms to try to warm it up a little bit.

"She okay?" Daniela asked.

Lizbeth touched Lyse's cheek.

"Can you hear me?" she asked.

Lyse wrinkled her brow, eyelids fluttering as she began to stir.

"Wake up, Lyse," Dev said, stroking the crown of Lyse's head.

"The circle . . ." Lyse murmured, forcing Dev and Lizbeth to lean close to hear what she was saying.

"It didn't break," Dev said, smiling down at her. "You were outstanding."

Lyse tried to get up, but Lizbeth saw she was too weak to manage it herself, and she and Dev helped her into a sitting position.

"It's gone?" Lyse asked, eyes focused on the edges of the circle, searching the darkness.

She thinks it's still out there, Lizbeth realized.

"It took off when you finished the spell," Lizbeth said, trying to assuage Lyse's fear.

Lyse nodded.

"Okay. Good."

"Because you closed the circle," Dev said smiling, "and reignited the wards."

Lyse took a deep breath, gathering her energy.

"Well, we still need to finish the ritual," Lyse said, crawling onto her hands and knees. "For Eleanora. So she can be free—and I want to do it now."

There was a power in Lyse's words the others could not argue with.

"The cardinal candles have been lit. Let's finish what we started," Arrabelle said, kneeling beside Lyse. "What are we waiting for, ladies? You heard what Lyse said. Lizbeth, go get the urn, please?"

They'd cremated Eleanora, and what was left of her physical body had been placed into a small brass urn that was now sitting in the grass beside the stone altar. The plan had been to do the Releasing Ritual, then spread her ashes here in the grove, allowing her spirit to move on to the next plane, if she so chose.

"I'm in," Daniela said. "But once we're done, I want us out of here."

"Agreed," Dev said.

Lizbeth picked up the urn, and it felt heavier than she'd

expected, the brass cold to the touch. She carried it into the center of the circle, where Lyse was sitting. As she joined them, she felt a calming presence fill the grove. It was like Eleanora was already there among them, waiting.

Lyse motioned for Lizbeth to hand her the urn, and Lizbeth realized she'd been holding it so tightly her fingers were white with tension. She watched as Lyse set the urn down in the grass, placing it dead center between the women. She took the moment to look each of her blood sisters in the eye, acknowledging that they were all in this together. She got up and, her gait still unsteady, walked to the stone altar, picking up the two white candles she'd lit earlier. One for each hand. She rejoined the circle, holding the candles out in front her, their flames guttering in the chilled air.

"We call upon the Goddess and her light to help our friend, Eleanora Eames, pass into the next realm."

She tipped both candles forward, so a few drops of wax dripped onto the urn.

"We release her from this plane and bless her with safe passage to the next realm," Lyse finished.

She passed the candles on to Dev, who was on her right.

"May she be blessed by the Goddess on her journey," Dev said, some of the wax spilling onto her fingers as she dripped it over the urn.

She handed the candles off to Lizbeth and began to pick the cooling white wax from the top of her knuckles.

Lizbeth's eyes were attracted to the twin flames, each dancing upon its wick like a tiny ballerina.

"The Goddess releases you from all of your earthly duties," Lizbeth said, dipping the candles too far forward, so that some of the wax missed the urn and landed in the grass.

"Sorry," she said, and handed over the candles to Daniela.

"Freedom is yours, Eleanora Eames, if you really want it. You have been the Maiden, the Mother, and the Crone—you have experienced the triple goddess in every incarnation,"

Daniela intoned as she repeated the ritual and gave the candles to Arrabelle.

"Do you really think I'm gonna bow out now when you need me the most?" Arrabelle's mouth was moving, but the words and voice were not her own.

"Eleanora? Is that you?" Dev asked, and Arrabelle rolled her eyes in a physical affectation that was pure Eleanora.

"Of course, it's me. I told you I wasn't going to curl up under the house like some dying old cat." Once again, the face was Arrabelle's, but from the animated way her features moved, the brow furrowing in good-natured consternation, it was clear that Eleanora was in charge.

"I'm not going. Releasing Ritual be damned. And you"— Arrabelle/Eleanora turned on Lizbeth, glaring at her—*"you could've been killed. They know we're here and they know one of you is the last of the Dream Keepers. Don't disobey the others. Listen to Daniela when she says that they need to look out for you."*

"I wasn't going to be taken," Lizbeth said. "I knew what I was doing."

She wasn't going to let herself get hurt—and no way was she going to stand there and let something terrible happen to Lyse and Arrabelle. Not if she could help it. She knew how to take care of herself. She'd been on her own for most of her life, and no one had taken care of her then. They'd just thrown her in that horrible psychiatric facility where she'd been totally alone, forced to fend for herself.

Lizbeth's brain sensed something was different in her thought process. At first, she wasn't sure what it was, but then she realized she'd never been able to go down this avenue of thought without her whole person shutting down. Never before had she been able to tolerate thinking about the past. Specifically about the psychiatric facility her father had placed her in after her mother died. Just the smell of the cleaning disinfectant they'd used at the facility could send her into a mental meltdown, but now all of that had changed.

It was as if the two parts of her mind had finally fused together and become one. No longer was the child brain in charge of her, and it never would be again. Not now that the adult part of her possessed all the power.

The past was the past.

"Don't look at me like that," Arrabelle/Eleanora said, interrupting Lizbeth's train of thought. *"We're just trying to do what's best for you, dammit."*

Lizbeth opened her mouth to reply, but Lyse beat her to the punch.

"Eleanora," Lyse said, changing the subject. "You're free to go on to the other side. Don't stay here for my benefit—"

"It's not just for you, my sweet Lyse," Arrabelle/Eleanora said. *"It's so much bigger than that. Hessika and I stay behind as Dream Walkers for a greater purpose. You will need us and we are here for you."*

It was true. Hessika had stayed behind partly to save Lizbeth's life.

The very first night she'd been taken to the institution, she'd cried herself to sleep only to be woken up by the most magical creature she'd ever seen: a giant lady with fluffy strawberry-blond hair and eyelashes as thick as beetles' legs. Only later did she realize it was a dream, but that didn't matter. From that night forward, Hessika's dreamlands appearances were the only thing holding Lizbeth's sanity together.

"Eleanora—" Lyse said, but Arrabelle/Eleanora merely shook her head.

"It's my choice, and my choice alone to make." Then Arrabelle's face went slack as Eleanora's spirit vacated its host body.

Then every candle within the circle extinguished itself.

Lizbeth knew the possession was over. Eleanora had made her choice and she, for one, would make sure her wishes were followed. To that end, she picked up the brass urn and held it tightly to her breast.

"Thank you," she whispered into the night.

Thank you, Eleanora and Hessika.

Arrabelle

Arrabelle turned the key in the ignition and the car shuddered once and fell quiet. In the silence, she heard the gentle ticking of the engine; the outside sounds—the rise and fall of the waves as they lapped at the boat, the insistent call of seabirds, the idling of the other cars lined up to board the ferry—seemed a million miles away. She felt cut adrift, as if she were a shade walking through the world of the living, a revenant returned from the grave and forced to wander the Earth.

The events of the previous night had left them all shaken, but hadn't deterred them from their plan. Arrabelle had taken a flight to Seattle; Lyse, Daniela, Lizbeth, and Weir had gone to Rome; and Dev had remained behind, but with the knowledge that her family was coming to stay and the Dream Walkers, Hessika and Eleanora, would also be available to her. Arrabelle tried not to let their parting feel like an ending, refusing to believe she might never see her coven mates again.

Instead, she held on to the belief they would be reunited again, and sooner than any of them expected.

She got out of the rental car, closing the driver's-side door behind her, the wind biting into her flesh, stinging her with cold air and salty sea spray. She wasn't thinking straight, her mind filled with memories, the past making it impossible to be alive in the present. The drive had been good. She'd found solace in the monotony of the road and the swish of the windshield wipers as the rain beat down on the red rental car she'd picked up at Sea-Tac—but now she had nothing to do. Just sit on the ferry and wait to cross the water.

She depressed the lock button on the keychain the young guy at the rental counter had given her, the subcompact now impenetrable, and began to weave her way through the sea of parked cars. Old rusted junkers, modest midsize cars, minivans, and SUVs . . . they mostly seemed to belong to people who lived on the island but worked on the peninsula.

Not a lot of tourists this time of year.

Except for her. But then she was really just a virtual tourist, lost in her own memories, traveling back in time as her physical body remained moored to the present. Soon her memories and reality would intersect: She'd be on the island where Evan had spent the last decade . . . precious years that did not, besides the occasional phone call or note, include her.

She ignored the rows of wooden benches bolted to the deck floor and made her way over to the side of the ferry, resting her elbows on top of the metal mesh railing. She was just another body wrapped up tight inside the wall of fog that rose up from the water, the late-afternoon sky above her turning charcoal gray as she stared out toward the fading horizon.

Evan.

She heard his boisterous laugh and almost turned around, her heart hammering out a chaotic, nervous beat. But the laughter was just a phantom, an echo inside her head. She closed her eyes as a wave of tears flooded past her eyelashes. She did nothing to wipe them away. She knew anyone looking on would think she just had sea spray on her cheeks.

* * *

They met at a used bookstore. Well, he was standing *outside* the bookstore, and she was *inside* shelving books in the romance aisle—but she figured it still counted. He only caught her eye because he was leaning against the building, reading a dog-eared copy of *The Man Who Mistook His Wife for a Hat* (a book she loved), and biting his thumbnail like a nervous child.

He was cute in a nerdy, grungy fashion—curly red hair, freckles, and the kind of round-rimmed glasses the Harry Potter books would popularize a few years down the line. He was beanpole thin in his baggy khaki cutoffs and oversized Screaming Trees T-shirt, black Chuck Taylors on his feet. He had the sole of one shoe pressed against the wall as he leaned against the brick, turning pages at a rapid pace. All the while silently mouthing the syllables of each word he read.

As she moved an errant copy of Victoria Holt's *The Legend of the Seventh Virgin* from the *P* section back into the *H* section, she kept glancing through the plate-glass window. Out on the sidewalk, the cute boy—she didn't know his name was Evan yet—was oblivious to her stares. He just kept reading and rereading pages, flipping back and forth between the beginning, middle, and end of the book as if it were a puzzle he was trying to figure out.

He scratched the side of his nose as he read, a very unconscious gesture that Arrabelle found amusing and kind of endearing. Part of her wanted to knock on the glass and get his attention, but she was working and responsibility was the touchstone of her existence. She just wasn't capable of slacking off, even though it was only a silly summer job, something to pay for food and incidentals while she decompressed from a rigorous spring semester of pre-med hell.

Her dad had wanted her to continue taking classes, but the thought of going to summer school made Arrabelle's teeth ache. She was so burned out from studying she couldn't see straight. She needed a break, but she also wanted to stay in Santa Cruz for the summer, so getting a job had been their compromise.

Arrabelle loved to read, was a total book whore growing up, her nose always in the pages of a novel, and it was thrilling to think she might fall in love with a stranger she'd seen only through the window of her bookstore. It made her feel like an Austen heroine all flush with excitement after her first dance with Mr. Darcy. Not that anyone threw balls in that day and age. And not that Arrabelle needed a husband—but having someone to talk about books and hang out with, well, it did sound pretty nice.

She'd never had a boyfriend before. She'd always been too busy. At least, that was what she thought, but then her freshman-year roommate, Allison, had told her the truth: Arrabelle intimidated the shit out of guys.

So many things had made sense after that—for all her book smarts, Arrabelle was naïve when it came to romance. She knew what she'd read in books and that was it; she had zero practical experience in the ways of love. She'd always been too busy reading, had missed some crucial real-world stuff because she was too busy getting lost in books. Not precious about what she read, she loved literature *and* genre stuff: westerns, science fiction, and fantasy. There was just something exhilarating about disappearing into another world. You were a voyeur, true, experiencing the stress and romance and misery of the characters you were reading about, but then when things got too intense, you could just put the book down and be glad the story wasn't your own.

When it came time for her lunch break, Arrabelle decided she'd let fate dictate what happened: If the cute guy was still outside on the sidewalk, she'd go talk to him. If not, then that was fate's way of saying to let it go. So she grabbed her brown bag lunch from the back room of the bookstore—she was too student-poor to eat out every day—and made for the front entrance.

The shop wasn't very big, but it was crammed floor to ceiling with bookcases. Tall wooden ones precariously bolted into the drywall, their skinny frames and shelves thick with books, making Arrabelle a little nervous should an earthquake decide to hit while she was standing under one of them. Jezzer was the only other employee working that Sunday afternoon, but he barely noticed when she walked by the register.

"I'll be back in thirty minutes," Arrabelle said, slipping a gauzy gray scarf around her neck and donning a pair of Jackie O sunglasses.

"Evs," Jezzer replied, pen in mouth, eyes glued to the *New York Times* crossword puzzle he was working. Jezzer wouldn't have been caught dead doing the *Times* in pencil.

She passed the curio cabinets by the front of the store, their glass fronts just out of reach of the sunlit glare from the windows. Full of first editions and other specialty collector's items, the cabinets held the items that were the store's real moneymakers—without them, they would have had to sell a metric ton of two-dollar paperbacks to pay the rent.

She stopped by the door to look at the signed German-language first edition of Hermann Hesse's *Journey to the East*, of which she was particularly fond. Her father had given her an English translation of the book when she was a kid, and she treasured it.

Even when she and her father disagreed, he was always the person she wanted to please the most. He believed in her, and for that she would be eternally grateful. He'd never treated her like a girl. Never told her there was anything she couldn't do or be. He saw the beauty in her brain, understood her innate curiosity about life (a quality they both shared), and he nurtured it.

A thoracic surgeon by day, her father was a magic story-teller by night. He knew how to weave together the greatest tall tales, and often dinner table conversation centered on odd cases from his work. Hearts with extra valves, hearts reversed so that they formed on the wrong side of the chest . . . her father had lots of juicy stories filled with blood and guts and macerated organs. It was a wonder anyone could stand to sit at the dinner table with the two of them.

She sighed, leaving thoughts of her father behind as she strolled toward the front entrance. The little bell nailed to the top of the doorframe tinkled when she opened the door, a light breeze catching the edge of her scarf and ruffling it. Arrabelle had always been a careful dresser, liking a certain style and taste of clothing. She had a penchant for jumpsuits and soft clothes that hung from her tall frame like drapery. She appreciated things that were elegant but comfortable—something that didn't change when she got older.

This day she'd decided on a pair of green linen pants and a silky tank top, her lean body on full display. She liked to run, feeling the muscles working like machines underneath her skin, and this outfit showed off her toned physique. She felt good about herself, was confident in who she was becoming— and all of this was due to her father giving her the greatest gift of all: the belief that she could do anything she wanted. That nothing was beyond the limit of her abilities.

Except there was one key piece of information she had trouble learning, and in this friendship with Evan, it would eventually prove to be her downfall. It was something a lot of strong-willed people could never really wrap their brains around . . . that try as you might, you couldn't make other people do what you wanted them to do just by sheer dint of will.

Arrabelle looked in both directions, hoping to see the boy, but there were only a few random shoppers on the sidewalk, following the flow of traffic. She stood by the doorway, her sack lunch in hand, trying to decide where to go. Usually she ate on her own in the back office, but now that she'd changed up her routine, she didn't relish going inside again. Not that

Jezzer knew or cared what she was doing. It was enough that *she* knew. That *she* felt stupid standing out there on the street with no plan.

"Hey."

Arrabelle lifted her head and saw the cute boy standing beside her.

"Hi," she replied, trying to figure out where he'd come from. She'd checked in each direction, searching for him like a hawk, but he'd been missing in action—and then, just like that, he'd popped into her view.

"You were in my Intro to Cultural Anthro," he said, his angular face a study in morose adolescence. No smile, thin lips slightly turned down. He had a curious expression in his dark eyes, thick eyebrows pressed together thoughtfully.

She thought back to the class, racking her brain to find his features in her memory catalog of faces, but she came up blank. She didn't think she'd seen him, or maybe he'd just been so unprepossessing she hadn't really noticed him.

"I liked that class," Arrabelle said, gripping her lunch bag tightly in between both hands. She felt a little nervous, something that wasn't normal for her.

"Me, too."

He took a step back and pressed his shoulder blades against the brick wall of the building.

"You work here?" He inclined a thumb toward the bookstore.

She nodded.

"Yup, I do. For the summer, a compromise with my father."

"You guys close?" he asked.

"Pretty much just him and me," she found herself saying, divulging more information than she normally did during the course of a first meeting. "So yeah, we're close."

"My parents are okay. Not really close to them, though. They're a little impenetrable."

"How so?" she asked, rocking back and forth on her feet.

"Can't get in their heads—probably because there's nothing in there, I guess."

He pulled a book from his back pocket. It was all rolled up, the pages bent into a cone. It was the book he'd been holding when she'd first spied him through the bookshop window, the one he'd read like a puzzle.

"You like to read?"

Arrabelle nodded.

"I do."

He nodded, the same thoughtful expression still on his face.

"My name's Evan. What's yours?"

After school, both Arrabelle and Evan had found themselves drawn into a new world, one neither of them had known even existed. They'd been shown their talents and conscripted into the world of the covens, and though it had come as a surprise to them both, each having grown up oblivious to the idea of magic existing, they'd both accepted their strange, symbiotic fates and never looked back.

This was how Evan had ended up in the Pacific Northwest on an island only reachable from the mainland via ferry, far removed from everything and everyone he'd ever known. It was this separation—Arrabelle hundreds of miles away in Los Angeles, a city she'd never in a million years expected to call home—that had ultimately made it impossible for their friendship to become anything more.

In her heart, Arrabelle had hoped their relationship might change, that Evan would start to think of her as more than just a friend—not that he'd ever given her a reason to suspect this was even an option. He'd never once let on that he needed or wanted to share his life with *anyone*.

The announcement over the loudspeaker letting everyone know the ferry was about to dock broke into her thoughts.

Arrabelle stood up, leaving the railing and the gentle sway of the sea behind as she followed the others back to where the cars were parked. She found her rental easily—it was the cleanest car there—and slid into the driver's seat.

The camper in front of her started its engine, and Arrabelle did the same. She took the few moments of wait time before they could disembark to program Evan's address into the GPS. She wasn't really worried about getting lost. It was a small island and she thought she'd be able to find the house without too much trouble. Still, she liked using the GPS because she appreciated being told where to go.

She followed the line of cars as they proceeded out onto the dock, turning up the defroster as the windshield began to fog up, obscuring her view. She tried to stay present as she drove, not letting her mind drift into the past as she rolled through the quiet island streets. It was a cute fishing village with rows of clapboard houses. Painted in shades of cream and blue and brown, they'd each seen their share of the powerful storms that seasonally broke across the island.

She turned right and the downtown stretched out in front of her. It consisted of about fifteen small stores and restaurants, and a gas station—all probably catering more to the tourist trade than the year-round residents. She wished she could pretend to be one of the summer people. No agenda, no responsibility, no stress . . . just vacationing in a beautiful place and enjoying herself. But her reason for coming to the island was the opposite of relaxing. She was here to find Evan and Niamh, the girl whose journal he'd sent her. She needed to see him, to make sure he was okay . . . or not.

Only then could she get her sanity back.

The GPS called out directions in its feminine monotone, and Arrabelle did as she was told, turning onto one tiny street after another until the voice announced they'd reached their destination. She pulled the car over and parked on the street but didn't get out. She needed to collect herself before she went in. She hadn't seen Evan in so long that the whole thing felt absurd. How could you share so much with another human being and then one day they were gone? Or, at least, they weren't there for you in the same way anymore.

There was a knock on the car window and Arrabelle jumped. She turned to find a painfully thin girl with long brown hair standing just beyond the glass. The girl's pale face was coated in a spackling of light brown freckles. Dark circles bit into the skin beneath her emerald and gold-flecked eyes, her cheekbones sharp as blades. Grief had cut deep hollows into the girl's face, and her oversized plaid shirt hung from her bony shoulders and fell across a shapeless chest.

Arrabelle turned the car back on and rolled the window down. The girl shook her head.

"You're Bell."

It wasn't a question.

"Yes."

"He said you'd come." The girl circled around the front of the rental car, eyes searching the woods and houses around them, looking for what, Arrabelle had no idea. "I'll take you."

The girl reached for the door handle, but then her head popped up like a cork, her behavior almost animal-like. She reminded Arrabelle of a doe whose soft brown ears twitched at the first sign of a predator lurking in the shaded woodlands.

She must've heard something, Arrabelle thought, and watched the girl crane her neck warily.

Arrabelle rolled down the passenger window.

"Get in, Niamh."

The girl stood frozen, hand on the door handle, too keyed up to pay attention to Arrabelle.

"Niamh, I read your journal. I know it's you. Get in the car."

No response.

"Please?" Arrabelle added—and this seemed to break the spell. The girl turned back around, eyebrows pinched together.

"Did you hear—" she began, but at that very moment there was a *crash* from the tree line.

Niamh screamed, her fingers scrabbling for the door handle. Arrabelle was out of the car in a shot, racing toward the sound, all thoughts of personal safety forgotten. She crossed into the grass beyond the sidewalk, eyes scanning the trees, but it didn't take long to discover the source of the sound.

The man was a giant—and like the humanoid creature that had attacked Arrabelle and her coven the night before, his skin was like melted plastic, burnt shoulders and chest covered in ropy scar tissue that looked even more grotesque in the daylight.

The creature wore no shirt, just long pants covered in excrement and dirt, their bottoms shredded after roaming the woods like an animal. His face was a ruination—no real features, just a gluey approximation of a human being. She didn't know how he could see. His eyeballs protruded from the ruined skin around the orbital cavities of his skull like two glassy-white marbles. His gaze flicked back and forth between them before finally settling on Arrabelle, who was closer to him.

"What do you want?"

He didn't respond, but a wicked grin stretched across his face. And then something strange happened. She felt him inside her head, placing his thoughts into her mind:

—*The girl. They want her.*

Arrabelle shuddered as the words slithered around inside her brain.

"You can't have her," Arrabelle said to the creature.

"What's happening?" Niamh asked, frightened by the one-sided exchange.

"He's a telepath," Arrabelle murmured, without looking at her.

—*I don't have any business with you, blood sister. Go and I will let you live.*

"Let me live?" Arrabelle almost snorted. "Fuck you. You're the one who better be worried about your life, my friend."

The man's body shook, and Arrabelle realized he was laughing.

"Get in the car," Arrabelle said, turning to Niamh.

"But—"

"Just do it," Arrabelle said over the girl's protests.

Niamh stood there a moment longer than Arrabelle appreciated, but finally she gave a nod and headed toward the car. Arrabelle heard the door open, the shocks squeaking as the girl climbed into the passenger seat.

"Close it and lock the doors," Arrabelle called back to her, glad the windows were still down. "Turn on the car, key's in the ignition, then roll up the windows. If he kills me, get the hell out of here and go to Los Angeles. My coven will take care of you. You know my address, right? The place where you sent the journal?"

Out of the corner of her eye, she saw the girl nod.

"Good. Now promise me you'll do it."

Niamh nodded.

"Say it," Arrabelle demanded, her eyes locked on the creature as he took a step toward her.

"I'll do it. I promise," Niamh called back to her.

And with the promise extracted from the girl, Arrabelle removed her long down jacket and dropped it in the grass. Steeling herself for a beating, she took a deep breath and ran for the giant.

Daniela

"I don't know," Daniela said, turning back around in her
seat to look at Lyse. "They're still whispering together
like they're plotting something."

Lizbeth had not taken well to being told what to do—and
maybe it was true, the old Lizbeth would've been bullied into
submission without comment, which obviously wasn't good.
But damn if this new and improved Lizbeth wasn't just a pain in
the butt to deal with. It would've been easier to handle her con-
frontational attitude at a time when they didn't need to work so
closely together. When splintering into hostile factions might be
the end of them.

Daniela intimated as much to Lyse, who was sitting beside
her. They'd boarded their flight a few minutes earlier, and
now they were waiting for the attendant to close the cabin
door so they could take off.

"So, yeah, is it just me, or is she like a different kid now?
One that talks back and doesn't listen?"

Lyse frowned, her blue eyes serious as she finished strapping on her seat belt. She sat back, resting her head against the foam headrest.

"Well, I don't think she's a kid anymore. Something happened to her back in Elysian Park," Lyse said. "Whatever it was. She's stronger now. She's not locked away inside herself—and I think it's necessary. For what's coming next."

Daniela had never heard Lyse speak so plainly before. It was refreshing, made her feel for the first time that Eleanora hadn't been wrong in her choice. That she'd made the right decision to hand the leadership of the coven over to her granddaughter.

"Okay," Daniela said, watching one of the hot flight attendants stride past her, leaving the scent of white jasmine in her wake. "I'll chill out and not take it too personally."

"There's nothing to take personally," Lyse said, and closed her eyes. "Lizbeth is going to do what Lizbeth wants. It's the coven's job to protect her—even when she's being difficult."

"I think I liked her better before she grew a pair of cojones."

Lyse laughed, opening one eye to look over at Daniela.

"You are a truly unique individual."

Daniela grinned.

"What can I say? I try."

Lyse smiled at this and closed her eyes again, her face relaxing. Daniela got the message: Lyse was done talking. Leave her alone and let her nap.

Well, so be it, Daniela thought. She turned around in her seat and looked back at Lizbeth and Weir, who were a few rows behind them. She wished they didn't look so chummy.

After the night they'd just had, Daniela was hyperaware of everything and everyone around her. She hated having an opponent she couldn't see, and it was even harder to wrap her head around a group like The Flood. She had no idea what their goals were. They seemed hell-bent on eradicating the covens and had chosen draconian tactics to do it. Their methods were straight out of the Dark Ages—witch burning, anyone? As far as Daniela was concerned, a real man or woman came at you with both fists up, ready to give as good as they got.

Too bad there were so many more cowards in the world than stand-up people, she thought as the plane finally taxied and took off.

She did not feel good about this excursion to Italy.

She'd been in Rome the last time she saw her mother. Those precious few hours she'd spent with Marie-Faith before she'd died, they'd wandered the streets of the very city to which Daniela was heading. She didn't know how it would feel to be back there so soon after her mother's death. It wasn't a trip she would've taken, but duty called. And now with Lizbeth behaving so strangely, she was starting to feel even more uptight about the excursion.

Daniela closed her eyes and let her mind wander.

Her thoughts returned to her mother. It was an automatic response, this slippage of time, and it was impossible to control. Given half a second, she would find herself sliding back into childhood, her brain free-falling into the past. There was nothing she could do about it. Ever since she'd learned of her mother's death, it had become an addiction.

She opened her eyes again, fighting the urge to disappear down the rabbit hole. She stared at the tiny television screen embedded in the seat in front of her. She turned it on, not bothering to plug in the headphones she'd found in the seatback pocket. It was some reality show with a series of forgettable men trying to date an overplasticized woman who giggled like an idiot at anything/everything they said to her—not that Daniela could hear the woman's laugh. She could just tell it was terrible by the way the woman's face and mouth hardly moved an inch.

Her mind drifted back to Thomas—who, presumably, was still tied up in the Mucho Man Cave. He was right about the hybrids. This was something she and her mother had spoken of, and, afterward, Daniela had been sworn to secrecy on the subject. When she thought back to the days before Lyse's arrival, her gloves had always been more than sufficient protection—but now she didn't trust herself around anyone.

Lyse was definitely the cause of Daniela's empath problems . . . but she was also the most alluring thing Daniela had encountered in a very long time. It was tough, seeing her with Weir and knowing he would be the winner were there ever to be any question about where Lyse's affections lay.

She sighed and looked past Lyse to the window, the scenery slowly beginning to change below her. She didn't want to do this, didn't want to play protector to an ungrateful kid. What *she* wanted was to go back in time to when her mother was still alive and stay there. She never wanted to let Marie-Faith go.

When Lyse lost Eleanora, it was Daniela who understood her pain the best. She knew what it felt like to be untethered and at loose ends, unsure of who or what you were anymore, or where you belonged. Unlike Daniela, though, Lyse could access her grandmother whenever she wanted because Eleanora had chosen to stay behind and become a Dream Walker.

Marie-Faith had not made the same choice. Obviously. Or Daniela would've encountered her mother again by now. But she did have something that eased her feelings of loss. A secret weapon that kept her from feeling completely alone:

Desmond Delay.

Desmond requested she not say anything to the others about their meeting. She'd agreed, deciding not to tell *him* that she'd been forbidden to talk to anyone outside her inner circle.

After all the craziness of the Releasing Ritual and then packing for the trip, meeting Desmond before she left meant that Daniela got very little sleep. Instead of resting, she found herself sitting at a sparkly red Naugahyde booth in a twenty-four-hour diner on Sunset, unopened menu on the cracked Formica table in front of her.

A mug of steaming hot coffee found its way to her, and she loaded it up with cream and sugar, ignoring the raised eyebrow she got from the hipster waiter when he realized she wasn't going to be taking off her gloves.

"You're here early."

She looked up and smiled. Desmond Delay took the seat opposite her and set his lion-headed cane against the edge of the booth. He looked more like a kindly old grandfather than a powerful member of the Greater Council, all white hair and craggy face, hazel eyes tired and sad—but he truly was a man to be reckoned with, exhaustion and kind eyes aside.

Desmond removed his gray fedora and set it on the seat beside him. He smoothed his hair, then rubbed at the salt-and-pepper scruff on his chin, a thoughtful expression on his face.

"So we're leaving today." She opened with the obvious, the thing she knew he would be most curious about.

"All right," he replied, ignoring the waiter, who was lurking nearby waiting to take their order. "Tell me more."

He pushed the menu away and rested his elbows on the tabletop, giving her another weary smile. Daniela leaned forward, her voice hushed.

"I think you know who I mean . . ."

He pursed his lips, then nodded before speaking.

"Ah, so Marie-Faith sent you here to protect her," he said, his tone so soft that at first, Daniela wasn't sure she'd heard him right. "I should've realized."

"I know that my mother confided everything in you," Daniela said. "When I saw her in Rome . . . before she died . . . she let me know what I'd be getting into. I wish I'd asked her more, but I didn't know it was the last time I'd ever see her."

It hadn't been her intention to let her emotions get out of hand, but there she was, sitting in a brightly lit diner at five A.M., crying like a baby. She didn't want to do this, so she picked up her paper napkin and dabbed at her eyes, trying to control herself. It was being with Desmond, one of her mother's oldest friends and a trusted compatriot within the highly political fishbowl of the Greater Council, that made it impossible for Daniela to hold on to her composure.

"No tears, my dear," Desmond said. "That's not what Marie-Faith would want to see."

He didn't reach out to touch her—he'd known her since she was a small child and was well aware of her powers—but he removed a monogrammed white handkerchief from his navy wool peacoat pocket and offered it to her. She took it, grateful for the small kindness. Not being able to use your hands to touch the ones you loved made these tiny gestures of affection extremely important to Daniela.

"Sorry," she said, and blew her nose. "I just . . . it's still difficult, you know?"

Desmond nodded.

"I miss her, too," he said, and beckoned the waiter over to their table, so that Daniela could have a few moments to collect herself.

The young waiter yawned, then pulled out his pad of paper expectantly.

"You need to eat," Desmond said to Daniela. "You look worn out." He turned to the waiter: "Two omelets, bacon, hash browns, and toast. Coffee for me. That's all, please."

Dismissed, the waiter skulked away like a dog with its tail between its legs. Daniela laughed.

"I don't know why everyone is always so intimidated by you. You're the sweetest man I know."

An omnipresent fixture in her adolescence, Desmond was like the father she'd never known. He was the person she went to when she fought with her mother, or when she needed to talk about something private . . . something no one else would understand. He was a great listener, and he never judged her—not even when she came out to him. He merely shook his head and said: "Of course. I've known this about you for a very long time."

If he didn't have her heart before that moment, he had it forever after.

As they ate, she told him everything, and all the emotions that had been trapped inside came rushing out.

"And then when the call came, I didn't know what to do," Daniela said, absently stirring her coffee with a battered aluminum spoon. "It didn't seem real. I couldn't process it, and I was stuck here in L.A., a part of a coven that didn't know me or trust me. I felt so lost. The only saving grace was Eleanora. She and Mom had been friends for ages, and I remembered her from when I was little. So she wasn't a stranger, at least."

Desmond set his fork down and pushed his plate away, finished with his meal. Daniela didn't think he looked well. He seemed exhausted, and the way he pushed his food around his plate, barely tasting any of it, gave her the impression that there was something wrong.

"I'm sorry. I've been babbling at you this whole time. How are *you*? I feel like I haven't really talked to you in such a long time." They hadn't spent any real time together since right after her mother's memorial service—and she'd been in such a daze, barely been functioning.

"I'm the one who should apologize," Desmond replied, sitting back into his seat. "There's been so much to do in your mother's absence . . . but I should've come sooner, regardless."

"Well, you're here now," Daniela said, pushing the eggs to the side of the plate, where they disappeared into a wall of uneaten ketchup and hash browns.

"Just so you know, I was part of the splinter group your mother created to find and protect the last Dream Keeper. I'm pleased she saw fit to bring you into our confidence," Desmond said, and smiled. "Of all the people in my life, I consider you to be my family, Daniela. That I can trust you and work with you as a peer has been one of my greatest joys. Thank you for your honesty in all things."

Daniela returned his smile. "Well, I figured you couldn't be frank with me until I was frank with you. How could you have known my mother had brought me into her confidence?"

"She spoke of doing so," Desmond said. "But then . . ."

He chose not to mention Marie-Faith's death again.

"She told me about the hybrids, but not what it was The Flood wanted with them," Daniela said, shattering the silence that hung between them.

Daniela watched as the sun began to coast over the horizon. It wasn't as dark outside as it had been and she felt exposed, worried that maybe one of her blood sisters would walk past the large plate-glass window. See her betrayal.

"That is something we don't really know ourselves," Desmond said, and sighed. "Well, I do know one thing. Your logic is sound. Not letting the Dream Keeper out of your sight is key. Now tell me what your plans are. I have people around the world ready to do your bidding at a moment's notice."

"We need to let the Council know that The Flood isn't just coming. It's here. We need to prepare—"

Desmond interrupted her, waving his hands to stop the flow of words.

"If only it were so easy. There are people on the Council who'd throw you out on your ear if you even suggested that. They believe nothing terrible could ever touch them, and they have no interest in someone like you, or your mother, crying wolf and upsetting the status quo."

"It's not true. We've been attacked with magic a number of times," Daniela protested. "And something or someone is out there burning witches . . . making monsters to do their bidding."

Once again, Desmond held up his hand for her to stop.

"Listen to yourself. You sound hysterical . . . though *I* know you're being anything but—"

"I don't think—" she tried to interject, but Desmond was still talking.

"—and remember how impenetrable the Council is, especially the high council: The more facts you collect, the more information you obtain, the easier it will be to convert the naysayers. That's all I'm saying to you."

Even though Daniela knew Desmond was just trying to make a point, she didn't like being referred to as "hysterical." She'd seen how difficult her mother's job had been. Getting anyone to agree on anything was an almost impossible task. And the Greater Council was not just one group of women governing their world, but a series of committees that each, in their own right, possessed a level of power.

The high council—where her mother had been installed until her untimely death—was like the Supreme Court, taking the opinions of the other committees, weighing them against one another, and coming to a final decision on the matter. Desmond was a member of the Autonomous Committee— an objective group of scholars and academics who didn't possess magic, but who acted in an advisory capacity to the high council. These men and women were highly important to the blood sisters but were not *of* them.

Desmond had spent enough time among the covens to know how they maneuvered and what would and wouldn't fly. As much as she hated to admit it, he was probably right.

"So how do we proceed, then?"

"You follow the Dream Keeper, see what she discovers in Italy, and then you bring everything to me. Together, we can go to the high council and make our stand . . ." He leaned forward in his seat, rheumy eyes alive with excitement. "If they believe us, then the rest of the committees will be more inclined to do so, as well."

He sat back again, having said his piece.

"I'm not as energetic as I once was," he said, closing his eyes. "It's almost too much for an old man."

Daniela wanted to reach out and touch him, reassure him he wasn't old—but she didn't want to lie to him. It would be a first in their relationship. Desmond had always inspired the truth from her. Instead, she chose to remain silent.

"I'll have people on the ground in Rome. They'll stay in the shadows, but they'll be there if you need them. Or if something goes wrong."

He was looking at her now, waiting for an answer.

She nodded.

"I know you can take care of yourself, but these are dark times and you're going to need all the help you can get to protect Lyse—"

"You mean, Lizbeth . . . ?" Daniela said, correcting him.

Desmond shook his head, trying to clear it.

"Of course, that's what I mean," he sighed, deep frown lines creasing the skin around his mouth. "Between the two of us, my mind isn't what it once was . . . it's not terrible . . . yet."

He stopped there, taking a deep breath, and Daniela's heart fluttered in her chest. Fear, as cold and mercenary as a vise, squeezed at her insides. She didn't think she could listen to what he was about to tell her.

"I didn't want to tell you like this," he said, looking down at the tabletop, unwilling to meet her gaze.

No. No. No. This can't be happening, Daniela thought. *I can't lose you, too.*

"What's wrong? Are you okay?"

She couldn't help herself. The words came out in a rush, her fear a living thing inside her.

"It's Alzheimer's. There's nothing that can be done. I've known for a while, but the disease is progressing faster than the doctors expected."

Daniela's face fell. It was like being kicked in the gut. She dropped her head, cupping her face in between her hands, and began to rock back and forth in her seat.

"Stop it," Desmond said, his voice stern. "I don't need you

to fall apart on me. I want the opposite. I want what's happening to my brain forgotten and for you to do the job that your mother gave you."

Daniela nodded, fighting back tears.

"Yeah, okay. I can do that."

She said the words out loud but had no idea if she'd be able to stand by them. This news was devastating: The last link to "family" was fading away right before her eyes.

"I think it's time for us to go," Desmond said, throwing a hundred-dollar bill down on the table and climbing to his feet.

Daniela followed suit, dragging herself from the booth, her legs unsteady beneath her. She rested a gloved hand on the Naugahyde seat and steadied herself.

"Oh, I forgot to ask you something . . ."

Desmond, who was already moving toward the front entrance, turned back around.

"Yes?"

"Does the name Temistocles mean anything to you?"

For a moment, Daniela thought she saw a flash of recognition in Desmond's eyes, but it was so fleeting she couldn't be sure she hadn't just imagined it. He made a show of thinking about the question for a moment and then shook his head.

"Outside of an historical context?" he asked, a curious frown on his face.

Daniela nodded her head.

"Then the answer is no."

Daniela woke up as the plane began its descent into the Leonardo da Vinci–Fiumicino International Airport in Rome. She'd watched a few mindless films, and then she must've just passed out because she didn't remember falling asleep.

"We're here," Lyse said, her head turned toward the window, watching the abstract geometric patterns slowly resolve into the trappings of the human world.

"Good," Daniela said, stretching in her seat.

"You were unconscious for hours," Lyse said. "I was jealous. I never sleep well on planes."

Daniela shrugged, the nasty taste of cotton mouth making her wish she had some water.

"Any word from the kids?" Daniela asked as she pulled a pack of spearmint gum from her pocket and popped a stick into her mouth.

Lyse shook her head.

"Weir slept. Lizbeth read through the journals I brought."

Lyse had removed Hessika's Dream Journals from their hiding place in Eleanora's closet and presented them to Lizbeth at the airport. Like the notebook Lizbeth had retrieved from the dreamlands, the Dream Journals appeared blank to anyone who did not possess a Dream Keeper's talents.

"Ah, more knowledge she may or may not share with us," Daniela mumbled.

Lyse shot her a disapproving glance.

"Please don't do that. We need to close ranks, not cause more rifts."

Daniela sighed.

"All right. Team effort from now on," she said.

Lyse smiled at her.

"Thank you."

Their pensione was tucked away from the center of the city in one of the quieter, more residential quarters of Rome. Once it had been a single-family home—a mansion, really, with Doric columns on the portico and the classical, clean lines of a Roman villa—but those days were long gone. Its latest owners had sectioned off the massive interior space into a number of charming, sun-drenched rooms, each one taken up by two single beds and a rococo desk and chair.

Lizbeth and Weir were bunked in one room; Lyse and

Daniela would take over another. But they didn't stay long enough to enjoy their new surroundings. They dropped their stuff off and headed out again with little delay, only making a pit stop at a small café to get paninis and coffee.

Daniela had insisted they move quickly, so they'd hopped in a cab and headed for the Villa Nomentana, the international home of the high council—and the very place where her mother had spent the last few months of her life.

"Drop us here, please," Daniela said to their driver, and the four of them piled out of the taxi. They were at a busy intersection, and Daniela threw the man far more euros than necessary before waving him on his way.

She and Lyse had decided not to take any unnecessary risks, not wanting to alert anyone to their presence here in the city. Which was why they'd chosen to get out of the cab a few blocks away from the villa, among the crumbling old buildings and tiny shops of the Trieste district.

The afternoon sunlight beat down on their heads as they wove their way through a sidewalk filled with pedestrians—and Daniela wondered what the local Italians thought of them.

With our American accents and backpacks, we must look like the worst kind of tourists, she mused. *Weir busy scanning the crowd like he's expecting to be pickpocketed at any moment, Lizbeth off in some fantasy land of her own making, Lyse's whole body as tight as a drumhead.*

Lizbeth and Weir had been strangely silent since their arrival in Rome, and Daniela tried not to let her suspicions about that silence influence how she behaved. She knew Lyse was right—creating an atmosphere of distrust wouldn't be good for anyone—but it didn't mean she ignored her gut feelings. She just put them aside for the moment—though they always remained within easy reach.

It was warmer than usual for October, and Daniela began to

sweat as they walked the remaining blocks to the Villa Nomentana. She'd spent some time in the city while her mother was in
residence with the high council, and she had a basic understanding of the layout of the area around the villa. She just
wished she knew a way to get to the catacombs without having
to enter the grounds.

"We'll just be tourists," Daniela said as they turned off the
crowded sidewalk, leaving the terra-cotta-colored buildings and
high stone walls to cross to the other side of the street. "We'll
walk around the grounds, looking as normal as possible. And
we stick together, don't split up—we're safer as a group."

"Sure," Weir said, but his tone was unconvincing. He pulled
his backpack up higher on his shoulders and let his gaze drift
away—almost as if he were too embarrassed by the obvious-
ness of his lie to look her in the eye.

I'm gonna have my work cut out for me, Daniela thought. They
reached the end of the sidewalk, and the rough stone wall separating the park from the street gave way to a wrought-iron gate
that led into the villa's manicured grounds. The high council
only used the main building, which was separate from the rest
of the grounds. Those were open to the public and many tourists could be found inside its gates, snapping pictures and
enjoying the bounty of its gardens.

It was an impressive piece of real estate. Sprawling lawns, cul-
tivated Italianate gardens leading to marble-sculpted fountains,
and Roman statuary intermixed with verdant shrubbery and lus-
cious floral beds in neon-hued pinks, yellows, and reds. The four
of them followed the dirt path through rows of statuary of
mythic Roman gods and goddesses, their human musculature—
long-limbed bodies, rounded bellies and breasts, massive hands
and feet—sculpted from aging white marble. A large oval fountain sat in front of the gated entrance into the main villa, and all
along its sparkling aqua pool, water burst in fanlike arcs from
urns held by lounging water nymphs, their budded breasts and

curving hips making them appear wanton and lazy in the heat of the afternoon.

"It's so beautiful here," Lizbeth said, spinning in place so she could get a three-hundred-sixty-degree view.

At that moment, she resembled a teenager again—only one whose wistful eyes had seen far too much suffering for such a short lifetime. Daniela found herself feeling sorry for the girl. Daniela knew what it was to be different. To be physically unable to connect to other people because reaching out was impossible.

Now she began to feel guilty for being so suspicious of the girl.

"Where do we go from here?" Lyse asked, brushing her thick black bangs out of her face.

"This way," Daniela said, taking a deep breath. "This is where we access the catacombs."

Devandra

Melisande and Delilah Montrose arrived with the dawn, the ring of the doorbell dragging Dev from the warmth of her bed. She threw on her chenille robe and headed downstairs.

"Mama?" A sleepy voice called out in the darkness, and Dev stopped at the head of the stairs.

Marji stood in her bedroom doorway, hair unkempt and eyes still half-closed with sleep. She yawned, raising a hand to cover her mouth.

"Yes, baby?" Dev whispered.

"Tell Grammie they wanna talk to her."

"I will, sweetheart. Now let me go let Grammie in . . ."

"Okay." And like a sleepwalker, Marji returned to her bed, leaving the door wide open behind her.

Dev waited until she could hear the rustle of Marji climbing back under the comforter, and then she continued down the stairs. She yawned as she hit the bottom step, her brain on autopilot. It didn't help that she'd barely slept the previous night, having been on guard duty in the Mucho Man Cave until three in the morning. Freddy had graciously called in sick to work in order to take over for her—but as exhausted as she'd been, sleep had proved elusive.

And now a bunch of little old dead ladies were using her elder daughter as a messenger service. Could her life get any more bizarre?

Dev pulled her robe tight around her middle as she padded through the sitting room, shivering a little in the chilly morning air. The heat was on, she could hear the gentle thrum of the compressor, but because heat rose, it was always warmer in the upstairs bedrooms than it was in the rest of the house.

There was a quiet comfort in being surrounded by the everyday familiar. The creaky old Victorian was like a tried-and-true friend—she knew every nook and cranny in the place, had played hide-and-seek with her sisters in all of the drafty high-ceilinged rooms, had cried herself to sleep in what was now Marji's room when the boy she liked in middle school wouldn't go to the Sadie Hawkins dance with her.

Its walls were privy to all of her sorrows and joys, from her idyllic childhood to the excitement of falling in love with Freddy to the birth of her two precious daughters. It was a part of who she was—in fact, was a part of each Montrose woman who had lived and died there before her.

"Coming," she called out softly as she crossed to the front door and looked through the peephole.

She blinked as her sister's patrician face came into view, features distorted as if Dev were observing her through a fish-eye lens. Dev was reassured beyond measure to see her tiny mother standing just beside Delilah, both women with overnight bags at their feet. She sighed with relief and reached down to undo the chain. She threw back the deadbolt and opened the door.

"I'm so glad you're here," Dev said, crossing the threshold and enfolding both women in her arms. They hugged in silence, enjoying the familial connection of being with people who loved you unconditionally no matter what. "Come in, come in."

She picked up her mother's brown-and-mauve floral carpet-bag, gesturing for them to follow her inside. Her mother, who was barely five feet tall, was a smaller, more compact version of Dev. She wore her gray hair in a chin-length bob, but it was so thick that it poofed out around her cheeks like a puffin's chest. She wore a pair of round spectacles on a silver length of chain that hung from her neck, holding them up to her eyes whenever she needed to read something, but otherwise ignoring them.

"It's just like a snapshot," her mother said as she stepped into the sitting room, her eyes roving from the dark oak love seat and settee to the antique empire rolltop desk to the Victorian green-and-beige tiles that lined the fireplace, offsetting the polished glow of the thick wooden mantel. "It never changes."

"And that's why we like it," Dev said, nodding as they passed through the wooden doorway leading into the kitchen.

"But do we *really* like it that way?" Delilah asked, half jokingly.

She was the youngest of Dev's sisters and the free spirit of their already very bohemian family. She'd joined the Peace Corps, traveled all over South America, and then taught English at a secondary school for girls in Rwanda. She'd never planted roots anywhere, was constantly in motion, never settling, always off on another adventure.

"I mean," Delilah continued, removing her green knit cap and revealing an inch of gold-blond stubble. "I love the old place. Don't get me wrong. I'd just never want to be tied down to it indefinitely."

Delilah had been in the middle of her yearly visit with their parents when Dev had called for backup. She was happy to have her youngest sibling there to help, but older sister and baby sister were about as different as two people could be.

"I'm not being mean, Dev," Delilah added, realizing by Dev's silence she'd offended her older sibling. "You know I love the house. I really do. I'm just not cut out for a sedentary existence."

Dev knew she shouldn't take umbrage at the word *sedentary*, but it rankled a little bit. Especially coming from her baby sister. She opened her mouth to reply and was interrupted by the pounding of small feet on the stairs. With a sharp squeal of happiness, Ginny burst into the kitchen, brimming with excitement at seeing her grammie and aunt Delilah.

"Grammie, Grammie, Grammie," Ginny cooed as she danced around the room. She was so full of energy that it made Dev tired just watching her. "You're here! I wanna show you my ant farm—"

Ginny took her grammie's hand and, because Melisande wasn't much bigger than her granddaughter, almost succeeded in dragging her from the room.

"Gin, let me talk to Grammie for a few minutes before you drag her off, please," Dev said, turning to shrug helplessly at Delilah. "Maybe your aunt Delilah wants to see the ants instead?"

Dev only felt a little bad for throwing Delilah under the bus—besides, Ginny just wanted a little attention and Delilah was amazing with kids. In point of fact, without further prodding she took Ginny's outstretched hand, tiny fingers slipping easily into Delilah's palm, and pulled her niece in for a bear hug.

"Show me the ants."

Ginny, pleased with her hug and the prospect of having her aunt's undivided attention, grinned.

"Okay!"

She pulled Delilah along behind her, leaving the warmth of the kitchen and heading back upstairs. Dev watched them go, relieved that Ginny had saved her from being rude to Delilah. She wished she could just let her baby sister's condescending tone wash over her without affecting her state of being, but it was almost impossible. Delilah was aces at making her feel like she was being judged.

"So shall I make us some tea?" her mother asked, already

starting to putter around the kitchen, which she knew as well as Dev did, if not better. "And then we can sit down and discuss what to do next?"

It was so rare to not feel the overwhelming yoke of responsibility around her neck that Dev *almost* enjoyed her mother trying to take over and fix everything—it was like being ten again . . . and she knew she'd only be able to handle it for a little while before it started to bug her.

"The tea is in the—"

"I know," her mother said with a smile, bustling over to the other side of the kitchen, where she opened a cabinet door to reveal a whole shelf full of tea tins. "You've changed less than you think."

Her mother winked at her.

"Now sit, sit and tell me what's happened."

Dev did as her mother asked, pulling out one of the spindle-backed chairs and taking a seat at the kitchen table.

"Lucretia's memento mori," Dev began, her hands busily pulling at a loose string in the tablecloth as her mother filled the kettle. "Well, it didn't start there, but it's where I found the letter . . ."

Dev pushed back her chair, careful not to scrape the wood floor as she stood up. She left her mother pulling teacups from the shelf and went into the living room. Dev retrieved a brown envelope from inside the antique armoire where she kept her good china and her grandmother's silver service, careful with its handling. She worried that too much jostling would damage its fragile contents. She carried the envelope back into the kitchen and set it on the table.

"It's from Lucretia. Addressed to me and written so long ago it boggles my mind."

Her mother stopped what she was doing and turned to look at Dev, brow wrinkled with concern.

"Why didn't you tell me about this sooner?" she asked—not angry, exactly, but definitely unnerved. Now Dev really *did* feel ten again, but with the caveat that this time she was a kid who'd done something bad and was about to get punished for it.

"I'm telling you now," Dev said, shrugging as she retook her seat. "The letter concerns a tarot spread—"

Her mother held up a hand for Dev to stop speaking, then crossed the kitchen and knelt down beside her carpetbag. She unzipped it, digging through a mound of clothing and toiletries before she spied what she was looking for. She lifted up a plastic Ziploc bag and held it aloft.

"Here," she said, handing the plastic baggie to Dev before climbing back to her feet. "Open it."

Dev did as she was told and pulled out a rectangular object wrapped in paper towels. As she unwrapped it, the kettle whistled and her mother turned off the eye of the stove and began to fill the teacups.

"I found the Russian tea," her mother said, spooning the sweet tea into the hot water. "Hope that's okay?"

Dev nodded, but she was hardly paying attention to her mother's words. Inside of the nest of paper towels was a slim stack of tarot cards. She began to lay the cards out on the tabletop, her hand shaking:

The World
The Magician
The Hierophant
The Devil
The Fool

It was Lucretia's spread. The one referenced in the aged and crumbling letter Dev had found hidden inside the frame of Lucretia's memento mori.

"Why . . . ?" Dev asked in wonderment.

It seemed like only hours since she'd pulled these very cards for Eleanora—it was hard to remember that those "hours" were actually many days ago and that Eleanora was dead now. She didn't want to hate the spread laid out on her table like a portent of death. She tried not to blame the cards for everything that had happened. They were only the harbinger of evil, not the evil itself.

Her mother set one of the teacups down in front of Dev and then took the chair opposite her.

"They've cropped up over and over again these last few weeks," her mother said, frowning as she lifted the teacup to her lips and found the liquid too hot to sip. "And it's not just me. Darrah, too."

Darrah was only eighteen months younger than Dev, so their parents had always called them the Irish Twins. She and Dev emailed frequently, but Darrah hadn't said a word to her about any of this.

"She never mentioned anything to me," Dev heard herself say, the defensive tone of her voice making her sound childish and petty.

"I don't think either of us realized the significance until you called—and Daphne and Delilah don't ply the trade, so they wouldn't have known one way or the other."

Dev realized that this was probably the case—the Montrose women were notorious for focusing on the positives and ignoring the negatives. Plus her mother was right: Delilah and Daphne were completely out of the loop.

Delilah led an itinerant lifestyle that seemed at odds with Dev's life, but at least she still believed that magic existed and being a Montrose woman meant you came from a magical heritage. Daphne, on the other hand, was willfully ignorant of this fact.

By far the most conventional of the sisters, Daphne had moved to Chicago and married a wealthy pediatrician. She loved playing society wife and mixing with the Windy City's movers and shakers, but she'd really found her bliss by working with charitable organizations across the city. Not just sitting on their boards, but going out into the city and actually getting her hands dirty. Dev admired Daphne greatly, but she didn't appreciate how her younger sister pooh-poohed their family's facility with the cards.

"Does the coven have any idea what it might mean?" Melisande asked, finally taking a sip of her tea. "Because I have some thoughts."

"Like?" Dev asked.

"The cards are both literal and not literal in this instance," Melisande said. "The World isn't just the human one, but ours . . . the world of the covens."

Dev nodded.

"And maybe it's even more than that . . . once upon a time, I knew someone from another world. It was similar to ours, but with marked differences."

Melisande stopped speaking, her eyes far away.

"But that was a long time ago. As for The Fool . . . this person is blinded by the sun, unable to see the truth right in front of them."

"A literal 'person'?" Dev asked.

"Yes, a real person. And they think they're doing the right thing," Melisande said. "But they're being used."

Dev's stomach turned, her mind trying to figure out who among them fit the bill of The Fool.

"I wonder if Eleanora and Hessika might have some thoughts on this."

Her mother set her teacup down in its saucer and stared at Dev.

"What do you mean?"

Dev swallowed, not sure how best to broach the subject, but then she decided to just be blunt:

"Mom, they're both Dream Walkers . . . and they want to speak to you."

Dev was glad Melisande had already set her teacup down. Otherwise, she was certain her mother would've spilled the hot liquid all over the table.

The information was no sooner out of Dev's mouth then Melisande had insisted they go upstairs and wake Marji. Now the three of them sat in a semicircle in the middle of Marji's bedroom floor—Marji and Dev still in their nightclothes—and waited for the ghosts to make themselves known.

"Mama?" Marji asked. "Why can I see them and you guys can't?"

Her elder daughter looked so tired and woebegone sitting in between them that it made Dev sad. She reached over and tucked a strand of loose hair behind Marji's ear.

"I don't know, sweet pea," she said. "But maybe it's because you're special. You can see things that others can't and it's a good thing, not bad."

Marji's face puckered up like she'd eaten something tart.

"But it's scary sometimes," she said, and rested her head on Dev's shoulder. "I don't like it."

Melisande reached out and patted Marji's arm.

"God only gives us what we can handle, Marji-May," she said, and smiled at her granddaughter. "The scary stuff is what makes us stronger. I promise you that."

Marji nodded, but her big eyes were wide with uncertainty—and then a cold chill shot through the room.

"They're here," Marji said, staring at something on the other side of the room. "The tall lady and Auntie E."

Dev caught her mother's eye.

"It's been so long, Eleanora," Melisande said. "I wish I could see you. I'm jealous of Marji's abilities."

Marji grinned, then looked over at her grandmother.

"What's so funny?" Dev asked.

"Auntie E said Grammie's haircut makes her look like the Flying Nun." She turned back to Dev. "Who's the Flying Nun, Mama?"

Melisande snorted.

"Ha! I'll take it. Just so long as she doesn't call me Gidget . . ." She winked at Marji.

"Auntie E says she wouldn't wish Gidget on anybody. Even Grammie," Marji said, but it was clear she didn't quite understand what she was repeating.

"C'mere," Dev said, patting the spot in front of her. Marji didn't need to be asked twice; she crawled into Dev's lap and burrowed in.

It was getting colder by the minute and Dev shivered, wrapping her arms around Marji.

"I'm not cold, Mama," Marji said, wiggling out of Dev's embrace. Then: "The tall lady says that we need all the Montrose women here—and that we have to listen to Thomas. Especially you, Mama."

Melisande shot Dev a look.

"Who's Thomas?" she asked.

Dev opened her mouth to reply, but Marji answered for her.

"He was good and then he was bad and then he was good again, Grammie. Mama tied him up and I think it hurt him a little."

"He's the one in the Mucho Man Cave," Dev added to clarify—which only made Melisande shake her head. "The one who broke into our house . . . ?"

She'd told her mother about the break-in, but what had been said on the phone was now clearly forgotten.

"No, I remember that, Devandra," Melisande replied, her tone sharp. "There was just . . . someone . . . a long time ago."

Marji began nodding, her eyes narrowed as she listened intently.

"The tall lady says that it's your Tommy. That's why they

wanted to talk to you, Grammie. So you didn't get your heart hurt when you see him. 'Cause he looks just the same."

Dev watched the color drain from her mother's face.

"*No.*"

Marji was still listening to the Dream Walkers, so she didn't see her grandmother's distress, but Dev did.

"Mom, are you okay—"

Melisande shook her head, then raised her hand for Dev to hold on.

"It's . . . just give me a moment."

Dev gave her mother some space, returning her attention to Marji.

"Uh-huh," Marji murmured, concentrating on whatever Eleanora and Hessika were saying to her. "Uh-huh. Okay. I'll tell her."

She turned to look at her grandmother.

"Grammie?"

"Yes, dear heart," Melisande said, managing a weak smile.

"It's not his fault. He couldn't tell you, but he's not from here. Auntie E says not to be mad at him."

"The tarot spread?" Dev asked. "Who is The Fool? Do you know?"

Marji shook her head.

"They don't know, Mama. Eleanora says she's been worried about that one. It's been on her mind a lot. She believes that Lyse is The Magician . . . but who The Fool is, she just doesn't know."

Dev nodded.

"Eleanora? What do you mean . . . it wasn't his fault?" Melisande asked, but Marji bit her lip and scrunched her eyebrows together.

"They had to go, Grammie. They're not here anymore."

Dev realized she was no longer cold, that the chill had left the room along with the two Dream Walkers she couldn't see. She squeezed Marji tight, proud of her.

"You did good, sweet pea," Dev said, stroking Marji's hair.

"Thanks, Mama," her daughter murmured, then quickly squirmed out of her lap. "I'm gonna go make Frosted Flakes."

Marji crawled to her feet and slipped on her fuzzy duck head slippers.

"It's not so scary," she added, and bounded for the door, leaving Dev and Melisande alone in the room.

"Mom . . . ?" Dev asked.

"I'm okay," Melisande replied. "It's fine. I'm just grateful to Eleanora for telling me."

Dev pulled at the hem of her robe, trying not to look at her mother as she asked the only question that was on her mind: "Who is he, Mom?"

Melisande sighed, rubbing at her mouth with her hand. Dev knew what this meant—her mom was trying to decide what information to divulge.

"He was . . . is . . . someone who was very important to me," Melisande began. "From before I met your father—and then one day he just disappeared and I never saw him again. That's it. There's nothing more to say that isn't personal between him and me. Stuff that's not for sharing. Even with one of my favorite daughters."

"Ha!" Dev said, and laughed. "We're all your favorite daughters."

Her mother smiled.

"You know all my tricks, Devandra."

Dev wished she could agree with her mom, but, sadly, she understood the opposite only too well: As hard as you tried, you could never really know *anyone*.

"Hello, Melisande."

Thomas was still mostly bound to his chair, but Freddy had taken pity on him and freed one of his hands. Now he was holding an aluminum can of Pabst Blue Ribbon that was ensconced in a foam coozie emblazoned with the words *Beer = Life.*

"*Freddy,*" Dev said, when she saw this. But he just cocked a dark eyebrow, as if to say: *Sorry, babe, but I felt bad for the guy.*

She sighed and shook her head, her annoyance at Freddy quickly dissipating when she caught sight of her mom's face. Melisande stood in the doorway, staring at the strange man, the sheen of tears in her eyes catching the twinkling yellow lights of the tiki bar.

Her mother swallowed and looked away, wiping at her cheeks with the back of her hand.

"Don't cry, Melisande," Thomas said. "It's not so bad, is it, really?"

She remained silent, but from the rapid rise and fall of her chest, Dev could see that her mother was working hard to control herself.

"Melisande, my love, let me get you a chair," Freddy said, working that ridiculous charm of his—the same charm that had captured Dev's heart the first moment she'd laid eyes on him.

He was compact and muscular, and even when he was exhausted—as he was now—he moved with the fluid grace of a dancer. One moment he was pulling out a chair for Melisande, the next she was seated and Freddy's handkerchief had been discreetly tucked into her hand.

"There you go," Freddy said, patting Dev's mom on the back, then stepping away to give her some space.

She was lucky that her parents had taken so well to Freddy. He was older than her, Filipino, and a nonpracticing Catholic—it could've easily been a fiasco when she'd brought him home to meet her parents. But his kindness and charm had won both her mom and dad over within minutes, and that was that. He'd become a part of their family. Though they'd never married—neither of them had ever seen the need to—he would be her better half for all of time.

She knew this because it had been Freddy's face she'd seen when she'd joined the coven and been metaphorically mated to the Horned God. The ritual induction ceremony was one of the most important rites of the coven, and it was here that each blood sister saw her true love's face imposed upon the visage of the great Horned one.

Freddy came to stand beside Dev, taking her hand and squeezing her fingers tightly between his own. She was happy for his presence, pleased that he had her back, no matter what. She didn't know many men who would just accept their partner's weird eccentricities without comment, who would get up at three in the morning to stand watch over a strange man their lady had tied to a chair and stashed in their converted bar/garage. She thanked heaven every day that the man she loved was as chill and patient as a saint.

"Melisande?" Thomas said, voice smooth as honey, but with a slight catch at the end. Like he was just as moved to see her mother as her mother was to see him.

Her mom cleared her throat, dabbing at her cheeks with Freddy's clean white handkerchief.

"I know you didn't go away on purpose."

Thomas let out a long sigh, beginning to tear up himself.

"Really? You mean that?" he breathed, his jaw clenched tight as he fought back the waves of emotion that seemed ready to overwhelm him. "Because it's the truth. I wouldn't have gone. I would've done anything to stay."

Her mom nodded, apparently not trusting herself to speak.

"That night at the Beltane fire . . . it was the greatest night of my life," he continued. "You were everything."

Her mom started to cry in earnest, and Freddy squeezed Dev's hand, holding her back, so she wouldn't rush to her mother's side.

"Let her be," Freddy whispered into Dev's ear, then followed his words up with a soft kiss on her cheek.

He was right, of course. If she'd intervened, she'd have ruined the moment, and it was obvious her mom needed this, needed the closure that this meeting would bring her.

"You're so young," Melisande murmured—at a loss for a better way to say it. "How can that be? I don't understand."

Thomas shrugged, a bit of his beer spilling out over his hand.

"Without going into the physics of the thing . . . time runs differently where I hail from," he said, sadly. "All those stories about humans getting lost in the fairy world, where no one ever seems to age? Well, those stories come directly from your people falling into my dimension. We're not fairies, of course, but the rest of those tales have their roots in the truth."

"But I've lived a whole life," her mother whispered, "*my* whole life without you."

Thomas stared down at his knees.

"I know. And it's been almost no time at all for me in my world."

Dev watched as the tears poured down her mom's cheeks. She wished she could go and comfort her, but Freddy's presence still held her in check.

"You've met my oldest daughter. I have three more. I'm a grandmother, even."

Her mom laughed, and the years fell away. For the first time, Dev saw how beautiful her mother must've been when she was a young woman—so beautiful that this strange young man from another dimension had fallen hopelessly in love with her.

"You've had a good life?" Thomas asked, and finally looked up at her mother again.

"Yes, I *have* had a good life," she said, grinning through her tears. "But not a day went by that I didn't miss you."

"Good," Thomas said, a little cocky now. "That makes it all right, then."

They smiled at each other, and Dev's heart ached for what could've been. Dev loved her dad, but this connection her mother shared with the stranger went beyond anything she'd ever seen between her parents.

"Now you have to listen to me, Melisande," he continued, letting his look encompass Dev and Freddy, too. "The Flood is coming to wipe you out. All of you except your granddaughter. Her, they want to control because she's special—"

"No," Dev cried. "They can't have her. I won't let them."

"They're coming. There's nothing you can do. Only the power in your blood will protect you. But you need the others, all of the Montrose women. Make that happen and we might still survive the night."

"Man, this sounds really out there," Freddy said, turning to Dev. "But if you tell me that's what's what, then I believe you. I mean, I haven't lived with you all these years without seeing some crazy shit."

Dev snorted, not fully believing what she was hearing.

"I didn't know you were paying attention—"

"C'mon, Dev, I'm not blind," he said, shaking his head. "The tarot cards are one thing, but sneaking off into the woods . . . let's just say, I may have gone after you once or twice to see what you were up to."

He looked over at Dev, sheepish.

"I may have also seen more of Eleanora than any man really wants to see of an old lady's—"

"Okay, I got it," Dev said.

Freddy grinned.

"So I guess we gotta get your sisters, then?"

But it was Melisande who answered.

"That's the easy part," she said, a strange resolve in her eye. "It's raising the dead ones that's going to be difficult."

Lizbeth

꧁

Daniela herded them out of the sunlight toward the shaded portico of the smaller structure across from the villa. They took the stairs in single file—like schoolchildren, Lizbeth thought—letting Daniela lead the way.

"C'mon—" Daniela began, but the words caught in her throat.

Daniela froze at the top of the stairs. The others, unaware of her distress, piled into her back.

A frail old woman in a gauzy dress stood in the doorway, her long gray hair flowing past her shoulders and down her back. Her face was deathly white, and there were deep fissures of age in her flesh. She lifted a paper-thin arm—the wrist as tiny as a child's—and waved in greeting.

"Buona sera, amore mio."

Daniela's face went slack with shock, and the old woman's wide grin quickly disappeared. She reached out with a frail hand, trying to touch Daniela's cheek, but Daniela stepped out of her reach.

"It's Francesca," the old woman said, frowning now. "Don't you know me?"

Daniela shook her head.

"No . . . this can't be . . ."

Lyse moved to Daniela, almost touching her shoulder. Then she swiftly retracted her fingers, remembering how dangerous even one touch could be.

"What's wrong?" Lyse asked—but Daniela wouldn't look at her.

Instead, she continued to stare at the old woman.

"But they said you were dead," she whispered, her face as white as a sheet. "That you died with my mother."

Her eyes rolled up into her head and she fainted.

Weir ran for Daniela, trying to catch her before she hit the ground.

"Weir! No!" Lizbeth cried, but it was too late—Weir had his arms around Daniela's unconscious form, careful to steer clear of her gloved hands as he gently set her down on the porch. Thankfully, there was no one else on the portico to see what had happened—just the strange old woman, who seemed as worried about Daniela as they were.

Weir moved Daniela's body toward the side of the porch, where a large hedge grew, blocking the view from the gardens into the portico. Lizbeth and Lyse ran to their friend, Lizbeth kneeling by Daniela's head and Lyse tucked in by her side. Both of them watched with bated breath. If Daniela started seizing, it meant Weir had triggered her empathic power and, though it wasn't horrible in the moment, the cumulative damage to her brain was irreparable.

"I hate that we can't touch her," Lyse said, and Lizbeth nodded. She knew exactly what Lyse meant—but then her mind went to Temistocles, who existed in the dreamlands and, as desperately as she wanted to, could not be touched, either.

"Was I wrong to catch her?" Weir asked, realizing that he might've done something wrong.

"She will be fine."

Lizbeth looked up as the old woman—*Francesca*, Daniela

had called her—squatted down on Daniela's other side, cradling Daniela's limp head between her hands. She realized that this was the same Francesca from Marie-Faith's notebook, and that she was a Dream Keeper just like Lizbeth.

"I've watched her since she was a baby. I know all about her 'difficulties'—and I know that when she is sleeping or not in her head," Francesca continued, stroking Daniela's hair, "that it is safe to touch her. Even the hands."

Lizbeth reached out a tentative finger to gingerly shift a few strands of pink away from Daniela's face. She looked over at Lyse, encouraging her to do the same.

"Are you sure?" Lyse asked Francesca. "I . . . I think I might be a different story . . ."

Francesca shook her head, her long hair a wispy cloud around her face, but the way she looked at Lyse was frightening. Lizbeth could feel the hostility pouring out of the old woman's eyes, her gaze fixed solely on Lyse.

"I know what you are. And even you can't hurt her now."

Her tone was even, but Lizbeth could sense her underlying hatred even as she tried to suppress it. Weir also picked up on the old woman's vibe, and he moved to stand over Lyse, offering her his silent protection. The old woman shook her head, the wind catching bits of her hair and blowing them across her face.

"I'm not the one you need to worry about, tall one," she said to Weir before pressing the back of a birdlike hand to Daniela's forehead. "We should wake her up now. I'll do a spell."

Lizbeth caught Lyse's eye and smiled because her friend's expression seemed to say: *This old bat is crazy.*

"Uh, so how do we do a spell?" Lyse asked, brushing her bangs out of her eyes.

Regardless of the old woman's strange attitude, Lizbeth—and Lyse—were curious to see her in action. Neither of them had ever witnessed someone treat magic like, well, *magic.* The coven performed rituals, meeting at preordained times, casting protective circles, reciting canon that had been passed down from the old covens of yore. But what exactly the rituals accomplished when compared to "real" magic, that had always eluded Lizbeth.

She knew all about the five talents—that Daniela could see inside of a human's soul, Arrabelle could manipulate plants, Eleanora could enter the past and present as if she were a thread in the woven fabric of time, Devandra gave voice to fate with her cards . . . and she, Lizbeth, was a Dream Keeper, who could walk in the dreamlands—she just didn't understand how "real" magic worked.

"No one teaches anyone anything anymore," Francesca muttered under her breath and, with creaking bones, hauled herself to her feet. "Spells and manipulating the fabric of time . . . all of that knowledge has been banished . . . leaving only the five weak forces. But maybe that will be changing."

She wiped her palms down her white shift, avoiding Lyse's proffered hands and heading straight for Lizbeth.

"Give me your hands," she said to Lizbeth.

Boy, she's really anti-Lyse, Lizbeth thought.

"Come now, don't be shy," the old woman said, her gnarled fingers searching out Lizbeth's youthful ones. "It's so simple, really, but none of you are taught the old ways . . . all these centuries the Council has been scared we'll get ourselves burned at the stake for witchcraft if we do anything out of line . . . and now this. The Flood coming and none of you can protect yourselves—it's just wrong."

"Is that the truth?" Lizbeth asked, her voice scratchy in her throat, reminding her of how blessed she was she could speak again. "What else is there? We want to learn."

She turned to Lyse, who nodded, blue eyes earnest. She was standing close to Weir, his hand brushing her wrist. It made Lizbeth happy to see them touching; Weir had been out of sorts since Eleanora's memorial service, and Lizbeth thought it had something to do with Lyse. Her brother wouldn't say as much, but he was usually so even keel that she knew he was upset. And then she'd seen how strangely he'd behaved around Lyse the other day. Acting as if they weren't an item, like he wasn't all gaga over her friend.

"It wasn't an option either of us knew existed," Lyse replied, agreeing with Lizbeth. "Show us, please."

Francesca frowned, then looked over at Lyse.

"You understand what it is, though," she said, staring into Lyse's eyes. "Magic . . . ? Where it comes from?"

"I will be as honest with you as I can be," Lyse said. "Until a few weeks ago, I didn't even know that blood sisters existed. I've been as in the dark as Weir, here, has been."

Lyse patted his arm, her fingers dancing across his bicep.

"Sorry to use you as an example," she added, smiling at him.

He shrugged and looked sheepish.

"S'okay."

"But I meant what I said," Lyse added, returning her attention back to Francesca. "We want to know and we'd be grateful for anything you can show us."

The old woman bowed her head.

"The rituals are to bring together the five powers in a place filled with the energy of the flow lines," she began, taking Lizbeth's hands in her own. "A coven of five—five feminine forms who possess the sacred blood: Earth, Wind, Fire, Water, Spirit—when brought together in these sacred spots, they hold the power to create and sustain life. Not just human life, but *all* life."

She stopped speaking and the everyday outdoor sounds of the world filled Lizbeth's ears. The bleat of a car horn in traffic, the roar of a plane as it passed overhead, the chatter of a group of men and women walking past the small round building . . . with her eyes closed, Lizbeth could almost "see" the sounds as images . . . almost see Francesca's face in front of her as the old woman's breathing grew more relaxed.

—You can trust no one but Daniela. Marie-Faith trusted and you can see where that got her—dead.

Francesca's voice was inside her, rattling around in her head. She opened her eyes and found Francesca's inky black irises boring into her own.

—*You're the last of us. You must go to the Pillar before the blood moon passes the meridian—only then can the truth go out to the rest of our world. You will dream them into knowing who we are, that the witches are here on this Earth and will not be ignored or forgotten ever again.*

The words rained down on Lizbeth's hungry mind like water—there was so much information, it was hard to take it in, but she let it all wash over her.

—*The one you call friend, this "Lyse" woman? She is a Judas. She has already betrayed you once and she will do it again before the day is through. Kill her if you can. Stop her from playing her part in their plans.*

Lizbeth was appalled. This was not the Lyse she knew. Lyse was her friend and would never betray her. She wanted to ask Francesca how she knew these things, but Francesca was not done.

—*Go down to the catacombs. The others are there waiting. They've been trapped for so long . . . set them free and their power will be yours to command. But first I must give you the word. Will you receive it?*

"I will," Lizbeth said—and then a searing, white-hot pain shot through her hands, up her arms, through her chest and neck, and into her head. She screamed as a million points of light burned like fireworks inside her skull, information downloading into her brain like she was some kind of human hard drive. Tears coursed down her cheeks, her body buzzing with enough energy to split her like an atom.

And then it was over.

Her head ached and she felt strange, kind of woozy on her feet.

—*Go to the catacombs. Take your brother and Daniela. Leave the Judas here for me. She will be taken care of.*

Francesca's voice was growing weak, her energy expended. "LB?"

Lizbeth blinked.

She was standing on the path, her back to the fountain, her hands in her hair. She released the strands of russet, and they fell like a fan across her throat, the spray from the fountain tickling her bare neck. The villa lay before them, a massive stone edifice with towering Doric columns and a wide flight of stairs that stretched like a beige skirt across the front of the building.

To her right the small stone circular building with its shaded portico and heavy wooden door was gone—in its place stood two alabaster obelisks sanded so smooth they appeared to gleam like pillars of water in the sunlight.

"LB? Are you even listening to me?"

Lizbeth turned her head. Daniela was standing beside her, pink hair falling around her face like a frame, a concerned expression on her face. Lizbeth realized this concern was directed at her. She shook her head, a subtle movement meant to clear her mind.

"I'm fine," she replied, smiling back at Daniela. "Sorry, what were you saying?"

As Daniela prattled on—rehashing the need to stay together, blah, blah, blah—Lizbeth's mind raced, trying to understand what had just happened to her. The whole experience had felt so real: Francesca, the small circular building, Lyse being a Judas . . . it had all been in her imagination.

Or had it?

She could feel the energy pulsing through her body, a heightened awareness of how her muscles and skeleton worked: The flutter of her eyelashes, the beat of her heart in her chest, the subtle rise and fall of chest as her lungs and diaphragm worked in tandem to make her breathe. It felt as if her body were just a flesh-and-bone vessel, carrying her thoughts and emotions . . . her essence . . . everything that made her Lizbeth.

But now she was so much more than that; Francesca had

burned *the word* into her soul and it swirled around, mixing with the rest of her thoughts and feelings. It pulsed and wove its way around her brain, enticing her forward, suggesting the next moves for her to make as if her life had become some kind of game.

Tell Daniela.

It was a command, and it pushed her to open her mouth. She looked up and saw that Lyse and Weir were still heading toward the villa's front entrance. Definitely out of earshot.

"Wait up!" Lizbeth called to Daniela, running to catch up to her. For someone so small, Daniela moved like a flash.

"What is it?" Daniela asked, barely slowing her pace. Lizbeth, who was head and shoulders taller than her pink-haired friend, had to jog to keep up.

"Was there ever a circular building? Over there, on the far side of the fountain. Where those two obelisks stand now?"

She knew the answer—the whole sorry event had been placed into her mind, like a movie on a loop. Daniela stopped midstride.

"Why are you asking me that?" Her tone was subdued, but she was gritting her teeth, working the muscles in her jaw.

"I don't know—"

"A long time ago. It was demolished a long time ago," Daniela paused, working hard to catch her breath—which didn't make sense, they hadn't been walking *that* fast—and then Lizbeth realized Daniela was actually trying not to cry. "But the obelisks, they're a tribute to my mother and the others that were killed in the accident with her."

"I'm sorry—" Lizbeth said, forgetting she wasn't supposed to touch Daniela and reaching out a hand.

Luckily, Daniela had enough on the ball to see what was happening and step out of the way before Lizbeth could get close enough to reach her.

"I always forget," Lizbeth murmured. "To not touch you."

"It's okay," Daniela said, using the distraction to pull

herself together. "They said it was a technical error, the train derailing? An accident. Officially. But I don't believe it. And everything that's happening now just confirms that for me."

She held her ground, waiting for Lizbeth to say something.

Tell her.

Lizbeth didn't like to be told what to do, but the thought was insistent and would not be put away without her addressing it.

"A woman named Francesca was with your mother—"

Daniela's face went ashen, but she nodded. "Yes, she was like family. She helped to raise me. She was with my mother when . . . they died together—"

Daniela frowned as a group of German tourists walked past them, their guttural tones breaking the sense of intimacy they'd shared. They were the first people Lizbeth had seen in the gardens since they'd arrived. Somehow it took away the air of mystery the villa possessed, making it seem like any other tourist trap.

"Go on," Daniela said, once the Germans had passed.

Lizbeth tried not to let her gaze drift in Lyse's direction, but it was hard. She and Weir were deep in conversation by the stairs, Weir's hand on her arm. Lizbeth sighed and dragged her eyes away.

Daniela was waiting for her.

"She came to me. She wasn't a Dream Walker, but more . . . a moment in time. Like an insect trapped in amber," Lizbeth said.

Daniela's eyes lit up like candles, two hungry flames searching for oxygen, or, in this case, a glimpse of someone she'd thought she'd lost forever.

"Is she here now?" she said. "Can we speak to her? Is my mother with her?"

Lizbeth shook her head.

"No. She's gone now . . . and your mother was never here."

The glow went out of Daniela's eyes and a sense of melancholy settled over them both. Navigating the minefield of another person's grief was delicate business, Lizbeth saw.

"But Francesca gave me a *message*. And I think it was the power of the message that kept her spirit here."

"And what did she tell you?" Daniela asked, shifting her bag from one shoulder to the other.

"That we can't trust Lyse," Lizbeth said, and she was surprised at how easily it rolled off her tongue.

"No," Daniela said. "That doesn't make any sense—"

"—Francesca says that she's already betrayed me once."

"No," Daniela murmured. "That can't be right. I don't believe it."

Judas.

The word sprang into her head and she wished she could punch Lyse in the back of the neck. Paralyze her, or better yet, *kill her.*

Lizbeth swallowed hard, nauseated by the dark turn her thoughts had taken.

I'm not this person, she thought. *Even if Lyse did betray us, that doesn't mean I should kill her.*

Besides, it didn't seem possible Lyse could be a Judas— but then Lizbeth supposed that was the point: You weren't supposed to trust someone who looked like they were going to betray you.

"We have to get away from her," Lizbeth heard herself saying. "Ditch her in the catacombs—"

Daniela shook her head.

"We can't do this. It's not right."

Lizbeth shook her head, the heat from the sun bearing down on the back of her neck, making her skin itch.

"She'll destroy everything," Lizbeth said—and then shook her head, not sure where the thought had come from.

"I just . . ." Daniela sighed, and Lizbeth could see how conflicted she was. "If this is what my mother wanted us to do . . ."

"It is. It's exactly what she wanted," Lizbeth said. "Lyse is part of the whole thing. She's in league with The Flood. With those that killed your mother."

Daniela's face was ashen.

"No," she said.

"Lyse is a Judas. She has to be stopped."

Daniela nodded, eyes shiny as she fought back tears.

"Okay. We ditch Lyse and get the hell out of here as soon as we can."

You're an open book, Lizbeth thought as she watched Daniela go, the rigid set of her friend's shoulders informing the world she was on a mission. *You give everything away.*

But there was nothing Lizbeth could do about it. She didn't really understand what was happening to her, but she knew she had to do what she was told. Saying no wasn't an option.

The four of them were huddled together in the semidarkness of the underground catacombs that stretched out beneath the grounds of the Villa Nomentana. The musty dampness filled Lizbeth's nostrils as they moved single file through the claustrophobic tunnels cut out of the soft volcanic rock. She'd tucked in between Daniela and Weir, Lyse leading the way. The group of German tourists from the gardens was ahead of them, chatting in their native language. Lizbeth had no idea what they were saying.

Their young Italian guide spoke in heavily accented English, stopping them here and there to point out certain frescoes, their colors aged and faded in the darkness. One was of two beautifully rendered menorahs surrounding a golden building Lizbeth figured was probably a temple. They followed the guide into another, larger room. It was a burial chamber and Lizbeth could see the graves hewn from the rock walls, the ceiling a muted watercolor painting awash with Judaic motifs.

As the guide chattered on about the burial practices of Roman Jews, the Germans listening attentively, Lyse came to stand beside Lizbeth. She'd slipped her red hoodie on when they'd entered the catacombs, and it was the brightest thing in the murky light of the burial chamber.

"Any idea what we do now?" Lyse whispered, keeping watch over the guide and the German tourists out of the corner of her eye. "You're the only one who's read the notebook . . ."

Judas.

The word invaded her thoughts again. She tried to push it away, but she wasn't the one in control.

"You don't trust me enough to share the info?" Lyse asked, teasing.

"I know what you are."

"Excuse me?" Lyse said, taking a step back from Lizbeth.

Lizbeth countered the retreat, moving into Lyse's personal space, anger consuming her and making her want to intimidate the smaller woman.

"You know exactly what I mean," Lizbeth growled, getting her face as close to Lyse's as she dared. "You're playing a game that you won't win."

Lyse shook her head.

"I don't understand, LB—"

Lizbeth's eyes flashed in the half-light.

"Eleanora may have left you in charge, but that's only because she didn't know what you were all about."

Lyse's blue eyes flared in anger.

"Something's wrong with you," Lyse said, shaking her head. "This isn't you."

Judas.

The word was a catalyst, enflaming Lizbeth, making her shake with rage.

"You want to wreck everything. To destroy what we've been working for," Lizbeth said, sneering at Lyse.

Weir had noticed something was wrong. He came over,

standing between the women and placing a hand on each of their shoulders.

"What's going on here?"

Lizbeth shrugged out of his grasp and took off.

"Ask your girlfriend, Weir. She's the Judas!" she called over her shoulder before disappearing into the darkness.

She headed away from the rest of the group, down one of the less well-lit tunnels that branched off from the burial chamber, following the voice in her head as it urged her to move quickly. To get away from Lyse.

She could hear Weir cursing and then the scrabble of feet in the dirt—probably him coming after her. She hated to do it this way, but Lizbeth had no other option. She needed to find the Dream Keepers and release them, channeling their powers into her own—whatever that meant. From there she would escape the catacombs and continue on her journey.

In her mind's eye, she could see her final destination calling to her. The Pillar was a lonely place, shrouded in cloud— and it was there she would meet her destiny.

Because the blood moon was on the rise.

And time was growing very, very short.

Lyse

ॐ

The next few minutes happened in slow motion, the flow from inaction to action, so smooth even someone trained to notice such things would've been hard-pressed to pick up on the cues. Lyse, who'd been blindsided by Lizbeth's odd behavior, missed it completely—and even if she had realized what was about to come, in retrospect, there really wasn't anything she could've done to prevent it.

Still, guilt had a funny way of perverting the truth. Especially when you were at your weakest. That was when the recriminations tiptoed in on silent feet and ripped your heart out—but that wouldn't come until later. At the precise moment that the German tourists ceased to be tourists and turned into militant commandoes, Lyse's brain stopped processing the past or future and just started reacting to the onslaught of insanity that had become her present.

One second Lyse was standing in the middle of the subterranean chamber watching Lizbeth disappear into the darkness of an unlit tunnel, one that was obviously not part of the tour; the next, all hell was breaking loose.

Two of the Germans dropped their backpacks and took off after Lizbeth. They raced past Lyse, pushing her out of their path with enough force that she was slammed into the wall, her left elbow and hip hitting the stone with a bone-jarring crunch. As she slid to the ground, pain ratcheting up her left side, she saw two more of the German tourists, a man and woman heading in Weir's direction.

"Behind you!" she screamed as the woman took her backpack and slung it at Weir's head. It was enough of a warning that he was able to dodge the blond woman's attack.

Out of the corner of her eye, Lyse saw Daniela slam the heel of her shoe into the solar plexus of one of the other Germans, sending the man flying backward into the hollow of an empty burial slab. The man caromed off the stone and landed at the feet of their Italian tour guide, who decided to cut his losses and take off toward the entrance of the catacombs.

The German woman grabbed the guide by the head and quickly snapped his neck, his lifeless body crumpling to the ground. Lyse stared at the man's body, in shock until she heard Daniela call out:

"I'll find Lizbeth!"

"Run," Lyse yelled back at her. "There were two of them after her—"

Daniela shot her a quick nod and then took off like a shot down the unlit tunnel. Lyse watched her go but was quickly distracted when the blond woman—the only female in the group—decided she was easy pickings and descended on her.

Shit, Lyse thought as the woman brandished her backpack over her head like a medieval flail.

Lyse pushed off the stone wall, leaping out of the way just as the woman attacked with the backpack. It smashed into the stone, breaking off a chunk of the frescoed wall—art that had survived for centuries now ruined in mere seconds.

Lyse had never been great in a fight. She'd survived the encounter with her uncle only because Eleanora had intervened.

Now she was on her own and whether she lived or died was solely up to her—but there was something about the immediacy of death that narrowed your focus down to a pinhole. Everything else fell away. All the worry and fear that were part of being human disappeared as instinct kicked in and your body became a tool to beat the ever-loving crap out of the thing that was trying to end you.

Her life had been upended, she'd found and lost the only family she'd ever known, and now Lizbeth was accusing her of God knew what . . . well, she was sick and tired of being life's whipping boy. Enough was enough.

"Screw you!" she screamed at the blond woman, all of the fury and fear she'd amassed over the last few weeks coming to a head.

She gave a guttural battle cry, the sound a visceral manifestation of the raw emotion percolating inside her, and, like a berserker no longer in control of her actions, she ran headlong into battle. A red haze of rage clouded her vision, her focus lasered in on the blond bitch with the backpack. The blonde hadn't expected Lyse to go on the offensive and was clearly thrown by this flipping of the script as Lyse's body barreled directly into her.

The backpack crashed into Lyse's head, the woman getting in one good blow before they both crashed to the stone floor. The bag was loaded down with something heavy, opening a gash in the side of Lyse's scalp as it connected with her head. Her vision pinwheeled, unconsciousness hovering at the periphery, but she managed to push it away as she fought to get back onto her feet. The blonde was in better shape, recovering more quickly. She was already swinging before Lyse could find her footing. Lyse ducked out of the way, evading the blonde's extended reach, the backpack millimeters above the top of her head.

This happened twice more, Lyse ducking out of the way just before the backpack could connect with her face. It was tiring work, but she knew if the woman hit her mark that would be the end.

Knockout.

"If you give up, you will not be harmed," the blonde said as she took another swing at Lyse's head. "We know who you are and we don't want to hurt you."

The German accent was gone, replaced now by the monotone of Middle America. Lyse didn't know which accent to believe—probably neither, she decided.

"Leave my friend alone and I'll go with you," Lyse replied.

"Can't do that," the blonde responded with a condescending grin that exposed crisp, white teeth and pink gums.

"Why not?" Lyse asked, playing along.

She and the blonde were both getting tired, and Lyse hoped that by talking she'd drag the whole thing out long enough to somehow get the advantage.

"Orders."

The woman slung the backpack at Lyse once more—but this time Lyse was prepared. She held her ground, reaching out and plucking the orange bag out of the air with both hands just as it was about to connect with her face. Without missing a beat, she pulled the bag into her chest, holding on to it for dear life. The blonde tried to yank the weapon out of Lyse's grasp, but Lyse had a firm grip on the Day-Glo orange material and there was no way she was going to let go of it.

The blonde was now within easy reach. Lyse used all of her strength and kneed the woman in the stomach. The blonde grunted, falling heavily against the backpack that separated them, but she didn't go down. So Lyse slammed her knee into the woman's gut again and again, fear driving her attack. Now the woman teetered and fell to her knees, still clutching at the bag. Lyse ripped it out of her hands and swung it like a bat. It connected with flesh and bone and the blonde fell forward, her face hitting the stone floor.

Lyse raised the bag and slammed it into the back of the

woman's head, ensuring that her attacker would be out of commission for the duration.

She heard Weir grunt behind her and turned to find him embattled. He was having trouble fending off the two men who surrounded him, each of them larger and more muscular than he was. She could see that he was already starting to tire, his face a mask of concentration as he dodged blow after blow that rained down on him.

He was going to need her help, sooner rather than later.

She picked up the backpack and unzipped it, instantly seeing why it was so heavy: It contained two pistols and a metal billy club. She pulled out one of the guns, then zipped up the pack, sliding it over her shoulder.

"Stop, or I'll shoot you," Lyse said, making sure the safety was off and looping her finger through the trigger.

The two men halted what they were doing, giving Weir a moment to catch his breath. Then the larger one, whose blond hair resembled the pale fuzz on top of a fleshy peach, made a move toward her. Lyse didn't hesitate; she pointed the gun at the man's feet and let off a shot. He jumped back as the slug went into the soft stone floor, shards of rock rocketing into the air.

She lifted the gun and quickly checked the chamber: four more shots, more than enough to take the two men out.

"You can see that I know how to shoot and I promise you I will make your life miserable if you mess with me," Lyse said, keeping the gun trained on the two fake German tourists. "Now back away from my friend . . ."

Using the barrel to indicate that they should move to their right, she waited for them to do what she asked. Peach Fuzz and his smaller but no less muscular friend looked at each other as if they were trying to decide what to do.

"C'mere," Lyse called to Weir, who was staring at her like she'd grown an extra head.

He stepped over to join her, and she saw that the two Germans had gotten him good. His nose was busted, a thin trickle of blood oozing from one nostril, and his left cheek was split, the gash raw and angry-looking.

"You look like crap," Lyse said, grinning at him.

"You look like you're about to kill someone," he replied, eyes still on the pistol in her hand.

"Eleanora taught me to shoot when I was a teenager. We used to go downtown to the gun club and spend Sunday afternoon there," Lyse said, keeping the two men within her sights. "I know what I'm doing, don't worry. Now here, take the bag."

He raised an eyebrow but refrained from saying anything she might mistake as disparaging. Instead, he took the proffered backpack and held it in between his hands, not sure what to do with it.

"Take out the other gun—"

"I don't know how to use it," he said, shaking his head. "And I don't believe in them."

Peach Fuzz snickered, and Lyse sighed, not willing to force the issue.

"Then just hold on to the bag, so none of them can get their hands on it."

He nodded, slipping the Day-Glo pack over his shoulder. When Lyse was sure the backpack was secure, she began questioning the men in front of her:

"Who are you and what do you want?"

She got no answer. They both stared back at her, unfazed by having a gun held on them. She wondered if this was an everyday occurrence in their line of work, or if they were just being stoic.

"Come on, don't make me shoot you," she said.

"You're not going to shoot me," the larger man replied, the corners of his mouth stretching into a lazy grin. "You don't have the—"

Lyse didn't hesitate, just took aim and shot the man in the foot before he could get out the rest of his sentence. He screamed as blood blossomed around the hole in his sneaker—and she imagined she'd taken off a toe or two with the shot.

"You dumb bitch," he shrieked, falling back against the chamber wall and using it to support his weight now that one of his feet was out of commission.

"I don't care what you call me," Lyse said, glaring back at him. "I will shoot you in the other foot if you don't answer my question: Who are you and what are you doing here?"

The temperature in the chamber dropped and Lyse felt a cold chill wrap around her body. Her teeth began to chatter as something wet dripped onto the crown of her head. She looked up, but there was nothing there, zero condensation on the stone ceiling that could've fallen on her.

Yet still the feeling of intense cold wouldn't go away. In fact, it began to get worse, spilling down the length of her body as if someone had poured a pitcher of ice water over her head.

She looked over at Weir and then at the two men, but they all seemed immune to whatever was affecting her.

"Tell me!" Lyse shouted, her blue eyes flashing.

The surge of anger she felt took her by surprise. Even Weir noticed and shot her a strange look.

"Sorry," she murmured to Weir, trying to shake off the impotent rage she was feeling.

These are not my feelings, Lyse thought, pushing them away. *I don't know what channel I'm tuned into, but it has to stop.*

She gritted her teeth and mentally pushed back at the oppressive feelings that were trying to fill her head—*Go away! I don't want you.* She imagined the cold pouring back out of her, returning to wherever it had come from—and she relaxed.

The wounded man kept his mouth clamped shut, a pissed-off expression on his ruddy face. But his friend, by far the quieter of the two, was watching her intently. The way his intelligent brown eyes stayed locked on her face, she wondered if he sensed what had just happened to her.

"We're here to get your little friend," he volunteered, more forthcoming than his partner.

Maybe he just doesn't want his body damaged irreparably, she thought. She supposed it didn't really matter why he was talking, just that he was.

"What little friend?" Weir asked.

"The one who took off into the dark. My two guys will catch her and then she's all ours."

The man spoke with a quiet authority, his dark eyes earnest. Lyse realized that he was the one in charge of the mission, not Peach Fuzz. Even if Peach Fuzz was the more physically intimidating of the two.

"You'll never find her," Weir said. "She'll outsmart anyone you send after her."

"No, it doesn't matter what he thinks," the man said about Weir before returning his attention to Lyse. "But you know that already."

"Know what—" Lyse started to say, but then she felt a sense of claustrophobia so strong that it was hard to breathe.

Whatever had tried to sway her emotions before, it was back and this time, it was playing on her fears. She felt an intense urge to escape the confines of the catacombs. To get outside and inhale fresh air again. She hated being in such an enclosed space. She was certain that the tiny burial chamber was far too small to hold all of these people.

She was having trouble focusing. She felt clammy all over, slick sweat breaking out on her upper lip and down her back. She closed her eyes, trying not to hyperventilate. She felt Weir's hand on her arm, his touch tender as his voice sounded in her ear:

"What does he mean? What do you know?"

She shook her head, wanting to explain that she had no idea what the man was talking about, but she was unable to speak. She couldn't open her eyes, couldn't open her mouth . . . couldn't do anything to defend herself from whatever was trying to take her over.

Judas.

It was an old woman's voice and it was full of rage.

"What do you mean?" she heard Weir ask the man.

There was a pause.

"Ask your girlfriend. She knows . . ."

Judas, trying to take the place of the rightful Magician. Now you will die.

In the darkness behind her eyelids, Lyse knew something terrible was about to happen, and that she was helpless to do anything about it. She heard the crack of a pistol firing—one of the Germans was shooting—once, twice, three times, and a spray of blood hit her face. Terror filled the burial chamber as the gunshots deafened her. She held her breath, waiting for the pain to blossom in her chest like a flower . . . but there was nothing, not even a twitch.

She opened her eyes slowly, the buzzing in her head making it hard to hear. Everything muffled, like she was underwater. She looked down at the gun in her hand and then at her body, realizing that she was covered in blood. She twisted her head to the side, not wanting to look, but knowing that she had to.

Lyse screamed, the sound of raw grief exploding out of her as she dropped to her knees. The broken keening that next escaped her lips was inhuman.

And then everything went red.

She didn't remember lifting the gun in her hand. Didn't remember shooting Peach Fuzz in the face. Didn't remember turning and shooting the blond woman in the chest. Didn't remember shooting the one man she'd totally forgotten about, the one Daniela had kicked in the solar plexus—but she'd caught him crouched near one of the burial slabs in a halo of smoke, a shiny black pistol in his hand.

The smoking gun.

The only one standing at the end of it all was the man with the brown eyes—and that was only because Lyse had run out of bullets.

When she came back to reality, she was curled in a fetal position on the floor of the burial chamber. She reached up and touched her face, felt the dried blood caking on her skin, her lips scaly as desiccated bone. She wanted to sit up, but her head was a bowling ball, so heavy she couldn't lift it. She tried to swallow and had trouble with even this simplest of tasks. Her tongue felt hairy and thick against the roof of her mouth, the foul taste of stagnant saliva turning her stomach as she tried to swallow and finally managed it this time.

She blinked, her vision fading in and out of focus, could make out a puddle of blood on the floor by her head. She reached out, hand shaking, and touched the gelatinous pool, her fingers coming back black. She closed her eyes, squeezing her eyelids shut tight, pleading with her mind to ignore the memories as they bombarded her—the flash of a gun muzzle, blood blooming like a rose on the front of Weir's shirt, his hand twitching once and then no more—but still they came, unbidden, and she couldn't stop them.

"No," she mouthed, mentally pushing the pictures away.

She forced herself to roll over. She took a deep, shuddering breath and opened her eyes again. The images in her mind ceased, replaced now by cold hard reality.

"No," she moaned in agony. "No . . ."

Weir lay sprawled on the ground, his back to her. When he'd fallen, the bottom of his blue T-shirt had ridden up, revealing a slash of smooth golden skin, the bony ridges of his rib cage, and the thick lines that spiderwebbed together to form the outline of the ghostly pirate ship that adorned his torso like a piece of art. The jewel tones—bright aqua and ruby and jade and banana—filled the inky black webbing with vibrant color, giving the ship a surreal Salvador Dali quality that Lyse loved. She reached out and touched Weir's back, smearing the blood she'd gotten on her finger onto the prow of the listing ship— but she didn't take her hand away. She continued to trace the ship's outline, surprised at how cold his body felt.

She was afraid to poke him, to try to prod him awake, because she didn't want to know what she already knew. Instead, she lovingly ran her fingers along the curve of his ribs and down the vertebrae of his back, stroking his bones like an instrument. Her flesh crawled as she touched him, her skin so alive it recoiled at the thought of connecting to something dead.

"Weir?" she whispered, still stroking his back.

She got an answer she did not expect.

"Over here."

She turned her head and saw Weir—or a ghostly approximation of the man—sitting on the edge of one of the rock outcroppings. He looked the same except for a dark stain on the front of his shirt.

"Hi," he said, and smiled sadly.

"Hi," Lyse said, swallowing back a sob.

"Don't cry over me," he said. He patted the rock beside him, indicating she should join him. "It's not like they said it would be, Lyse. Nothing scary about dying. It didn't even hurt."

"Yeah?" Lyse asked.

He nodded.

"Come sit by me."

She shook her head and looked over at his body.

"I don't want to leave you alone."

He nodded sadly.

"I loved you, Lyse. I hope you know that."

She didn't trust herself not to cry if she opened her mouth, so she shook her head.

"No, you don't know that?" he said, his brow furrowed.

She shook her head again. *No, I didn't know,* she thought. *I'd hoped, but I didn't know.*

"You're the funniest thing," he said. "So strong and determined, but so childlike, too."

"I love you, too." She managed to choke out most of the words before the tears came.

A wave of nausea crashed over her, but she fought it off. The tears were another story. They leaked from her eyes at will, trickling across her upper lip, down the side of her face and onto the ground. She could taste them, hot and salty.

"Don't cry," he said.

He was kneeling beside her now, his hand stroking her long dark hair. She felt him there, the nearness of his warmth and smell making her cry harder.

"It's tough," she whispered, grief swallowing her words. "So tough."

"I know," he said, touching her cheek. "I know."

She never wanted this time with Weir to end, but nothing lasted forever. He leaned down and kissed Lyse's forehead.

"Take care of LB," he whispered into her ear. "She needs you. No matter what happens, love and protect her the way I would."

Time came to a standstill as Lyse's grief ebbed and flowed. How long she lay there on the cold ground, letting the stone leach her body heat away, she didn't know. Weir was gone now and that was all that mattered.

Eventually she pulled her hand back, letting it fall to her side, the fingers extended, so that they did not touch the rest of her.

Dead hands, she thought, rubbing her bloodstained fingers together, mesmerized by the soft swish of skin on skin.

She wanted to roll Weir over, to see the place where they'd shot him, but she couldn't bear it. Imagining this simple action caused her tears to flow again.

A voice spoke out of the darkness:

"Enough."

A pair of rough hands slipped between her arms and her torso, lifting her up in the air. She felt weightless, a feather floating in the air, so light it would fly forever.

"Stand up."

The voice was stern, authoritative, and in her daze, she did what it said. Her feet touched the ground; the stone floor was the only solid thing in the whole world.

"You did this to yourself," the voice said.

Unseen hands turned her, so that she was face to face with the man in charge, the one with the dark brown, earnest eyes. He shook his head, jaw gritted together so tightly Lyse wondered if his teeth would shatter.

"This was your doing," he said, driving his words into her like a sword. "Do you understand? You did this."

He raised his hand in a sweeping arc, pointing to the carnage surrounding them. Five human bodies in their death rictus, blood spray on the walls and floor, a wanton murderess . . . it was a scene fit for the burial chamber of a Roman-era catacomb.

"Screw you," Lyse said, and spat in his face.

The man pulled a black hood from his pocket and slipped it roughly over Lyse's head. She tried to breathe, but fabric filled her mouth. She fought, kicking and screaming at him, but his grip was too strong. After a while, her body stopped working. Panic turned to acceptance and her brain stopped screaming for oxygen.

Unconsciousness came swiftly.

Lyse

⌘

Lyse began the slow climb to wakefulness.

As if she were trapped in a drugged dream, the languid fingers of oblivion stroked her brain, making it difficult to slip the tether of unconsciousness. She wanted to stay in the darkness, wanted to hide in the emptiness of her own subconscious because it was safer there. No one could reach her where she slumbered. She had no responsibilities, no needs, no wants . . . she was free.

For the moment.

But that didn't mean she was alone.

When you wake up, Lyse, the clock will begin to tick again . . .

The familiar voice—Eleanora's voice—slipped into her fractured mind like an eel, galvanizing her unconscious brain with an electric buzz. As soft as a whisper in her ear, it burrowed its way into the darkest recesses of her subconscious, becoming one with her own inner thoughts.

. . . and once that happens, I cannot help you. We will be fighting the battle on another front—and that will take all of my energy . . .

She was on the cusp of awareness. She couldn't scrabble back

into the darkness, couldn't dig in her heels like a braying don-
key and refuse to return to reality. That was the way it was;
once her brain woke up, it would not be put back to sleep.

*I love you, Lyse. Take that with you. And know that I will see
you on the other side.*

There was a finality to Eleanora's words that tore at Lyse's
heart, rending the muscle into useless bits. The tears came
unbidden, wet warmth that trickled down the smooth curve of
her cheeks and collected in the hollows of her collarbone. Lyse
realized then that she was about to be alone, waking up in a
place she knew nothing about, other than that she would be
surrounded by the enemy—and with this thought the last of
her grandmother's ghostly presence dissolved like a spoonful of
honey in a mug of hot water. The essence of the woman who'd
raised Lyse—and loved her more than anything or anyone else
in the world—was gone now except for a slight melancholy
aftertaste.

"Elyse MacAllister, it's a pleasure to finally meet you."

The man's voice seemed to come from a thousand miles
away—the cadence so unlike Eleanora's warm dulcet tones
that it made Lyse shiver. She cracked open a blue eye and, as if
she were carefully twisting the focus ring of an old film camera, the world slowly slipped into sharpened relief.

The room was cold, not just in temperature, but sterile like
an operating theater. A naked lightbulb hung from the ceiling,
dangling like an incandescent jewel on the end of a long cord.
It dipped into the darkness, a frozen teardrop bathing the rest
of the room in deep shadow. There was something wrong with
the voltage, and the bulb emitted a low-pitched hum—*phaaar-
rooooah, phaaar-rooooah*—that mimicked the song of a lone
cicada. This was a sound Lyse was familiar with after years of
living in semirural Georgia—and she'd always had pity for the
poor bastards . . . alone and awake while all of their brethren
were still in the deep throes of hibernation.

Now that she was almost fully awake, the brightness of the

light made her eyes water, but there was nothing she could do about it. Cold stainless-steel restraints cut into the delicate skin of her wrists, and as much as she strained against them, she was unable to do anything to release herself from their bite. They did a good job of keeping her immobilized on her metal chair.

At least she could move her legs—her captors had been kind enough to allow her legs to remain free.

"What do you want from me?" she asked, rage crashing over her like a wave, the rush of blood under her skin making her cheeks flush bright red.

The words slid out of Lyse's mouth without her thinking them. Her lips were dry and cracked, her mouth and tongue parched as a desert—but she didn't have any trouble making herself understood. Anger had a way of cutting through the bullshit.

The man sat across from her, a rectangular aluminum table separating them—but it was a divide that did nothing to ease Lyse's mind. An air of menace permeated the space. As if a grotesquerie of monsters sat locked within the shadowy confines of the room just waiting for the man sitting in front of her to snap his fingers. Would they descend on her in a heartbeat? Rip her limb from limb before sucking the very marrow from her bones?

Even though she knew (she hoped) monsters didn't exist, the train of thought made her shiver.

"What a vague question," he replied, leaning forward on his elbows, so that he could settle his chin on the tops of his clasped hands. "What do I want from you? Why, merely your company, my dear."

He did not look at her as he spoke, and his eyes seemed unable to settle on anything for longer than a few seconds before moving elsewhere. At first she assumed this was a sign of weakness, that he was too insecure to look at her directly, but then he smiled and their eyes locked. Now he would not drop her gaze but held it with an unwavering attention, his pupils dilated an inky black. It made her skin crawl to imagine him trying to breach her mind via her eyes, sending out tendrils of his soul to slip inside her and carry away intimate, personal information.

Eyes are the windows to the soul, someone had once said, but she'd never taken the sentiment seriously until now.

She wanted to look away, but her inborn stubbornness wouldn't let her. She was determined to force his hand, make him drop his gaze first.

"Why are you doing this?" she asked after a protracted silence, still unwilling to break their impromptu staring contest. "Murdering blood sisters, destroying covens? What're you trying to do here?"

The man's eyes were rheumy, snaking red capillaries crisscrossing the jaundiced sclera. He opened his mouth, then closed it again, compressing thin beige lips into a straight line. The action caused his chin to slip into the crevice between the second and third fingers of his still-clasped hands, and she noticed a tremor in his arms that hadn't been there before.

"You and your kind are in our way—and like a disease, you must be stamped out before you can spread."

"You murdered my friend," Lyse said, and the full weight of the words settled over her as she spoke them—*she did not cry, she would not cry*—there'd been too much of that during the past few days and she was done with it. "Your people have killed so many of us and we've done nothing to you."

It wasn't that she'd made any kind of peace with what had happened back at the catacombs; it was that she could do nothing to change that moment . . . that precious second in time when everything had changed. So she disassociated herself from her feelings, pushed away the pain and grief—even though she knew that once she found her way out of this place, she would be overwhelmed by her emotions and would have to give in to them, or lose her mind.

"Kill or be killed . . . I think you know this old adage

well," the man said, smiling again, so that the skin around his eyes crinkled in a charming way. "But I don't want to bring up all that nastiness. What can I do to make you feel more comfortable?"

He'd put on an imaginary mask, magically transforming himself into a sweet old man to try to fool her—not that she was buying the act. But she didn't want him to know, so she put on a neutral expression, behaving as if she were unaware that this was all a charade.

Besides, she wanted to buy herself some time. Needed it to think about her next move.

"I want some water."

"But of course," he said after a moment, his smile widening to reveal hideously worn-down yellow teeth, the front incisors the only ones still holding their sharpened edge. "I can refuse you nothing."

He turned his head, breaking the connection between them, and his face disappeared into shadow. Lyse released her breath, her whole body shaking. She hadn't realized how much he'd unnerved her, how rigid and tense her body had become until he was no longer looking in her direction.

"Bring us some cold water, please," the old man said, speaking to someone Lyse couldn't see. Somewhere in the darkness she heard a heavy door slide open on ungreased tracks. Whoever was in the room with them . . . until now they'd been as quiet as a corpse.

With no eyes upon her, she took the free moment to collect herself and tamp down her unsettled feelings.

Maybe he really does have monsters all over this room, Lyse thought. *Just another way of trying to unnerve me*.

She put those thoughts away, realizing she needed to start thinking logically, to observe more of her surroundings if she were going to form an escape plan. Dropping her chin, she let her eyes scan the dark gray floor, raising a brow at the deep scratches etched into the poured concrete—probably made by the bottoms of other metal chairs whose occupants tried to escape torture and confinement.

She didn't doubt this place had been privy to some horrible atrocities. Hell, as far as she knew, *no one* had ever made it out of this room alive—then add to that a strange heaviness in the air, a sense that something unseen was pressing down on you, making it hard to breathe.

It was enough to make Lyse wish she'd remained unconscious indefinitely.

Not really an option, she thought as her skin became clammy and she felt sweat break out under her arms, the stink of her own fear permeating the room.

From her vantage point, Lyse couldn't tell the dimensions of the space, but it had to be huge, bigger even than she'd realized . . . especially if someone had been standing undetected in the shadows watching and waiting to do the old man's bidding.

"You would like to know where you are? Yes?"

The old man was watching her. *Had been* watching her.

She didn't want to look at him but felt compelled to take in his presence, to inspect everything on the surface that she could see: the graying hair a shade too long, curling around the lapels of his black suit jacket and starched white dress shirt. The boxy cut of his jacket swallowed up his gaunt frame, and the incandescent light made his body appear drawn and sallow. He was gripping a cane in his right hand—it must've been leaning against the back of his chair before, but now he was holding on to it for dear life, his fingers white and bloodless where they curled around the silvery head of a thickly maned lion.

"First, I'd like to know why I'm cuffed to this chair, actually," Lyse said, and swallowed hard, trying to encourage the flow of saliva back into her mouth. "And then, yeah, where I *am* would be nice, too."

The old man laughed, a phlegmy choked thing that made

Lyse flinch. She'd liked him better before she'd heard the sound.

"Excuse me," he rasped, then cleared his throat and coughed—the laughter had taken something elemental out of him.

He seemed diminished now.

"One, because I don't want you doing anything you'd regret," he said, squeezing the head of the cane and drawing it in closer to his torso. She could see the thickened nail beds of his right hand, the striated keratin as yellow as old parchment. "And as for why—that is the important question, Lyse, and so I shall answer it—you are here because of what you are . . . what's in your blood. And also what you will mean to a movement that is only now beginning to grow. I don't need you to martyr yourself for their cause, so we will keep you here for the duration."

Lyse chose not to roll her eyes at the old man's pompousness.

"What I *am*? What's in my blood? I don't know what any of that means," she said, her words laced with feigned innocence.

The old man leaned forward in his seat, hazel eyes narrowed.

"Oh, I think you know exactly what it means . . . *witch*."

He spat the word out as if it were a curse.

"But that's not all you know, now is it?" he continued. "There's so very much for the two of us to discuss—"

He was interrupted by the *click* of a door unlatching, and then the rickety growl of metal casters running on track. The old man did not look up, but Lyse could see something moving in the shadows. She shrank back in her seat, fear and adrenaline coursing through her veins as a tall man in a dark blue suit crossed the threshold from darkness to light, revealing himself.

Lyse gasped as she stared up into the startling ice blue eyes of the first person she'd killed.

Her uncle smiled down at her, bright white teeth as even

and unmarred as if they'd been cast in a dentist's office. He was exactly as she remembered him from the last time they'd met—only this time he was alive, not crushed underneath a stone statue.

His posture was ramrod straight, his long arms held at attention by his sides; the close-cropped silver-gray hair remained the same, as did the tan skin and the gleam of menace behind his eyes. It was as much a part of him as the sneering pull of his upper lip, a feature that made him look mean even when he was trying to play nice.

"Hello, Lyse," he said in a voice as taut as piano wire.

Fear cascaded through her, and she gritted her teeth to keep him from seeing her lips tremble. The violence of her reaction to him was palpable, and she could smell the raw, feral scent of herself coming off her body in waves: under her armpits, at the small of her back where her flannel shirt hung over the waistband of her black jeans. She wanted to reach up and wipe the moisture from her lip, but she was held in place by her bindings.

She let her gaze drift to the tan flesh of her uncle's exposed neck, her eyes focusing in on its smoothness. She would've done anything not to have to stare into the dead man's eyes ever again.

Not that she regretted killing him.

He'd kidnapped her from Eleanora's bungalow on Curran Street in Echo Park and hidden her away in a place where no one would ever have found her body. His intent: to kill her slowly and with as much mortification as possible.

Yet here he was again, alive and breathing and less than three feet away from her.

Lyse remembered how crushed and dead he'd looked underneath the ruin of the Lady of the Lake. It just didn't seem possible for him to have survived—but somehow he had, or at least some incarnation of him. It was as if she'd imagined the whole horrific nightmare . . . and maybe she had.

Seeing him now made her question her sanity once again.

There was the clatter of metal on metal and then a small, mousy woman stepped into the light. She held a tray carrying a metal pitcher and two glasses, the pitcher sweating with condensation.

The woman's eyebrows pinched together in concentration as she walked, the pitcher clattering against the tray as she slowly maneuvered her misshapen body closer to the table, her gait unsteady as she tried to keep a safe distance between herself and Lyse's uncle.

As she approached the table, the woman lifted her gaze to catch Lyse's own. What Lyse saw there almost turned her stomach. The woman's once-beautiful face had been transformed by a livid pink scar that ran down the right side of her cheek and cut through her eye, the skin puckered from jaw to brow. The instrument that caused the wound had left behind a milky white iris that was a ghostly twin of the untouched forest-green one that was still intact. Her brown hair was cropped close to her scalp, revealing a small dark hole where what was left of her right ear's cartilage curlicued around like a nautilus shell. The damage to her face and ear continued down her body, the right side—arm, torso, hip, and leg—gnarled and twisted. The effect was magnified by the thin black cotton dress she wore, the fabric clinging to her deformed frame, enhancing rather than hiding her disability.

Because of all the scarring, it was hard to tell how old the woman was, but as she set the tray down on the table between Lyse and the old man, Lyse caught a glimpse of the woman's good left hand—unblemished and smooth, the fingers supple, well-shaped and unlined by age. She realized the woman couldn't be much older than she was.

The woman sensed Lyse's interest. She raised her eyes, dark lashes fluttering.

—Escape if you can, or they will do the same to you.

Lyse started as the words came into her brain, unbidden.

She forced herself not to look around, but to hold the woman's gaze.

—*Fire and a knife,* the woman said without physically moving her lips. *Cut and burned for my supposed "crimes." And I'm one of the few lucky ones they've allowed to come and serve them.*

Lyse wanted to respond, but she didn't know how. She tried thinking her response, but the woman just stared back at her, unblinking.

"That's enough staring," Lyse's uncle said, grabbing the woman's twisted right arm and dragging her away from the table, the sheer violence behind his grasp clear to anyone watching.

"David—" the old man said, his tone a warning.

The woman's face spasmed in pain, but when she opened her mouth to cry out, no sound escaped her lips—and Lyse saw that there was only a nub of fleshy pink skin where her tongue had been brutally cut from her mouth. Despite the pain, the woman caught Lyse's eye one last time, her telepathic presence returning for a final parting shot:

—*We are here when you need us.*

The words were either a promise or a threat, Lyse did not know which—and then Lyse's uncle dragged the woman off into the shadows, the darkness swallowing them whole.

Before she could stop herself, Lyse found herself speaking.

"What happened to that woman?"

The old man nodded, as if he had been expecting the question.

"She was tried as a witch, but she confessed to her crimes and begged for absolution."

"*That's* absolution?" Lyse asked, incredulous. "Taking someone's tongue, burning them until they're half dead?"

The old man held up his lion-headed walking stick, shaking it at Lyse to emphasize his point:

"The tongue ensures that the lies of her past are never spread, and the burning is to cleanse. Fire cleanses best of all. Better even than water. Once we learned that lesson, that water was not the easiest of ways to destroy your evilness, we went back to the work of our forefathers, and things changed quickly."

Lyse shook her head, trying to clear it of the images the old man had called into being in her mind's eye.

She woke up the first time underwater. Eyes bulging from lack of oxygen, she screamed, but no one could hear her, the sound muffled by the water . . .

These were the words she'd read in her grandmother's journal. By some strange trick of exhaustion or magic, as Lyse had read the manuscript, she'd fallen into the slipstream of Eleanora's memories. Here, she'd seen and felt the torture her grandmother had endured as a young woman, when she'd almost been drowned by a group of religious zealots just like the one sitting in front of Lyse now. They, too, were trying to *cleanse*, to destroy some imagined evilness they saw inside the woman who'd raised Lyse.

It was a defining moment in Eleanora's life, and it had culminated with her leaving Massachusetts, never to set foot again in the state of her birth. It had also brought Eleanora to Echo Park and to Hessika and the coven, sealing her grandmother's fate forever.

As these thoughts ricocheted inside Lyse's head, she began to get a very strange feeling.

"She never told you about me, did she?" The old man asked, becoming excited for the first time since the bizarre interrogation had begun. "About *her* and *me*?"

Lyse's blood ran cold. She did not want to believe what the old man was implying.

"No," Lyse said, the softness of her tone forcing him to lean farther across the table to hear her. "No, that's not possible. *You* can't be possible."

The old man's face split into a wide grin, his pleasure evident.

"Yes, what you are thinking," the old man said, then cackled with glee. "It's all true!"

Lyse fought back her revulsion, not wanting to give him the satisfaction of seeing how much he'd upset her.

"I am the bringer of the end, the crest of the wave, a follower of the only truth . . . I am a rider of The Flood . . . *and I am your grandfather.*"

Lyse realized that her senses hadn't been wrong. There *was* a monster in the room with her.

Only it wasn't hiding in the shadows.

It was sitting right in front of her.

Arrabelle

⁊⊃

"You think I'm scared of you, you've got another thing coming," Arrabelle said as she crossed the space between herself and the creature, closing the gap in a few long strides.

She wasn't going to let this Frankenstein wannabe intimidate her—she'd laid waste to men his size before, and she thought nothing of fighting dirty if the situation called for it.

The words were no sooner in her head than the giant was slamming his entire body weight into her. She'd hardly seen him move and suddenly he was pinning her to the ground, crushing her rib cage with his deadweight, his body convulsing over her.

She felt the dirt pressing against her back, errant shoots of brown grass scratching at her neck. Her lungs screamed for air, but her hands were pinioned underneath her and were already beginning to go numb.

"*No!*" She heard Niamh scream as the car door opened and then slammed shut.

"It's okay. I've got her." A new voice.

Upon its arrival, all of her instincts kicked in and a surge of adrenaline shot through her body. She was fighting again—and she hadn't even realized she'd given up.

"Help me roll him off her." That same, oh-so-familiar voice.

"But . . . he's so heavy," Niamh said—and Arrabelle knew she was close by, maybe even beside her, though she couldn't see the girl.

"We'll both push. It'll work. I promise."

"Okay," Niamh said, though she didn't sound too sure about this plan.

The man stopped seizing, and now Niamh could get her hands under the man's deadweight. Arrabelle felt the man's body began to shift, and, for a moment, she had enough space between her chest and the man's body to enable her to draw a breath—but this was short-lived as the weight crashed back down on top of her.

"One more time," she heard the voice say—and then there was a massive push from her rescuers and the man was pushed off her.

She rolled onto her side, gasping for breath and coughing at the same time. The grass tickled her cheek and nose, but she didn't care. She was just so damn happy to be alive that she could barely contain her joy.

"Bell?"

The voice. He was right there beside her. All she had to do was sit up and look at him . . . but she was scared. She didn't know if she had the wherewithal to deal with the reality of what was happening. Arrabelle, who was never scared of anything, was terrified to face the person she loved more than anyone else in the whole world.

"Bell . . . open your eyes . . . please."

She did as she was told, and all the feelings she'd held at bay rushed to fill the void that had been created in her heart by Evan's absence.

"Evan," she said, his face swimming in front of her like a dream come to life. "I thought you were gone . . ."

The same liquid brown eyes she'd always loved—chocolate irises ringed in a halo of gold, thick lashes that belonged on a catwalk model, not a skater punk dude—stared back at her. She reached up and touched his face, fingers brushing across one cheekbone, following the line of his angular jaw until she reached the soft flesh under his chin. He smiled down at her and she saw the familiar empty space where his right eyetooth should've been.

It had happened when he was ten, showing off for his younger sister by hanging upside down from an apple tree in their grandparents' orchard in San Luis Obispo. Swinging back and forth and laughing like an idiot, pleased as punch that he was doing something he knew would piss his grandfather off—and then the branch had snapped in half and he'd fallen on his face.

A cracked skull, a missing tooth, and a fat lip . . . his parents had been none too happy, and his grandfather had forbidden him from playing in the orchard for the rest of that summer.

"I knew you'd come," Evan said, grabbing her hand and helping her to her feet.

It was then that she noticed how skinny he'd become. The kind of emaciated that was terrifying to see on someone you loved . . . because it meant they were sick.

"Evan . . . ?" The question was there in that one word. Once upon a time, they'd known each other so well that they hadn't needed words to communicate. Arrabelle hoped that there were still vestiges of that old connection left between them.

"Don't," Evan said, brushing the dirt from his hands onto the sides of his olive drab khakis. "I'm okay. It looks worse than it is."

The blue wool fisherman's sweater he wore swam on his gaunt frame, and Arrabelle could see the cords of his neck standing out in bas-relief. He'd jammed a woolen knit cap onto his head, but Arrabelle could see that he'd recently shaved his head. There was a little bit of red stubble on his chin—he'd never been able to grow much in the way of facial hair—and the dark circles under his eyes were very defined.

"What's happened to you?" She couldn't stop herself from asking. Worry was making her sound hysterical, but she didn't care. "What can I do?"

He shook his head.

"Nothing. At least, not for me."

"But—" she began, and he shook his head.

"Please, we'll talk later. I promise."

She nodded, not wanting to capitulate. She would never give over to anyone else, but this was *Evan*. He was different. She realized she'd do anything he asked her to do, *had* done things for him that she'd do for no one else.

The wind had picked up just in the few minutes they'd been standing there, and Arrabelle shivered. Evan nodded to Niamh, who handed over the thick down jacket Arrabelle had dropped before wading into the fight. It warmed her instantly when she slipped it back on, and her teeth stopped chattering.

"We should go. There are more of these bastards hanging around the island," Evan said, gesturing to Arrabelle's rental car. "That you? Mind if we take it?"

Arrabelle shook her head.

"Of course."

While Evan and Niamh made their way over to Arrabelle's car, she stopped to check on the monster, and to see what Evan had used to subdue it. She knelt down in the grass beside the giant man, palpating his neck until she found his carotid artery. She found a pulse, albeit a weak one, but it was slowly fading. As much as she didn't want to get crushed to death, she also didn't want Evan killing anyone on her behalf—but that seemed to be a moot point now.

"Now what did you use?" she muttered to herself, and was quickly rewarded with an answer.

She pulled a small dart free from the only smooth tissue

on the man's back, careful not to touch its tip, and wrapped it in some tissue she dug out of her coat pocket. Thus, safely concealed, she slipped it into a zippered pocket on the outside of her coat and stood up. There was nothing she could do now for the giant. Death made its way on swift wings and it would not be deterred.

She said a little prayer to the Goddess and left the monstrous man to his fate.

They drove the first few miles in silence.

Niamh was in the driver's seat, having already been there, waiting, when Arrabelle came back from checking the giant's body. Evan was in the backseat, and when Arrabelle started to open the front passenger door, he stopped her:

"Come back here with me."

He patted the seat beside him, and Arrabelle didn't hesitate. She closed the door she'd just opened and climbed into the back with him.

"I'm really happy to see you," Evan said, reaching over and taking her hand. He squeezed it between his own thin fingers.

Niamh put the car in gear and it lurched forward.

"Sorry," she said, catching Arrabelle's eye in the rearview mirror.

"Don't worry about it. It's a rental."

After that, no one said a word. Niamh seemed to know where she was going, but her long hair was like a veil hiding her face from Arrabelle's view. A few times she fiddled with the control of the heater, adjusting the defrost, and once she accidentally pulled the seat too far forward when she tried to get her legs—which were shorter than Arrabelle's—closer to the pedals.

Arrabelle slipped off her coat and gave a silent *thank you* to the younger woman for doing the driving, allowing her and Evan to reconnect. As the heater flooded warmth through the car, Arrabelle closed her eyes, savoring Evan's presence.

They were sitting almost on top of each other, so near that she could feel Evan's bones through his clothes; hip bones touching hip bones, arms and shoulders pressed tightly against one another.

The hand that Evan held tingled, his flesh on her flesh. His skin was so thin that she could feel the pulse at his wrist as it beat sluggishly beneath her fingers. She closed her eyes, realized how rigidly she was holding her body, and let out a shuddering breath as she forced herself to relax.

"Okay?" Evan asked, and Arrabelle smiled.

"Yes, of course."

There was so much she wanted to say, so much she wanted to ask, but nothing came out. She was terrified of breaking the spell, of Evan going away again. She just wanted to live in the present moment, filing every second into a secret compartment in her heart to be taken out and savored at her convenience.

With Evan, there was no such thing as the future. He was an elusive creature, unwilling to be pinned down by anyone—especially Arrabelle. He may have told her that he loved her in that note, but she doubted he would ever tell her the same to her face. That was his nature, to stay silent about his feelings. He'd never said as much to her, but she'd always had the impression that he didn't trust emotion, that being vulnerable was anathema to him, and he'd do anything rather than give over to sentiment.

No one would ever call Arrabelle romantic, but there was something about Evan that brought out the feminine in her, heightening her need to love and be loved. A heart that never wanted or needed anything was useless, she now knew. She *wanted* and *needed* Evan both, the two things becoming one overarching passion where he was concerned.

"Where are we going?" she asked, choosing a neutral topic. She knew asking about his health or about their relationship would just make him clam up.

"Away from here. It's not safe," he replied. "We were just

waiting for you. I'd hoped you'd go to the general store like I'd said in the letter—having people around is helpful, stops me from having to take out things like that giant back there. But you never do it the easy way, do you?"

That was the truth. She'd never been able to just follow directions, wanting to be independent and blaze her own trail at every turn. It made her life more difficult, that was for sure, but it kept things interesting.

"No, I guess not," she said, unapologetically. She'd never seen the need to be sorry for who or what she was.

Evan squeezed her hand.

"Well, you're ever constant, Bell. I should've known better than to tell you what to do."

He'd given her the nickname one day almost as an afterthought. There'd been no buildup, no teasing or testing out of possible nicknames . . . just a casual reference to her being a "beautiful belle" and that was that—she'd been Bell ever since.

"I hope you know that it's not just happening here," Evan said. "It's everywhere. They're taking the covens apart, bit by bit—"

He stopped talking and the color drained from his face. He went rigid beside her, gripping her hand hard. He grimaced in pain, and she watched, unable to do anything, as his whole body was racked by an intense seizure that rippled through him, dissipating as quickly as it had come.

After a few moments, he began to breathe normally again.

He released her hand and she looked down at her fingers, wiggling them a little to make sure they still worked.

"Sorry . . . about that," Evan whispered, a sheen of cold sweat breaking out across his brow and upper lip. "I'm fine. So don't even ask."

Arrabelle hated that he knew her so well, had called out her next move before she could make it. She glared at him and reached for his wrist. He let her take his pulse, and she frowned; his heartbeat was wild and erratic.

"You're not well."

He grinned.

"Very observant of you."

"Evan—"

He shook his head. "Not now. Later."

She sighed, releasing his wrist even though she hated to let go, to not be touching him, somehow.

I'm like a teenager, she thought. *My brain is a mess when he's around. It's not good. It's gonna get someone killed.*

"I know what you're feeling, Bell," Evan continued, lifting her chin with his finger so he could look into her eyes. The tension between them was palpable. "I feel it, too, but it's for another time."

She swallowed, her mouth dry. She was having trouble focusing because her entire body was reacting pleasurably to Evan's admission of attraction. She could feel it in her breasts and belly . . . between her legs. It was a delicious warmth and it washed over her like an ocean wave cresting against the sand. This was the most he'd ever said on the subject, the only time he'd ever acknowledged that there was something potent between them.

She'd tried to force his hand once, had ambushed him before he'd realized what was happening . . . had kissed him—and that kiss had ignited a flame inside Arrabelle that had never gone out. After that, Evan had made it clear there was no future for them as a couple, that they were friends only.

Even now it still hurt to think about that night, and how devastated she'd been by his words.

"I know," she said, agreeing with him. There was a much bigger threat that needed to be addressed, and her feelings would have to come second to that.

"Bell, we know where they've taken Niamh's sister, Laragh—and it's not just her. There are others there, as well," Evan said, his face slack with exhaustion. "So many more than can be imagined, held against their will. We have to go and help them."

They were back on the main drag, passing the cute tourist boutiques and restaurants, the road straightening out as they neared the dock.

"I don't think you should be trying to help anyone right now," Arrabelle said, shaking her head.

It was true. She was surprised that he was as functional as he was . . . the seizure had taken its toll on him and he looked done in for the moment. She really didn't think it would be humanly possible for him to do anything as physically exerting as this jailbreak he was informing her they were about to attempt.

"I'll be the judge of what I can and can't do," Evan said, the fierce determination Arrabelle remembered from their years of friendship rearing its head. Evan was not one to be dissuaded from something he wanted to do.

"I'm not your mother and I'm not responsible for you choosing to abuse yourself when you're obviously ill," Arrabelle said, folding her hands in her lap and fixing her gaze on something, anything that wasn't Evan. She didn't want to fight with him. Especially not now, when things were so unsettled.

Through the window, she saw that the ferry she'd arrived on was still there, waiting to load up those who'd spent their time on the island and were now ready to depart.

"Good," Evan said, clearing his throat. "Then that's settled. You mind your business and I'll mind mine."

Arrabelle felt like rolling her eyes. Evan's stubborn streak had always driven her mad and, all these years later, it still made her want to punch him.

"Fine," she said, still not looking at him. "But on one condition. You promise to tell me what the hell is going on with you"—he started to protest—"not now, but soon."

He had no argument. He could hedge all he wanted, but if he didn't promise now, he knew she would hound him with questions until they got in a nasty fight. Which would only be counterproductive.

"Fine," he said, and sighed. "I told you we would discuss everything later—"

Arrabelle turned away from the window and looked at him, searching his face for answers.

"I think it's pretty obvious that we know each other very well," she began. "With that said, you will do everything in your power to keep me in the dark for as long as possible. If you promise something, though, that means you've given your word and I know you won't go back on that."

He stared back at her, his frustration evident.

"Fine. I promise. I give my word. Whatever you want, Bell."

Arrabelle could see Niamh's worried face in the rearview mirror.

"I accept," Arrabelle said. "And I will hold you to it. That's my promise to you."

Evan's shoulders slumped, but he gave her a wan smile.

"I know you will, Bell."

With that Niamh navigated the rental toward the line of cars waiting their turn to board the ferry and put the gear into park. Now they waited.

The rolling of the choppy sea did not seem to faze Evan but, like a lullaby, had lulled him into slumber. Stretched out across the backseat, he looked angelic, all the sharp angles and hard lines smoothed away by sleep. Arrabelle closed the car door softly behind her, making sure the catch clicked into place. Then she wove her way through the parked rows of cars, looking for Niamh.

She wasn't sure what she expected to learn from the younger woman. She was Evan's coven mate, knew more about him now than Arrabelle did . . . Really she just wanted to talk to her. It was as simple as that.

There were fewer cars on the return trip to the mainland than there had been on the voyage over. Fewer cars meant fewer people, and Arrabelle was able to find Niamh easily. She was sitting on one of the wooden benches, legs tucked up underneath her, arms wrapped around herself for warmth. Arrabelle crossed the deck and took the empty seat beside Niamh, slipping off her own jacket and draping it over the girl's shoulders.

"Oh, you don't need to—" Niamh started to say, but Arrabelle waved her words away.

"Please, you're freezing, take it."

The girl debated internally for a moment, unsure of what to do, and then finally nodded. She shifted the puffy jacket so it draped around the front of her like a giant down-filled bib and slipped her arms backward through the sleeves.

"Thank you."

Arrabelle smiled at her.

"You're welcome."

They sat together quietly, neither speaking, just listening to the crash of the waves against the ship's hull as the ferry knifed through the water. It was pleasant there on the deck, the sun warming their skin for a moment before that warmth was pilfered by the lashing of the cold, wet cross-breeze.

Niamh spoke and, at first, Arrabelle did not hear the words because the wind kept stealing them away.

"What?" Arrabelle asked, moving closer to Niamh, leaving no space between them on the bench.

"He won't tell you," she almost whispered.

"Won't tell me what?" she asked, placing a hand on the girl's shoulder. To her surprise, she found that Niamh was shaking.

"That he's dying. Anyone can see it, but he acts like it's not happening—"

Arrabelle's heart froze, Niamh's voice fading out until there was only the buzzing inside of her own head to keep her company in her terror.

No. The word came to her unbidden.

"—he was so sick that night, I was sure that was the end. So I sent the package."

Arrabelle forced herself to refocus, to pay attention to what Niamh was saying.

"How long has this been going on?" she asked, curious at how calm her voice sounded even to her own ears.

"The night *they* came. The night they took my sister . . . and murdered Yesinia and Honey . . ."

Niamh's voice trailed off. She looked so miserable that Arrabelle felt compelled to loop an arm around the girl's shoulder and pull her in tight.

"I'm so sorry," Arrabelle said as the girl's whole body began to shake, tears falling down her cheeks like raindrops. "I can't even imagine what this has been like for you."

"My sister," Niamh murmured. "I feel everything they do to her . . . and then two days ago, she began to talk to me. That's how we know where she is. She told me."

Arrabelle frowned, her fingers nimbly stroking the girl's long, tangled hair.

"How is that possible?"

Niamh shrugged and shook her head.

"I don't know. I can't ask her . . . she doesn't hear me. She just talks . . . like she hopes she's reaching me, but isn't sure."

"Okay," Arrabelle said, nodding. "That's good. She's still alive. And that's something."

Niamh's lower lip trembled.

"She sounds bad, though. Really, really bad."

"Then it's good we're going to help her now."

"Evan . . . he shouldn't come with us," Niamh said, her mind moving quickly between subjects. "I'm afraid of what they'd do to him. It would be worse than death."

Arrabelle wasn't quite sure that anything could be worse than death, but she understood that Niamh was scared of something her sister had shared with her, and she didn't want that fate for Evan.

"Because what they've done to Laragh is worse than death," she said, another onslaught of tears sliding down her face. "It's inhuman."

"We'll stop them—" Arrabelle began.

"But will we?" Niamh whispered, interrupting her. "Really?"

As much as Arrabelle wanted to reassure the girl that everything would be fine, she realized only a hypocrite would say that. Because Niamh was right, Arrabelle did not know the future. She could make an educated guess, could hang her hat on hope, but, in the end, there was only *what would be* . . . and that was for the fates to decide.

Instead, she chose to speak the only truth available to her: "I don't know."

Daniela

Dammit, Lizbeth, Daniela thought, the steady sound of her own pulse a syncopated beat in her ears. *Where the hell did you go?*

She jogged down the unlit path, her footfalls echoing in the confined space, the close quarters making her feel claustrophobic. With its lack of overhead lighting, it was obvious that this particular tunnel was definitely not supposed to be traversed by visitors, and Daniela had to be careful not to trip over the natural rises and dips in the rock floor as she navigated the empty catacombs. She could hear the pounding of feet up ahead, and hoped that meant Lizbeth was proving elusive to the two mercenaries who'd taken off after her.

She has no idea they're coming for her, Daniela thought, and then she careened into a ledge protruding from the wall, something she'd missed in the low light. It slammed into her thigh and she bit her tongue in order not to cry out.

She instinctively smacked the ledge with the meaty heel of her palm, lashing out in anger at an inanimate object.

"Bastard," she murmured, placing both hands over her thigh

and applying pressure to stanch the flow of pain, sharp and almost sweet in its intensity, that radiated from the injured area.

She knew it was going to leave a nasty bruise, but she didn't have time to wallow in the pain. She started moving again, walking off the injury, and then she forced herself to run, ignoring the ache in her leg.

She could still hear the heavy thud of running feet and was pleased the two men hadn't gotten so far ahead that she couldn't follow them—but then she hit another of the burial chambers, and everything changed. Though this one was smaller and brighter than the last, with flat stone walls that reflected back the artificial light, making the rock seem to sparkle beneath the faded mosaics . . . there were *five* exits from this new chamber.

"Dammit," Daniela murmured as she stood in the middle of the chamber, unsure of what to do next.

She scanned the room, looking for a sign, anything to tell her which way to go, but there was nothing. The symbols covering the walls were indecipherable to her, and the images were just as useless: egg-shaped pomegranate fruit and arcing plant fronds. These were painted on the stone above the empty graves, each one having long since been relieved of its human remains.

She spun on her heel, the mazelike catacombs offering her no help. She checked the floor, but there were no footprints to lead her in one direction over another. She continued the search, desperate for a clue—when one presented itself to her almost by accident.

"Wait a hot minute," she said, jogging over to one of the empty graves and squatting down beside it.

It was nearly invisible, so neatly had it been cut into the soft volcanic rock, but there in front of her eyes was an ouroboros. She reached out a tentative hand and pressed her finger into the center of the symbol. There was a quiet hiss as some kind of metal clockwork sprang to life—then the ground shifted as a trapdoor opened beneath Daniela's feet and she was plunged down into darkness.

"Where is Weir?"

Daniela sat up, letting the water pour off her like a waterfall. She was dizzy from the long ride down and it took her a minute to catch her breath.

"I don't know," she replied after a moment, her eyes adjusting to the low light as she climbed out of the pool, her shoes squelching with each step.

"We have to go back and get him," Lizbeth said. She, too, was wet, having arrived by the same means, but somehow Lizbeth managed to look presentable while Daniela did not.

She was standing beside an intricately carved wooden doorway. It appeared that once upon a time there'd been a door to go with it—probably carved in the same detailed design—but it had been removed at some point, leaving only the lintel and frame.

"I don't know how you propose to do that," Daniela said, moving to the doorway in order to study what she now realized were ancient runes cut into the wood. "There's no going back the way we came."

The trapdoor had shunted Daniela down a lightless shaft cut into the rock. *This is it,* she'd thought, expecting to fall until her body was smashed into smithereens at the bottom of a deep hole in the ground—but, instead, her ass had slammed into something hard and she'd found herself snaking down the cold, polished surface of a man-made stone slide.

It had looped in circles like an amusement park ride, sending her deeper and deeper beneath the Earth. She'd immediately given over to the feeling of being out of control and after a few minutes, the slide had straightened out and she'd been jettisoned into a pool of warm water.

Where Lizbeth had been waiting.

"I can't leave him here," Lizbeth was saying as she glared at Daniela.

Daniela was too busy studying the runes to pay Lizbeth much attention. She'd seen many of them before and had a vague understanding of what they meant. Besides, as far as she was concerned, the burial chamber where they'd left Lyse and Weir was totally unreachable from the place they were now standing.

"You're not even listening to me," Lizbeth continued, her anger rising.

To Daniela's shock, Lizbeth's control slipped away and she slapped Daniela across the face.

A fiery ache shot through Daniela's body and her eyes rolled back into her head as a wave of red-hot anger slammed into her, knocking her off her feet. Though to outside eyes, it must've looked like she was having one of her normal, empath-related seizures.

This wasn't the case. Lizbeth's emotions were to blame, pummeling Daniela like a fist. Anger, fear, anguish, lust . . . they walloped her until Daniela could barely form a coherent thought—and then something strange happened: The beating stopped and Daniela's soul began to float into the air.

Daniela stood on the portico of the small circular building on the grounds of the Villa Nomentana.

Why am I here? she wondered—and then the answer presented itself to her.

She turned and saw Lizbeth. She was holding hands with an old woman in a long white dress.

"The one you call friend, this 'Lyse' woman?" the old woman was saying. "She is a Judas. She has already betrayed you once and she will do it again before the day is through. Kill her if you can. Stop her from playing her part in their plans."

Lizbeth's eyes were unfocused, her lips slack. She looked like a zombie.

Daniela crossed the portico and touched the old woman's shoulder.

"Francesca? What're you doing to Lizbeth?"

The old woman held tightly to Lizbeth's hands but twisted her neck so she could look back at Daniela.

"What're you doing here?" she asked. "This is no place for you."

"I'm here because she touched me. And now I get to make a few changes in her head."

She grasped Francesca's wrists with her gloved hands and squeezed. The old woman cried out in pain but released her death grip on Lizbeth's hands. Lizbeth opened her eyes and blinked, confused. She opened her mouth to say something to Daniela, but, at that very moment, she disappeared.

"You can't control her anymore," Daniela said. "She's free of you."

Daniela spun Francesca around so they were facing each other.

"Why were you doing that? Saying those things about Lyse?"

Francesca wouldn't meet her eyes.

"It's not true, then. What you told Lizbeth? You lied to her—"

Francesca glared at her.

"That girl . . . she is stealing your place. You were supposed to be The Magician. Not The Fool."

"I don't understand you," Daniela said. "What're you even saying?"

Francesca's shoulders drooped and she sighed, beaten.

"I was left here to give the word to the last Dream Keeper. I was to do that, then tell her to release the others before she began her journey . . ."

She looked down at the ground, unhappy.

". . . but I decided to play with fate. To change things so you were the good daughter instead of the bad . . ."

Before Daniela could decipher what any of this meant—

—she was in an interrogation room.

It was a metal box that contained a metal table with one sad lightbulb hanging above it, bathing the tabletop in a soft yellow spotlight. Desmond Delay sat on one side of the divide, his lion's-head cane propped against his knee. Across from him sat two prisoners, each one wearing a sackcloth over their head—and Daniela wondered how they could breathe. One of the prisoners sat ramrod straight against their seat back; the other was not doing so well, had slumped over in their chair and was looking the worse for wear.

"*I wish it had not come to this,*" *Desmond said, resting his elbows on the smooth, level tabletop.* "*I was hoping you'd see it my way, that you would understand the deeper truth and join us . . . but that was naïve of me.*"

Neither of the prisoners responded to him—and even though Daniela wanted to jump in and stop whatever was happening, she didn't possess a body here in this memory (because that was what she reasoned it was) so she wasn't allowed to move, or speak or breathe. Instead, she was forced to watch silently, and take it all in without comment.

"*Of course, you will join us, just not in the way I had hoped.*"

He turned in his chair, catching the eye of someone standing in the shadows behind him, then swiveled back to face the prisoners.

"*Your powers are very useful to us—as abhorrent as they are— and they will help to bring The Flood into this reality,*" *he continued.* "*Yours is a personal loss to me, Marie-Faith—*"

Daniela didn't hear the rest of Desmond's speech. She was too focused on processing what he'd just said to pay attention.

My mother, *she thought, and reached out with her mind—but neither of the prisoners moved a muscle. It was just a memory.*

Though whose . . . *Daniela couldn't have said.*

Grief poured through Daniela, a pain so raw and alive it threatened to eat her up. All these years Desmond had been a father to her when she had none. When she was small, she'd prayed he would marry her mother and they'd live happily ever after. She'd wanted him to be a part of her family, had often daydreamed that he was—and now if she could've, she'd have happily ripped his head off his neck and fed it to a real lion, and not just the one on the walking stick she'd given him.

Oh my Goddess, *she thought—another, more immediate horror occurring to her: She'd given Desmond information he hadn't had . . . she'd told him that Lizbeth was the last Dream Keeper when he'd so obviously believed that it was Lyse.*

She was mortified. Yes, she'd been tricked into releasing the information, but that didn't make the damage any less severe. She, and she alone, had placed Lizbeth into mortal danger.

"Bear with me, ladies," Desmond was saying as Daniela forced herself to listen in again to the one-sided conversation. *"This will only hurt a bit."*

A man stepped from the shadows, his close-cropped hair as silver as the moon. Daniela recognized the handsome face, with its eerily familiar features, knew how he would move before he even took a step because she'd seen his brand of predatory feline grace before. When he'd shown up to Eleanora's memorial, claiming to be her long-lost son . . . and Lyse's uncle.

"David, please make our guests more comfortable. I want them to understand what is about to happen to them," Desmond said, *a sense of sadness belying the triumph in his words.*

Lyse's uncle circled the table until he was standing behind the prisoners— behind my mother, *Daniela thought, her misery building. He wore a fitted green sweater over olive-drab pants, the thin fabric showing off his muscular body and impeccable posture—but all Daniela could see was the evil emanating from him like a plague.*

He reached for the prisoner who was slumped over, pulling them bodily back against the chair before grabbing a swatch of the fabric and lifting it over their head. The woman slumped forward again, her body slack as a corpse—but Daniela saw she was breathing . . . that she was conscious.

Francesca.

She was older than Marie-Faith, and had always been a grandmother of sorts to Daniela. She'd lived with them when Daniela was little, looking after her while Marie-Faith traveled on Council business. For a long time, Daniela had believed that Francesca *was actually her mother because her real mother had been in such short supply. Of course, all of that changed when Marie-Faith had realized Daniela's empathic talents were destroying her . . . that was when her mother had taken center stage in her life. She'd made her daughter the priority, taking a leave of absence from the Council so that she and Francesca could look*

*after Daniela properly, show her how to protect herself from her powers,
how to use the gloves as a barrier from people.*

*David moved to the other prisoner, grasped the ends of the sack-
cloth, and roughly pulled it over Marie-Faith's head. Her mother
was alert, her brown eyes flashing with rage. She'd fought her capture, that much was apparent. She wore her split lip and black eye
like prizes. The thin gag between her lips had prevented her from
talking before now, but as soon as David untied it and it slipped
from her mouth, a wave of invective poured out of her.*

*"You lousy goddamned son of a bitch," she seethed, her words a
poison wraith. "If I could slip my hands around your throat, I'd
crack your windpipe and watch you die slowly and painfully—"*

*David slammed an elbow into her back and she gasped with the
pain, her body shoved forward against the table by the impact. She took
the blow, unable to defend herself because her hands were bound behind
her back. She gritted her teeth, refusing to cry out, but the tears that
filled her eyes and slipped down her cheeks could not be stopped.*

*"David, please, control yourself," Desmond said, admonishing
the younger man.*

"I apologize, Father. I didn't care for the way she spoke to you."

*But he moved back from Marie-Faith and Francesca, keeping
his distance.*

*"Father . . . ?" Marie-Faith groaned and blanched, the color
swirling away like pigment down a drain. "And who is his mother?"*

Desmond closed his eyes and sighed.

"A youthful dalliance. I believe you know her. Eleanora Eames."

*Marie-Faith's eyes flared and she gathered herself enough to
stare across the table at Desmond.*

"And you never said a word. Not even after all these years . . ."

*She shook her head, unable to wipe away the tears that formed
at the corners of her eyes.*

"It had no bearing on us, Marie-Faith," Desmond replied.

"No bearing? That Daniela had a sibling—"

No, no, no, *Daniela thought.* Not possible.

The scene in front of her froze . . . and then Francesca lifted her

*head. She spoke directly into Daniela's brain—and it was extremely
clear that this was her memory:*

*"Doesn't matter," she whispered, eyes full of fire. "Your mother
wanted you to know, and now I have fulfilled my duty. But it's of
no consequence. Get the Dream Keeper to the sacred Pillar before the
blood moon passes the meridian. I have given her the knowledge of
what to do to pass the word on to the world."*

*Francesca dropped her head again. Marie-Faith and Desmond
and the horrible interrogation room began to fade out and Daniela
was no longer a witness to the past . . .*

Lizbeth was standing over her, her cheeks pale as milk. She
blinked, relief flooding her face as she realized that Daniela
wasn't dead.

"You . . . you weren't breathing," she murmured, all the
cockiness drained out of her. "I . . . I think I hit you. I'm so
sorry . . . I haven't been myself."

Daniela inhaled, and the air filled her lungs, recharging
her brain . . . her *brain*. There was definitely something
wrong with it. One eye was sharp and clear, the other—not
so much. She closed the bad eye and felt a little better, but
the massive headache throbbing behind her temples and at
the base of her skull instantly took over, the pain jackham-
mering itself through her sinuses and into her jaw and teeth.

"Are you okay?" Lizbeth asked, sounding worried.

Daniela sat up and the thrumming ache in her head got
worse. Instinct made her press the heels of her palms into her
temples, hoping to alleviate the pain, but it was a stopgap,
barely stifling the pounding—and now she was feeling nauseated, too.

"*Headache*," she said, and it came out as a whisper. She
wanted to say more, but she just couldn't summon the energy.

All Daniela wanted to do was lie back down and press herself against the rock floor, letting the cold absorb her agony.

"Daniela?" Lizbeth said, kneeling down beside her—though careful not to physically touch her.

Daniela swallowed back a wave of nausea, the edges of her vision tunneling into darkness. She fought the urge to pass out, grabbing hold of reality and desperately trying not to let go.

"*I . . .*" Daniela began, but had to stop in order not to vomit.

"I can't help you," Lizbeth moaned. "I'm scared to get any closer than this to you."

Daniela managed a weak shake of her head.

"*No . . . no closer.*"

She, too, was terrified of what would happen if she were to come into contact with Lizbeth's flesh.

"It's just supposed to be your hands," Lizbeth said, guilt permeating every word. "I didn't know. I really didn't."

Daniela tried to smile at her, to reassure the kid that everything was going to be okay, but it came out as a grimace. Besides, she wasn't sure anything *was* going to be okay. Not after what she'd just learned.

"*I just . . . need to rest,*" Daniela managed to get out before the last of her energy reserve was tapped and she rolled onto her side, eyes closing of their own volition.

When she opened them again, the nausea had passed, and she was on her back, staring up at the rock ceiling. The weird vision quirk was still there, making everything seem slightly fuzzy, but the headache had lessened. Now she felt strong enough to crawl onto her knees and look around.

"You're awake," Lizbeth said, eyes ringed with worry. She was sitting with her knees tucked up under her chin, her back against the rock wall.

"Yup," Daniela murmured, covering her bad left eye with her hand. "My eyes are all messed up."

"I think something burst in your head," Lizbeth said,

unprompted. "I think it was really bad, *is* still really bad. Bad enough to go to a hospital."

Daniela almost laughed out loud, but the balance between functioning and not functioning was too precarious and she didn't want to do anything that would push her over the wrong side of the divide.

"No hospital," Daniela whispered as she slowly dragged herself over to the same wall Lizbeth was seated against. "We have to get you out of here."

"But you're not well—"

"No hospital," Daniela said, interrupting Lizbeth. "Not happening."

Daniela ignored Lizbeth, and, using the rock wall for support, she gingerly began to inch herself up onto her feet. She dug her fingers into the rock face, grasping the craggy stones like handholds, careful not to push too hard, and to treat her body with delicacy. When she was finally standing again, she leaned back against the rock. After a few minutes, her sense of balance—for the most part—had returned and she was able to stay upright on her own.

"You were out for a while," Lizbeth said, climbing to her feet. "I did a little exploring. You were right. There's no way back up the slide."

Daniela wasn't surprised. Glancing at the pool of water in its rocky basin, she knew it had been dug there specifically to stop a person's forward momentum. To have that kind of velocity, you had to be moving pretty fast, and that required a slick surface like the one on the stone slide . . . which meant there was no way in hell they would be able to climb back up without help.

"What's through the doorway?" Daniela asked, careful to stay well clear of Lizbeth.

She didn't trust her enough yet to get within slapping distance. She understood why Lizbeth had gotten upset, but that didn't make the girl's outburst all right.

"You should see for yourself," Lizbeth said, walking over to the rune-encrusted doorway. This left Daniela no option but to follow her. "It's where they keep them . . . *all* of them."

Daniela sighed and trailed after Lizbeth, her energy ebbing even though she was starting to feel better. At least her vision had finally begun to stabilize, the bad eye less fuzzy and out of focus. But now there were these strange neon flashes of light—probably floaters of some kind—that were really annoying.

Ahead of her, Lizbeth slipped through the doorway and disappeared.

"What the hell . . . ?" Daniela murmured. One minute Lizbeth was there and the next she was missing in action. "Lizbeth?"

She heard Lizbeth's disembodied voice coming from the other side of the doorway:

"Come in. It's safe. I promise."

Daniela was not faint of heart. She'd always been fearless, was always ready to jump into the fray and get the shit kicked out of her if necessary. An enchanted doorway did not scare her, but her lack of energy did—she was winded just crossing the small chamber to get to the door's threshold.

"I'm not freaked out about it being safe," she called back to the invisible Lizbeth. "I'm just old and beaten. My body's not really listening to me right now."

She'd never experienced anything like this malaise before, and it was beginning to unsettle her. She was thinking that maybe Lizbeth was right about her going to the hospital.

"Okay, coming through."

She placed her hand on the doorway and felt something instantly come to life beneath the fingertips of her black leather gloves. The runes were not just decoration. The swirling curlicues and angular geometric shapes had been cast for protection. She yanked her hand back, afraid the door would cause something else to go haywire inside her head. Then she realized how stupid she'd just been . . . if the door were going to affect her, it would've already done so with that first touch.

"*Idiot,*" she mumbled to herself—and then she placed her hand back on the doorway and stepped through to the other side.

The room was actually a small alcove hewn from the same volcanic rock as the rest of the catacombs. But it was full of a thousand man-made nooks and crannies, each one containing a small earthenware jar. Over each one was a flickering candle set into a holder in the wall above it. Among them was not a single matching taper; each was a different size, shape, or color . . . and the flames, too, were in a rainbow of hues.

Lizbeth stood in the middle of this magical cavern, eyes lit with excitement. She was looking at Daniela expectantly.

"What?" Daniela asked, having no idea what it was Lizbeth wanted from her.

Lizbeth frowned and clasped her hands in front of her. Daniela could sense the change . . . now it was guilt, not excitement that Lizbeth was feeling. The emotion was so bold Daniela could smell it like an animal musk. She wished she could tell Lizbeth to forget feeling bad, that everything was fine between them—but it would've been a lie. Daniela did not trust Lizbeth fully anymore. Would never be one hundred percent comfortable around the girl ever again.

"You don't hear them?" Lizbeth asked, scrunching her brows together thoughtfully. "Nothing? Not a sound?"

Daniela cocked her head, listening.

"Not a thing," Daniela said, finally, shaking her head. "What is it?"

Lizbeth paused for a moment before speaking. As if she were weighing exactly what to say before answering:

"Dream Keepers. There are so many of them. Each of these jars contains one."

She sighed, listening again to something that Daniela could not hear. Then she laughed softly, a sense of wonderment on her face.

"And they're singing to me. They want us to set them free."

Devandra

evandra thought her mother ought to write a pamphlet
called *I Know Everything about Everything*.

It would make a mint.

No, I'm just being snarky, she thought as she stood over the
antique O'Keefe and Merritt stove in her kitchen, stirring a
large stockpot of chicken soup she'd made to feed her steadily
growing household. *I'm glad she's here and that she and Thomas
seem to know what to do. I just wish she'd give me a little more
responsibility. Making soup wasn't quite what I had in mind.*

While her mother and Thomas went to Arrabelle's house—
with one of the keys Dev kept for emergencies—to collect the
necessary herbs for their "raising of the dead" spell, Dev was
busy holding down the fort. In the only moment not fraught
with drama, Freddy had taken the girls to the L.A. Zoo for the
day. It meant pulling them out of school, but they'd decided it
would be the best way to keep them safe and entertained.

Dev did *not* want them running around the house, asking
questions about why their grandmother, mother, and aunts

were doing crazy magic spells in the backyard. It was bad enough they'd been exposed to Thomas—a man her mother seemed to trust implicitly, even though Dev still had her doubts about him.

Freddy had appeared to like him, too, but that only meant her partner had felt sorry for the guy. Because as kindhearted as Dev was, Freddy was even more of a softie. Everyone thought he was all charm and machismo, but that was just a façade. Inside, he had the gooiest of centers.

She'd once seen him buy twenty bucks' worth of tacos from the taco truck next to the Walgreens and give the food to a homeless old man, who'd wolfed the carnitas tacos down like no one's business. It was in moments like these when Dev was most reminded of why she loved Freddy. Even though he was just as flawed as the next guy, he could always be counted on to try to do the right thing.

The sound of the front doorbell spooked Dev, and she dropped her wooden spoon into the stockpot.

"Darn it," she mumbled, pulling a pair of metal tongs from a drawer and fishing out the spoon.

She set the spoon and the tongs down on the counter and wiped her hands on the floral print apron she wore, then lifted it over her head. She smoothed out her pale yellow skirt and laid the apron over one of the spindle-backed kitchen chairs before hurrying to answer the front door.

"Coming!" she called as she ran through the living room.

She undid the locks and threw the door open to find her sister Darrah standing on the porch smiling up at her. She was wearing a gray trench coat and a stylish beret, her copper-colored hair tucked into a chignon at the back of her neck. She and Dev had the same eyes, but her mouth was thinner and her nose more hawkish. She set her overnight bag down on the ground and the two sisters ran into each other's arms.

Darrah was the nearest of Dev's siblings in age, and this

had made them much closer. Because of their ages, they'd shared a lot of the same experiences—doing their bonding before Daphne and Delilah had even been born. In fact, Darrah had been with Dev the first time she'd met Freddy.

It had been a warm summer night and the two sisters had gone skating at the Starlight Rollerway with a group of friends, neither knowing that it would be an evening both of them would never forget. Dev had met Freddy and Darrah had ended up in the emergency room with a broken ankle, the aftermath of a roller limbo competition gone horribly wrong.

"You look amazing, lovey," Darrah said once they'd broken apart and Darrah had pushed Dev an arm's length away, so she could get a better look at her. "Scrumptious."

Dev grinned, ridiculously happy to see her younger sister.

"You look amazing yourself," Dev replied. "And everyone and everything is good at your house?"

Darrah nodded and followed Dev inside.

"All the kids are well and accounted for."

Like Melisande, she stopped in the front room and inhaled the scent and feeling of the house. But unlike their mother, she didn't comment on what had or hadn't changed. That this was now Dev's home was an implicit understanding between the two sisters; there was no mention of wanting things to remain unchanged. Darrah respected Dev's choices and if she had any criticisms, she kept them to herself.

"There's just something about the old homestead that fills you with a sense of longing," she said, instead. "Not for the house, but for what it represents. For being a Montrose."

Dev nodded in agreement. Her sister was correct. No matter where she went, or how she changed, the old Victorian in Echo Park was the heart and soul of who and what she was at her core. She knew deep down that her mother and all of her sisters felt the same way.

"Is Daphne coming?" Darrah asked, Dev leading them into the kitchen so she could check on the soup.

"She says so. Mom spoke to her earlier. She's supposed to get in to Burbank in a few hours."

Darrah sat down at the kitchen table and Dev saw that her sister looked tired.

"Long flight," Darrah said, catching Dev's worried glance. "I'm fine."

"Mom said you've pulled the same spread . . . ?" Dev launched in without preamble.

"Yeah, I didn't think too much of it at first, but then when I mentioned it to Mom," Darrah said, shaking her head, "she seemed to immediately intuit that it was important."

The back door leading to the mudroom opened and Melisande, hair mussed and complexion ruddy, stepped through into the kitchen, holding a small wicker basket in her arms. Dev heard the back door close and then Thomas was there beside her tiny mother, his hand on her shoulder. He grinned at Dev and then let his eyes drift to Darrah, giving her a small nod.

"This is Thomas. An old friend," Melisande said to Darrah, blushing. "This is my second eldest, Darrah."

"Pleased to meet you. You are as lovely as your mother and sisters." Thomas intoned, reaching out and plucking Darrah's hand from the table in order to kiss it.

Darrah raised an eyebrow at Dev, who shrugged. She would let her sister come to her own conclusions about the stranger.

"We've got the yew and the belladonna," Melisande said, setting the red-cloth-covered basket on the table and patting Darrah's shoulder. "Any word from Daphne?"

"Soon," Dev said.

This seemed to reassure Melisande, and she set about uncovering the basket and placing its contents onto the table. She'd taken a number of corked vials from Arrabelle's large antique apothecary cabinets and a small black iron cauldron. Dev wondered how unhappy Arrabelle would be when she got home to find that her stuff had been unceremoniously rifled through.

"All dangerous stuff, so please be careful, my dears," Melisande said, removing the final item from the basket: a pair of industrial-strength rubber gloves. "Use the gloves. Even a few seconds on the skin would be enough to make you seriously ill."

Dev and Darrah shared a look—they didn't need to be talked to like they were small children. They'd both had experience in these things.

Now I remember why I was so happy my parents decided to buy the Airstream, Dev thought, amused.

"We should get started, Melisande," Thomas said, pushing his hair out of his eyes and then smiling at Dev and Darrah. "Maybe Delilah would join us, as well?"

Dev sighed and turned off the eye of the stove, setting the heavy metal lid on the stockpot.

"I'll get her and we'll meet you outside," Dev said.

"We call those beyond us into being."

The yew was pungent and warm, but so damn toxic they had to burn it outside. Even being near the smoke made Dev uncomfortable—but it was a necessary evil.

Darrah and Delilah had walked widdershins around the Victorian three times, placing black candles along the foundations of the house. Each of the candles—taken from Dev's own stores in the attic—had been dipped up to their wick in pig's blood, an item Dev had gotten at one of the local *carnicerias* on Sunset. The man behind the counter had looked at her funny when she'd asked for a gallon of pig's blood, but he'd obliged her odd request without comment.

She was pretty sure he'd experienced weirder demands.

"We call up all the women of the Montrose line who have passed on . . . we have called up Hessika and Eleanora, two of our blood sisters who have chosen to walk the dreams of humankind . . ."

They stood in a circle around the tall black marble-and-bronze brazier that held the burning yew wood. Rarely was Dev's brazier used for its true purpose—in fact, until that afternoon, it had been a makeshift birdbath that Marji and Ginny liked to decorate with tree branches and sparkly odds and ends they'd found, thinking this helped attract the birds. As Melisande spoke, the fire grew in size and strength—yew was known for the intensity of its burn—and the smoke began to form a straight column that shot up into the air but did not disperse with the wind.

"Take each other's hands," Melisande said, catching each of her daughters' eyes, in turn.

The three of them did as their mother asked. Dev looked at her two sisters, surprised at how strongly they resembled each other.

We truly come from the same place—even if our coloring differs, so many of the features are the same, Dev mused, taking Delilah's fingers in her left hand and Thomas's in her right.

She still wasn't sure about the strange man, but she'd watched him with her mother these past few hours, and there was such tenderness between them, a feeling of connectedness that made Dev feel better about him. He was here, helping them to raise the spirits of their ancestors, and he didn't seem to mind at all that a bunch of women were bossing him around and telling him what to do.

As soon as Melisande took Darrah's hand and closed the circle, the smoke became invisible. At first, Dev thought it was a trick of the light, but then she realized it was truly transparent—and the smell had changed, too. There was a darker, loamier scent in the air and she quickly recognized it for what it was: the stink of the grave.

"It's working, my fair ladies," Thomas murmured, smiling at each of the women. For the first time, Dev began to feel the excitement of what was about to happen. "When they come, and they will come as they did in my world, we will be ready."

"We've done what we can," Melisande said as they released each other's hands.

Dev's palms felt sweaty, and she wiped them on her skirt. She'd been nervous without realizing it and had probably been squeezing everyone's hands way too hard.

"We'll need the girls, though, for everything to work correctly," Thomas said as they turned to go inside.

It was an offhand comment, but Dev froze. No one had said a word about this to her.

She frowned, turning to her mother.

"We need *all* of the Montrose women, Devandra," Melisande said.

Suddenly, the backyard—a place that had always been a safe harbor for Dev—had been desanctified. The floss tree with its magical chandelier of sparkling candlelight that she and Freddy had rigged up one summer morning when she was pregnant with Ginny now seemed malevolent in the darkening afternoon light. The Mucho Man Cave was empty and shuttered, as if nothing light or gay might be hidden inside. Everything had taken on a surreal, sinister quality and Dev wasn't sure if it was the spell at work . . . or if it had come about when Thomas had asked for her daughters.

"I don't want them here, Mom," Dev said. "It's not safe. You didn't see what happened before. What Hessika and Eleanora did to protect them. It was terrifying and he"—she pointed at Thomas—"was the instigator of that. So, I'm sorry if I don't feel comfortable with this . . ."

No one had gone inside. Her sisters were watching the conversation with unease. But when Dev was done speaking, Darrah placed a hand on her arm:

"Dev, if I didn't have boys . . . if my sons were daughters, you know I'd have them here right now."

Darrah was the one person in the world that Dev could not argue with. Darrah had no ulterior motives, no need to manipulate or confuse. If she believed it was important—*necessary even*—for Marji and Ginny to be there, then Dev had to submit to Thomas's will.

"Call Freddy," Darrah said. "Tell him to come home with the girls. It's safer here, anyway. I promise you that Delilah and I will do whatever it takes to protect them."

Dev cast her eyes to Delilah's face and saw that what Darrah said was true. That her sisters would move heaven and earth to make sure her daughters remained unharmed.

"Okay," Dev said. "I'll call him."

"And Daphne will be here soon," Melisande said, smiling at Thomas. "We'll have a full complement then."

As much as she wanted to believe that everything would be all right, her mother's words sent a chill up Dev's spine. With a real sense of disquiet, she took out her phone and texted Freddy, telling him to come home . . . and to bring the girls with him.

The moment she stepped foot into the house, Dev knew that things were very, *very* different. For one thing, the interior of the house was darker than she'd ever seen it—and she realized that there was not just one reality contained inside the Victorian, but many. Electric lights were laid over gas lamps, furniture was in one place, yet if you blinked, it would magically reappear in another spot. The rooms shimmered as different varieties of wallpaper fought for supremacy on the walls, as carpets changed color and patterns when you blinked—and the most surreal part of it all . . . the ghostly images of every Montrose woman who had ever lived in the house were there, lounging around the rooms.

They stared at Dev and her mother and sisters but did not speak. They did not appear to notice Thomas's existence, which Dev appreciated. She was starting to really resent his presence among her family.

"This is amazing," Delilah said, reaching out and trying to

touch one of the living room walls. As soon her fingers made contact, the wall stopped shimmering and the wallpaper from their reality appeared. When she pulled her hand away, the oscillations between the different realities/times began again.

"I guess whatever belongs in our time will stay fixed in place as long as we're in contact with it," Darrah said, and she plopped down on the settee, putting her feet up on the old horsehair ottoman, pinning both pieces of furniture into permanency with her touch.

"Where are Eleanora and Hessika?" Dev asked, searching the room for the two Dream Walkers.

"They're different than the others," Thomas said, shrugging. "We can't see them in this dimension."

Dev frowned.

"Then why did we name them in our spell?" she asked.

Melisande came to stand behind Thomas, her hand instinctively finding his.

"We want them bound to the house, sweetheart. It's the only way we can assure ourselves of their cooperation."

Dev hoped she'd misunderstood.

"They're here to help us, Mom," she said. "We don't need to coerce them or bind them to us."

Melisande brushed Dev's worries aside.

"That's not what I meant," she said. "It's to help us keep everyone safe. That's all."

Dev felt bristly after that, but she didn't want to fight with her mom. They needed to stick together in these dark times. It was imperative that they presented a united front in the face of something as powerful as The Flood—because whatever it sought to do on Earth would not be for the betterment of mankind.

"Maybe we should eat now," Melisande said.

Her mother was right. They'd all been up for hours and none of them had eaten a thing.

"We'll all feel better if we do that," Thomas agreed, looking at Dev.

Dev nodded.

"I guess that's my cue to go ladle out the soup," she said, trying to mask her unhappiness underneath a chipper tone.

"I'll help you," Delilah said, and she followed Dev into the kitchen, where someone, possibly Melisande, had already retrieved a stack of bowls and laid them on the counter.

Dev realized that though the kitchen lights changed back and forth as they shuffled through the different realities, the kitchen itself remained very much the same in each time. Apparently, this room had not often been changed. Only the copper rack hanging from the ceiling above the center of the room appeared and disappeared. But that wasn't so strange, seeing that it was something she and Freddy had added to the space a few years earlier.

"He's a weird guy," Delilah whispered as soon as they were out of earshot. "I know you feel the same way. I can totally see it on your face. You're not buying his schtick, either."

Dev let out a long sigh—she didn't even know she'd been holding her breath. It was a relief that she wasn't alone in her thoughts. That Delilah felt the same way she did about her mother's friend.

"There's something odd about him," Delilah continued. "Do you think we should say something to Mom?"

"Ha," Dev said, and snorted. "She's so in love that she can't see reality at the moment. I don't think either of us saying anything disparaging about him is gonna help our cause."

Dev reached for the lid of the stockpot but paused when she saw that it was a little askew. She turned to Delilah.

"Did you take the top off this pot? To stir it or something?"

Delilah shook her head.

"Do I look like I'd take the top off that thing and stir it?"

Dev had to laugh. Cooking was definitely not Delilah's forte.

"It was probably Mom," Delilah added. "She's gotta be in charge of everything. As usual."

Dev laughed. It was so true. The Montrose women came by their bossiness honestly.

"You speak the truth," Dev said, and she removed the lid and placed it on the counter. She opened the drawer next to the sink and plucked a copper ladle from inside, dishing up the soup as Delilah held out the ceramic bowls to be filled.

"It's nice having us all together under one roof," Delilah said, reaching for another bowl.

"Never thought I'd hear such a sentimental sentence come out of your mouth."

Delilah laughed and set the second bowl down on the counter.

"I've always been in the Montrose shadow, Devandra," she said, and Dev knew her younger sister was speaking seriously now. "I had to get as far away as I could so I wouldn't get lost."

There was a sad truth behind the statement.

"I didn't know that."

Delilah shrugged, as if to say: *How could you?*

"And I probably wouldn't have told you back then, anyway," she replied, shrugging. "Even if you *had* asked."

It's funny how strange times bring out the confidences we should've shared long ago, Dev thought, and put the ladle down. She pushed away from the stove and took her younger sister's wrists, pulling her in close.

"I'm sorry I wasn't there for you more when we were kids," she began, but Delilah shook her head.

"Please, don't," she said, and sighed. "That's not why I said it. For you to pity me. I've made my peace with it and that's that. It's fine."

Dev bit her lip and nodded.

"Okay, yeah. I get it. I'm just . . . glad that you're telling me now. I love you and I don't want us to be so removed from each other anymore."

Delilah smiled.

"I appreciate that. Which is why I wanted to talk to you about something . . ."

She paused.

"Anything."

"I . . ." Delilah's eyes slid to the side—a holdover from when she was a little girl and was too shy to ask for something she really wanted. "I want to come home. Back here with you. I know you'd need to talk to Freddy and—"

"Yes," Dev squealed, interrupting her. "That would be wonderful. I would love it. Freddy would love it. The girls would be beside themselves."

Delilah shook her head, surprise written across her face.

"Really?" she said, eyes narrowing in disbelief. "You're serious."

Dev threw up her hands.

"Of course, I'm serious. It's a done deal. Whatever, whenever you want or need—you're part of the family."

"Okay," her sister said, still looking a little shocked. "If you're sure . . . ?"

"One hundred percent," Dev replied. "We'd love to have you. You can stay in the guest room downstairs. It's perfect."

With that settled, Dev grabbed Delilah in a bear hug and squeezed her tight.

"I'm so excited," she whispered in her sister's ear.

"Me, too," Delilah replied, returning Dev's enthusiasm.

She released her sister from the embrace, having to stop herself from reaching out and stroking Delilah's head as if she were one of her daughters. Delilah, shying away from being mothered by her eldest sister, ducked out of further reach and backstepped over to the round oak table with the yellow damask tablecloth. The tablecloth was another item, along with the copper pot rack and the small appliances on the counter, that kept flickering in and out of existence as it fought for supremacy with a red gingham one and cornflower blue one.

"Shall I set the table, then?" Delilah asked, already reaching toward what used to be the cutlery drawer when this was their mother's kitchen. Dev shook her head.

"Two drawers over and, yes, please."

The sisters worked in harmony, the room shifting in and out of time like a carnival house of mirrors. While Dev ladled the last of the soup into the bowls, Delilah brought them to the table, where she'd already laid out soup spoons and napkins—and both sisters tried to ignore the pinwheel effect of color and patterns going on around them.

"I'll go get them," Delilah said, leaving Dev alone in the kitchen.

As soon as Delilah was gone, Dev's stomach began to rumble. She really hadn't eaten anything all day and she was starving. She picked up the ladle and swallowed a huge mouthful, not caring if she burned her tongue. The soup tasted sweeter than she'd expected, but it was still delicious. *Or maybe that's just my hunger talking,* she thought.

Behind her, Dev could hear the others enter the room and take their places at the table, or, at least, it sounded like that was what was happening. She could've sworn she heard the scraping of chair legs as seats were pushed back from table . . . but when she turned around, there was no one in the room with her.

That's not right, she thought, frowning. *I know I heard something.*

But there was only an empty table staring back at her, its tablecloth shifting from gingham to yellow to blue so quickly that it was hard for her to focus on it. The whirling of the different fabrics abruptly sped up, and as much as she wanted to drag her eyes away from the frenzied cotillion of colors, she could not.

Stop it, she thought. *Stop it.*

She fought whatever force was trying to hijack her brain. Screamed at her body to do as she wished, her world spinning out of control—and with the greatest of effort, she was finally able to drag her eyelids shut.

The darkness she found there was calming after such a riot of color. She relaxed, wanting to stay in this placid place for as long as she could.

Something's wrong, she thought. *You know it. You just have to open your eyes to see what it is.*

The part of her that always did the right thing was trying to make her leave the darkness, but the rest of her was dead set against it.

The girls are coming, she thought. *Open your goddamned eyes!*

The image of Marji and Ginny walking into something bad, something she could've prevented, drove her to listen to the still-rational part of her brain. She opened her eyes:

Everyone was sitting around the kitchen table . . . Eleanora, Hessika, Melisande, Darrah, and Delilah. They were eating her soup and talking together—and not one of them had even looked up to acknowledge her presence.

"Hello?" she said, a little peeved that they were acting like she wasn't even there.

They kept their own company, and it appeared that Dev was not going to be included in the conversation.

"Excuse me? What gives here? Am I invisible—" She stopped talking as she noticed for the first time that there was an empty seat between her sisters. "Oh, is that for me?"

At this, the conversation stopped and they turned as one, finally looking in her direction. Dev screamed when she saw that none of them had eyeballs . . . just gaping black holes where their eyes should've been. She took a step back, wishing she could erase the horror she had seen, and closed her eyes.

When she opened them again, the scene had shifted:

Melisande, Darrah, and Delilah were facedown on the table. The bowls of soup Dev had made were mostly untouched, but it appeared that they'd consumed a few spoonfuls each. Dev began to inch toward the table, holding her breath. When she reached Darrah's chair, she placed her hand on her sister's shoulder and Darrah's head lolled to the side, revealing a blacked tongue protruding from shriveled lips.

Dead.

"No . . ." Dev moaned, clutching her hand to her mouth.

She couldn't believe what she was seeing, didn't want to believe it.

"Mommy?"

She whirled around at the sound of Ginny's voice—but the doorway leading into the kitchen was empty.

"Ginny?" she called out.

"Mama!" Now it was Marji calling out for her.

She spun around, searching for her daughters, but there was only an empty room.

"Devandra, come with us."

She stopped spinning to discover that the scene had changed one more time:

Now Hessika and Eleanora had joined her mother and sisters again, but they were all wearing long black dresses and pointed black hats. Each woman carried a homemade broom in her right hand.

"You look like witches," Dev blurted out before she could help herself.

"We are *witches," Eleanora said. "We're going to ride our brooms to the other side."*

Dev nodded as if she understood what this meant.

"Can I come?" she asked, itching to hold her own broom.

Eleanora shook her head.

"You didn't take enough to join us . . ." She looked at something behind Dev and smiled sadly. ". . . and now Freddy's here to get you."

Dev felt a pair of strong arms encircle her waist and she was being pulled backward, away from the women.

"No!" she cried, not wanting to be parted from them as they hopped onto their broomsticks and were lifted up into the air.

"We love you!" Darrah and Delilah called over their shoulders, their voices melding into one as the five women flew, single file, out of the house and into the darkness of the evening.

"Leave me alone!" Dev yelled at whoever was holding her back, the tightness around her chest making her cough—

"Dev, stop it. It's me."

She opened her eyes and she was outside, lying on her back in the grass. The acrid stink of burning things filled her nostrils and she began to cough wildly, her whole body convulsing.

"Babe, you're okay," Freddy said, and his face loomed over hers.

"My family," she cried, in between gasps of air.

But Freddy's face was stricken.

"It was you. I could only get you." And he began to cry.

Dev wanted to reach out and comfort him, but her own heart was breaking. She pushed herself onto her elbows, found that she was in the across-the-street neighbors' yard, and that her own house—the Victorian that had been in the Montrose family for over a century—was a funeral pyre of burning timber.

"Oh, lord, no . . ." she cried, and she felt Freddy's arms wrap around her shoulders, squeezing her tight.

"I'm so sorry, baby," he whispered in her ear, his voice choked with sobs.

The girls.

It was a whispery voice—one she could not place.

Where are your girls?

Dev pushed Freddy away and climbed to her feet.

"Where are Marji and Ginny?" she almost screamed at Freddy, who looked askance.

"They . . . they're over there with Thomas," Freddy said, pointing behind them.

"No!!" Dev screamed as she followed Freddy's gaze.

Thomas stood underneath their neighbors' weeping willow tree, a hand on each of her daughters' shoulders. Both girls appeared to be asleep on their feet.

No, Dev thought. *He can't have my babies.*

"Don't worry," Thomas called out to Dev and Freddy. "We're just going on a little trip to the dreamlands. They'll be safe there. No one bad will hurt them."

"No!" Dev cried. "You bastard! What have you done?"

"It wasn't me," Thomas said, a look of utter despair on his face. "I would never have hurt your family . . ."

"I'll kill you," Dev screamed, and ran toward him—but Thomas snapped his fingers and the three of them disappeared right before her eyes.

Dev fell to her knees, a scream of anguish filling her ears . . . and it took her a moment to understand that the sound was coming from her own mouth.

Lizbeth

They wanted to be free. They were singing, begging Lizbeth to let them return to the world and become one with her so that she might spread *the word*. The word that magic was real and that the witches were coming to take their due.

There were so many different voices and timbres and tones all playing at the same time; it was like listening to a symphony without a conductor: all cacophony and discord. She tried to separate them out, but it was a near impossible task. Instead, she turned to Daniela, her eyes pleading for help.

"They need us to let them go."

Daniela, who'd looked like death warmed over, leaned against the doorway, eyes wide with curiosity despite her utter exhaustion.

"We should leave them alone. They're obviously here like this for a reason . . ." Her voice trailed off.

"They've been trapped here. Someone wanted them hidden away, so that their magic couldn't be recycled back into the world in death."

She closed her eyes and rested her forehead on the rock wall.

Lizbeth had hurt Daniela terribly—and she had this strange idea she'd done the same thing to Lyse . . . if only she could remember. But large chunks of her memory were missing.

"You have the weirdest look on your face," Daniela said, her eyes open again. "What were you just thinking?"

It was apparent from her concerned expression that she'd been staring at Lizbeth for a while and Lizbeth had been oblivious.

"Nothing. Just that we have to free them," she said, indicating the vials surrounding them. "They're here against their will. So many Dream Keepers. Trapped to prevent them from continuing on to the next phase of their soul's journey."

Daniela's face brightened and she looked more alive than she had in the last few hours, restored by the energy from whatever realization she'd just had.

"They're here to stop the transmigration of their souls. I bet it's why no more Dream Keepers are being born, because their energy is trapped here on Earth. It knocks things out of balance on a cosmic level."

"But—" Lizbeth began.

"No *but*s," Daniela replied, grinning like a starving hyena about to eat its very first good meal in days. "These guys have been here for a long time. We need to let them go."

She reached out and grabbed the vial closest to her. Lizbeth expected her to uncork it, but instead, Daniela smashed it to the ground.

"Yes!" Daniela cried, as a cloud of pure green energy burst from the broken vial and shot toward Lizbeth, slamming into her chest. Lizbeth felt no pain when it happened, but one of the singing voices got louder than the others for a moment before slowly fading away.

She smiled—the soul's parting song had been a beautiful one.

"It worked," Lizbeth said, nodding her head in excitement. "It rejoiced. I heard it."

"It's inside you," Daniela said, her voice full of wonderment.

"Yes, they are going with me to help me spread *the word.* After that, they will be free."

"Then what the hell are we waiting for?" Daniela asked, plucking another vial from its nook in the wall. "Let's set these babies free."

And, together, the two of them began the arduous task of setting the Dream Keepers free. They worked in tandem, grabbing handfuls of the vials and smashing them to the ground, working until there wasn't a single one left.

Lizbeth saw Daniela pluck a slender pink vial from one of the last crevices and slyly slip it into her pocket. She assumed the vial contained the last essence of Marie-Faith Altonelli, Daniela's mother, and so she held her tongue.

The sense of purpose that had infused Daniela while they were destroying the vials had all but left her now. Her face was wan and her neon-hued hair hung limply around her cheeks. Lizbeth also noticed that her friend's right eye was dilated, making her features appear asymmetrical.

"Are you sure you should be walking?" Lizbeth asked.

They'd searched the room that held the vials—actually Lizbeth had searched and Daniela had rested—but they'd found no means of escaping the underground prison. Finally, in a moment of frustration, Lizbeth had slammed her fist down on one of the outcroppings of rock, and, without warning, the wooden doorframe began to glow.

"The runes," Daniela said, letting out a long sigh. "I'm an idiot."

She crawled to her feet and ran her hands along the glowing symbols, pressing one here and another there.

"What're you doing?" Lizbeth asked.

Daniela turned her head and smiled back at her, continuing to press on the glowing runes.

"Well, unlike Arrabelle, I don't read runes well enough to write a sentence, so I'm just gonna keep pressing on these guys until something happens."

As if the Goddess had heard her words, there was a sharp *click* and then the back wall of the room slid open like a gaping maw.

"Wow," Lizbeth said, her mouth falling open in shock.

"You can say that again," Daniela murmured, pleased as punch.

They hadn't needed to be encouraged further to follow the gentle upward slope of the dimly lit corridor.

They were in luck. Someone had been there recently, lighting the white tallow candles inside the medieval, black iron candleholders placed intermittently along the walls. In this half-light, Lizbeth could see Daniela flagging, could sense the high amount of energy she was exerting just to put one foot in front of the other. It would be a miracle if they got topside before Daniela collapsed.

"How much farther?" Daniela asked, the physical strain of walking uphill taking her breath away.

"I don't know," Lizbeth said. "But it can't be too terribly far. At least, I hope—"

Lizbeth heard a low wheezing gurgle and then the sound of Daniela's body hitting the ground. She didn't need to turn around to know what had happened: Daniela had fainted. She retraced her footsteps, surprised to discover how far behind her Daniela had fallen as they'd been walking.

"Dammit," Lizbeth said as she knelt down beside Daniela's unconscious body.

She didn't know what to do. She was terrified to touch her friend but even more terrified not to help her. Lizbeth had the worst feeling that if she left Daniela in this corridor, she would die—and there was no way in hell she was letting that happen.

Lizbeth sat down on the rough rock floor, her long legs

aching from too much physical exertion. She was exhausted and too confused to know what the best course of action should be.

"Well, it's either utterly destroy you, or save your life," Lizbeth said out loud—though she knew Daniela could not hear her.

She climbed to her feet and took a deep breath. Fear coursed through her body like adrenaline. For the first time ever, Lizbeth was glad she was tall. Her height and weight were the only things that made what she was about to do even possible.

I'm sorry, Daniela.

She squatted down beside her friend and rolled her over onto her stomach, then hooked her hands underneath Daniela's armpits. With a tremendous grunt, she lifted the smaller woman onto her feet.

"You sure weigh a lot for being so small," Lizbeth said, gritting her teeth as she took another deep breath and, using all of her strength, hoisted her friend up and over her shoulder.

She exhaled loudly, her thighs burning, as she raised herself to a standing position, holding Daniela in a modified fireman's carry. She felt the world tip to the side, all the blood rushing from her head to her feet, but she fought the urge to pass out. After a few seconds, the vertigo eased and she was able to think clearly again.

Time to get us out of here, she thought, and with the heavy burden of her friend's life in her hands, Lizbeth headed out into an uncertain world.

They'd been nearer to the end of the corridor than she'd realized and, after about ten more minutes of walking, they'd emerged from semidarkness into the bowels of a defunct fountain that had been built over one of the many exits from the catacombs. She'd hefted Daniela through the small trapdoor in the bottom of the fountain and then pulled herself through—to the consternation of an elderly gardener who had pointed his rake at Lizbeth and hissed a stream of Italian invective at her.

She'd ignored him, sliding Daniela's unconscious body back over her shoulder, and carrying her friend through the villa's gardens while a handful of tourists stared after them. She didn't stop to try to find Weir—cursing her idiocy for being too timid to own a cell phone. She promised herself she would find her brother later. But she knew he was smart and tough and that he could take care of himself.

At the entrance to the gardens, she somehow flagged down a taxi, scaring the man half to death with her wild shouting for a "*hospitali*"—because she had no idea how you actually pronounced the Italian word for *hospital*. He'd seemed to understand what she'd wanted and had driven accordingly. Luckily, she had some euros in her pocket and was able to pay the man his fare when they got to the hospital entrance.

With a frown, the nut-brown man waved away her cash and instead helped her carry Daniela through the sliding glass doors and into the waiting arms of a cadre of stone-faced nurses and doctors. They'd put Daniela on a gurney and taken her away, leaving Lizbeth alone in the middle of the whitewashed hall.

The taxicab driver was still there waiting by the entrance when Lizbeth stumbled back out of the hospital. She looked up at him.

"ATM," she asked, pleased that now she'd finally be able to tell Weir she'd used a cash machine without freaking out. "And then to the airport after, please."

She held up her arms, letting them tip up and down as she tried to simulate the wings of an airplane. The driver nodded, once again seeming to understand what she wanted, and opened the back door for her. He seemed entranced by her presence, almost unwilling to let her out of his sight. She smiled at him and he blushed, removing his cap in a gesture of respect.

"Thank you," she said, and slid into the car, the door closing softly behind her. The vinyl was warm to the touch as she settled into her seat. She closed her eyes, exhaustion settling over her like a shroud. She let her thoughts drift as they drove away from the hospital, her mind flying over many miles to a far-off locale in the middle of the former Soviet Union. A place called the Republic of Georgia. Here, there rose a towering pillar of red rock hewn from the guts of the Earth itself. This was part of the information Francesca had burned into her brain back at the villa in Rome. This, she knew, was where she would fulfill her destiny and spread *the word*.

She just needed to get there.

Unbeknownst to her, a long black limousine followed closely behind the taxi, marking her every move.

When her flight from Rome arrived at the Tbilisi Airport in Georgia, she was surprised at how modern everything looked. She didn't know what she'd expected, exactly, but this was a welcome surprise. She made her way through the crowd going to collect their baggage and headed for the exit. She'd barely made it through the sliding glass doors when a woman approached her, grasping at her wrist. Not with any aggression, just wanting to get Lizbeth's attention.

"We've been waiting for you," the woman said, smiling up at Lizbeth. Her British accent was tinged with South London. She was a head shorter than Lizbeth and had a frosted blond pageboy underneath a fedora and the kind of soft, white skin that smelled of talcum powder. "Few of us who received the word from Marie-Faith a long while ago, that is. We knew when you'd be coming and so we've been waiting and watching the airports and bus stations here these last few weeks. Hoping we'd be the ones to find you first."

Lizbeth let the woman pull her away from the crowd and lead her over to a small red Ford minibus that was idling nearby. She could see that inside the minibus were more ladies kitted out against the blustery October night in light beige trench coats and dark sweaters. Lizbeth almost laughed when she saw they were *all* wearing fedoras.

It's as if they think they're in a spy novel, Lizbeth thought—but instead she said:

"How did you know who to look for?"

"Your aura. Could see it a mile away," the woman leading her said, smiling again to reveal yellow smoker's teeth. "We all could. Now come along, you. It's only getting colder and darker—and the blood moon won't wait for no one."

She stopped midstride and held out her hand.

"Sorry, that's rude of me. I'm Patsy Louise Kendrick"—Lizbeth couldn't help but shake Patsy's hand—"and that there's a minibus full of my Slough coven."

So Lizbeth had gotten into the little red minibus full of very chatty British women. They'd used the whole two-hour-forty-eight-minute ride to regale her with stories of how much Slough was changing, and how one day soon it might be a part of London proper instead of a less desirable suburb. As they talked, Lizbeth let her gaze stray to the minibus window. It was so dark out that she had a hard time seeing the landscape as it passed her by, but here and there she could make out quaint little villages, isolated houses and farms, and long stretches of empty green.

"Marie-Faith let a few of us trusted ones know that you existed. We knew you were American, but not which part of the country or who was taking care of you."

This was Pernilla, a short bulldog of a woman in her late fifties who smelled of crushed mugwort—which Lizbeth took to mean that she was the coven's herbalist. She was sitting closest to Lizbeth, and the brim of her fedora had made it difficult for her to see Lizbeth as she talked, so she'd taken it off and set it on her lap.

"We aren't the only ones," Pernilla continued, caressing the top of the fedora as if she were petting a cat. "There are others out there and we will all be waiting below for you, a line of blood sisters there to lend to you whatever powers we possess."

Lizbeth was grateful for these women, out of their element, scared and uncertain just like she was—but still they'd come for her, come to be a part of something bigger than themselves.

Lizbeth stared up at the towering monolith of rock, the sky a tumultuous dark cloud that seemed hell-bent on spilling rain. It would make the climb she was about to attempt even more arduous.

She was scared and alone—though there was a ring of power waiting beneath her if she only called for it—but she tried to ignore the fear gnawing at the pit of her stomach. The others were with her in her heart . . . and they were thinking of her. Sending their love to her in these dark hours. She could feel it. She didn't know where exactly they were, but she knew that she had to keep moving forward or everything they'd sacrificed would be in vain.

She couldn't think of her blood sisters without tears filling her eyes. She felt no different than the great storm cloud above her, and then, as if Mother Nature could feel her pain, the clouds split open and delicate drops of rain fell upon her.

She is crying with me, Lizbeth thought. *Of course Mother Nature knows what it means to mourn alone and she can't bear to watch.*

She stopped thinking, stopped letting the fear take over, stopped feeling alone . . . because she wasn't anymore. Something greater than her, something elemental, was at her side, had been given as a gift by Francesca and Marie-Faith. The power of all the Dream Keepers, even the ones she and Daniela had rescued, was inside her.

She grabbed the first rung of the ladder and began to pull herself up the sheer rock face. Her palms and fingers hurt as she looped them around the wood. The higher she climbed, the more her skin began to blister, becoming raw and bloody, the flesh burning.

For some reason, she decided she wouldn't shed another tear—and she let the rainwater, which was now more of a downpour than a trickle, wash them away. She felt exhausted by her task. The sheer physical effort needed to climb the hundred-and-fifty-foot ladder was daunting. She wasn't small and compact; she was large and ungainly, and she was carrying all the height and weight of a giant's body with her as she climbed.

Her heart beat harder the farther she ascended, and her breathing came in ragged huffs that made her chest hurt. She was soaked, the rainwater plastering her russet hair to her face and scalp. She was forced to pause every few feet to push the wet strands out of her eyes, and the green leather jacket she'd bought at the airport did nothing to stop the deluge of rain from chilling her to the bone. Her sweater and jeans were soaked, and the thick woolen socks inside her hiking boots (another airport purchase) squelched with every rung higher she climbed.

I should find this view spectacular, she thought as a few rays of light broke through the clouds, illuminating the mountains that surrounded her. *I'm not afraid of heights. I should pause and take it all in. I may never be in this place again.*

She wished she were just a tourist, that she *could* stop, but every second counted. She had to reach the top of the rock pillar, had to be standing by the base of this celestial lightning rod when the blood moon crossed its meridian. Only then could *the word* reach the rest of the world; only then could The Flood be stopped.

So onward she climbed, letting the rain lash her skin like a cat-o'-nine-tails. She ignored the breathtaking views of the luxuriant green mountains that surrounded the Rock of Astarte. Kept her eyes on each successive rung as she scaled the tall wooden ladder by nothing more than sheer dint of will.

She imagined a village of women cutting and stripping the wooden boughs of a great birch tree, lashing together the rungs and side rails with hand-woven rope. She felt their energy, their strength flooding into her, urging her upward even as exhaustion made the task seem impossible.

She was halfway up the ladder when her right hand grasped a broken rung, and it snapped in half. Her arm flew away from the ladder, her hand still wrapped around the now useless piece of wood. The other half of the rung fell away from the rock face and disappeared into the darkness, cracking against the pillar as it fell to Earth. She stared at her hand, at the piece of ruined wood, and then instinct kicked in and she dropped it, letting it join its other half on the long descent to the ground.

She still possessed a good grip with her left hand, but the muscles were starting to shake. She looked upward, saw that the next unbroken rung was within her grasp, and reached out her right hand, her whole body stretching as she tried to catch hold of it. Her raw hands protested, but then her fingers slipped around the solid wooden rung, and she choked back a sob of relief.

She thought back to the Slough coven as she thrust her arms forward again, grasping onto the next unbroken rung and the next and the next, pulling herself up into the clouds.

She reached the edge of the cliff and used a rope handhold to drag her body up and over the side, where she lay panting on the ground, exhaustion flooding through her body and begging her to stop. If she thought she'd been tired before, this added a whole new level of fatigue to her repertoire. She closed her eyes, letting the cold air fill her nose and lungs, and then she opened them again, slowly, wishing she were back in her own bed in Echo Park.

She rolled over on her stomach and crawled to her feet, ignoring the cold and wet as it blew against her, peppering her face with condensation. She looked around and saw a lone church at the edge of the rock. It was a Gothic structure made of red stone and it looked menacing in the darkness—but it wasn't why she was here. Something else that lived atop this rock was her goal, and she needed to find it before the blood moon reached the meridian and revealed itself.

Only then could it be seen.

And only for five minutes.

This was her tiny window, and if she missed it, all would be lost.

She walked across the rock island, which to her resembled a magical castle in the sky surrounded by a moat of cloudy gray, and easily found the set of standing stones she'd been looking for. There were five of them embedded in the Earth, each signifying one of the blood sisters' five magical powers. In the middle of the ring of stones was a small depression in the ground, and this was where she was supposed to be standing when the blood moon crossed the meridian.

This was where everything that Francesca had poured inside her would finally be released.

She walked over to the stones, marveling at how small they were—barely reaching her thighs—and then stepped in between them. She threw her head back and looked up at the sky, the wind buffeting against her.

That was when she heard the sound of a helicopter approaching.

Lyse

Time was a sieve and the hours of Lyse's life poured through it as slowly as blackstrap molasses drizzled from a spoon. Hours of trying to extract herself from a very bad situation had, at least, whiled away some of the time she'd been trapped inside the sterile metal room. Treated like an animal, caged and alone, she'd felt her anger swelling to a fever pitch. But then it had ebbed away as she'd tried—and failed—to free her arms from their bindings, getting nothing but raw and bloody wrists and a massive headache for her troubles.

When she was focused on something, Lyse worked with a single-mindedness that was unsettling. All she could see was the task at hand. But now she was done trying to get away—exhaustion clogged her brain and made it impossible to focus. Instead, she stared at the unblinking glow of the overhead bulb and the long shadows it cast along the sharp edges of the metal table in front of her.

There was so much information to parse through; so many things had happened in the last forty-eight hours that she felt overwhelmed. She worried about Daniela and Lizbeth, about Dev and the girls left alone in Echo Park . . . and she had no idea where Arrabelle was—hopefully out bringing others to their side in case everything else failed. And then there *she* was, trapped in an interrogation room, alone with her thoughts . . . thoughts she didn't want to deal with.

Weir.

No, she wouldn't go there. *Couldn't* go there.

She heard the sound of a latch being undone, and then the heavy door slid open. It was a welcome distraction from the misery of her thoughts.

She looked up, eyes searching the darkness for her visitor. It was the mutilated woman. The one who'd brought her water. Only now she carried a tray laden with food: baked salmon, a salad, steamed green beans, and coffee.

Obviously they didn't want to starve her to death . . . they were just putting her on a diet.

Her first inclination was to refuse the food, to tell the woman to throw it all away, that she wouldn't eat it. But now that they were finally deigning to bring her something, she found herself ravenous—making it difficult to refuse the food on principle alone.

Her stomach growled.

"I wish I could tell you to take the food and shove it," Lyse said, eyeing the pink salmon, her mouth watering.

—*Eat. You're starving.*

The woman's voice came into her head, unbidden. The same telepathy as before. But she was right. Lyse had no idea how long it had been since she last ate. The only meal she could remember eating was a sandwich she'd shared with Daniela in Rome before they'd gone into the catacombs. The panini was a mere memory, and she'd been running on its fumes for God knew how long.

The woman set the tray down on the table in front of Lyse, and without thinking, Lyse reached for the utensils. She grimaced in pain as the restraints caught her wrists, trapping her to the chair. The woman's scarred face didn't register any emotion as she reached into the pocket of her black dress and extracted a key.

—I can only undo one hand.

Lyse gave an almost imperceptible nod that she understood.

—They are watching you. Just so you know.

The young woman looked up into the shadows with her one good eye.

—A camera behind you and one directly in front.

Lyse started to follow the woman's gaze, but the woman frowned.

—Don't look. They have no idea that we can communicate. You'll give me away.

Keeping her face neutral, the woman undid the handcuff encircling Lyse's right hand.

"I'm a lefty. I make a mess with my right."

The woman nodded and returned Lyse's right hand to its binding before reaching for the other wrist.

"Thanks," Lyse said, shaking out her left hand. She rolled her wrist back and forth, trying to get some circulation into her fingers before picking up the plastic fork where it lay on the tray in front of her.

The woman bowed her head as if to say *You're welcome*, then moved toward the exit, disappearing into the shadows.

But not before Lyse heard these words:

—We will help you.

Lyse held the fork in her hand, but the sound of the door sliding closed behind the woman almost took her appetite away.

You're gonna need the energy before this night is through, she thought. *Damn, I don't even know if it* is *night anymore.*

She attacked the food. She was so hungry that she couldn't stop herself from shoveling it in. She ate fast, barely tasting what was going into her mouth, but at least her stomach wasn't growling anymore.

Finished, she pushed the plate away—and that was when she noticed what the woman had done. The metal restraint around Lyse's right wrist was now loose enough that she could easily slip her hand out of it. Not wanting to give anything away, she rested her head on the tabletop and pressed her cheek into the cold metal. Closing her eyes, she was able to hide her excitement, the nervous glee she felt as a wave of adrenaline surged through her.

I have one chance. One try to get it right and that's it—so what the hell's my plan?

She opened her eyes and lifted her head, running the possibilities through her mind. Her hands were free, but there were at least two cameras and a metal door to get through before she could attain her freedom. Her eyes fixed on the naked overhead bulb, the only light in the room, and she knew then what she had to do.

Have a little faith, she thought, and slipped her right hand out of its shackle.

She jumped up on the metal chair and punched the bulb out with her bare left fist, the glass shattering in a shower of orange sparks.

Holy shit, she thought as darkness blanketed the room, and her hand throbbed where tiny pieces of glass stuck into her skin.

She brushed the back of her hand against her jeans and jumped off the chair, the food tray clattering to the floor. It was dark as night in the room, but she had a general idea of the layout and a good idea of where the door might be. She placed her fingertips on top of the metal table to orient herself, then took a tentative step to the side. Once she gave over to the idea that she was going to slam into a few immovable objects on her way to the door, she progressed quickly.

"Damn," she mumbled, tears of pain springing to her eyes. Whatever she'd just run into was sharp and metal, and now her left shin ached. Another leg wound to add to her growing collection.

She did her best to ignore the pain, and after a few failed attempts—her fingers finding empty air where she'd expected metal—she finally located one of the walls, using it to guide herself toward the door. Sliding the tips of her fingers along the metal surface of the wall was like touching an iceberg; the cold was so intense it burned.

Just a little farther, she thought—and then her fingers stumbled across the long perpendicular doorframe and she almost shouted with joy. She stayed put, one hand on the frame, the other fumbling around for the latch. But after a few seconds when she still hadn't found anything, she started to get nervous. It had only been a few minutes in the dark, but it felt like forever.

Behind her, Lyse heard a strange scratching sound, like long nails on a chalkboard, or, more likely, long nails on a metal wall. The hair on the back of her neck rose to attention and she began to sweat, the salty liquid pouring out from underneath her arms and drenching the pits of the red flannel shirt she was wearing.

Ignore it. Whatever it is doesn't matter. You need to get out of this fucking room, she thought, but fear had ratcheted up her nerves to the point where she'd begun to shake.

She let go of the doorframe, blindly inching her way along the wall until she found the opposite side of the door. She ran her hands up and down the cold metal surface, searching for the door latch, but there was still nothing.

She moaned under her breath as she felt something come up behind her. She let out a soft whimper as the scent of rose petals wafted underneath her nose and the moist heat from a living creature's breath tickled the nape of her neck. The scratching sound came again, much closer now—almost inside her head—and the claustrophobia she felt was enough to make a sane person go crazy. To be trapped alone in a dark room with a monster was every human being's nightmare. One shared by the collective unconscious of humanity.

"Go away," Lyse murmured, her tongue moving of its own volition.

Whatever the creature was, it could understand her words. She heard a guttural chuckle, but one that sounded as though it had been run backward through a blender and stuffed into a pig's throat. It made Lyse's skin crawl, and now she really couldn't stop shaking.

Something heavy touched her shoulder—*a cloven hoof, possibly,* Lyse thought as the image of a giant minotaur penetrated her brain—and she shuddered.

"Please," she whispered.

The hoof, if that was even what it was, dug into her shoulder, cutting the flesh. She couldn't see it, but she could taste the salty scent of iron as blood poured down her sleeve. She redoubled her efforts, her fingers scrambling to find the door latch, but without success. The beast removed its hoof from her shoulder, and the pain lessened. She slid away from where she thought the creature was and dropped down to a squat, her back pressed against the wall.

She felt something digging into the small of her back, and her first instinct was to crawl away from it as fast as possible, but she stopped herself. She swallowed her fear and slipped her hand behind her back. Her fingers found the offending object and she almost laughed out loud: It was the stupid door latch.

She depressed it and pushed with all her might, but nothing happened.

She wanted to cry.

Then she realized she was trying to open the door the wrong way. She changed tactics, sliding the door instead of pushing it, and it rolled to the right with a gentle squeak.

Lyse crawled through the crack in the doorway. As soon as she was on the other side, she quickly slid the door back into place, the lock catching with a *click.* She pressed her ear to the metal, but she couldn't hear anything coming from the other side.

She squinted, eyes adjusting to the meager light as she checked out her shoulder, expecting to find blood everywhere.

"No way," she said, pushing the flannel fabric around, looking for tears.

She could find nothing. No blood, no rips in the material of her shirt. The lack of a wound was unsettling. Especially when she'd so clearly felt something tearing into her skin.

She took a minute to check her surroundings, eyes running down the length of the gray concrete hallway. She noted the closed metal doors that were spaced out evenly on both sides of the walls and wondered where they led. She had no idea where she was, or where the hallway would take her once she started walking, but she knew that she needed to get moving, or risk being caught and thrown back into that awful room with whatever the hell monster she'd left in there.

Time to go, she thought, and climbed to her feet.

She decided to head north—a smart choice, as it turned out, because a few moments later she heard the sound of footsteps coming from behind her. Fear licked at her insides as she sped up, the soles of her sneakers making a soft *shushing* sound as she ran, the sound echoing down the hall.

She tried to open a couple of the doors, stopping just long enough to discover that they were locked from the inside before moving on. The light got murkier the farther down the hall she got, but this ceased to be a problem as her eyes began to adjust.

She felt like she was going nowhere fast. Every step she took just led her farther down a seemingly endless hallway. She was starting to get worried. Would she ever find her way out of there?

Without warning, she passed two doorways directly across from each, both of them standing wide open. She stopped in her tracks and doubled back so that she could see where they led: One opened onto another, smaller interrogation room. The other was the entrance to a long hallway very similar to where she already was, but more brightly lit.

She stood there feeling indecisive, not sure which path to take. Continue going down the first hall, or try the new direction that had been presented to her?

Behind her, Lyse heard the faraway echo of feet drumming on concrete.

She had to make a choice.

"Eleanora?" she whispered. "What do I do?"

She felt a hot tear slide down her cheek and wiped it away with the back of her hand. She was exhausted and scared and she wanted to go home—back to Georgia and a time before Eleanora was sick.

She closed her eyes, slowing the trickle of tears.

"Dammit," she moaned, and slammed her fist into the concrete wall, putting all her frustration into it.

The release she felt was unbelievable. She felt so much better, despite the fact that her left hand now hurt like hell.

"Sorry," she whispered to her damaged knuckles, watching blood pool inside the abraded skin.

A rivulet of bright red slid down her wrist and fell onto the floor. She stared down at it, surprised by how black it looked in the low light. She couldn't have said why, but for some reason she felt compelled to kneel down and examine it in more detail.

"What the hell," she said, as the blood drop began to quiver.

She got even closer, watching it shimmy on the concrete floor. She was fascinated by the droplet's strange behavior. She'd never seen anything like it before . . . and then, without any warning, the blood drop began to roll down the hall.

Lyse opened her mouth, but no words came out. Instead, the corridor was filled with the mind-numbing scream of a high-pitched alarm.

Someone must've engaged the emergency warning system for the building, she thought as an army of rotating red lights flashed on and off, up and down the corridor.

Lyse climbed to her feet, still not sure which way to go.

Screw it, she thought, and began to follow the blood, curious to see where it would lead her.

There was no real illumination now. Even the meager overhead lighting was gone; just the intermittent flash from the emergency lights was all she had to show her the way. But it was enough for Lyse to keep an eye on her guide . . . the droplet of blood.

It's in the blood.

She had no idea where the phrase had come from. Yet there it was in her head. It sounded familiar, as though she'd heard it before.

What's *in the blood?* she wondered.

The alarm siren was pervasive, a trilling whine that rose and lowered in pitch, the pattern repeating again and again, and she'd had to cover her ears with her hands or risk going deaf.

She'd gotten a smear of blood on her cheek for her trouble and had unsuccessfully tried to wipe it away with the tail of her flannel shirt. This had only made it worse. She'd given up, hoping there weren't any more monsters in the hallway to drool over the scent of her blood.

Eardrums protected by her palms, she continued down the corridor, following the blood droplet through the first hallway. She was glad she hadn't had to make the choice herself. Glad the blood had decided which direction to go, which hallway would be her fate.

As much as she racked her brain, she'd never seen blood behave in such an odd way. The closest she could come was that once in middle school, when they'd studied the periodic table, her Earth/space science teacher had shown the class a droplet of pure mercury. It had caught Lyse's attention because it was so pretty. A metallic silver, it reflected your face back at you when you looked into it, and rolled around the surface of its container, always returning to its original shape no matter how the teacher manipulated it.

The blood reminded her of that mercury.

She watched it slide and curl around itself as it rolled down the length of the hall, moving with a graceful fluidity. It was as if it were being pulled toward something greater than itself. It made Lyse wonder if she was in the bowels of a particle collider whose giant magnets were attracting the iron in it.

Not that there was enough iron in her blood for any magnet to catch hold of—even the big ones in a particle collider.

Maybe she was in an underground lab buried deep beneath the deserts of Los Alamos, or in some kind of top-secret military base right out of a twisted, wannabe *Dr. Strangelove* remake.

It's in the blood. It's in the blood. It's in the blood.

That phrase again. A persistent whisper repeated in a voice she didn't recognize.

Lost in her head, Lyse had to pull up short when the hallway came to an abrupt end in front of a large hangar door. She'd been so focused on following the little droplet that she hadn't realized the corridor had changed its shape, the floor dropping away from the ceiling and the side walls expanding until it was now big enough to drive a jeep through.

It was colder here, too, which made Lyse suspect she was being led even farther underground. She was pretty sure a facility like this one, with its myriad locked doors, strange layout, and emergency alarm system, would not be mappable by the likes of Google Earth.

The hydraulic hangar door blocked the droplet's path, and the poor thing was vibrating like crazy as it tried to find a way through the door to the other side. Lyse knelt down and touched the ground in front of the door, her fingers coming away coated with dirt.

Only the dirt didn't feel right.

No, it was darker and smoother than normal dirt—and Lyse understood then that it was ash.

She stood up and swiftly began to wipe her hand on her pants, something cold snaking through her heart. She didn't want to know where the ash had come from. She didn't want it on her fingers, or sticking to the bottom of her sneakers.

The incessant screeching of the alarm seemed to have lessened, or Lyse had gotten used to it—she didn't know which—but she felt more cognizant now, more awake and functioning. She began to search for a way to open the hangar door and quickly discovered a large yellow button built into the wall beside it.

Here goes nothing, she thought, and depressed the button, hoping it wouldn't alert someone to her presence.

Pale golden light trickled across Lyse's feet, expanding up the length of her body as the door rolled into itself, leaving everything on the other side of it illuminated. Lyse gasped as she saw what lay before her.

The droplet of blood—which didn't seem to care what was inside the new space—shot forward, crossing the threshold and resuming its journey onward.

Lyse

❧

Lyse blinked as her eyes tried to adjust to the bright white light, but it was like being thrust into another universe after all that darkness. The scream of the alarm system faded away behind her as the heavy hangar door rolled back into place, basically trapping her inside this new environment. Even as she was grateful to have made her escape from the people pursuing her, Lyse's brain began to fully process what she was seeing, and she began to feel a pit of fear opening up in her stomach.

It's a laboratory, Lyse thought as she took a step away from the interior of the massive room, the cold metal of the hangar door pressing into the small of her back. *But it's* wrong. *Something is very wrong here.*

Cages lined the walls as far as the eye could see, but inside them weren't lab rats or chimpanzees or dogs. No, these heavy-duty steel cages were filled with human beings. Some sat listlessly in puddles of their own excrement; others were curled up in the fetal position, their limbs pressed against the bars of their cages. They wore hospital smocks that barely covered their nakedness, their heads shaved down to fuzzy stubble.

To her horror, Lyse realized that all of them were female.

Whereas the human element was soiled and unkempt, the rest of the lab was pristine: a state-of-the-art medical facility with various apparatus that Lyse could barely describe, let alone understand what they were for or how they worked. There were stand-alone, concrete block rooms built within the lab, each with a long observation window cut into its side, so that someone could monitor what was happening in the interior of the room.

Above her a sea of fluorescent, commercial-grade light fixtures flooded the giant space with white-hot light that cast minimal shadow, though it was caught and reflected back at Lyse in every one of the lab's chrome and steel surfaces.

It was like looking into an alternate-universe version of Josef Mengele's lab at Auschwitz. Because only someone or something as monstrous as the Nazis could've created what she was seeing here in this place.

In the face of such horror, Lyse had forgotten about the blood drop—and when she looked down at the floor, she saw that it was gone. She scanned the ground, trying to catch sight of it, but it had disappeared.

"Damn," she murmured, frowning. She was annoyed with herself for not paying more attention. It was the blood drop that had led her here in the first place.

Without her little scarlet guide, she felt uncertain of where to go next—and then she realized it didn't matter. The first and only order of business, she decided, was to free the women.

On silent feet, Lyse moved toward the first row of caged women, her breath coming in short, hollow gasps. She tried to calm herself down but discovered that fear was one thing that would not be quieted. She gave up and just focused on remaining calm as she approached one of the near-comatose young women.

"Hello?" Lyse whispered as she knelt down beside the bars, her lips as close to the woman's ear as she could manage. "Can you tell me who you are and what's happening here?"

The young woman didn't move. She stayed curled into a fetal position, her shorn head a Brillo pad of coarse hair that Lyse wanted to reach out and smooth down. Lyse got even closer to the bars, her eyes taking in the girl's pale brown skin—and then her heart lurched: One of the girl's eyes had been burned away, ropy scar tissue covering the side of her face. Lyse sat back on her heels, thrusting her hand into her mouth to stop herself from sobbing.

She stayed like that, motionless and trying not to cry, for a while—how long exactly, she wasn't sure, but when she was able to think straight again, she stood up and backed away from the cage. She hadn't heard a sound since she entered the lab, and she was pretty sure that meant the women had been sedated. No roomful of living creatures was this quiet unless there were drugs involved.

She looked for a way to jimmy the padlock on the woman's cage, but without a key or lockpicking tools—which she had no idea how to use, anyway—she couldn't open it. In anger, she grabbed the lock and began to pull on it, yanking it back and forth as she took out her frustration on the stupid piece of metal keeping her from helping the poor, tortured woman in front of her.

A *cracking* shot ricocheted across the lab, echoing off the floor and walls. Lyse threw herself to the cold tile floor before she realized it was only the sound of a door opening somewhere on the other side of the massive room.

My best bet is to just stay down and out of sight, she thought as she kept her body parallel to the ground and began to crawl away from the cages, keeping her movements as quiet as possible. Across from her was a long metal cabinet covered in computer monitors, and she decided that it provided the largest hiding space she could get to without crossing the open floor of the lab. So she headed toward the cabinet, still crawling, reaching it just as she heard the echoing footsteps of her pursuers.

"She's in here. Start looking by the cages."

A man's voice caromed through the space, the acoustics in the lab carrying his words straight to Lyse's ears. She could feel her heart rate increase, every muscle in her body throbbing in terror as she tried not to breathe. They knew where she was, had probably seen her on their monitoring system, and it was only a matter of time before they found her.

I need an out, she thought, racking her brain for any kind of plan that might save her.

She began to scan the space, looking for an escape route.

"Check those cages. Make sure she's not hiding inside an unlocked one."

Whoever was leading the search was smart. If she could've figured out a way to get into one of the cages and play pretend "science experiment subject," she would've done it—but her clothes and healthy coloring would've given her away instantly.

Lyse blinked as something bright flashed across her plane of vision. She searched for its source, hoping it wasn't one of the people pursuing her, maybe their watch face catching the fluorescent light and reflecting it back. But then it appeared again, more insistent this time, flashing back and forth across her face, then shooting away before returning once more. This time it moved away from her slowly, trailing across the floor at a speed she could follow with her eye.

Someone is trying to show me something.

The light twitched as it caught up to the droplet of blood, staying with it as it continued its journey across the floor. She realized that the light was helping her, showing her where the droplet was so that she might follow it. She didn't hesitate, not wanting to look a gift horse in the mouth, and began to crawl away from the shelter of the cabinet.

The floor was cold, its hard surface digging into her knees and elbows, but she ignored it, pushing forward. The blood took a circuitous route, weaving in and out of the workstations and between lab tables. She followed as best she could, keeping her eyes locked on the droplet as it progressed in its slow and meandering fashion. She could hear the men looking for her, hear the *scrunch* of their tread as they fanned out across the floor, but she kept going.

The droplet led her away from the center of the lab and past another row of caged women. Lyse tried not to focus on their pathetic faces as she passed them by, not wanting to see what horrible torture they'd endured. She felt a hand clamp on her ankle and she almost screamed, but fear kept the sound locked inside her throat. Instead, she pulled her leg free—which she was easily able to do—and then turned around, prepared to fight off an attacker.

But no one was there.

She checked to make sure the blood droplet was still visible, then returned to the row of cages—and that was when she saw the long, pale fingers retracting back between the metal bars.

"Hey," Lyse whispered. "Don't go."

She crawled over to the bars, searching out the woman's face.

"Who are you?" Lyse asked, her voice so low that she didn't know if the woman could hear it or not. "Please, I want to help."

The woman was probably Lyse's age, but the dark circles under her eyes and her dry, cracked lips made her look older. Her face was unharmed, but she was extremely thin and had a gray pallor to her skin.

"Get away," the woman murmured. *"Tell them what you've seen."*

Her eyes were so full of desperation that all Lyse could do was nod.

"They burn the ones who don't have the blood . . ."

Lyse got closer to the bars, forgetting where she was for a moment.

"Burn them?"

"To death."

Lyse felt nauseated, bile rising in her throat.

"No . . . they can't. That's . . ."

Lyse had no words to describe what it was, so she stopped without finishing the thought.

"Worse for the rest of us——"

"She's over there!"

Lyse turned and saw a tall man in camouflage pointing at her. She reached out and grasped the woman's fingers, giving them a quick squeeze.

"I'll come back. I promise."

Then she climbed to her feet and began to run.

She immediately slammed her left hip into the edge of a metal table, the pain shooting up her side. She bit her lip to prevent herself from crying out and kept moving. There were four men in camouflage at her back and if she stopped, that would be it. They'd capture her.

She tried not to think about where she was going; just let her instincts guide her. She'd lost track of the blood droplet and felt bad about that. If she hadn't stopped to talk to the woman in the cage, things might've turned out differently. She could've found out what was calling the blood, attracting it like a magnet—something she'd never seen before.

Aside from the slap of her shoes on the ground as she ran and the pounding of her pulse inside her head, Lyse could also hear a low murmur that, at first, she thought she was just imagining. But the sound began to grow, getting louder and louder as Lyse threaded her way through the lab. As the sound swelled around her, Lyse became cognizant of the fact that the murmur was actually a *hum*—and it was coming from the women. They were knitting a spell with their voices, using magic to try to help her.

They are blood sisters, Lyse realized, finally understanding. *The Flood is experimenting on us, using us to further some miserable end of their own.*

She wanted to cry. To scream at what she could not un-know. Instead, she chose to push the knowledge away for the moment. Dwelling on it would only slow her down.

There was a visceral *ripping* sound and Lyse looked up to see the heavy metal door ahead of her being pulled from its frame by unseen hands. She kept running, dodging as the door was yanked from its last hinge and thrown across the room, hitting one of the freestanding concrete block chambers with a percussive *crash*.

The humming stopped abruptly. Their job was done—the women had given her an escape route.

"Cut her off!" one of the men behind her yelled. "Before she hits the damn corridor!"

She gave a silent *thank you* to the women for their kindness and, with an extra surge of energy, picked up speed and headed for the exit.

Here goes nothing, she thought, and launched herself through the doorway before any of her pursuers could get close enough to grab her.

She found herself running down a dimly lit corridor, flying past dozens of open doorways, inside which were tiny prison cells in various states of disrepair. Each one contained a cot, its rotten bedding shredded or stripped away. Whatever this place was now, once upon a time it had been some kind of prison, probably housing hundreds of men at a time.

It gave Lyse the creeps.

She could hear the men pursuing her, but then, as if by magic, their footfalls ceased and silence reigned. A moment later, she heard them dragging something heavy across the lab floor, the sound of metal scraping against metal making her teeth ache. Suddenly, it got much darker in the corridor, and Lyse realized it was because the men had blocked the empty doorway with something large and heavy.

Terrified this was some kind of trick, Lyse kept running—but after a few minutes of continued silence, her curiosity was too great. She slowed down enough so that she could check behind her. To her surprise, not only was the corridor empty, but all the doorways she'd just passed were now closed.

She didn't know how that was possible. All of those rusted old metal doors, and she hadn't heard a single one shut? It didn't make any sense.

She stopped to catch her breath and was tempted to double back but decided against it. The men who'd been chasing her hadn't just been called back to home base, or given up on catching her. No, there was way more to it than that. Lyse could feel it in her bones. Those men hadn't wanted to come down this corridor for a very specific reason, and she was pretty sure it had something to do with whatever entity closed all the doors. Those tough guys in their camouflage outfits and heavy black boots were unsettled by whatever was now trapped in here with her.

"Hello?" Lyse called out, the hair on the back of her neck rising as the overhead lights in the corridor began to flicker.

No one answered her, but there was now a noticeable chill in the air. Lyse wrapped her arms around herself, grateful that she was at least wearing a flannel shirt and long pants. Exhaustion filled her entire body, and she let out a sigh, frowning when she realized she could see her breath hanging in the air.

It had been chilly in the lab, but not *this* chilly. From experience, she realized something supernatural was approaching.

Then all the lights went out.

Lyse could sense the creature before she felt it. It was sentient, alive and moving more quickly than anything human had a right to. She screamed as it passed her, its speed and size knocking her off her feet. She hit the ground hard, the back of her head bouncing off the concrete floor. The pain dazed her for a moment, but then the present started to seep back into her brain. She remembered the lab and the women and the giant scary creature that was now trapped inside the corridor with her.

She realized that it was probably the very same beast that had been with her back in the interrogation room.

"Please don't hurt me," Lyse whispered as she rolled onto her stomach and crawled over to one of the walls.

She pressed her fingers against it, using it to help herself climb to her knees and then, finally, onto her feet. Hands still grazing the wall as a guide, she began to walk.

"The enemy of my enemy is my friend!" Lyse yelled. "They're your enemy, too, or you wouldn't be down here in this horrible place with me."

There was a slight *hiss* in Lyse's ear—as though someone were breathing softly against her earlobe. The numbness came next as that side of her face began to freeze. She reached up and brushed her fingers across her cheek, but the skin felt normal. Warm to the touch, even. The creature was screwing with her perception, but it wasn't harming her physically.

"What are you?" Lyse murmured as a wave of sadness so intense washed over her that she felt her eyes prickle with tears.

I'm feeling its emotions, she realized. *This is like the telepathy, but so much more intense.*

"No," Lyse said out loud. "Not *what. Who* are you?"

This appeared to be the right question. The sadness melted away and then, as if the creature were beaming images directly into her brain, Lyse *saw.*

blink

Identical faces. Sisters. Twins.

The words *REMEMBER THIS* flash across Lyse's mind.

blink

Men and women in dark robes, holding horrible weapons of murder and mutilation. A pyre; two women are lashed to a wooden stake in the middle of the flames. One of the women screams and the sound rips through the air as the stench of burning flesh fills Lyse's nostrils.

blink

A young woman, her dark hair shorn from her head. A ragged suture line across her forehead where her skull has been split apart and then sewn back together, electrodes spilling from her head like hair. She lies on a metal gurney, strapped into place—though where anyone thinks she might go is a mystery. She's so thin, the flesh hanging from her bones, no muscle left on her skeletal frame to hold it in place. Like a petrified woman, she's atrophied into one position, her chin pressing into her collarbone, a feeding tube inserted down her throat, an IV in her left arm. Everything necessary to keep a husk of a person alive, but to what end?

Like in a horror movie . . . she looks up, the movement so fast it's impossible to follow. Haunted eyes, full of suffering.

And then Lyse is being pulled away, leaving the woman's bedside, being dragged out of the room where the woman lies . . . and Lyse realizes the woman is in one of those concrete chambers in the lab, trapped in there—and that there are women trapped inside *each* of the concrete block chambers of the lab. These women are all strapped to gurneys, being sucked dry of their life force . . . literally wasting away.

The words *I AM ALL OF THEM. THEY HAVE MADE US ONE* flash across Lyse's mind.

blink

Whatever had had hold of Lyse was gone. Her mind was her own again and she'd never felt so happy to be herself. She'd borne witness to terrible suffering, and the knowledge now filled her with a grief so palpable she could sense it taking up residence inside her body, overwhelming her brain.

They were killing her blood sisters, using them for their powers . . . basically draining them dry and then discarding them. The ones in the cages, they were just waiting for their turn on the operating table. The whole thing made Lyse's blood run cold.

I AM ALL OF THEM. THEY HAVE MADE US ONE.
It's in the blood.
I AM ALL OF THEM. THEY HAVE MADE US ONE.

It's in the blood.

Lyse was beginning to understand more about magic. That hybrids, like herself, had evolved in such a way that they were born with aspects of each of the five magical talents: Clairvoyance, Divination, Dream Keeping, Empathy, and Herbalism. There was something special in their blood, something that The Flood wanted. The others, the witches without this special blood, The Flood murdered outright—burning them at the stake to "cleanse" them in some awful tip of the hat to the witch trials of the Dark Ages. It was archaic and torturous, but it made a very firm point and scared the hell out of anyone who opposed them.

"Where are you?" Lyse called into the darkness—and then, one by one, the lights began to pop back on. The ghostly creature that had frightened the men away was allowing things to return to normal.

Except it's not a ghost, Lyse thought. *It's the collective psyche of my blood sisters, a creature born from their suffering that is more powerful than anyone realizes—and I bet The Flood has no idea that they've created it.*

Lyse wasn't sure where she was supposed to go. There was no magical blood droplet to follow, no angry camouflage mob to chase her, no one to tell her what to do.

"Lyse? Is that you?"

Up ahead, a figure emerged from one of the old prison cells. As the figure moved out of the shadows and down the long hallway, its features resolved into a face that Lyse had never expected to see here, in this terrible hellhole.

Lyse

⌖

"Oh my God," Lyse said as Arrabelle crossed the space between them and wrapped her arms around her. "I don't . . . how did you . . . ?"

She couldn't finish the sentence. There was just too much emotion clogging her throat, making it hard to breathe, to speak, to think properly. How Arrabelle had ended up here in this place with her was a miracle—and one she almost didn't want to question for fear it would turn out to be a dream.

"I'm not here alone," Arrabelle said, and she looked back down the hallway. Lyse followed her gaze and saw two bedraggled-looking people camped out in the shadows. "C'mere. This is my coven mate, Lyse. One of my closest blood sisters."

She gestured for her two friends to join them. Tentatively they came forward: a young woman with long brown hair and a face that felt vaguely familiar to Lyse. The other was a man whom Lyse had never seen before—and from the pained hunch of his shoulders and the gauntness of his frame, Lyse was almost sure this would be their only meeting.

"This is Niamh," Arrabelle said, indicating the girl, "and this is Evan . . ."

Lyse knew the name. Remembered how distraught Arrabelle had been when she thought he was dead—and she recognized that soon Arrabelle would have a repeat of that same grief. Lyse wanted to hold her friend tight, tell her that this was not the end, and Evan would go on (she knew this from her experiences with Eleanora), but now was not the time. Later, she promised herself, she would be there for Arrabelle. After they were long gone from this horror show.

"Any friend of Arrabelle's is a friend of mine," she said, nodding to Niamh and Evan. "I don't know why you've come to this terrible place—"

"My sister is here," Niamh said, her eyes plaintive. "Have you seen her? She looks like me. She is me . . ."

And Lyse realized where she'd seen the young woman's face before.

I AM ALL OF THEM. THEY HAVE MADE US ONE.

The young woman in the concrete chamber in the lab— that was how Lyse had recognized Niamh's face. She took the girl's thin wrists and held them in her hands.

"I know where your sister is, but . . ." She paused, not sure how to go on. "I don't think she's wholly your sister anymore."

If there was one place Lyse did *not* want to go back to, it was that fucking laboratory. But saying no to Arrabelle and her friends was out of the question, so as they made their way back down the shadowy hall, Lyse explained what the place was and what The Flood had done to the blood sisters they'd kidnapped.

"No," Niamh said, as she kept pace with Lyse. "That's not possible."

"They steal their powers, but what they don't realize is that when they pool all of the psychic energy together in one place, they're creating a connection," Lyse said. "And it's something more than just a connection. It's built a living thing . . . a sentient creature that's in this place, stalking the halls and scaring the shit out of the bad guys. It will protect us if we need it. It's on our side . . ."

"I just want my sister," Niamh said.

"No, we want to set them all free," Evan disagreed, coming up behind them with Arrabelle at his side.

"There are others here, too," Lyse said. "They use them like servants. They've cut out their tongues."

"Damn," Arrabelle said, looking sick. "Well, I think they've been experimenting for a while. And on their own followers . . . I think that's where the creature that attacked us at the eucalyptus grove came from."

"God, that's not something I'd wish on my worst enemy," Lyse said. "That they'd do that to their own people. Well, the blood sisters are different. They're not scary and they'll help us. They promised me."

"How do you know that?" Niamh asked. "If they have no tongues . . . ?"

"They're connected to the creature. They can link into your brain, speak to you telepathically."

"My sister . . ." Niamh said. "It's how we communicated when we were little. They said it was because we were twins."

This made Lyse start to wonder if the creature's abilities were an amalgamation of all the talents it had acquired. If the creature had soaked up Laragh and Niamh's telepathy and was using it to link all the blood sisters. It was a fascinating idea—and a terrifying one.

"We're here," Lyse said as they reached the end of the corridor.

The doorframe was still barricaded—the men in camouflage had done a fine job of sealing off the entrance with a heavy metal filing cabinet.

"Now what?" Niamh asked.

"If we get this crap out of the way, the lab and your sister are right on the other side."

Niamh nodded and began to attack the cabinet. Lyse and Arrabelle joined her, trying to shove the heavy metal filing cabinet out of the way, but it was a losing game.

"I think it needs all of us to shift it," Evan said.

"No—" Arrabelle said, trying to dissuade him, but he shook his head and lent his weight to the endeavor.

Lyse could see the toll it took on him. His already pale face became ashen and he could hardly catch his breath, but he didn't complain, just kept throwing his weight against the cabinet with the others, willing it to move. After a few minutes, the cabinet began to inch forward and then, before they knew it, there was enough of a gap for each of them to squeeze through.

"I'll go first," Lyse said as she crawled through the gap and climbed out into the fluorescent-lit lab. It was just as she'd left it, the horror of the place still as real and frightening as before.

"Oh, lord," Arrabelle said as she followed Evan out into the light.

"What've they done?" Evan asked, his voice cracking with emotion as he stared at the rows of cages, his face a mask of disbelief as he realized there were women trapped inside them. "We have to get them out of here."

He started to move toward the first grouping of cages, but Arrabelle caught his arm.

"Wait. Let's do this efficiently—"

But Arrabelle's warning came too late. Niamh was already making her way into the lab, searching for her sister.

"Niamh!" she called, but the girl ignored her. Lyse sighed and turned to Arrabelle: "There are cameras everywhere. I'm ninety-nine percent sure they already know we're in here."

"Jesus," Arrabelle said, looking truly frightened for the first time since Lyse had known her. "We have to get her back here."

"Too late," Evan said, his eyes focused on the far corner of the lab, where two men in camouflage were pushing through the doorway.

"Fuck," Lyse said.

"Let's get Niamh and go back into the hall," Arrabelle said. "This was insane to break in here without a plan—"

"No."

Evan grabbed Arrabelle's arm.

"Yes," Arrabelle replied. "You're sick and you can't—"

Evan reached over and touched Arrabelle's cheek.

"Bell, I'm dying. There's no need for me to run anymore."

"You're going to be fine," Arrabelle said, tears flooding her eyes. "We'll find something that'll—"

"Bell, I've tried . . ."

And he lifted up his shirt.

Arrabelle gasped when she saw the rotten black wound. It had eaten up Evan's whole side, digging into the flesh of his stomach and down toward his pelvis. But what surprised Lyse was something else . . . not the necrotic tissue, but the long, thin scars that ran underneath each nipple. Lyse had a friend who'd undergone sexual reassignment surgery, and his scarring had been very similar.

Arrabelle's friend Evan had not been biologically born a man.

"Oh, Evan," Arrabelle said, shutting her eyes and shaking her head as she realized how bad the wound was. "No, no, no . . ."

Evan let his shirt fall back into place.

"There's nothing we can do except not let my death be in vain."

He pulled her to him, and she let his hand caress her face.

"I love you, Bell. I'm sorry I was too scared to give you what you needed," he said—and then he leaned over and kissed her.

Lyse looked away, wanting to give them privacy, and her gaze locked on the two men with guns slowly moving toward them.

"We have to go," Lyse said, turning back around in time to see Arrabelle hand Evan something small and wrapped in tissue. Lyse didn't know what it was, and she wasn't sure if she wanted to find out.

"Go find Niamh," Evan said, pushing Arrabelle toward Lyse. "Help her find her sister."

He took off, heading toward the men in camouflage.

"Evan, no!" Arrabelle said, and Lyse had to hold her back to prevent her from going after him.

"Do what he said. Let's help Niamh and the others," Lyse whispered into Arrabelle's ear. Her friend stiffened and then finally nodded.

"Okay."

Lyse grabbed Arrabelle's hand and they took off through the lab, bypassing metal surgical tables and threading their way through the rows of computer workstations.

"This place is a nightmare," Arrabelle said, and Lyse nodded.

"It's hell."

Lyse had an idea of where Laragh was being held, but she didn't know which of the concrete rooms housed Niamh's sister. She realized that she and Arrabelle were going to have to split up.

"Those concrete rooms," Lyse said, pointing to the closest one. "She's in one of those. Find her and I think we'll find Niamh."

"All right," Arrabelle said. "I'll see you shortly."

Arrabelle took off, and Lyse did the same. Lyse's path led her in the same direction Evan had taken, and she was glad Arrabelle had chosen to go the other way.

Up ahead, Lyse saw one of the concrete rooms and jogged toward it, hoping to find Niamh or Laragh inside, but when she looked through the small window she saw it was empty. It was at that very moment she caught Evan's reflection in the window, his body moving like a speeding bullet as he ran toward the two men in camouflage.

Lyse whirled around and began to sprint in Evan's direction.

He was acting like a kamikaze pilot hell-bent on death and destruction—and she didn't think his life should be sacrificed just yet. Whether he knew it or not, he was going to get her help.

"Wait up," she called to him as she picked her way through the maze of medical tables and workstations. "I'm your backup."

Evan slowed down but did not stop.

"I don't need backup," he yelled at her.

The two men with guns were moving forward in stealth mode, careful not to expose themselves to an attack. Apparently, they seemed to believe that Lyse and Evan were some kind of a threat. The idea almost made Lyse laugh.

"What was in the tissue?" Lyse asked, as she finally caught up to him.

"Poisoning agent on a dart."

"Can you use it on these guys?" Lyse asked as she followed Evan into a crouch behind one of the metal surgical tables.

"If I can get close enough."

"Consider it done," Lyse said, and stood up, waving her arms at the two men, who were also hiding behind another of the surgical tables.

"Hey, over here, assholes!" she screamed.

She felt Evan's hand on the side pocket of her jeans, trying to pull her back down, but she stayed on her feet, ignoring him.

"They don't know what to do," Lyse whispered down to Evan as across the room, she saw the two men conferring. "I think they've been told not to hurt us."

"Lucky us," Evan whispered back, his words dripping with sarcasm.

Lyse had to agree that death was a far kinder end than getting locked up in one of those god-awful cages.

"If I had a white flag, I'd be raising it right now!" Lyse yelled at the men. "I give up and I'm unarmed."

"Are you crazy?" Evan said, shaking his head.

"Just trust me," she whispered down to him.

He looked as though he'd rather do anything but what she'd just asked. Yet he held his tongue.

The two men rose from their position slowly and began to move through the maze of workstations. Lyse noticed movement in her peripheral vision and realized that her yelling had woken up some of the women in the cages. They were stirring now, opening their eyes. Some were sitting up, following Lyse's movements, tracking her with their haunted eyes.

"They're waking up," Lyse said, cocking her head in the direction of the nearest row of cages.

"I can see," Evan said, looking around him. "Jesus, they look like they've been tortured."

"They have been," Lyse replied.

More and more of the women were waking up now, and as they came to consciousness, they began to murmur among themselves.

"They want to help us," Lyse said, recognizing the sound as the murmuring grew in pitch until it was a driving hum.

More voices joined in until Lyse could feel the hum racing through her body—and she wasn't the only one. Evan was feeling it, too. Lyse reached down and touched her calf. The cut on her leg was gone.

"I . . . The pain is less," Evan said, frowning in confusion.

Lyse fought back tears as she realized what they were doing. Sacrificing their own existence to ease her and Evan's suffering.

"They're taking our pain from us, taking it into their own bodies, so we can fight."

"I don't want them to—" Evan tried to say, but Lyse cut him off.

"They're doing it because they want you to help them. Let them help us in return."

Evan rose to his feet.

"Okay."

The two men were still moving toward them. Lyse realized,

with a start, that they couldn't hear the women. *They're not attuned to the frequency,* she thought.

"Let's go," Lyse said, and took Evan's arm, guiding the two of them in the direction of the armed men.

"We don't want anyone to get hurt," Lyse called out to the men as they drew near them. "We come in peace."

The closer they got, the more Lyse could see of the men's faces. She was frightened by the soulless emptiness in their dark eyes, as if there were no humanity left in them, just the need to fulfill their duty. One of the men reached for Lyse, grabbing her arm and pulling her roughly into him. At the same time, Evan removed the dart from the tissue paper and stabbed the other man in the throat. The man screamed, his hands clasping at his neck, and then he fell onto the floor, writhing in pain.

"What the—" the man holding Lyse started to say, but Evan had already stabbed him in the back of the neck with the same dart.

The man released Lyse and stumbled backward, slamming into a surgical table before sliding to the ground, scratching at the spot where Evan had stabbed him.

"Two down," Evan said, pushing Lyse ahead of him. "And if you're right about them seeing everything, more will be on the way."

Lyse followed Evan, the humming growing even louder as they ran. It was like being out in the woods in Athens on a hot summer night, the song of the cicadas wrapping itself around you like a blanket.

"We need to find Arrabelle and then get these women out of here," Evan said—and Lyse couldn't have agreed more.

They ran as fast as their legs could carry them, scanning the lab for their friends. Then Lyse saw a flash of Niamh's long hair off to their right, and she grabbed Evan's arm to stop him.

"This way," she cried, and now she was in the lead. "I see Niamh."

Arrabelle and Niamh were standing outside one of the concrete block rooms, staring through the small rectangular window. Niamh was banging on the glass, trying to break it, but to no avail.

"What's wrong? Why can't you get in?" Lyse called out as she approached them.

"It's locked," Arrabelle shouted back.

Lyse didn't hesitate, she opened her mind and offered up a plea:

You who are one, help us, please!

She heard a dry whistling in her head, like a billion leaves rolling across a wide-open plain—and then the humming stopped.

The women in the cages opened their mouths and *screamed.* The sound was titanic and Lyse fell to her knees, covering her ears to block it out. The window shattered, pieces of glass showering down on them like raindrops.

As the scream faded away, Lyse climbed back to her feet.

"Let's go!" she cried, and gestured for the others to help her climb through the window.

Arrabelle and Niamh boosted her up and she shimmied through the broken frame, careful not to cut herself on the long shards of glass.

She dropped into the room and her skin began to break out in gooseflesh as she recognized the smell: Death was here in the room with her.

The girl she'd seen in her mind was definitely Niamh's twin—and Lyse found her waiting on a hospital gurney, her skeletal body tucked underneath a thin white sheet. She looked up as Lyse crossed to her and smiled.

You came.

She was in Lyse's head, her voice soft.

"We all did," Lyse said, moving closer to the bed until she was standing by the young woman's side.

She's at the Pillar, but they won't stop her.

Lyse frowned as she took Laragh's emaciated hand and held it gently.

And once she's spread the word, the world will know us finally. Isn't that a miracle?

Her voice was light and giddy, full of childish awe.

Our power is in the blood, Lyse. It's what connects us all. It's what will save us, too.

"God, I hope you're right," Lyse said, and she found herself wanting to believe the young woman's words more than anything else in the whole world.

You can let Niamh in now. They've gone. You will be safe here now.

Laragh's face remained immobile, the ability to move her body long since gone. Lyse leaned down and kissed her pale brow. Her skin was dry as bone.

"I'm so sorry," Lyse whispered.

Don't be.

Lyse stood back up, wiping at her cheeks. The ache in her throat was almost too much to bear as she walked over to the door and undid the lock, the metal hinges creaking as it swung open.

Niamh was inside in a heartbeat. She'd already seen her sister's face through the window and was prepared, so there was no shock. Without a word, she climbed up onto the hospital bed and held her sister's body tightly to her, rocking them both back and forth.

Only Niamh knew when Laragh finally left the world.

While Lyse stayed with the twins, Arrabelle and Evan began the long and arduous task of busting open each and every cage.

Lizbeth

> ❧

The helicopter hovered above her, but Lizbeth ignored it. She closed her eyes and willed herself to go to sleep—

—she opened her eyes and she was still standing exactly where she'd been, only above her now was not a helicopter but a monumental wave poised to crash down upon her head.

"Don't look up, silly child."

And then Temistocles was standing before her, grinning like an idiot. As happy to see her as she was to see him. She wanted to race over to him, to have him catch her in his arms and hold her tight, but he sensed her intention and held up a hand for her to remain where she was.

"Stay. It's not time to leave the safety of the stones just yet."

"I'm afraid," she said, looking back up at the wave, which had moved incrementally closer to engulfing her.

"I told you not to look," he scolded her. "When you look, it lets them get closer."

She dragged her eyes away from the wave, refocusing them on Temistocles.

"Only two more minutes and the blood moon will reach the

meridian—then everything will be out of your control," he said, rubbing his hands together thoughtfully. "The men in the helicopter will try to stop the message from going out. If they fail, then it's the army's turn."

"Army?" Lizbeth asked, fear snaking through her.

He nodded, his head bobbing up and down like a marionette.

"Of course there's an army down there," he replied. "They're ringing the Pillar, waiting to apprehend you as soon as the message goes out."

Lizbeth couldn't help herself. She looked up at the wave again—this time it was only a foot or so above her head, frozen in place, but ready to break at any moment.

"Stop it, I say!" Temistocles shouted, and she was forced to look back at him. "Now. Do you trust me?"

She didn't have to think about it. She nodded that she did.

"Good. Because when the message goes out, you are going to escape the only way I know how—through the dreamlands."

"Okay—" Lizbeth said, and then she heard a loud crash *above her. She looked up at the wave—*

—and felt the weight of a man's hand on her shoulder, his fingers digging into her skin.

"Come on now, you stupid cow—"

She knew that voice. It was Lyse's uncle—the traitorous bitch had sent him to find her. Of course, she hadn't killed him. It had all been a lie.

"Leave me alone!" she screamed, and turned, kneeing him in the groin. He fell to his knees and she shoved him away from her.

Above her the clouds broke and an oxblood orb appeared in the sky. It was massive, descending over the nearby range of mountains like an unbroken, bloodied egg yolk. She felt heat in her feet and hands, her toes and fingers blistering—and she screamed in pain. Then Lyse's uncle was back, grabbing at her ankle, unseating her, so that she tripped backward, her upper body falling out of the stone circle. The pain instantly went away.

"No," she cried as he crawled over to her and grabbed a handful of her hair, yanking her head back.

"You've failed," he whispered into her ear.

I can't, she thought as a horrible idea entered her head.

She swiveled around, so that they were face to face, his soulless eyes boring into hers—and then she did the unthinkable. She opened her mouth and sank her teeth into the cartilage of his nose, pulling at it until the tip came away in her teeth and blood filled her mouth.

He screamed in agony and released her, clutching at his ruined face.

She looked up and saw that the blood moon was already starting to wane.

No, she thought—and quickly threw herself back into the stone circle. Woozy, she climbed to her feet and raised her hands in the air. The same burning began to consume her body again and she felt like a roman candle about to be lit into the atmosphere.

She bit back a scream, but then she heard the singing—all the power of the Dream Keepers filled her up with their love, cocooning her in their protective magic.

Then everything around her exploded as *her* dream became the *world's* dream.

Well done, my love, she heard Temistocles whisper.

She felt him take her hand.

Well done, he repeated.

And they disappeared into nothingness.

Epilogue

Around the world, awake or asleep, all of humanity dreamed the same dream.

Lizbeth's Dream.

It went out into the universe like a shot, infecting every sentient being with its message: *Let it be known that witches are real.* And like that, the scales fell from humankind's eyes and magic was once again awake in the world.

Only now could the real battle begin.